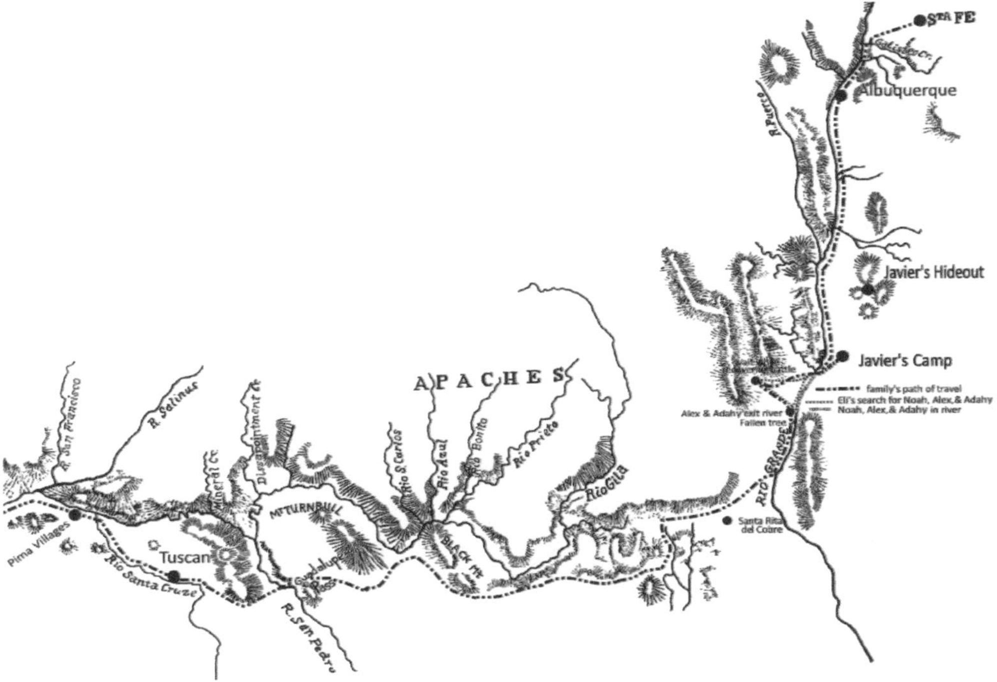

Puma Village

R. San Francisco

Rio Santa Cruze

R. Salinas

Tuscano

Mineral Ck.

Disappointment Ck.

R. San Pedro

NATURAL BRIDGE

Rio S. Carlos

A P A C H E S

Rio Azul

Rio Bonito

BLACK Mts.

Rio Prieto

Rio Gila

Sierra Rica del Cobre

RIO GRANDE

R. Puerco

Alex & Adalin raft river
Father's Trail

Javier's Camp

Javier's Hideout

Albuquerque

STA. FE

family's path of travel
Eli's search for Noah, Alex, & Adalin
Noah, Alex, & Adalin in river

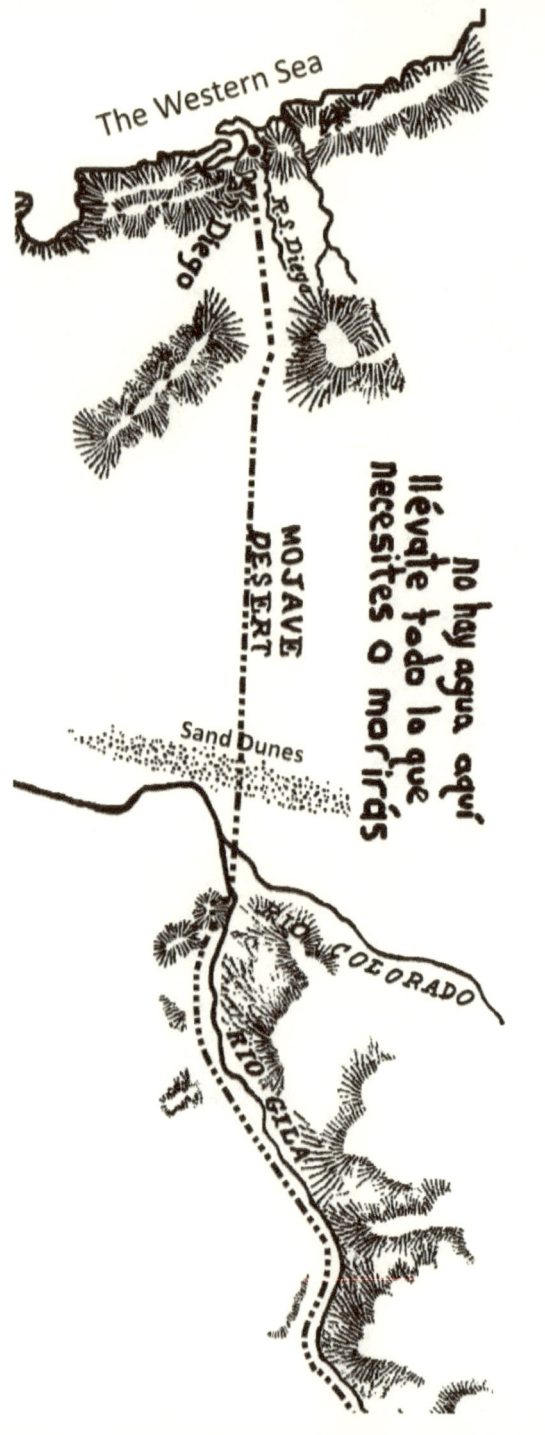

THE

WESTERN

SEA

A Chance and Choices Adventure
Book Ten

Lisa Gay

Illustrations by
W.R. Michael Mattingly

Chance and Choices

This book is a work of fiction. The names, characters, places, and incidents are either the product of the author's imagination or used factitiously. Any resemblance to an actual person, living or dead, business establishment, or event is entirely coincidental.

ISBN-13: 978-1-945858-24-6

The Western Sea

San Diego

Milk box

Otey River

Tijuana River

Sweetwater River

Alamar River

Ejido Mtn

Cottonwood Cr.

Tecate Cr.

Kuuchamaa M.

Campo Cr.

Hot Mineral Spring

Cerrizo Cr.

Those Involved in these incidents:

Place of Origin – Albuquerque
Manuel Ortega – leader of the San Felipe de Neri
Church and convent
Friar Emil– friar at San Felipe de Neri convent
Javier – uncle of girl at fountain

Place of Origin – Alexandria, Virginia
Micah Clemont - His Honorable Justice of the
United States Supreme Court
Corporal Fisher – assigned to records room
inspections

Place of Origin – Eighth District
Rufus Knapp - Warden of Arkansas Penitentiary
Alger Dickerson – the guard assigned to assist with
records room inspections

Place of Origin – Fort Arbuckle
Joy – a baby found beside her dead father
Arbuckle – a cow found in the barn

Place of Origin – Fort Smith
Promise – army horse purchased by Noah
Biscuit – army horse purchased by Noah

Place of Origin – Guadalupe Pass
Tarak – leader of the Apaches encountered when
cutting down Spanish bayonet
Awinita – Tarak's wife and Spanish bayonet
processing instructor
Baishan – son of Awinita and Tarak
Lozen – cousin of Awinita
Itza-chu – man with Gila monster bitten toes

Place of Origin – Harmony
Ann Williams – oldest sister and Noah's wife
Stephanie Yates – middle sister and Eli's wife
Sally Williams – the youngest sister
Eli Yates – Stephanie's husband
Tom Yates - Eli's father/owner of Yates Mercantile
Eyanosa – Noah's horse
Spirit – Tom's horse

Place of Origin – Indian Territory
Quapaw Land:
Noah Swift Hawk – Ann's husband
(Tahatankohana)
Christopher – Noah's and Ann's baby son (Chris)
Ehawee – Noah's sister

Cherokee Nation:
Adahy - Ehawee's husband
Paint – Adahy's horse
Mojave:
Tálpo

Tipai-Ipai:
He Who Talks- man who brought Noah's family to
his village at the western sea
Duro- He Who Talks' father
Bly - He Who Talks' wife

Place of Origin – Javier's Banditos
Lucky- the horse that they pulled out of the river
with a rope
Miracle – the horse that got itself out of the river
after going over the rocky rapids

Place of Origin – Little Rock

Daniel Hall – State Judge of Arkansas

Richard Atwood –State Judge of Arkansas

Parley Taylor – Sheriff of Little Rock

Captain Miles Cornish – commander of the Little Rock arsenal

Christmas Bell – lawyer (Chris)

Cornell Hillcrest – the owner of Hillcrest Inn

Bessie Hillcrest – Cornell's wife

John Peabody – the owner of Peabody Inn

Colt Barrett – bounty hunter

Bruce McHay – drunkard

Mavis McHay- Bruce's wife

Tom Henry – caught looking at the wrong female

Augustus Pexels – sawmill owner

Owen – son of a convicted murderer

Beauty – a mule given to Sally

Dolly – a mule purchased by Sally

Edwin - a mule purchased by Sally

Martin - a mule purchased by Sally

Honor- a mule purchased by Noah

Justice - a mule purchased by Noah

Place of Origin – Mexico

Filipe Espinoza – commander of the Mexican Army detachment

Jorge Bueno – second in command of the detachment

Place of Origin – New York

Helen Yates – Tom's mother

Place of Origin – Pine Bluff

Roscoe Bacon – the first owner of Bacon's Trading Post/adopted grandfather of the family

Roscoe's donkeys:

Little Jenny – miniature donkey

Little Jack – miniature donkey

Big Jenny

Shaggy

Spot

Blanco

Chocolate

Smiley

Honey

QuickSilver

Roscoe's mules:

King

Rose

Hector

Molly

Jumper

Blue

Chief

Diamond

Roscoe's goats:

Bella

Billy

Eli and Stephanie's mules:

Redeemed

Ace

Place of Origin – Raton

Alejandro Divine – grandson of man being buried
(Alex)

Domingo -man given guardianship of Alex

Juan – village tailor

Pedro – village blacksmith

Esmeralda – the woman who cared for the flocks
Blackie- Alex's quarter horse
Goliath – Alex's draft horse
Azúcar - horse Oscar traded his wild ponies for
Leche - milk cow bought with two steer

Place of Origin – Republic of Texas
Dennison – commander of the Texas militia
Johnson – insubordinate soldier
Carmichael - soldier
Carlyle – scout
Stanley Cornwall – the soldier picked by baby
Chris (Stan)
Tennessee Trivet – the soldier picked by baby Joy

Place of Origin – San Luis Valley:
Kanneatche – met on the Sangre de Cristo
Mountains
Chipeta – Kanneatche's wife
Kanosh – Kanneatche's first son
Maykh - Kanneatche's second son
Miguel Lopez– the owner of the gold mine
Fernando – trapped miner
Paco – trapped miner
Alberto Perez – trapped miner
Efren– trapped miner
Roberto – trapped miner
Antonio Vega – Pueblo's doctor

Place of Origin – Santa Fe
Joaquín Hernandez- store owner
Carla Hernandez – Joaquín's wife
Patrick – Sally's alternate identity as a sheep drover

José Luis – the man who made the map and one of the men who harvested plants

Hector – one of the men who harvested plants

Alvaro Salazar – one of the men who harvested plants

Karmen Salazar- Alvaro's wife

Rosa Salazar – Alvaro's sister

Camilla – mother of the Arrogante sheepdogs

Samantha – Arrogante sheepdog (Sam)

Blondie– Arrogante sheepdog

Blackie– Arrogante sheepdog

Honey– Arrogante sheepdog

Frisky– Arrogante sheepdog

Bliss– Arrogante sheepdog

Tiger– Arrogante sheepdog

Place of Origin – The prairie

Emily Stringer– Tom's wife

Oscar Stringer –Emily's son

Nicholas Wolfgang Krüger – found on the prairie (Nikki)

Greta Adele Krüger – Nikki's sister (Adele)

Courageous – lost cow rescued from wild animals

Gimpy – the cow with a leg broken in a dust storm

Ahyoka   -wild mustang Ann and Nikki helped to deliver a breech colt

Tsayi - Ahyoka's colt

Place of Origin – The Quarry (Missouri hard labor camp)

Forest Ronan – Warden of The Quarry

One

"What a fool I am! Oh well, I didn't have much of a life in store for me anyway," the young man lay on his belly in the tall grass. "You can shoot me, but you won't get anything. All I have is the clothes on my body."

Noah Swift Hawk, one of the two men with a nocked arrow, informed the person claiming destitution, "You're waiting to ambush my family."

"Ambush them?! Why?"

"We have many animals, and you think our wagons are full."

What an idiot I am. "I was hiding because I'm out here without any way to defend myself, and I thought you might try to kill ME."

"Nobody in his right mind would go off without a weapon. What if a puma came after you? Get on your feet."

The captured man rose. "I'd probably ask God to have it kill me fast."

1

"What's your name?"

"Alex Divine."

Noah directed the other man holding a weapon. "Check him over."

Adahy, the sixteen-year-old Cherokee who had married Noah's sister, frisked the fellow who was only a year older than himself. "He has nothing but his clothes."

Gus had that shiv. Noah ordered, "Kick off your boots."

Alex did so. "I'm not going to kick you to death, and it's going to hurt to walk without them."

"Keep your bow on him." Noah returned his arrow to his quiver and slung his bow across his back. He examined the inner seam of each boot for a long, slender blade but found none. He handed the footwear back to their owner. "It's a good thing we came along. Pumas will try to eat you. I have ten scars on my chest to prove it. Why ARE you out here?"

Alex slipped his foot into a boot. "I don't want to live in Raton anymore. This place took my parents, and now it's taken my grandfather. He was all I had left."

"We've lost a lot of people too. There must be other people in Raton who love you."

"Nobody anywhere cares about me."

A caravan of five wagons, eleven adults, two seven-year-old boys, five babies, twelve hens, one rooster, forty-three horses, twenty mules, seventeen donkeys, six goats, ten sheep, five cows, and one cat arrived at the place where the three men stood.

Alex sighed. Even though she had a baby in a cradleboard on her back, Alex couldn't take his eyes off the girl with waves of hair shimmering with reddish hues. He looked into her hazel eyes. *My word, her face is shaped just like a heart, and her lips are too! Gorgeous!* "Very nice to meet you."

Sally Williams, the person whose appearance spoke to Alex without an audible word, said, "Pleased to make your acquaintance."

Without saying her name, Noah identified the slender teenager consuming Alex's thoughts as his sister-in-law and then stated the relationships of the rest of his large family to himself and each other. He didn't identify anybody as the beautiful girl's husband.

Noah requested, "Come back to Raton with us."

Alex turned back to the town he had tried to escape while folks lowered his grandfather into the grave he had dug. He walked beside the man who could have, but had not, skewered him with arrows. "When did a puma attack you?"

"Not too many months ago. I didn't realize a puma was stalking me as I was stalking a bear. The next thing I knew, both of them were after me. If other people hadn't been there, I would be gone." He pulled the edge of his shirt to the side and showed Alex the wounds arched above his breast.

Alex glanced over Noah's shoulder at the loveliest girl he had ever seen. Noah noticed Alex wasn't exactly looking at the scars he was displaying. "Any idea where you were going?"

"East, I guess. It's only July. I figure I can make it across the prairie before winter. I'm surely not going down to Santa Fe. Twenty years ago, my father and grandfather went there to do some trading. When Father saw my mother, he talked Grandpa into staying, so he could court her. When my parents married, her father disowned her, so my folks came here. I've lived in Raton my whole live, but those people have never wanted me. I'm not good enough because I'm not a full-blooded Mexican."

"I know exactly how you feel."

"No, you don't. Your people accept you."

"These specific people do. Not everybody does. I'm a Quapaw."

"Indians have brown eyes. Your eyes are blue!"

"My mother has blue eyes. The people of my village say my family is at the bottom because my father married a white woman, and because I married a white woman, certain white folks have tried to kill me. Some are still hunting me. That's why we're going west."

"I guess you do understand. Now that Grandpa is gone, nobody loves me."

"Don't your parents?"

"People were always mean to my mother because she married my father. He built our house away from the town beside the mountain to guard the rear. Three years ago, a landside buried them inside our house. I had been with my grandfather at the time. We heard the mountain fall apart. I've

4

never heard such a loud noise. When we got there, the house was under that." Alex pointed toward a massive pile of rubble at the foot of the towering Sangre de Cristo Mountains in front of them.

Noah looked into Alex's brown eyes. "Life hasn't been kind to you."

"No, it hasn't."

Two

Several dogs yipped and barked and swarmed around the wagon train. Nikki, the brown-haired boy who Noah and his wife found hiding with his sister inside the enclosed seat of a wagon, tried to calm his agitated animals. He hugged the neck and breathed into the nostrils of Ahyoka, the prairie horse he had helped capture, and its colt, Tsayi. Even though Nikki had learned quite a bit of English since Noah and Ann had come across his parents serving as dinner for vultures, he spoke to his horses in his native language. "Wir sind jetzt gute Freunde. Ich werde mich um dich kümmern."

Oscar, the blond-haired seven-year-old, looked at his friend touch what had been wild horses. "You say your horses are your friends, but mine aren't friendly with me at all."

"You must blow in the nose. Like this." Nikki demonstrated.

"I can't get close enough."

"Ask my Ann."

A fortyish-year-old Mexican returning to town from the graveyard grabbed Alex. He barked in Spanish, "Where have you been?"

Alex answered in the same language. "I didn't want to say goodbye, so I walked into the prairie." He did not attempt to free himself from the man pulling him along by his shirtsleeve

Why is he letting that man treat him like that? Sally wondered.

"Whether you say goodbye or not, it's time for you to get to work. You are under my care now, and you're going to work for your keep. Hook up Goliath, and get the manure spread over the fields!"

Alex hung his head. He muttered, "I hate him!" as he walked toward a barn.

Sally had heard Alex tell his story to Noah. *Alex lost all his family, and now, when he's feeling down, that lout is taking advantage of him. I despise people like that!*

A frown grew on Noah's face and his brow furrowed. *It's not my place to get involved.*

The man, who had sent Alex off to work, spoke to Noah in Spanish. "Mi nombre es Domingo. Deberías mantenerte alejado de ese chico. Él es nada más que un problema."

Noah shrugged his shoulders.

Domingo bellowed in Spanish. "¡Alejandro! ¡Vuelve aquí!"

Alex turned back.

Noah requested, "Alex, may we buy a meal and a hot bath anywhere in town?"

"I will show you the cantina."

"Much obliged," Noah put his arm across Alex's shoulder and brought the young man along.

In the cantina, the locals chatted with each other in Spanish. To keep an eye on their wagons, Roscoe Bacon sat at a table beside the window. Assuming the sixty-one-year-old gray-haired man was the father of the whole group, a fat woman asked Roscoe, "¿Quieres comida para tu familia?" She waved her hand toward the people and then acted as if she was putting something into her mouth.

In 1821, twenty years earlier, when Alex's father had been in Santa Fe, Roscoe had also been there. He had eaten a delicious meal. This year 1841, as they had approached the mountains, Roscoe had told the family he had adopted and then married into about cornmeal cooked inside a cornhusk and then covered with a spicy tomato sauce. They'd all decided to try some. "Tamales," he swept his hand toward the members of his group, "for everybody."

Ann Williams put a small taste into the mouth of Adele, the year-old baby she and Noah had found with Nikki. The child spat the offending substance and looked at Ann as if she were thinking: I thought I could trust you, and now I have this in my mouth! Ann attempted to spoon cornmeal without the sauce.

When does Alex get to eat? Wondered Sally. *Probably not until he's done spreading manure.*

Sally put a silver coin on the table. She tried to sign what she wanted. "Make me a double portion. I'm taking it out of the cantina."

The woman nodded. When the second batch arrived, Sally had finished what had been on her plate. She went out the door with the new serving, jumped on her mule, and then rode to the field. "I brought you something to eat." Sally held out the big bowl.

Alex took it and the spoon. "This manure smells awful. How can you stand it?"

"I've shoveled manure most of my life, and I don't like Domingo. I'd rather not be in the same room with him. May I get on the wagon?"

"How could I say no after you brought me supper?"

Sally stepped directly onto the wagon from Beauty's back. She tied on her mule's reins and sat beside Alex, who happened to be splattered with the object of his work. "I'm sorry you lost your family," she said. "I lost my parents three years ago. For a long time, I was furious at God for taking them."

"I don't understand why He took away my grandfather, especially after He had already taken my parents."

"I don't know why God takes people we love, but last summer, my sister asked me if I liked myself. I realized that I do, and then it occurred to me that losing my parents allowed me to become who I am. I don't want to have lost my parents, but God gave me something back. He's given me the family I have today. I wouldn't have them if I still lived on the farm with my parents."

"You're lucky. God hasn't given me a single thing. When Grandpa knew he was dying, he signed over his house to Domingo. Domingo is supposed to take care of me. I'm old enough to take care of myself. I could have had a house. Instead, I'll have a life of slavery to Domingo. I guess I do own my quarter horse, Blackie."

"All that's left of my parents are two rifles, a tintype, two candle holders, and a music box that doesn't play."

"Why don't you have anything else?"

"Some awful men burned down our farm, including our house. We barely got out alive. We had to climb a rope of sheets out a bedroom window. We didn't have time to get anything else except a few clothes and blankets."

"You said you have a music box."

"I guess the only useful thing Gus ever did was to steal it, but he didn't do it to do good. Later, we got it back, but it doesn't play. He's probably the one who shot and broke it when his gang tried to kill us."

"Why would somebody want to kill you?"

"I think they didn't like us saving the life of a man one of them had tried to kill."

"Was he the man with the puma scars? He told me white people had tried to kill him because he's part Indian."

"Yes."

"People here don't like me because my father was a white man."

"They're stupid! That's all there is to it."

Alex swallowed the last of his meal. "If you're going to be here a few days, I might be able to fix your music box."

"Would it play the same music?"

"Depends on what's broken."

"I'll show it to you. Come to the cantina after you're done here."

"I will."

Alex had thought about something while he had been spreading animal feces. "One of Grandpa's books said it's best not to breed your animals within a small group. We've never had anybody come through with sheep and goats before. I wonder if your family would be willing to exchange some of your male animals for some of ours. You probably wouldn't exchange any of your donkeys or horses, would you?"

"You can talk to my family about it." Sally took the empty dish. "I'll see you later." She climbed onto Beauty and headed back to Raton but turned and waved.

Alex waved back. *Beautiful outside and inside.* He felt something he hadn't for a long time. He felt happy.

In Raton, Sally walked into the cantina.

Ann asked her youngest sister, "Why do you have the music box?"

"Alex is going to fix it."

"How?" her other sister, Stephanie, wondered aloud.

Sally told them the only important thing. "I don't know, but he says he can. He's going to come and look at it after he's done working." Sally sat at the table humming as she inspected the workings of her mama's music box.

Ann looked at Noah. He gazed into her green eyes and ran his finger through the edge of his wife's wavy, black hair. He shrugged his shoulders and mouthed, "Maybe."

Ann nodded her head and smiled.

A few hours later, manure-free and in clean clothes, Alex came into the cantina. Sally pulled over a seat and then patted it. Alex sat in the chair. "Let's take a look." He poked around. "You see this?"

Sally leaned closer. "What am I looking for?"

"What a music box needs are the cylinder with the bumps, that's where the melody is, the comb that makes the sounds, and a windup spring that turns the cylinder, a crank, and the box to amplify the sound."

"So where is the windup spring?"

"You're a natural. You've already figured it out. The spring is gone. It's just a coil of metal that the crank tightens. I can fix this for you."

"Lovely! How much will it cost? I'll get the money."

"Nothing."

"No. I must pay you."

"You paid me by bringing supper. If you can stay overnight, I'll return it to you in the morning."

Sally looked up from the music box. Her cheek almost touched Alex's. She blushed. "May we stay until morning, please?"

Sally's family, pretending they hadn't noticed her happiness, responded, "Yes."

"Grandfather's house is large. If I owned it, all of you could have stayed at my house." Alex looked at Domingo and then asked if they could.

Domingo immediately stated, "La tarifa será de dos dólares por una noche."

Alex translated for Noah, who pulled out a money bag. He paid the cantina owner and then turned to Alex. "We still have two Pieces of Eight. I assume Domingo will accept these."

Domingo held out his hand. "Alejandro, enséñales la casa y las habitaciones."

Three

On the way to the house, Alex asked Noah, "Would your family swap some male animals for some of ours?"

"They don't all belong to me. Why do you want to trade?"

Roscoe overheard the question. "That's not a bad idea. It's better to get fresh blood into the flock and the herd. We could at least put males with the opposite group of females overnight. I don't know if the timing is right, but it couldn't hurt to try. Who owns the animals here?"

"Different people, but we keep all of them together. We wouldn't have to tell anybody. After dark, we could move males around and change them back in the morning. As you said, though, "Nothing may happen over one night. It would be better to trade some."

"We would have to speak with the owners." Roscoe looked at Noah. "I wouldn't mind trading any of the young ones. They're all weaned now."

Noah negotiated, "I won't trade my son's horses. Also, we don't have a bull to help you, but I would like to put our females in the field with yours. Let's talk with the rest of the family. Maybe we can move some tonight and work out a trade."

Alex replied, "It's best not to mention it to anybody here until tomorrow. I don't want anybody to prevent our plan for tonight. Also, some people came through Raton last winter and stole from us, so it would be best if you put your wagons in the town's barn. That building is big enough to hold all your wagons, and it can be locked. Then, we'd also have a reason to take your animals to the barn at Grandpa's house. It's closer to our animals and farther from town."

Ann followed with her two littlest babies on her hips. "What did the thieves take?"

"They took Grandpa's clocks, tools, and supplies, stole all Juan's cloth and thread, and Pedro's blacksmith tools. Pedro hasn't been able to fix anything without his billows. Those louts gave a celebration to thank us for fixing their wagon. While everybody was in the cantina, they somehow sneaked around town and carried everything away."

"What will the townsfolk do?" Roscoe stepped into what was now Domingo's adobe house.

"Pedro has been praying for somebody to come along who has what he needs and will sell it to him, but nobody's been here since everything was taken." Alex showed Sally and her family the entire house. "Grandpa always rented rooms to people going west. Sometimes, folks got here so late they had to stay all winter." *Before Domingo moves in, I wish I could find where Grandpa kept his money.*

They sat together in the sitting room. By the light of oil lamps, they discussed and then agreed on an overnight animal placement strategy. Afterward, Alex told stories about the various people who had passed through Raton. He carefully avoided speaking of his family because he didn't want to think about them and miss them even more.

Four

Roscoe stood. "Even though it's summer, the pass will be deep in snow and hard to climb. We need plenty of sleep, so let's get started."

Alex held out his hand to Sally. "It's been very hot the last few years, and we haven't gotten much snow. I'd guess it's down to twenty feet, but I don't know. The trail goes behind the ridge, and I haven't gone up there."

"We'll find out tomorrow." Noah carried Adele and his seven-month-old son, Christopher. Ann cradled Joy. Nikki brought their calico cat into the room. Noah pulled a trundle bed out from under the extra-large bed. "I'll be back as soon as we get done."

Sally had no children to care for, so she went out the door with the men. In the barn, she separated the male from the female animals. Noah got his stallion, Eyanosa. Eli rounded up their three female cows while Tom got their ram and the oldest male goat. Even though Shaggy wasn't their largest donkey, Adahy led it away because Alex liked the donkey's long, thick twists of hair.

Roscoe went with Alex to select which of the town's males he thought would be best to breed with their females.

The bull grazed with his herd. The horses, donkeys, goats, and sheep shared the larger of the two fields used by the village animals.

Alex and Roscoe returned with the selected Raton animals in tow. Alex opened the gate. "Wait for us to get back before taking the cows into the field with Diablo."

At the barn, Roscoe opened the stall with their female sheep inside. Alex released the lead rope from Raton's oldest ram. It trotted in. They did the same with the goats and then left the jack in the central part of the barn with all the jennies, except for Roscoe's miniature donkeys, which he had in a different compartment. On their way back to the cow field, they released Domingo's powerful white stallion into the paddock with the mares.

Farther out of town, Eyanosa reared back on his hind hooves and then charged toward the cluster of horses gathered at the far end of the field. They released Shaggy, Billy the goat, and the ram right after the horse.

Everybody met at the gate. Diablo snorted and pawed the ground on the other side of the fence. Eli held the ropes to their cows. "I think at least one of our cows must be ready. Diablo sure is! I don't know if we'll be able to get them in there. He looks like he's going to charge out the gate."

"He's let us take cows in and out of the field before." Alex started to release the latch.

Eli called out, "Wait! Everybody go away."

"You too. I'll do it." Alex took the ropes.

Noah peeked out from behind the corner of the barn. Sally watched from behind her oldest sister's husband. The rest of the men stood behind the other corner. Alex saw his new friends safely out of goring range. "Diablo, stay put, and you'll have these girls in a second."

Diablo let out a big snort. Alex positioned the cow the family had acquired at Fort Arbuckle and therefore named Arbuckle. He released her from her line, cracked the gate, and smacked her rear. She darted into the pen and across the field. Diablo charged behind her. Alex let the other two go in.

The rest of the family came back to the fence. Across the field, they saw Diablo doing his business. Sally commented, "We'll have Arbuckle to give us milk again. Maybe we'll be lucky, and Courageous will come into estrus tonight. Gimpy's broken leg seems healed, but maybe Diablo would be too heavy for her right now?"

"It's not likely either will be receptive," Roscoe added, "but Gimpy's been walking fine this week."

As the group returned to Domingo's house, Sally asked, "Do you think anybody in town noticed what we're doing?"

Alex answered, "I don't think so. If somebody did, Domingo would be here wringing my neck!"

Sally walked close to Alex. "You're very brave, and it's very nice of you to take a chance to help people who don't even like you."

Five

Before Sally shut the door to the room she occupied alone, she asked Alex, "Would Domingo trade books with us?"

"They aren't his, and he doesn't even know what's here. Grandpa always traded books, especially when people were here for a long time. Swap one for one and take what you want."

Alex went to his grandfather's workroom. The thieves had taken all the clocks Alex and his grandfather had already made, tools, gears, and most of the inner workings. *I have some scraps.* Alex looked for the proper tools and a clock spring. He opened boxes, moved things from here to there, and then attempted to pull out a drawer he and his grandfather had never used when they had built clocks together.

The drawer didn't open but a few inches. Wedged between the drawer and the bench top, Alex discovered a small bent screwdriver preventing the drawer from sliding out. *It's small enough to remove the mechanism from Sally's music box. I need to get it out.*

Alex forced the tool down. *That felt strange.* He bent over, held his lantern to the drawer, and pushed on the screwdriver again. A three-inch lip at the bottom of the drawer hinged open. He tried to see into the wedge-shaped opening. The lip blocked his view. *This didn't open for no reason.* He stuck his hand into the space but didn't feel anything inside. He peered into the opening again. He couldn't see any better than the first time he had tried.

Alex felt in the void and looked over the drawer for thirty minutes. *I don't know.* He gave up, dumped their scrap box onto the worktable, and found a quarter-inch wide strip of metal. He fed one end of it into the slot of the crank handle bolted to the heavy boards of the workbench, turned the handle, and wound the metal into a coil.

Alex couldn't free the screwdriver from the drawer, and all the other tools had been stolen. He had the part he needed, but he couldn't remove the crank from the broken music box or install the new spring. He had no idea what to do with the mysterious space he could partially open by pressing the screwdriver in the stuck drawer, so he gave up for the night and went to bed.

Six

The sun rose. Alex spoke with the only other person in the house who was already awake. "My grandfather's tools were stolen. I need to borrow a small screwdriver to fix the music box."

Noah opened the jockey box on the side of his wagon. Alex pushed tools around and found one he hoped was small enough.

"We need to get the animals moved." Noah locked the wooden box. "My horse will come when I signal. It should be easy to get your animals back into the field. We'll get our cows last." Noah hoped he was far enough away from town so the people would not hear but close enough to Eyanosa for his horse to do so. He whistled a short sharp note. Eyanosa galloped to Noah.

"I've never seen an animal do that." Alex opened the gate.

"Bring your stallion around this side. I'll take mine on the left side of the barn into the paddock. Neither will know the other was with their mares."

"All right. I'll come right back and meet you in the barn."

Securing the animals to lead lines, the two men

had no problem moving Raton's animals back to their field and Noah's into Domingo's barn. Alex looked at the tight cluster of cattle. "I don't know if Diablo will let us take your cows."

"I'm not leaving them. Maybe we can get the whole group to walk past the gate and draw mine out without him realizing it."

"They ARE going to walk past the gate when they go into the barn for milking. Esmeralda will be in the barn putting out grain. We might be able to get them before they go in."

"Wait, I thought we locked the barn with our wagons in there."

"Esmeralda has the key."

"You didn't tell us that!"

"She won't take anything."

"You should have told us."

"She's the one you should talk to about trading the young animals. Everybody else will do what she agrees to."

"She's probably going to realize we put our cows with the town bull and then not agree, and who knows what else she'll do."

"She's the most reasonable person in Raton. The animals are heading to the barn. I'll see if I can get your cows to this side of the herd." Alex climbed over the fence and walked into the field. Diablo spotted the intruder. With new cows to protect, he charged. Alex sprinted to the fence. "Help!"

Noah pulled Alex over as he scrambled up the wooden rails. Diablo slammed into the fence as

Alex fell to the safe side. Noah's cows moseyed into the barn with the rest of the herd.

Triumphant, Diablo followed his harem to the feeding trough. Alex could do nothing but watch his plan fall apart. "Let me talk to Esmeralda. Wait outside the door."

Noah followed. "I'm not leaving my cows!"

Seven

Esmeralda heard keys jingle at the barn door. *I didn't think they'd leave this early. I don't know English. What am I going to do?* She hid behind a stack of hay.

Alex came through the door. "Me explico."

What has he done now? The tall, slender woman stepped into view. "Explain what?"

She hasn't noticed. Well, she will soon. "As smart as you are, I'm sure you know how important it is to get new blood into our herds. It was too late to ask you last night, and these people are leaving this morning, so I thought it would be good to get our animals with their animals last night, and, well, now we can't get their cows away from Diablo."

Without hesitating, Esmeralda asked, "Did you get our animals with their males?"

"Yes, the rest are in the right places."

"If you hadn't gotten their cows trapped, you'd never have told any of us, would you?"

25

"Probably not."

"You wouldn't have gotten the gratitude of the people of this town, and yet you did the right thing for us anyway. Diablo just went into the stall with the grain. Shut the door. You can take their cows after I get their milk."

"None of them are making milk right now."

"So, Alejandro, do you have any other ideas about these animals?"

"It might be a good idea to trade some of our animals for some of theirs. What do you think?"

"Is the old man outside the door waiting for my answer?"

"He's not the old man."

"Tell him to come in."

Alex opened the barn door. "I think she wants to trade."

Esmeralda instructed the men, "Both of you help me do the work, and then we can look at the animals and decide."

Alex translated. Noah said, "Give me a pitchfork. I'll give hay to Diablo first."

Even with Alex and Esmeralda milking, Noah finished putting out the cow food before they were done. "Do you want me to help milk or shovel manure into the wagon?"

Alex knew the answer because it would be him if not Noah. "Shovel manure."

Everybody was awake before Noah, Alex, and Esmeralda completed the negotiations. They walked into Domingo's house together and confirmed the trade of their two steers for one cow currently producing milk and the swap of most of their young animals. Although nobody knew how successful the night had been, since those unions would have been the adults, even more different blood would be added into their herds by swapping the juveniles.

Oscar leaned close to his mother. "My horses don't like me. May I trade them?"

"They belong to you. You can if you want to, but get your new father to help you pick."

Oscar turned to the man who sat on his other side. "Will you help me, Tom?"

"Alex, ask Esmeralda if we can trade a mare and its colt. They are unbroken prairie mustangs."

Alex passed on the request. Esmeralda walked toward the door and waved for them to follow.

Oscar stood on the third rail of the fence and held out an apple. A white mare took it from his hand. She allowed Oscar to rub her face while she crunched the yummy fruit. He blew into her nostrils. "She let me! Will she let me sit on her?"

Alex looked at Tom. "I'm sure she will. You want to put your son on her?"

Tom climbed the fence with Oscar right behind him. He set Oscar on the horse. "Hold tightly to the mane." Oscar squeezed in his heels. The horse gently walked into the field with Tom beside her and Oscar on her back.

Oscar's smile spread across his face. "I want this one, but what about a baby?"

Alex spoke to Esmeralda, "He wants your horse and a foal too. Azúcar is yours, but you don't have any foals. What do you want to do?"

"She is pregnant. I put her with Domingo's stallion. He doesn't know it. As you said, we need new stock. The mustangs are an excellent breed. I'd like to do it if they will trade for Azúcar only."

Alex waved for Tom and Oscar. "Azúcar is pregnant. Esmeralda will trade her for your two horses. In English, her name is Sugar."

Oscar looked into Tom's eyes. "I want Azúcar. I can't even touch the wild ponies. Please!"

Tom looked at Esmeralda. "If you'll also sell me a bridle and saddle."

"Ustedes vienen." Esmeralda walked to the tack room.

Eight

Once back in the workroom, Alex fiddled with the screws of the music box until he got them out. Then came the hard part; he attempted to take the spring off the winder and get it into the housing in the music box. It decompressed too fast. He tried with gloves on, but he couldn't manipulate it into the metal chamber. Without the tool he needed to keep the coil of metal from unwinding, every attempt cut his fingers.

Except for Alex, the people in the house went to the cantina to get breakfast. After eating frittatas made with habanero peppers, Roscoe and Noah went to speak with Pedro. Since the man couldn't operate his forge, the blacksmith languished in his home.

Pedro stood in the doorway as Roscoe spoke. "I have been told you speak English and that you might be interested in some blacksmith tools."

"I surely am. Do you have some?!"

"Come out here. I'll show you what I have."

"These bellows aren't quite as large as what I had, but you have many tools. How much of this will you sell?"

Roscoe had already removed the tools he needed and had the leather bellows Eli had made to fit their small mobile forge. "I will sell any of the blacksmith tools in this wagon."

"How much for all of this?"

"Do you have lead? We also need many horseshoe blanks and nails."

After completing the trade, Pedro went with Roscoe to get Tom before he took them to see the man whose cloth had been stolen. They hoped the man would trade what they had brought from their stores back in Arkansas for good walking shoes to replace the several sets they had worn out crossing the prairie. Later, Pedro took the women to a lady who sold long strings of dried hot peppers, cornmeal, and hay from the fields around Raton.

The women returned to Domingo's boarding house to get their bags. Sally opened the door and heard music. "He did it!" She hurried to the workroom with the other women behind her. "Alex, you're the most wonderful person in the world!" She threw her arms around him and pressed her head to his chest. "You know how much this means to us!"

"That's why I didn't give up."

Sally saw Alex's bleeding fingers. "Oh my, what happened?"

"I had a hard time getting the spring to stay wound, but I finally did it."

The music box stopped. "Play it again," Stephanie requested.

30

Sally picked up the wooden box, still with a bullet hole but once again with a working spring. She wound it up and sat it on the bench. The women listened to the melody that Sally, Ann, and Stephanie had not heard for over two years. The third time they listened, Helen hummed along. "I saw this song in one of the music books I got at the pit houses. Let me get it."

Helen returned. As the melody played, she sang.

"Farewell, but whenever you welcome the hour
that awakens the night-song of mirth in your bower,
then think of the friend who once welcom'd it too,
and forgot his own griefs to be happy with you.
His griefs may return, not a hope may remain,
of the few that had brighten'd his pathway of pain,
but he ne'er will forget the short vision that threw,
it's enchantment around him, while ling'ring with you.

"And still on that evening when pleasure fills up,
to the highest top sparkle each heart and each cup,
where 'ere my path lies, be it gloomy or bright,
my soul, happy friends, shall be with you that night.
Shall join in your revels, your sports, and your wiles,
and return to me beaming, all o'er with your smiles.
Too, blest if it tells me that 'mid the gay cheer,
some kind voice had murmer'd, "I wish he were here!"

"Let Fate do her worst, there are relics of joy,
bright dreams of the past, which she cannot destroy,
which come in the night-time of sorrow and care,
and bring back the features that joy used to wear.

Long, long be my heart with such memories fill'd,
like the vase in which roses have once been distill'd.
You may break, you may ruin the vase if you will,
but the scent of the roses will hang 'round it still. "*

"I never knew the song!" Ann exclaimed. "Now, Mama's music box is an even sweeter remembrance. Alex, how can I thank you?"

"Just knowing somebody's pain is lessened is the best payment."

The workroom door slammed open. "I told you to get to the cherry orchard first thing this morning."

"Yes, sir. I'm going right now." Alex ran from the room.

Suddenly able to speak English, Domingo said, "He will never be good help."

Sally informed the man. "He is not your help. You are supposed to be caring for him as a son."

"Is that what he told you? I'll have to speak with him about talking to my guests."

I could punch you. Sally walked to the door. "Excuse me. I need to get out." She packed her small bag then went to speak with Noah, who had just returned from moving the traded animals. "We can't leave Alex here."

"It's not up to us to decide what he does, but I'll ask him if he would like to come with us." Noah had seen Alex in a grove of trees. He loaded their bags into the wagon, went to the orchard, and stood under the tree where Alex picked cherries. He looked at the young man on a ladder. "Why don't you come with us?"

That would be the nicest future I can imagine, but I can't pay my way. I'm not going to take advantage of these nice people. "Thank you for offering. I'd better stay here."

"Are you sure? Domingo doesn't seem like a very nice person."

"I'm sure."

As Noah walked away, a tear fell from Alex's eye.

"Is he coming?" Sally asked.

"No. I'm sorry, Sally."

A layer of loneliness and pain wound tighter around Sally's heart. She choked it back. "I don't care anyway. I just thought he might want to go with us since he had already tried to run away once."

Alex watched the family round the ridge on the wagon path into the mountains. "I hate you!" He shook his fist at the sky.

Nine

The animals slowly pulled the wagons, no longer hauling blacksmith tools, cloth bolts, or thread crates. They climbed the trail, which had been much smoother when covered with packed snow. During the preceding three years, the snow had softened and slid away in avalanches. All the new snow had fallen across the prairie in Arkansas. Jagged stones littered the bare ground.

After two hours of ascending, they still hadn't seen any snow. Here and there, the exposed mountain dropped away and barely left enough space for the wagons to pass. At every place for potential disaster, one of the men stood at the edge so wagons and animals wouldn't fall off.

Roscoe walked at the front of the wagon train. "Looks like a wagon ahead."

Helen commented, "Maybe it's those people who stole everything. If it is, we should go back and let the townsfolk know."

"The canvas cover looks rotted and ripped up. This wagon has probably been here for years." Roscoe called out, "Halt!" He opened the puckering strings and looked inside. "Oh, my!"

"What is it?" Helen walked toward Roscoe.

"Maybe you shouldn't look."

Helen did anyway. "How sad! I think they were trying to keep the baby from freezing."

"Unfortunately, they all did. They smell terrible."

Ann joined them and looked at the heartbreaking scene. "Why hasn't anybody taken any of the supplies?"

Nikki stood on the wagon seat and looked in through the front opening. "Very hard to get over mountain. Some people can't do it?"

"Some didn't. Alex said there's always deep snow. Maybe the wagon had been buried. Now, there isn't any snow, and it's uncovered. Get the rest of the group, and we'll get the usable supplies. I'll dig a hole and bury these folks." Noah went to his wagon to get a shovel.

"I'll clean away this mess." Helen pulled back the canvas lying over a corner of the contents. She picked up a sack of flour full of worms and tossed it out. Next, she opened a bag of what appeared to be undamaged black-eyed peas. She passed them to Stephanie. "Do you think these are good?"

Stephanie scooped out a handful and examined them. "I don't see any mold. They don't smell bad." She carried the sack away.

They divided pots, tools, a rocking cradle, and other items kept intact under a blanket of snow between their wagons. Ehawee picked up a pair of scissors. "I'm going to take all the long hair from this horse and start another net."

Hours later, all the rotten food had been tossed over the precipice, and the unfortunate family whose journey had ended on a frozen mountain had been respectfully interred. Everything good had been recovered, and the small empty wagon left behind.

Ten

In Raton, Alex carried another basket of cherries into the barn. The crowbar in the corner caught his eye. *I'm going to rip that workbench apart.* He strode over and grabbed the long iron bar and a sledgehammer. He ran back to the house, threw open the workroom door, pushed the bent screwdriver, and jammed the pry bar into the slot. It remained firmly in place, so he grabbed the hammer and swung with all his might. Wood splintered as he drove the wrecking bar into the workbench. The next stroke, Alex applied a downward force. Ruptured boards and the spring winder flew across the room.

Alex looked inside. "I knew it!" He pried until he made the opening large enough and then drew out a locked strongbox. *Grandpa always had that little key in his pocket. I put it in the wooden box my father made. If I take Blackie and go full speed, I may be able to catch up.*

Curiosity overcame Alex. He examined the broken table to determine how his grandfather had gotten the metal container in and out of the drawer.

He discovered the side of the drawer could be pushed out and then pulled forward, which released a catch behind the back of the drawer. *This would have been easy for a clockmaker to think up. I should have known Grandpa did something like this.*

Alex hurried to his room with the metal container he hoped held his grandfather's life savings. He grabbed the key out of the small, inlaid wooden box. With shaking hands, Alex inserted it into the strongbox keyhole. He turned the key and then opened the lid. "Praise the Lord!"

I might need to fix the spring again. Full of anticipation, Alex snatched the spring winder, dashed to his grandfather's room, and grabbed the carpet bag. He sneaked to the barn with the satchel containing his clothes, the spring winder, the wooden box, the strongbox full of money, the Bible his mother had given him, and the book on animal husbandry, which his grandfather had used to teach him how to read and write English.

Alex secured his saddle on Blackie and then slid on her bridle. *I'm going to miss Goliath, but Grandfather specifically gave him to Domingo. I'll say goodbye.* Alex looked at the baskets of cherries. *Those trees belonged to Pa.* He hung a set of the large transportation baskets on his horse, poured in all the cherries he had picked, and then led her to the backside of the barn.

He called for Goliath. Alex had always been the one who had cared for and fed the giant draft horse, so it walked to the fence expecting to receive a handful of grain. The horse ate from Alex's hand. Alex rubbed Goliath's neck. "I'm sorry, but I can't take you. I hope Domingo treats you better than he has me. I'm going to miss you."

Alex mounted Blackie. "Let's go." He drew his heels into the horse the whole town knew he owned and flew toward the mountains.

Goliath watched Alex race away. Behind the barn, Esmeralda did too. The horse stared at the mountain for several minutes and then frantically paced beside the fence. Esmeralda casually strolled over and opened the gate. Goliath charged to the mountain gap and then disappeared behind the ridge. "Goodbye, Alejandro. Goodbye, Goliath. Be happy."

Blackie ran and ran. Alex urged her on until the slope was too much for the horse. *I'll catch them when they stop for the night.* He allowed his horse to walk.

Behind him, Goliath did not slow. His mighty muscles powered him on. Alex heard the heavy clomping of hooves. *They're coming to drag me back!* He frantically looked for a place to hide himself and Blackie. One side of the trail was a shear rock face. The other was a precipice of hundreds of feet. *I'm not going back!* He kicked his heels into Blackie. "Run!"

Alex looked over his shoulder. The larger horse with longer legs came around the bend and overtook the human he loved. "Goliath!" Alex pulled Blackie to a halt and jumped off. He pressed his face to the shoulder of the giant horse. "Well, all right. I didn't steal you. You came on your own. You can come." He allowed both horses to rest for half an hour before he resumed his ascent.

At the empty wagon with a one-horse harness lying inside, Alex saw the newly turned-over soil. *They stopped to bury the people. They might not be much farther ahead. I wonder how many people didn't make it over these mountains. I think this is the first time these mountains haven't been capped in deep snow. Things that were buried under the snow will be out in the open. There might be a better wagon ahead, but I'll take this one in case there isn't.* Alex quickly hooked Goliath into the harness. He put his satchel and the baskets of cherries into the wagon and took away the last evidence of the catastrophe.

Eleven

When the wagon train stopped for the middle of the day rest, Alex caught up. "Hello ahead, Alex here!"

Sally jumped to her feet. "Hello!" She dashed down the trail and stopped beside Blackie with Alex on her back. "You came!"

Alex touched Sally's face. "How could I let the owner of the music box get away?"

"I'm glad you didn't. Join us. We brought tamales from town. Several of them are waiting for you."

"Welcome!" Noah asked, "Is that the wagon that was beside the trail?"

"Yes. I can use it, so I hooked up Goliath and took it."

Sally walked beside the wagon. "What do you have in the baskets?"

"Cherries. My father planted the trees, and I picked these cherries, so when I found the money, I figured I could pay my way, and there is no reason for me to stay in Raton. More than just these few cherries should be mine, so I'm giving the town a

41

gift by not taking every fruit on those trees." Alex reached into the basket and drew out a handful. "They are very tasty. Try some." He dropped them into Sally's cupped hands.

Alex got off Blackie and carried one of the baskets to the group sitting beside the fire. While Alex ate tamales, everybody else ate cherries and divulged their names.

Eli asked, "Is Domingo going to come looking for you because you stole his horse?"

Alex replied, "I didn't take him. I left with only Blackie, and she is mine. Goliath is too smart of a horse and must have realized I wasn't coming back. He escaped on his own and followed me. I don't know if anybody will come looking for him. Domingo is very lazy. I don't think he'd make the effort."

Sally rubbed the large horse's neck. "We had a big draft horse like Goliath, but his name was Samson. Unfortunately, he was killed." Sally walked to Blackie and patted her too. "I'm very glad they've joined us."

Ann knew what Sally really meant about whom she was happy had joined them, but Ann was sure Sally liked the horses as well.

Due to the altitude, the air was cool, but grass and spring flowers grew in the sunlight that warmed the ground for the first time in decades. Alex strolled through the flowers with Sally. "Up here, it's fresh air. I feel like I can breathe again." He picked a violet-colored bell-shaped flower

42

hanging on a slender stem and handed it to Sally. "This Bluebell is for you, but you're putting it to shame with your beauty."

"Don't be silly, Alex. I'm not more beautiful than a flower."

"Yes, you are."

Sally blushed. "Thank you for thinking so."

After allowing the animals to eat all the grass within a safe range of their camp, they resumed the climb.

Tom led them. At the next sheer drop, he called to the wagon behind him. "Alex, let Sally guide Goliath. You stand beside the edge and keep the animals from getting too close."

Alex handed the reins to Sally, who had been walking beside him. He looked over the edge. *I saw the wagon down there in Pedro's shop.*

After everybody and the last group of tied-on animals had passed, he climbed over the edge and dropped onto a pile of gnawed oxen bones lying at the front of the wagon. *I better keep a close watch.* He stepped into the wagon. *Some animal was eating on these bones too.* He pushed them around with his boot. *There it is.* He slid the knife he found behind his belt.

They had a lot of money. He searched until he found the bag. He heard a sound outside and shoved it into his pocket. *I don't have a gun. I don't want to fight a wolf with a knife.*

"It's me, Eli."

"Thank you, God! Come on in."

43

"Are those canned peaches? My wife loves them."

"I don't know how we'd carry them. We'll need both hands to climb."

"I tied a rope to a mule and dropped it over the edge."

"Let's take the cover and load it with what we want. Your mule can pull it up. You'll have to wrap those jars pretty good, or they'll break." Alex held a silver mirror. "Do you think Sally would like this?"

"I happen to know she would love it."

"I'll take all of these and give them to her."

"Alex, you should know, if you try to take advantage of Sally, I will kill you, so don't try to have your way with her."

"Of course not! I wouldn't do anything to hurt her or any of you."

"I'm glad you decided to come with us, but I want you to understand completely. Be a gentleman. Stephanie has her mule attached to the rope. She named it Redeemed because she redeemed it from stubbornness. Do you want all of this?"

"Let's see what we can get in one load." Alex untied the canvas cover and laid it in one end of the wagon. He already had all the jewelry he had found in his pants pockets. He slipped the fancy hair combs and the silver brush set into the large coffee pot and placed them on the canvas.

While Eli gathered scattered coffee beans, Alex stacked intact sugar sacks. "Should we see if any of the eggs in the broken cornmeal barrel are good?"

"No, we don't know how long this wagon has been here."

"It came through the beginning of last winter. I was in the blacksmith shop when the man bought this knife from Pedro." He drew it and handed it to Eli.

"It looks like blood on this."

Alex took it back and looked closer. "And it wasn't in the sheath. Do you think one of them stabbed the other?"

"Maybe they went over because they were struggling."

"Then it was the man. The woman owned all the money. The husband told Pedro not to tell his wife he had bought it."

Eli shook his head. "Bless her heart. She believed he loved her, and now she's down here stabbed and then eaten by wolves."

"At least she took him to the grave with her. I don't know how strong this canvas is. Let's send light things and see what happens."

"Stephanie!" Eli hollered.

"I'm here."

"Pull up this load."

Alex and Eli sorted while Stephanie retrieved the first load with most of the non-food items. "The wolves tore into the bran barrel and ate all the bacon. It's a mess, and so are the cornmeal and eggs. Let's only take what the animals left alone."

After Stephanie sent the canvas back, they loaded the wagon jack, axle grease, linseed oil, wagon repair tools, unbroken wheel spokes, and the kingpin. They sent sugar, salt, coffee, tea, rice, canned peaches, and spice jars on the third and last load. They also took the coffee grinder and silverware but left the smashed china in the wagon with all the tainted food and human bones.

Eli and Alex climbed to the trail as Stephanie and Redeemed retrieved the final load. They loaded Alex's new possessions into the rear wagon and resumed the ascent.

Near the end of the day, they found another abandoned wagon in a large open field. Oscar looked in. "Nothing except a big hole in the floor. How many people didn't make it over this mountain?"

Nikki looked at Noah. "Will we?"

Noah assured his adopted son, "We will definitely make it over. All the others had extreme cold and deep snow. We have nice weather, and there isn't a speck of snow anywhere. This wagon has been here even longer than the others. The bows are gone, and the canvas has rotted away."

Roscoe didn't think it had been that long. "The wood of the wagon isn't weathered. I think somebody shot the hole through the floor when he shot the people inside then stole everything except the actual wagon. Even the harness is gone."

"Must have used a shotgun to make a hole this big." Eli examined the wagon. "This is a better wagon than the one you have, Alex. We should stop here for the night. We'll take your little wagon apart and use the floorboards to repair this one. You can take the wheels and such as spare parts."

"I'd need help, and maybe you shouldn't work hard when you should be resting."

"This is a big field. We can block it with a wagon and let the animals eat grass tonight and tomorrow while we fix this. We'll save our hay for the places where there isn't anything else for the animals to eat."

Roscoe added, "Probably as we get higher, there won't be grass along the trail. We should stop here, so we might as well work on the wagon."

"Well then, thank you for being willing to help me."

Sally placed her hand over Alex's hand on the edge of the better wagon. "I'll help too."

Twelve

Since they would be staying more than just overnight, they set up the cast iron stove that Noah had earned helping injured people in a different wagon train. Emily, Sally, and Helen cooked supper while Ann, Stephanie, and Ehawee nursed their babies.

Oscar pried nails from a board of the smaller wagon that the men were deconstructing. "I like destroying this."

"We aren't destroying it. We're just taking it apart." Tom handed Nikki a board.

Oscar clarified, "I mean that I don't have to think hard about how to do this."

Alex took a floorboard to the pile. "I'm paying close attention to how this wagon comes apart. I might have to put one back together."

"We are going very far." Nikki put the plank from Tom in front of Oscar. "It's my turn."

"Where are you going?" Alex asked.

Oscar handed Nikki the hammer. "The Western Sea."

"What a long way!"

Inside the wagon, Noah removed another floorboard. "You can stop any time you want as long as you don't keep Sally."

"I'm not saying I don't want to go. I was just saying we're going very far. To tell you the truth, the farther from Raton, the better."

After they had taken apart the wagon, Alex ate salted goose legs. Sally took him a slice of the cherry pie she had baked in the stove's oven. "May we prepare some cherries for drying and keep the seeds?"

"What a good plan. You may." After the pie, Alex prepared to sleep in a place other than the town of Raton for the first time in his life.

A day passed as they rebuilt the wagon's floor. They attached both axles and all four wheels from the smaller wagon to the sides of the larger one and loaded the parts they had not reused. Except for the canned peaches that he had given to Stephanie, everything Alex had brought from the ravine, along with the drying cherries, more in their baskets, and his bag were loaded into his new, long, narrow wagon.

There was something else Alex didn't put in his wagon. He sat beside Sally. "I found something I thought you might like." He handed her his present.

"A coffee pot? We already have several."

"Look inside."

Sally removed the lid and carefully withdrew a mirror with an intricately fashioned silver frame and handle. "This is so beautiful." With a faraway look, she caressed the mirror for a second then put it back into the pot and handed it back to Alex. "I don't take anything from men. I know what you'd be thinking it would entitle you to." She abruptly walked away.

Alex looked at Eli. "You said she would love it."

Eli moved closer to Alex. "A year or so ago, a man we were traveling with offered Sally an orange. She asked for five more. The man gave them to her then sneaked into her tent and tried to force himself on her. I got there just in time to stop him. I had to threaten to shoot him. I should have told you not to give them to her until she got to know you better."

"Is that why you told me you'd kill me?"

"It is. Give her some time and assure all of us that you have only good intentions."

"I'll go apologize."

"Leave her alone tonight. I'll speak with her."

In the first light of day, Adahy gently set a crate of the dynamite they had gotten in Dover onto the ground beside Roscoe. "I think it would be good to have the mules carry this. It looks rough ahead. I'm sure bouncing in a wagon would set it off."

"I don't want to kill any of my mules. However, better a few mules than all of us," Roscoe tightened the strap of the pack saddle he filled with the dangerous sticks and diatomaceous earth from the first crate.

All four crates of dynamite were ready to be safely transported when Sally again spoke with Alex. "I don't think I should take anything so expensive from you. I understand that you had no ulterior motives. Please forgive me for being rude. Don't be upset with me."

"I'm not. I didn't understand how you would take it. I would never do anything inappropriate. It is just that you were so kind to me when I was hurting a lot. I wanted to do something nice for you. Forgive me for upsetting you."

"Let's forgive each other and forget it."

"All right."

The mules gently traversed the uneven terrain. However, the wagons bumped over the extremely stony and rough trail for hours. Repeatedly, one wheel or the other of every wagon went up on a rock and slammed to the ground until the sound of splitting wood rang out.

The group stood around the wagon from which the sound had emanated. All the males slid under the wagon.

"We'll have to replace the axle," said Roscoe.

Oscar had seen this before. "Yep, we'll have to replace the axle."

Alex said, "I don't know why it had to be my wagon that broke, but I'm glad I have the spare part. We haven't gotten very far. I hope we can make it all the way to the sea!"

"It won't be a problem. We've done this before. I'll get some jacks. Oscar and Nikki, get wagon chocks. We can use the broken axle to cook dinner when we get it off." Tom looked at Noah and nodded his head in Alex's direction. "Let's get started."

Eli slid out from under. "I'll look for something to hold up the wagon." *It could easily fall off jacks at this angle.*

Noah whispered to Alex, who still lay under the wagon with him. "It's going to be tough getting over these mountains, and this is just the beginning. We need to try not to scare the boys. You don't know everything they've been through."

"Haven't you been through it all together?"

"No. Their parents were killed horribly. Here they come. I'll tell you about it later."

With all the men working together, they replaced the axle by the time the mid-day meal should have been ready. However, they had ascended to an altitude where the water took a very long time to boil. They were still waiting for Alex's salvaged rice when Roscoe came back from scouting ahead. "There's a small stream not much farther ahead. We can let them eat hay."

"I'll do it." Oscar headed to the wagon crammed full of hay. Nikki followed to help.

The rice finally cooked, and they sat to eat. Roscoe cautiously tasted the spiced rice. "It's fine." He dug in. "We should start clearing the large rocks."

Eli said, "Only if we can't get around them."

They watered all the animals at the stream and

filled their water containers before they got under way. Every few yards, large rocks blocked the path. Moving them tired them all. They climbed the trail at less than a snail's pace. Night drew near, but only half a mile more lay behind them. Ahead lay a long, rocky gap between two high craggy walls.

Noah looked at the cliffs. "It's much wider higher up. Previous travelers would have had more space. I hope it doesn't become too narrow to get through."

Alex stood beside him. "Maybe somebody should ride through and find out. It's still early enough. I'll go."

Sally felt unsure of Alex's abilities. *Noah can handle any problem.* "Take Noah with you."

Thirteen

Alex rode Blackie into the space between the high rock walls. "While we're away from the others, please, tell me everything I should know. I don't want to keep saying or doing the wrong thing."

Noah led the way on Eyanosa. "I guess I should start at the beginning. Two years and three months ago, I left the village where I grew up...."

The men followed the winding path as Noah related the family's experiences. Alex asked questions, commented, or added relevant tales from his own life. "It looks too narrow here."

Noah removed the looped rope from the horn of his saddle. "Hold this end at that side." He fed out the line as he went to the other side. Before he got to the knot that marked the width of their widest wagon, he reached the other cliff. "We can't get through." He tied a knot to mark the width of the canyon. "We should keep going. It may be even narrower before we come out."

An hour later, the gulch ended. They had not seen any other place that appeared too narrow. Alex suggested, "Perhaps we should hold the rope to each side as we return. You know, to make sure nothing is worse than what we already measured."

Noah handed Alex one end of the rope. He rode to the opposite cliff and resumed the tale he had been asked to relate. "So, the snow wasn't here because it was in Pine Bluff, Arkansas…"

When Alex and Noah arrived back at camp, they had verified the narrowest width. "That isn't every detail, but basically, it's our story." Noah rode to the corral, where the other animals ate hay. He carried his saddle, bridle, and rope to the narrowest wagon. "Alex, hold an end."

Alex pulled the rope across the rear. "I guess we can do what you suggested."

While they ate super, Noah told the group about the problem he and Alex had discovered. "Only Alex's wagon will fit through a sixty-foot section."

In the chilly air, Alex held out his cup for more hot coffee. "We'll have to unload then take the wheels and wagon boxes off the frames. We can carry the pieces in my wagon. Some of us will put the wagons back together while others bring our supplies."

"That's going to take days," Helen informed them.

Sally stood with Alex's plan. "It will take as long as it takes. There isn't anything else we can do."

Emily gathered plates. "We probably have enough time to unload a wagon into Alex's tonight. Tomorrow morning, we can take the first load of supplies across while you take apart the wagon."

"While the wagon is gone," Helen handed Emily her empty dish, "we can unload another."

"We should take turns driving the wagon, unloading, taking apart, and rebuilding. That way, everybody can rest a little," added Eli.

"Don't move the supplies until the end. We can't protect everything and us if we're divided between two camps." Ann handed Noah a bowl of cherry cobbler.

"Nobody is up here," Stephanie informed her sister.

Ehawee took her dessert. "What about wild animals?"

After their discussion and the evening Bible reading, they unloaded the first wagon onto the ground.

The following day, Noah, Nikki, and Alex built a skid with some of the boards from the first wagon Alex had recovered. Goliath drew it into the gap. Along the way, the horse pulled as the two men and Nikki pushed boulders onto the skid. Once the rocks that would prevent a wagon from passing were on the wooden sled, they hooked the harness to it and took the stones to a broader place where they could place them out of the way. Those that were too large to be tucked away, they dragged all the way through the narrow gap.

Back in camp, Roscoe, Tom, Oscar, Adahy, and Eli took apart the empty wagon and loaded it into Alex's skinny wagon. The women unloaded another wagon before Sally offered, "I'll take the wagon in a wagon to the other side." She got to the constriction. *It's narrow but open at the top and the ends, and there is plenty of light.* The thought didn't consciously come into her mind, but part of her motivation to travel into the terrifying space, despite her fear of caves, was because she wanted to see Alex. She called into the crevasse. "I'm here with the first wagon."

Alex hollered, "Just one more large stone to move, but you can come on. We're going to take it out the far end."

Sally drove in with a pounding heart. Her breaths came shallow and rapid until she saw Alex pushing a large boulder with his foot against the canyon wall and his shoulder against the stone. She didn't care about anything except how wonderfully powerful Alex appeared. Noah struggled beside Alex. Sally barely saw him or Goliath straining to pull the tug chains around the giant boulder.

The stone scraped across the pebbles onto the skid. Alex stood and saw Sally watching. Smiles for each other lighted their faces.

Noah looked from one to the other. *Maybe I'll get to use my last marriage certificate after all.* "Come right behind us." Noah disconnected the traces from the straps around the stone and secured them to the holes they had bored into the skid.

Alex directed his horse. "Forward ho, Goliath."

Sally followed. "Goliath is beautiful. Samson was the same color. Our horse was murdered. Don't get me wrong; I'm glad we have your horse with us. It's just that he reminds me of Samson, and then I wish I could dig up Gus and kill him myself."

"I don't want to dredge up bad memories, Sally."

"Don't think that. It will help me to deal with it and get over hating Gus."

Alex directed Goliath beyond the narrow passageway. "We should leave the boulder on the skid and start unloading the wagon."

Once all the wagon parts lay on the ground beside the tools needed to put it back together, Sally drove Alex's empty wagon back into the narrow channel that no longer felt constrictive. The exhausted draft horse went to food, water, and, most importantly, rest.

The others had another wagon unloaded and apart when Sally returned. Roscoe, Adahy, and Eli went on the second trip, but only Eli returned with the empty transport wagon. The other two men remained to help reconstruct the wagons on the far side.

They got five wagons unloaded, four deconstructed, three on the other side of the passage, and two reconstructed. All their supplies remained with them.

On the second day, they unloaded the hay,

moved the last wagons across, and put the discombobulated wagons back together.

They worked eleven hours on the third day to shuttle and load their provisions and supplies into the wagons on the western side of the pass. Everyone was too tired to get the hay from the Raton side.

Three hours into the fourth day, Tom and Roscoe returned with the last load of hay in Alex's wagon. They immediately resumed travel through the treacherous passageway. The wagons rocked up, down, and sideways on uneven, rocky terrain. The hidey-hole wagon, in which Nikki and Adele had been found, smashed against the cliffs. The bows cracked. The weight of the pots and pans hanging from them finished the destruction. The canvas imploded as it dropped into the wagon. Noah screamed, "Halt! Take down the tops."

Oscar sat beside Tom as they exited the two-mile-long constrictive gorge under the setting sun. "My father never would have gotten us through that." He hugged Tom. "I'm glad we have you."

Emily whispered to Tom, "I'm glad we have you for other reasons too, and I have something to tell you later."

Fourteen

Emily made love with Tom after Oscar was asleep. Afterward, she lay beside him. "I have something to tell you."

"I'm listening."

"I hope this will make you happy."

"Everything about you makes me happy."

"We're going to have a baby."

"How wonderful! I thought we couldn't because Hattie never got pregnant again after Eli, and you didn't have another child after Oscar."

"Please don't think less of me. We had tried so long, and Warren wanted a child so much. I heard him crying in the barn one day, saying God hadn't found him good enough to allow him to have a child. Warren had a temper and could be a bully, but he was a good man. He was hurting so much over it. I knew a man who had a child almost every year. He agreed to my request. It was only until I was pregnant with Oscar. Warren never knew, neither did that man's wife, and I don't want Oscar to know."

"Do you think Eli isn't mine?"

"Of course, Eli is your child. He looks exactly like you. I want you to know I wouldn't ever do it again. I wasn't trying to be with the other man. I only wanted to give Warren something he desperately wanted. Was I completely wrong?"

"Did Warren still have the love of his wife?"

"I'm not saying he never irritated me or never made me mad, but I always loved him."

"Then maybe it wasn't a horrible thing, but now you're my wife. Don't ever be with another man. I wish you hadn't told me." Tom rolled away from Emily.

"Can you no longer love me?"

"I don't know right now."

Both of them silently cried.

Oscar played with Nikki as they prepared breakfast. Tom watched him. Tom had not only wanted Emily; he had wanted the boy too. *I'm glad Oscar is in my life.* He looked at Emily. *I don't know about what she did.* He sat across the fire and not next to her.

Everybody noticed the change. Nobody could imagine what had happened. Ann whispered to Noah, "What's happened between Tom and Emily?"

"I don't know."

Two very tense days later, they stood at the rocky crest of the Sangre de Cristo Mountains.

Fifteen

Alex looked at the sharply descending path ahead. "It must not have been like this when there was snow."

Sally stood beside him. "We've tested all the brakes, learned to put a log through the wheels, and been down a much steeper hill. We can do it."

"I don't want the same results as the Little Rock descent!" Eli rubbed his ribs. "Let's not all go at the same time."

"We should stay together. It's too far to the valley. We can't protect everybody if we're too spread out. One of us should scout ahead." Tom looked at Emily. "I'll go. I'm the expendable one." Spirit started down the trail.

Oscar glared at his mother. "What did you do, Ma?"

As the man she loved rode away, Emily yelled, "You are not expendable, Thomas Yates! You had better come back to me!" She told the people around her, "He misunderstood something I told him, and now he won't talk to me. Still, it's between us, and I'm not going to explain."

Noah looked at Ann. "It's not safe for one man to go alone, especially in that state of mind."

Ann nodded. "There's nothing for an animal to eat here. Let's set up camp and put out hay." She walked to a wagon.

Noah followed Tom.

Nikki asked Ann, "I'm so tired. Do I have to help?"

In the thin air at the top of the skyscraping mountains, they all felt as if they had walked for an entire day, even though it had been only a few hours. "Lie in the wagon where it's safer."

Sixteen

Tom didn't like what Emily had done, but he wasn't about to malign her. "I don't want to talk about it, Noah."

"I didn't ask you to. It's not safe for one man to be alone on this trail."

"Much obliged for you coming. Even though I don't want to talk about it, it's nice to have somebody with me who I know loves me."

"I surely do love you. Everybody does."

"I didn't say she doesn't love me."

"I didn't say that either."

"It's something that happened long before I met her. I shouldn't let it bother me. Besides, I don't want to talk about it."

"I'm not trying to make you."

A long, silent time later, Tom remarked, "This trail is very steep."

Glad to be talking about something, Noah assured Tom and himself. "Still, I don't think a wagon could run away like what happened at Little Rock."

"The hard part will be making all these turns with a log through the wheels. Maybe we should only put one through the rear wheels, and we shouldn't go very far in one day. The animals get very tired, and to tell you the truth, so do I. I'm not getting enough air."

"I'm not either. I hope we can get to a good place to stop every day. We'll probably have to stay on the trail, and we should chock the wheels even if we leave the logs in the spokes." Noah rose in the saddle to get a better look at their surroundings. "I see a valley WAAAAY down there. It looks even flatter than the prairie."

"And there's a silver ribbon down the middle. It must be the Rio Grande." Tom got off Spirit and measured the width of the trail with their rope, knotted and marked with ribbons. "We should be able to turn the wagons a little and roll them against the cliff. I hope we'll have enough hay to get back to grass."

"We've only had five days without grass coming up. If it's not many more getting back to pasture, we should be fine. Still, we should give them a little less each feeding, just in case. We better start back to camp. It'll be harder going up."

They'd barely gotten several yards before Spirit stopped. "He can't breathe." Tom stroked his horse's neck.

"Eyanosa doesn't look any better. I'll go alone. You and the horses wait here." Noah handed Tom an ammo belt. "With the Lefaucheux revolver, the bullets you already have, and these, you should be fine. You probably won't need them, but take them just in case. Besides, it will be less weight for me to carry."

"Wait a minute, Noah." Tom stared at the rock wall in front of him. "If I'm not here when you get back, tell Emily I decided I don't care. Tell Eli I love him and everybody else too."

"It's going to take me a long time to get there, and we can't bring the wagons down in the dark. I don't think we can get back until tomorrow. I changed my mind. We need to stay together. We'll go as slow as we need to."

"All right. I think Spirit is ready to go a little farther."

Every ten yards or so, the four of them rested. As they climbed, the distance they traveled grew shorter and the rests longer. Darkness descended on a moonless night. Tom tripped.

Crack.

"Are you all right?" Noah heard no reply. "Tom!" He knelt beside the fallen man and put his fingers to Tom's neck. A pulse beat strongly. He put Tom's head in his lap, stroked his friend's hair, and told the unconscious man, "I learned a tough lesson. I thought you had learned it too. You can't run away from heartache. I hope we get back to the women we love soon, but I'm staying here as long as we need to."

Thirty minutes later, Tom groaned. "My head hurts."

"You hit your head when you fell."

"Then, it's a good thing I'm so hardheaded. I hope that stone knocked some sense into me. She did the loving thing, and it was long before me. I love her, you know."

"I do. When we get back, you can tell her."

"I'm going to be a father again."

"Are you upset about that?! I think that's wonderful."

"I'm thrilled to have another child. It's something else. I'm not going to spread what she told me. She's a good woman, Noah. That's all any of us needs to know."

"Agreed!" Noah asked, "Can you walk? We've had a long rest, and I'm sure the others are worried."

"Let me try." Tom stood slowly and then took a few steps. "Let's go."

"We can't get separated. Give me one of Spirit's reins. I'll walk in front, keep my right hand on the cliff, and go very slow."

Tom held out the strap. "We'll make it."

Noah slid his hand along the stone cliff. Something else touched him. He jerked his hand back. "I don't know what that was, and I can't see a thing!" He gingerly felt around. "It's only a small tree growing out of the cliff. Forward ho." Not long after. "Ouch! How did I not feel this huge boulder until it hit my shin? Go a little to the left. Be very careful. I don't know how close we are to the edge."

"Let's stop. This side is much harder to climb. I need to rest. No scouting ahead in the future."

"Agreed."

Hours after nightfall, Noah saw a dim light. "I see our campfire."

Tom raised his head. "We made it! But let's not hurry and kill ourselves in our joy to be home."

They struggled on, avoided what they could, banged into what they didn't, and bled where the impact with mountain objects was forceful enough to break their skin. Bloody and exhausted, they saw the shapes of people by the fire. Noah called out, "Do not come down here! We'll be there in a few minutes."

The men stumbled into camp and fell to the ground. Ann knelt beside Noah. Nikki held a cup of water. Sally hovered over them. "Are you all right?" Ann asked.

"Just exhausted, bruised, and a little cut. See to Tom. He hit his head."

"Emily is with him. She'll take care of him. She's been out of her mind with fear."

Noah gulped the water. "Help me into our wagon. I need to sleep."

Emily held Tom's hand. "You're hurt!"

"I don't care about that or the past. I love you, and I want you. Nothing else matters."

"I'm very glad. Eli, help me get Tom into our wagon. Stephanie, bring bandages and a first aid kit. Come on, Oscar, I need your help."

Seventeen

The morning light crested the Sangre de Cristo Mountains and glittered off Noah's tin cup. "We have to go together. It's exhausting climbing back."

"It's going to be slow going. Every rock that was in the layers of snow is now on the path." Tom ate the few eggs their chickens had laid.

"We don't have much hay left." Roscoe poured coffee into Noah's cup.

Eli held his out. "Since we're going downhill, we should be able to take shorter breaks. I hope we'll get back to grass fast enough."

"I'm done eating." Stephanie stood up. "I'll get the shovel and bury the fire. We'll be able to get going quicker that way."

"And the animals had nowhere to roam off to last night." Emily snuggled beside Tom.

Tom patted her knee. "When we get there, three wagons need to pull in diagonally against the cliff at the far end of the wide area. The other wagons should pull to the cliff at the top end. We can keep all the animals between the wagons roped away from the edge."

They packed quickly, got the first set of animals into the harnesses, and started down the western slope with a pole through both sets of wheels. The rocky terrain kept the wagons from sliding. Even so, the animals pulled Tom's wagon with less of a burden than when they had pulled it uphill. The others spread not too far behind but not too close.

A couple of hours later, Tom chocked the wheels at the first tight turn and pulled out the front log. "Now, we should be able to turn. Hopefully, we won't slide too fast. You ready, son?"

"Ready." Eli pulled the wheel stop from his side of the wagon.

Tom removed the other. They needed to hug the cliff on the left. The wagon slid to the right. "Gee," he told his horse. The wagon started into the curve. Spirit and his team easily did as commanded. Suddenly, the horses struggled to pull the wagon, no longer skidding behind them. Tom looked back. "Halt!" He crawled under the wagon and examined the pole wedged between the rock cliff and a boulder on the right. He instructed the team, "Back." The wagon didn't move. "We'll have to pull it out. It's good that we made a hitch on both ends of our wagons. Eli, uncouple your team and get them attached to the rear of this one."

Eli hollered to those behind him, "We're stuck. We'll have to shorten the poles and figure out a way to keep them from sliding out."

Father and son set to work on the problem at the front of their caravan. The others contemplated how to make the poles short but secure.

Ehawee asked, "Roscoe, if we bored a hole through the ends of the poles, could you make metal rings big enough, so they couldn't pull out from between the spokes?"

"At least one of them on each pole would have to be able to come off. We'll have to spend at least a day here and use the metal bands of our spare wheels to make enough."

Farther back in the wagon train, Noah looked around. "We didn't get as far as Tom and I went yesterday, but we can tie the nets between the wagons and keep the animals away from the cliff. Chock the wheels."

Eli dropped the kingpin into the hole of the falling tongue he connected to the rear of the jammed wagon. "I'm ready. Are you disconnected, Pop?"

"We're good to go."

Eli commanded his mule. "Ace, forward ho." The wagon came out from between the cliff and the boulder. "Tell me when we're far enough for the team to get around."

After only a few yards, Tom informed, "We're good. I'll block the wheels before we come around."

Noah unharnessed the mules from his wagon. "We only have a few spare wheels left, and we still have a long way to go. We shouldn't use their rims. Let's think of another way."

"We don't have anything else. Help me get the forge." Roscoe walked toward the rear of the caravan.

Helen followed her husband. "Roscoe, before you start, we need to pray. God, show us another way to get off this mountain or give us more wheels. In Jesus' name I pray. Amen. Did God give anybody any ideas?"

Everybody shook his or her head.

"I'll get started." Roscoe handed out the fire pot of the mobile forge he had built while crossing the prairie. "Start breaking up the wheels. I'll use the wood for the fire."

Noah pulled a pole from the spokes. "I'll cut these shorter."

"I'll get the drill." Adahy rummaged for the largest of their auger bits.

Once put together and fired up, Roscoe forged a rim section into a rod and formed it into a ring. With tongs, Tom and Adahy drew the red-hot metal through the hole in the pole. Eli and Noah clamped the ring ends tightly together. While it cooled into an unbendable circle, Roscoe started the second.

Ann approached the forge carrying several long sticks with dough wrapped around them. "There's a lot of heat coming off your fire. Would these be in your way if I put them here?" She pointed to the ground.

"They wouldn't. We can cook your bread and make these rings if you keep the bellows going. I hope we'll be able to get both done before we run out of wood."

"How are we going to get the rings off?" Ann jammed one of the sticks into the dirt.

"I figure we can tie a rope to the ring and loop it to the spokes on the bottom side of the hub. The hub will hold the ring. All we have to do is untie the rope, turn the pole, and slide the ring out between the spokes."

Ann placed the last stick of dough. "Too bad we have only one anvil. I'm sure the other men would help make some if we did."

Before the sun set, they installed the twentieth ring into the end of the last pole. They read the Bible as each of them ate an acorn-meal bread-spiral cooked on a stick and buffalo pemmican soup cooked by the forge's heat.

Eighteen

The shortened poles efficiently prevented the wagons from rolling, allowing them to turn and fit through tight places. Well beyond the planned stopping place, the front end of the lead wagon precariously leaned on a sloping ledge over a rocky drop-off. Sally yelled, "Stop! It's going to tip over!" She peered over the edge of the precipice. "I can't even see the bottom. How did other people do this?"

Alex commented, "I always thought the snow was a horrible hindrance to the people trying to get over this mountain. I guess it wasn't. Fifty feet up from here, they wouldn't have had to come this way."

Stephanie offered a possible solution. "If we could tie a rope on the uphill side, we could use the harness we've used to cross rivers."

Roscoe looked back up the trail. "There was a boulder not that far back that we could use. We don't know if there's anything on the far side."

"I'll take the rope and go look," offered Alex.

Sally hurried toward a wagon. "So you can go

across safely, we'll tie a rope to you. If you slide, we'll still have you."

Alex barely breathed the crisp air as he hugged the rock wall above the ledge sloped at an angle a free-standing wagon would not be able to navigate. Too far around to be seen, a pebble rolled under his foot. Alex clutched a crack in the cliff face. His foot sent a cascade of stone over the edge.

"Are you all right!" Sally called out.

"I'm fine," Alex gripped the bare rock and planted his feet on solid stone. *I'm going to need to measure the width. I could have gone over the edge in a second.* He pushed the small rocks littering the ledge out of the way, took another sideways step, and inched his way around the mountain.

Five minutes of torture passed. Everybody prayed the rocks Alex walked over would not roll out from under his feet again.

Finally, the land again ran directly downhill. Alex heaved a heavy sigh and then started the search. Frustrated, he made his way back to the wagons. "We can't come this way. I couldn't find any place to secure the rope. I'm not even sure it's wide enough in some places. I'll need the measuring line to test it, but I think we have to go back and find another way."

"What choice did we have?" asked Stephanie. "We have to ask God to keep the wagons from tipping over."

Alex assured her, "No amount of praying will work."

Noah spoke up. "I agree with you both. This is

the only way we could have brought the wagons, and we can't drive them across that slope unsecured. There might have been another way a person could have gone. Maybe one of us could go and see if there is a way to tie the rope higher up on the other side."

Tom remembered his last attempt to climb the steep mountain trail. "Even if there is a way for a person to get over there, it will take a long time, and this isn't a good place to stop."

Ann took the cradleboard holding their son off Noah's back. "Since we have no choice, we'll wait here while you go back. Alex, measure the width before Noah goes."

Sally spoke up. "I don't want Alex to go across again. It's not safe."

"And then what? I can do it, Sally." Alex wanted to show not just Sally but the whole family that he was competent. Now familiar with the terrain, he walked the sloping curve again, dangling the measuring rope below him. At the far end, he told himself, "At least the width isn't a problem."

A sliver of sunlight shone between a slab of stone and the cliff. "What? I didn't see that before!" He examined the tall stand of stone separated from the rest of the mountain. He pulled it and pushed it and then untied himself from the rope. Alex swung it back and forth and then attempted to hurl it over the top into the slot. After several attempts, the line dropped behind the slab. He jerked and then hung from it. "Good, it's not breaking off." He tied a knot in the rope so it couldn't pull through, tied it back to itself around the hunk of stone, and then made his way across the slope for the fourth time.

"I found a place, but we should shuttle supplies. I think lighter will be better."

Eli already held the river crossing harness they planned to repurpose into a mountain safety device. "Let's get this attached." He held the traveling board as Ann and Stephanie looped the "C" bolts around the line and then slid the ends through the board. Sally and Helen screwed on the nuts. Tom and Roscoe slid its thick leather straps under the edge of the canvas. Inside the wagon, the boys dropped the straps out the other side. Underneath it, Noah and Adahy buckled the bottom strap to the top one. Ehawee and Emily got King, Hector, Big Jenny, Ace, Quick Silver, and Redeemed into the animal part of the harness.

Alex led the team. The wheels skidded sideways. The rope stretched. The outer wheels approached the edge. "Stop!" Sally ordered, "Tighten the rope."

Adahy and Eli tied Spirit, Promise, Honey, and Biscuit to the rope around the boulder on the upper side. "Start again." As Adahy walked the horses downhill from the boulder, the rope tightened.

On the ledge, the wagon rose closer to the cliff as it rolled forward. Mule hooves and the wagon wheels constantly slid on the pebbly slope. The animals on the safe part of the trail held the rope tight enough to keep the narrow wagon on the ledge. As the mules in the harness crossed the treacherous curve of the mountain, King's hooves went out from under him. The hard jerk on the rope pulled Biscuit over.

Eli and Alex both shouted, "Halt!"

Also fastened to the line and jerked off his feet, Alex got up and drew King's harness rope shorter as the mule rose. "King's leg is cut."

"Up, Biscuit," commanded Eli.

Once they all stood on their feet, they resumed the slow transit of animals, wagon, and supplies. Alex, six mules, and a half-full wagon finally arrived at the opposite side of the curve. Alex released the harness.

When Noah felt the tension leave the rope, he went across and inspected their anchor. "This is plenty strong, and the ledge is wide enough. We'll bring some of the little animals in a wagon and then take it back to get the rest. I'll start sending them over. Keep all the animals. We can draw the empty wagon back."

Noah easily returned. Without the wagon's weight, they pulled the line much tighter, secured it, and unhitched the horses on the upper side of the curve. The next wagon was wider, but it rode closer to the cliff and made the passage safely. However, the animals pulling it along the dangerous path frequently slipped and arrived at the far side with torn flesh.

The people and animals slid on every crossing. However, harnessed to the line, neither wagon, person, nor animal went over the edge. At the end of a tedious day, Tom released the rope tied to the boulder on the upper side and crossed, fastened only at the lower end. "I'm glad we got everything over today." He attempted to remove the rope from the slot of stone. "This is really wedged in there. I can't get it."

All the men tried to free it. The rope did not come out. Alex pulled the knife he had gotten from the first wagon wreck. "I'll cut it." The caravan continued on the much easier slope.

Before long, they arrived at an acceptable stopping place. "Don't forget to pull in diagonally against the cliff," reminded Tom.

Nineteen

The descent became easier, but it took too many days. The animals ate the last of their hay. Alex walked beside Sally. "I see trees. We might have made it to grass. Look at the valley way down there."

Sally pulled out her looking tube and surveyed the trees below, but still high above the valley. She inhaled deeply. "I love the refreshing scent of cedars. Too bad I can't smell them yet. Crimony! I thought this was the only mountain. I see more on the far side of the valley."

Alex looked through his telescope. "You're right. Maybe we can go around them."

Sally started around a stone column. "Halt! There's a group of wagons. I thought you said nobody had been through since last winter."

"There wasn't. Let me look." Alex again peered through the spyglass. "We better tell the others." He chocked his wagon's wheels. They walked toward the rear of their caravan. Alex informed the others, "There are wagons ahead."

Roscoe went forward and peered around the rocks. "Whoever it is, they probably already know we're here, and there is no place for either group to go. It's a sheer drop between us and the land below. All the women and children, get in the last wagon." As he approached, he repeated, "Friends here," but got no reply.

Expecting a shotgun blast, Roscoe knelt behind the rearmost wagon. He jerked open the puckering strings. No lead flew above his head. He shifted to the shadow side of the wagon before he carefully and quickly peeked inside. Nobody was home, but bolts of cloth were. "Alex, come here! Is this Raton's stolen cloth?"

"I'm not sure. It could be."

Behind the rear of the next wagon, Roscoe and Alex found a mass of rotting human flesh with a rifle on the ground beside it. Inside, a shotgun perched on top of another body. What looked like a money bag lay beside the corpse. "I recognize the hats. These are two of the men who robbed the town. There's a third person somewhere. Keep a sharp lookout."

The two men carefully approached the last wagon. Alex exclaimed, "My clocks are here! This one's head is beat in. I assume with that blacksmith's hammer!" He pointed. "They killed each other. They got what they deserved."

Roscoe stood beside Alex. "And God replaced

81

the blacksmith tools and cloth we gave to the people of Raton, plus our wagon wheels and bows."

Notified that it was safe, the others came to the cluster of wagons. Sally examined the falling tree of the wagon. "Looks like the animals kicked loose. They didn't deserve to die. I'm glad they got free."

"May I have a wagon and everything inside?" Nikki asked.

"What do you think, Noah?" asked Ann.

Noah replied, "We should leave the bodies."

"I don't want the dead people," clarified Nikki.

"Nobody can have everything." Noah put his hand on Nikki's shoulder. "Let's take an inventory and then decide who gets what."

"But you got a whole wagon with everything inside, and I didn't."

"I worked for that wagon."

"S—" Nikki stopped before he repeated the cuss word Ann had ordered him never to say again. "All right."

The people made camp. The animals drank water poured into ten-gallon tubs as Sally wrote the description of each item taken out of the thieves' wagons.

While they ate supper, they decided on the division of goods. All the money, food, and general supplies were added to the family inventory. One rifle, one shotgun, a bullet mold, and all the lead were also designated for communal use.

Roscoe got all the blacksmith tools and took

the same number of bolts of cloth and spools of thread as he'd had before he'd arrived in Raton. Tom also replenished to his pre-Raton level. The rest went into the family's trading inventory.

"Until you've learned how to care for and fire this, you can't use it unless you're with me." Noah gave Nikki a black powder pistol and the gun belt it was in, along with a powder horn and all its other accessories.

"My very own gun! Much obliged!" Nikki accepted the offering.

Tom gave a pistol along with the same instructions to Oscar.

One leather and one felt hat, the clothes and boots that fit Alex, the second rifle, the third pistol, a gun belt, and all their paraphernalia went to Alex because he had very little or none of his own. He also resumed ownership of the clocks, clock parts, and tools. "I'll keep the grandfather clock, but I want each family to have a table clock."

Roscoe looked over the offerings. "If the horses were still here, we could take the wagons, but I don't want to tire our animals more by making them pull more. However, we should replace everything we broke coming over the mountain."

Helen added, "There won't be much left." She picked the clock she liked best. "What do you think of this one, Roscoe?"

"It's fine with me." Roscoe loosened a wagon cover tie. "They were so stupid. They stole so much but not a single rope, and that's the only way down from here.

"I guess it was too much for them to deal with, so they killed each other instead." Helen went to pack the clock with their other personal possessions. "Nikki and Oscar, you WILL get to destroy some of these wagons."

"We will?" asked Oscar.

Tom passed him a hammer. "We'll use two of them to build a contraption to lower everything."

"Nikki, you want to work with Tom and Oscar? I'm going to lay the bows on top of our wagons before I close them with the canvas." Noah held out a mallet.

"I'll help bust this up." Nikki reached for the tool.

"Don't forget to keep one wagon box for tomorrow." Noah walked away with the first bow.

That afternoon they used two of the thieves' wagons to build the tower they hoped would make their descent much easier.

Twenty

The morning sun bounced off the bare stone. "Everybody, get your goggles!" Noah put on the green-glass eye covering he had used to protect his eyes from the blinding glare of the prairie. Ann put on blue-glass goggles from Dr. Pennyworth's wagon. "It's a beautiful blue world." She gave other blue goggles to Ehawee and Adahy and the smaller ones to the boys. Everybody else donned the green goggles they'd had since the beginning of the journey.

Looking through colored glass, Eli surveyed the green cliff. "This shouldn't be hard with our ropes. It's a good thing we got so many of them at the pit houses. Do you think it's more than a hundred feet?"

Tom stood beside his son. "Probably, but even if it's only a hundred, we'll still have to tie ropes together because we have to run them around a wagon. We'll only be able to lower one at a time."

"We couldn't do more anyway. We have only one pulley," remarked Noah, who surveyed the green-tinted drop-off below him. "It will be easy until the end. Who wants to go with the first wagon?"

"Pop and I will. We'll wait below. You draw back the empty wagon and then we'll unload the next group you send down." Eli gazed into his wife's aqua eyes, tucked her long, green hair behind her ears, and then kissed her green lips. "These goggles make your eyes an amazing color." He bent his head and kissed his baby's green forehead. "Love you and Hattie and everybody else. See you at the bottom." He crammed goats and sheep into the wagon at the edge of the precipice.

Tom squeezed in and blocked the open end. "Ready."

A long way up the trail, King, Quick Silver, Big Jenny, Hector, Blue, and Ace stood in the harness. "Forward, ho," commanded Ann. The animals climbed the mountain. The makeshift wagon-elevator rose beneath the newly built tower. Noah, Roscoe, and Adahy pushed the wagon beyond the cliff's edge.

Adahy shouted, "It's out!"

One after the other, Ehawee, Helen, Stephanie, Sally, and Emily relayed the message to Ann.

Ann told the harnessed team, "Backward, ho." They reversed the entire length of the one-hundred-foot rope. Not far from their lowering contraption, Ann didn't have to holler. "Are they down yet?"

"No, but it looks like they would touch the ground if the wagon had wheels." Noah yelled to the men below, "That's it! Jump out!"

On their bellies, Eli and Tom slid off the end onto their feet. "Come out," the men commanded. The animals jumped from the wagon to the ground five feet below.

Tom looked up. "We need more rope!" he screamed.

"We know!" hollered Adahy. He turned to Noah. "What should we do?"

"Pull it up, my wife."

Ann led the work team back up the hill.

"We could hook nets to the wagon corners, fasten two ropes to the long sides of the nets, and tie another to the rope hitched to the team up here. That way, we'll have more than enough length on both ends," answered Noah.

Roscoe nodded. "The nets are close to the rear of the hidey-hole wagon. I'll get them."

Not over an hour later, they got the juvenile animals into the wagon. Roscoe signaled to those below and then told Helen, "I'll ride with them and make sure the animals don't jump out too soon or fall out. I'll come back with the wagon. Send the message to lower us."

When the wagon touched the ground, Noah commanded, "Halt."

The message made its way to Ann, who stopped the team a long way from the wagon departure point.

Until midday, each of them guided the pull team, swapped the animals doing the hard work, secured the wagons to be lowered, and unhooked them at the bottom. Noah studied the cliff every trip but couldn't see into the crack that seemed to run from the ledge to the grassy field.

Since they had not gotten everything down, they ate their midday meal on the high stone ledge. Most of their animals grazed in the grass they had finally reached below the cliff. After dinner, they got all but the men, the partially disassembled wagon, and the last team to the land below.

From the heaviest to the lightest, they unhitched the animal members of the pull team and sent them down. They lowered the last mule by slowly allowing the ropes to side through their gloved hands.

Tom dug a hammer from the toolbox. "It's time to take down the tower."

The men had constructed the device to come apart once they had lowered their family, wagons, and animals. They made short work of the job. Adahy loaded the last piece of the deconstructed tower. "We should keep this wagon for when we have to carry the young animals." The other men held the rope tight as he and Tom slid the full wagon over the edge. The weight jerked the men to the ground.

Roscoe yelled, "It's gonna pull us over!"

Every hand on the rope let go.

Sally saw the speed of the approaching wagon. "God! Save our men!"

Everybody below turned.

"We'll be stuck up here!" Tom grabbed. "Don't let it get away!"

He and the other men got control of their lifeline just as the wagon and tower parts splintered against the hard ground.

Tom dropped to his knees. "Thanks be to God."

Eli crawled to the cliff edge. "Disconnect the net. We'll pull it up."

"All right," answered Sally as everybody below gawked at the spectacle.

Once the ripped net was free of what was now nothing more than firewood, Tom pulled it up. He climbed in and made his final trip down. Eli was lowered second. Alex rode third, then Adahy, and then Roscoe. As planned, only Noah remained above. It would have been simple for those below to hold one end of the line and bring him down like the others if there had been a place to loop the rope. That, however, was not the case.

Twenty One

Blessedly, Noah had climbed the rock cliff in his home village many times. *I can do this.* Noah threw the rope over the edge and then lowered his body into the deep, musty fissure. His foot felt for the protuberance he had seen from the ledge. Once Noah made contact, he wiggled his foot, made sure it was stable, and then let his weight settle onto the small bump. One at a time, he dropped his hands and tested lower notches.

Several moves later, Noah clutched a shallow hold and sought the last foot support he had seen from the top. He had observed the smoothness of one wall of the crack below his current position. He stood on the protrusion of stone, searched with his other foot, and discovered another knob that held him. It was large enough, so he reached for the stone lip behind him with his right hand, clenched the rock securely, rotated on his toes, and faced the opposite way.

I don't see another handhold. Maybe there's something inside that narrow crack. He tried to see into the slit at his left. *There's not much light, but there are **a lot** of webs.* No light at all illuminated the space behind them. *I've got to try, or I'm stuck.* He ran his fingers through the tangles and felt a large bump. *I hope it's part of the mountain and not a creature.* He gritted his teeth, drew his lower lip down, closed one eye, sucked in the smell of wet dirt, and squeezed. *Rock. Thank you, God!*

Noah scanned the crevasse for his next foot perch. *I have a very long way to go in this spider-filled tunnel.* He steeled his mind and lowered his foot into a narrow hole. Still grasping the same bump in the dark crack, he hunted for a place for his other foot. He found nothing. *I've done it before. I can do it again.* He pushed a foot against the stone behind him, placed his free hand against the surface in front of him, and held himself in place by pushing against the two sides.

He again explored the spider-filled crack for a new handhold. Sticky strings wrapped around his fingers. He felt a tickle. "Oh, no!" He jerked his hand, almost lost the pressure keeping him from plunging to his death, and flung a tarantula into the air. *I've got to get out of here. I doubt there's another one in the same spot.* He gingerly reached through the hole he had created, felt a vertical lip of stone, and slipped his fingertips behind it.

Noah sought a bulge in the cliff with the foot no longer pressed against the wall, whacked webs with it, and hoped that he had scared away any lurking eight-legged menace. A gigantic furry spider scurried away. To be sure, he smacked the vacated space again before he lowered his foot onto the web-covered lump of stone. Supported on his foot, he reached for an inch-wide lip of spider-free rock. Meticulously, Noah cleared his path.

Suddenly, a sliver of stone upon which he stood broke loose. *I'm done for!* Still too high for the small cascade of stone to be heard, he dangled from his hands just below a red hourglass on the belly of a shiny black spider as long as the lower joint of his finger beside it. *Help me, God!* He pressed his foot against the wall behind him, gritted his teeth, clutched a lip of stone, and slowly drew away from the black widow paying him no attention as it ate its mate. *Thank You!*

Little by little, he descended until he arrived exhausted at a wide platform. He lay on his belly and examined the fissure and the dense spider homes around him.

His right hand burned. *The tarantula wasn't on that hand.* He reached out into the light. Red skin surrounded two tiny spots of missing flesh. *One of them got me. I feel a little dizzy too.* Noah looked down. Nikki and Oscar picked white flowers at the edge of the cedar forest below him. *Much closer, but a fall from here will still kill me. I need at least one hand, and I need to be able to keep my balance. My hand's not numb. I can make it, but I can't get bitten again.*

Noah resumed his descent with a plan of travel for two feet and one hand for as far as he could see. Not far beyond the ledge, the fracture in the cliff narrowed. It became easier to wedge himself between the two sides without significant places to put his feet or holds for the hand he could still use.

He quickened his pace and made his way until the slit was too narrow to descend farther. Ten feet from the bottom, he called out, "Come here!"

Everybody ran to the voice. The fastest member of the family looked up at his brother-in-law. "You stuck?"

"Yes, Eli. Bring something I can use to get the rest of the way." Noah didn't mention his hand.

Ann soon stood below her husband. "I'm sure that was a very hard climb. Thank God you're safe. I was worried, but I trusted you to know if you could do it. You look tired."

"I'm exhausted. I didn't know the way, and there were spiders everywhere. One of them bit me. My hand is in a bad way."

Eli returned with one of the sides of the broken tower. "Can you get onto this?"

"I think so." Noah whistled for his horse and then stepped onto the top cross board. Eli and Ann held it tightly. "I'm plumb tuckered out." Noah descended the ladder. Eyanosa arrived in time for his owner to step off a rung onto his back. The horse carried his weary rider to their camp in the grassy field.

"You ready to eat?" Stephanie asked her brother-in-law.

"I'm too tired." Noah slipped off Eyanosa.

"A spider bit his hand. He needs help." Ann got their feather mattress, blankets, and pillow. "What medicine do you need, Noah?"

"Willow tea and Tapco told me to make a poultice of crushed bladder pod leaves for spider bites. We harvested some. I'm not sure exactly where it is. Look through our supply of medicinal plants."

Roscoe poured boiling water into a pot with the inner bark of a willow tree. Sally found and cooked bladder pod leaves. After several minutes, Ehawee examined the contents of the coffee pot in which the willow bark steeped. "Ann, it looks like blood."

"Good. It's ready." Ann took Noah a cup of the painkiller. "The bladderpod is still cooling. Go to sleep. I'll put it on your hand and join you after I feed the babies. Rest well, my husband."

Before it was dark, Ann wrapped a bandana with the warm poultice around Noah's hand and then laid Christopher, Joy, and Adele beside him. "Nikki, get between us when you come to bed." She slipped under the covers. "Goodnight, my love," she told the man who snored beside her.

Twenty Two

Noah couldn't help as they broke camp. Ann informed the group. "Noah's not able to stand, let alone walk. He doesn't want to do it, but I'm insisting that he ride in the wagon." She poured another dose of the painkiller.

"It's all right to ride, Noah." Roscoe helped his friend into the wagon before Ann handed Noah the willow tea.

"We just added all those supplies to the wagons. I hate to make the load even heavier. It's just that I can barely breathe, and my guts really hurt." Noah sweated profusely.

"You're not well, my husband, our animals are strong, and we've taken good care of them. They'll be fine." Ann kissed the bandana around Noah's hand and took back the empty tin cup.

Nikki looked at the man who had found him after his parents had been killed. "Ride and get better. I need you."

"As soon as I'm able, I'm going to ride Eyanosa." Noah lay on the feather mattresses.

Roscoe called out, "Ready!"

Leading the way, Adahy listened for everybody's signal that they had completed their assigned tasks and were ready to go. He heard the fourteenth ready. "Forward, ho."

The family moved out completely restocked with the supplies and spare wagon parts of the thieves, along with a load of broken boards for fires, fresh juniper, and a crate of their tasty berry-looking cones.

Oscar rode Azúcar at the slow pace of their four cows and the newly acquired juvenile animals. The family descended the mountain, followed by hundreds of pinyon jays cawing to each other as they weaved through the forest of rocky mountain junipers and Colorado pinyons. Ehawee watched the flashes of blue as the birds darted from tree to tree, caching seeds in the bark. She breathed in the calming scent of the cedar forest as she walked behind the wagon that carried her brother. "It's so much nicer walking on the soil of this forest than on the bare stone."

Ann agreed. "That mountain was hard. My feet ached at the end of every day. Can you imagine how bad it would have been if we hadn't gotten new shoes in Raton?"

"I'd rather not. I didn't know we would wear out so many shoes. I hope we have enough to get to the western sea."

"So far, God has given us everything we need."

"And He's done it more than once!"

Noah's head suddenly appeared out the back of the wagon. "Move!" He spewed his breakfast.

Ann stroked the back of her husband's head. "I'll get a wet rag to put on the back of your neck."

Noah emptied his stomach again. His mouth tasted like metal. He groaned in misery. "I hurt so bad. I don't know if I'm going to make it. I need ginger."

"What if we make ginger tea at dinner?"

"I need some NOW. Bring me a piece." His stomach ejected more of its contents. He moaned as Ann hurried to the wagon containing the requested item.

Ann handed Noah a hunk of ginger plant rhizome. "Should we put you to sleep?"

"No, I might choke on my vomit. Ugghhh!" He lay back onto the mattress. "Horrible spiders!"

Twenty Three

Adahy climbed into a wagon and poured rice into a duck cloth sack. He filled the remainder of the space with black-eyed peas and then waited for their wagons to pass. He quietly instructed his wife and Ann. "Get in the middle wagon right now." The women with their babies in cradleboards quickly made their way to the designated location. Adahy stood behind the last wagon and signed into the woods, "This is for you. We welcome friends to our mid-day meal. We have many guns if you choose to attack us." He spoke into the wagon. "I know you feel bad, but you have to get your revolvers and keep watch on our rear. I've left a gift. I hope it's accepted." Adahy hurried to gather the rest of the family to the most protected wagon.

Noah peeked out from under the wagon cover. He saw nobody. As they descended away, it wasn't long before he could no longer see the peas and rice bag.

Ann stepped onto the wagon's seat without any of her babies. "I'm here. Keep watching."

"Where are the children?"

"They're with the women in the middle wagon. Soon, we're switching back across the slope. I'm going to move this wagon to the middle. All the women and children will get in here with us." Ann pulled the left rein and then flipped them to direct her mules.

A few minutes later, a wagon drove past several yards below them. After the second wagon, Ann slipped her wagon into the line with the last two coming close behind. "They're going to pass in the babies from the lower side and then Eli is going to help the women get in."

Nikki appeared beside Ann. "I here."

"We're coming in." Ann pulled a crate to the front. "Nikki, stand on this and drive."

On the wooden box inside the wagon, Nikki held the reins and looked through a narrow gap between the drawn puckering strings. Noah peered uphill from a tiny opening between the canvas and the top sideboard. Ann untied the cover from the bows on the opposite side of the wagon. She raised the cloth. "Ready."

Ann pulled in Oscar before she took Hattie. Oscar slipped over to watch the babies as they were placed on the floor. Eli carried Stephanie as he walked beside the wagon. She leaned into the wagon under the cover and slid in. Ann brought in Christopher as her sister took Ehawee's baby, Etu. Eli lifted Ehawee and helped her go in while Stephanie and Ann brought in Adele and Joy.

Outside the wagon, Emily raised Sally. Ehawee

turned and helped Eli get Helen in. Helen and Sally slid in together. Eli got Emily in last.

Inside the front wagon, Adahy entered a protective ravine and turned downhill. The rest of the caravan followed with their unharnessed animals on the inner side.

When the sun finally approached its zenith, a campfire burned below them in the narrow valley. Adahy looked through his spyglass. Four people with long braids at both sides of their heads stood around a newly-built fire wearing brightly decorated buckskin leggings, shirts, and moccasins. Four horses ate the foliage around them. *Hanging in that tree is the bag I left.* From another branch dangled a gutted mountain sheep missing the two legs that roasted over the fire.

One of the people below looked toward the wagon train and signed, "We welcome friends at our mid-day meal."

"Halt!" Adahy stopped his wagon. He went alone to the group at the fire.

The Ute signed, "We offer your family meat for the beans and rice."

"We are peacefully passing through this land. We intend no harm, but we will protect ourselves," signed Adahy.

"We also intend no harm. Either of us could have attacked the other on our long journey off this mountain. Neither of us did. We offer to share our midday meal just as you did."

If they had wanted to harm us, they could have long before now. "Join us!" Adahy called out.

The women, children, and Noah remained in the wagon. The other men went to the fire. Tom looked at the shiny material stitched onto the Ute clothing. "What is that decoration made of?"

"Porcupine quills."

"We have trade items."

"We will look while meat cooks. Your women can cook at this fire too."

"We will protect them." Eli's rifle hung from its strap around his shoulder.

"We mean no harm," signed the man who had been the only one of the four to speak or look at the invaders of their territory. "I Kanneatche. Wife, Chipeta. Our sons, Kanosh and Maykh."

"The rest of our family will join us," replied Eli.

Roscoe asked, "Do you have treatment for spider bite?"

Kanneatche answered, "Maybe. We came up mountain to gather chuchupate. It powerful medicine. What kind of spider?"

"We don't know," answered Adahy.

"Bring," said the Ute woman.

"He hurts too much to walk." Roscoe walked toward a wagon and signaled for the Ute woman to follow.

As they neared the wagon, Noah draped his body over the wagon's rear and vomited. He clutched his abdomen, laid his head back into Ann's lap, and moaned. "I can barely breathe."

"Where bite?" Chipeta signed.

Ann removed the bandana holding the bladderpod leaf poultice then Nikki held out Noah's hand.

"When?"

Ann signed, "Yesterday, sun down four fingers."

"May not help. Still drink bear root now. Use four-wing salt brush when in valley."

Nikki sat beside Noah. "Bears do not have roots."

"It plant," explained the woman.

"Papa needs help." Nikki followed Chipeta. He signed, "What bear root look like?"

The woman brought out a ball of fern-looking leaves wrapped around wrinkly brown roots. Dome-shaped clusters of small white flowers appeared as she unrolled the three-foot-long plant.

"Where I find some?"

"Not down here. Must go up under juniper trees. Other plants look close, but kill you. Must not eat or touch. Must be very careful to get right plant. This have hairs and red at bottom of leaves by root." Chipeta pointed. "You see? And brown roots." She raised the plant close to Nikki's nose. "Smells like this."

"You take me."

Chipeta shook her head and waved her finger back and forth. "Too far away. Help make medicine." She ripped a root from the leaves, held it out, and raised her outstretched fingers up and down above it. "Chop."

Nikki did so and then dropped the pieces into boiling water. "Leaves and flowers good too?"

"We eat."

"Call me when ready." Nikki walked away from the fire. *Maybe I got some for my Ann.* He stood behind the wagon, where Noah moaned in pain. "Do you still have the flowers I gave you, Ann?"

"Of course. I'm going to keep them forever. They're drying with our other plants."

"I want to look at them."

Standing under the plants hanging from a bow, Nikki examined the hairs coming up from the parsnip-shaped chocolate-colored root. The reddish hue on the stems of the leaves revealed that he and Oscar had unknowingly harvested a valuable plant as love offerings to Emily and Ann. *I can't get more. I need to keep these for later.* He jumped but couldn't reach the plants. Nikki squatted low and sprang up again. He still came short of his goal, so he sauntered to Oscar and whispered. "Do not say anything. Come with me."

Once again standing under the plants, Nikki explained what he needed. "This is bear root. Kanneatche said it's strong medicine. Chipeta said it only grows under junipers high on mountains. We can't get more. We need to use what they have. If they see this, they'll make us use ours. We need to hide it, but I can't reach it. Hold me up."

Oscar wrapped his arms around Nikki's hips and raised him a few inches. He looked up. "I can't get you up there. Maybe we can sneak a branch in and pull it down."

Nikki peeked out. "It's clear this way."

Oscar surveyed the other exit. "We'll go your way."

The boys crept far into the woods, searching for a long, strong branch. "Here's one!" Nikki reached for a stick about two inches around. He pulled it out from under the leaves. The boys turned to hurry back to the wagon. All they saw around them were identical trees. They started back in the opposite direction from the way they currently faced.

After walking for what seemed to have been long enough to have gotten back to the wagons, Oscar knew they had no idea which way to go. "We're lost." He called for the man he wanted to save them. "Tom!"

Nikki let go of the branch he had been dragging. "Maybe we can see them from up there. Get me up to that branch." Oscar elevated his friend once again.

Nikki started up a pinyon tree while Oscar looked up from the ground. "Don't fall."

Sticky sap stuck to Nikki's clothes. The rough bark abraded his hands as he grasped one closely spaced limb after another and drew himself up. All he saw as he looked around were more trees. *What are these stuck in the bark?* As he climbed, he picked out what looked like small nuts here and there and dropped them into his pocket. He stopped and looked around again. *Oh, no! That's bad!*

Twenty Four

It is ready to mash. Chipeta looked around. *Where is he?*

"Boy!" she called out in Ute. Nikki did not arrive. Chipeta looked into the wagon where the spider-bitten man lay. "Where son?" the woman signed.

He asked about those plants. Ann replied, "I will get him." She kissed Noah's forehead, "I'll be right back," and then climbed out of the wagon. Nikki was not inside the plant wagon. She yelled, "Son!" but heard no reply.

Emily looked around. "My son is gone too!"

Noah soon stood beside a tree and looked into the forest. "I'll go find them."

"You'll pass out in the forest and then we won't be able to find you either. You have to let somebody else search for them."

Kanneatche had already circled the camp and found evidence of the boys' departure. "They went this way. I find them. What their names?"

The family never told their names, but this could mean his son's life, and Judge Daniel Hall wouldn't know anything about the boys. Noah gave up the information, "Nikki and Oscar."

"I'm going with you." Tom followed Kanneatche. "Oscar!" he screamed, "Nikki!"

"Nikki is my son. I should be out there looking for him." Noah leaned against the tree. "But I can barely breathe. God, please guide Kanneatche and Tom to our boys. Wife, help me get back into our wagon."

Noah lay in the wagon. As his body tried to survive the black widow bite, his mind tried to bear the anguish of knowing the boys were unprotected and that he was unable to do anything about it.

Twenty Five

Nikki called out, "Oscar, climb now!"

"I don't want to try," replied Oscar.

"A really big cat is not far away! Get up here fast!"

Oscar jumped. His fingers barely touched the lowest limb. "I can't."

"I'm coming down to help." Nikki climbed as fast as he could.

The puma paused and sniffed the air.

"Jump higher. It's coming this way now."

"I'm trying!"

At the lowest branch, Nikki screamed, "You have to jump, Oscar! Now!"

The puma ran toward the prey only yards away. Oscar put all the force he could into his legs and sprang toward Nikki. Nikki grabbed Oscar's wrist with one hand, clutched the branch above with his other, and pulled.

Oscar rose as the hungry cat bounded toward him. "I think pumas can climb."

"Maybe not far. Come on." Nikki scrambled up the pinyon. The puma slowly forced its large body between the close branches. The smaller children quickly weaved along the path Nikki already knew. The cat continued behind them.

Far from camp, Kanneatche stopped. "Two sets small feet. One dragging branch. Going wrong away."

"We'll find them soon." Tom screamed, "Oscar!"

"Nikki," yelled Kanneatche as they trotted along the easy-to-follow trail.

The top of the tree bent under Nikki's weight. He glared at the approaching animal. "We can't go any higher."

"It's going to keep coming. There's no hope." Oscar wrapped his arms around Nikki to get as high as he could.

"Ann always prays. God, I know you don't save everybody. You let my parents die and Oscar's father, and Ann's parents too. People trying to get over this mountain died. Why didn't you let us die with our parents? Why let this cat eat us?" *SCREAM NOW* popped into Nikki's mind. "We need to scream." He yelled, "HELP!" at the top of his lungs.

Oscar joined. "SOMEBODY, HELP!"

Kanneatche faintly heard. "Run!" He and Tom raced along the trail of disturbed leaves.

The men saw the menace drawing near to the boys.

108

"AHH!! GO AWAY!!" insisted Nikki.

"Too high. Too many branches in way. Cannot kill from down here. No time to climb." Kanneatche drew an arrow anyway.

Above them, Nikki frantically screamed, "YOU CAN'T HAVE US. GO!"

Oscar kicked the air above the puma.

Tom aimed his rifle.

BLAM.

The bullet sunk into the pinyon. The boys looked beyond the animal, planning no mercy. Oscar yelled, "TOM, KILL IT!"

Tom aimed above the giant cat that would soon snag a human foot.

BLAM.

The puma jerked, paused, and then continued to climb. Tom rammed balls down both barrels. The feline carnivore placed its rear foot on the limb that would take it to its final destination. Tom shot through the foliage blindly. A metal projectile entered brains. The puma crashed through several branches before it hung from a limb.

"Come on down!" yelled Tom.

Nikki didn't budge. "Are you sure it's dead?"

"I think so."

Oscar didn't move either. "I'm afraid."

Tom raised his gun and fired. A new hole in the puma dripped blood, but it hung unmoving. "It's dead."

Nikki and Oscar both pleaded, "Get it away."

"I go," offered Kanneatche.

"Much obliged."

With his knife in his mouth, Kanneatche prodded the wild cat's paw with an arrow, climbed above the animal, grabbed the cat's head, pulled it back, and slit its throat before pushing it to the end of the branch with his foot. The puma dropped several yards before snagging on a lower branch.

The three people started down the pinyon. Nikki saw Kanneatche pluck a nut from the bark and pop it into his mouth. "Get these." Nikki pointed. He and Oscar stuffed pine nuts into their pockets as they descended.

At the cat, Kanneatche slid out along the branch. The boys passed him.

"You saved us!" Oscar jumped the final distance into Tom's arms. "I love you!"

"I love you too." He put Oscar on the ground and then reached up to catch Nikki. "And you too. What on earth were you two doing out here? Don't ever leave the group again. Do you hear me?"

Nikki clung to Tom's legs beside Oscar. He looked up. "May I tell you later? I promise I won't ever leave again."

"It comes!" Kanneatche kicked the carcass.

The three below backed away as the animal crashed to the ground.

Oscar examined the shot, bruised, and torn animal. "It's big. It would have eaten us both if you hadn't gotten here."

Kanneatche joined them. He opened the giant feline's belly, removed its innards, and then hung the carcass around his neck. "We go."

Twenty Six

Nikki picked up the branch's end and followed Kanneatche to camp.

Tom realized the branch had something to do with why the boys had gone into the woods. However, he let Nikki drag it along without questioning him.

In camp, Ann called out, "They're safe!" so Noah could stop worrying. She ran to the children and hugged them tightly. "I'm so glad you're safe. You scared us! Don't ever go off like that again!"

Emily knelt beside Ann and put her arms around the boys too. "What were you thinking? Why did you go off alone?"

"Emily." Tom slightly shook his head when the women looked at him.

Ann told Nikki, "Go hug your Papa." She followed her son. They climbed into the wagon through the front.

Noah lay on the feather mattresses. "Nikki, I wanted to go find you. Forgive me for not going."

"I know you're sick. That's why I went to get the branch. We have to hide those plants we gave Ann and Emily. They're bear root. They'll make us

111

use ours if they know we have some. I need you, and you need the bear roots to get better."

"Lie here beside me." With Nikki snuggled against his side, Noah assured him, "If this spider bite was going to kill me, it would have already. I appreciate that you want to help me with the medicine, but if we have to use what you gave Ann, we do. Besides, we can get more."

"We can't. We're too low now. Chipeta said it only grows high on mountains under junipers. She said they are far away."

Ann left the wagon.

Noah assured Nikki, "We'll be going over more mountains. We can get more."

Nikki started to cry, "I don't want to. Somebody will die!"

"Nobody is going to die."

"Yes, they will. We saw all those dead people, my parents were killed, you're almost dead, and that puma almost ate me and Oscar. We can't do it. Nobody can!"

"What puma!?"

"Oscar and me had to climb a tree, and it came up too. Tom got there just in time to shoot it."

Noah spoke sharply. "Don't ever leave the camp without an adult. Do you understand me? Promise me right now, Nikki!"

"I'm scared! You don't love me because I was bad," wailed Nikki.

"I love you very much. Everybody will get to the western sea alive. I promise."

"I'm afraid."

"Stay here beside me. Let's name my big revolver. It will keep us safe. All right?"

"May I name the pistol you gave me too?"

"Of course."

"Did your father always keep you safe?"

"He did."

"I want to give your revolver your father's name."

"My father is named Chetan, and now my Lefaucheux revolver is too."

Ann came back into the wagon with a cup of bear root tea that had finally brewed. "I want Noah to have bear root." She handed him the cup. "So I did what you suggested, my son, because we both love Noah very much. Chipeta said she will show you how to make this and a poultice if you're ready, Nikki."

"Much obliged, Ann. My father made the hidey-hole under the wagon seat and kept me and Adele safe in there when the Indians killed him und Mutter. I love them, but you two are my parents now, and I love you too. I want to call you Papa and Mama and my pistol Otto. Papa, I want you to teach me how to shoot Otto and everything you know about taking care of people. May I go now, Papa?"

"After you promise you will never go off like that again."

"I promise."

"As soon as I'm well enough, we'll start your lessons." Noah hugged Nikki. "I love you, and I'm glad you're safe. Go on and learn from Chipeta."

Twenty Seven

That afternoon, the suffering spider-bitten man, his family, all their animals, and their six wagons rode into the San Luis Valley with the Ute family. Chipeta showed them a five-foot shrub covered in fruits with four thin pale yellow wings. She dug up the plant, chewed its flowers and a piece of root, and then spit the plant material into her hand. "Put on spider bite. Get many whole plant."

As the group traveled north across the flat plain, they shoved four-wing saltbushes into their wagons. At a shallow flow of water, Kanneatche drew a gill net from his bag. "We fish here. My sons go hunt."

"Kanosh and Maykh, may we join you?" Eli held his bow and arrows. Adahy stood beside him with his.

"Come," the Ute boys signed.

Roscoe watched two mountain trout entangle in the mesh Kanneatche threw into the water. "I'm getting one of our horse hair nets." Soon he and Alex cast it into the water downstream from Kanneatche. Tom and Oscar did the same.

Chipeta spread her blanket on the ground,

tossed one of the bushes on it, and signed, "I show you what we do."

Nikki sat on the edge of his blanket with a saltbush. Ann held a wet rag to Noah's forehead. The rest of the women set up to learn.

Chipeta spoke in her native language as she demonstrated. "Cut off roots." She sawed at the plant with a stone tool.

Stephanie rose and walked to the wagon loaded with their trade goods, returned, and handed their instructor a hunting knife in a leather sheath. "For you," she signed.

Chipeta examined the blade, drew the sharp tool across the plant, smiled, and then continued the lesson.

When Eli, Adahy, Kanosh, and Maykh returned three hours later, each had several grouse. Fifty-four large, red fish fillets hung in the smoke of the fire over which several whole trout cooked. Kanosh signed, "You didn't get very many, Father."

Tom exclaimed, "He didn't!?"

"Many people. Fish see us," explained Kanneatche.

A lone rider hollered as he galloped toward them.

Stephanie turned. "What is he saying?"

Alex dashed toward the approaching man.

The man stopped beside Alex, who looked intently into the frantically jabbering man's face. The upset man resumed his approach to the group.

Alex ran beside him. "The mine collapsed. People are trapped. Their pueblo is too far south. They need help now."

Sally looked up from the bush in front of her. "What can we do?"

Stephanie answered. "First, we pray. Heavenly Father, there are people trapped. We ask that you keep them alive. Show us what to do to get them out and how to help them with any injuries. Let us know what they need to make them more comfortable while we try to save them."

"The miniature donkeys can get in there and pull the cart out of the way," suggested Alex.

Having not caught a fish for the last hour, the owner of the requested tiny animals pulled in his net. "Little Jack and Little Jenny are strong enough, and maybe last year's foals, but the one born this spring is only a foot high. Where are the miners?" asked Roscoe.

Alex spoke Spanish with the man and then answered. "Miguel says his mine is an hour's walk up the valley from here."

Sally rose. "The food isn't cooked, but let's go."

Chipeta motioned to sit and signed. "I know where the mine is. Some go now. We go after finish."

"How did you know what they said?" Sally signed.

"Many Spaniards live in this valley with us. I learned how speak their language." She pointed at Alex. "I didn't know you do."

116

"Only him." Sally smiled. *Everybody is blessed because Alex is here.*

"Will we need Goliath too?" Alex pointed at his horse.

Miguel shook his head. "He won't fit."

Even though the littlest donkey was weaned, it didn't like to be separated from Little Jenny, so Roscoe prepared all five of his miniature donkeys to move out. He, Alex, and Tom followed Miguel north. The rest of the family remained where they were.

Twenty Eight

Close to the high dunes of the San Luis Valley, Spaniards mined gold in the western flank of the Sangre de Cristo Mountains. The timbers of the entrance looked stable. "I don't want to take a chance." Roscoe kicked one. It remained firmly in place.

"How far in are they?" Alex asked.

"Deep enough that we'll need lanterns." Miguel moved the top off a wooden crate not far inside the shaft and drew out a small oil lamp attached to a leather strap around a hat. He pointed at the container. "Everybody put one on."

Alex repeated the command in English. Once all of them wore a lamp, Miguel struck a lucifer match and started them burning. Leading the miniature donkeys that lugged cans of oil and other supplies, their faint lights glowed in the quickly darkening tunnel as they proceeded away from the entrance. The men slid their hands along the rope that guided them to the men trapped deep inside the mountain. Roscoe noticed cracked support timbers here and there. "You haven't been maintaining the tunnel. How much farther?"

Alex repeated in Spanish.

Miguel ignored the comment and answered, "Not much."

A long way from there, Miguel still led them toward the disaster. Roscoe complained, "I don't know what his definition of not much farther is, but it's not the same as mine."

"Nor mine," remarked Tom.

"Do you want to go back?" Alex hoped they didn't. "Because people need us no matter where they are."

"Of course not. It's just that we are risking our lives, and our family needs us too." Roscoe still held tightly to the reins of his little donkeys, which seemed to trust him completely and not care that they could barely see.

Thirty minutes later, they stooped to fit in the damaged tunnel. Shortly after, they arrived at the blockage. Miguel called out in his native language, "Fernando, are you still alive?"

"Yes, but some of us are hurt," came a muffled voice from the other side of the obstruction. "We tried to shore up the hole around the cart while we had light. Did you figure out how to pull it out?"

"I have help." Miguel and his team examined their side of the fallen stones. "What do you think?" he asked Alex.

Alex translated the question for the other men.

Roscoe put his hand on Little Jack's

packsaddle. "I brought dynamite, but I don't think that's the answer."

Tom lay on his back with his head in the open space beneath the jammed cart. "It looks like the cart might come out if we raise this rock." He touched the boulder straddling a larger one and the cart.

Alex slid in beside Tom to add more light. "It does look like this is what's holding it. Right here, we might be able to wedge one of these broken timbers in from the back side and then use the donkeys to pull the bottom our way. We only need to get the weight off." He repeated the statement in Spanish.

Roscoe looked at the other side of the ore trolley. "This side might slide in."

Everybody looked. Miguel moved a rock off a snapped timber. "It might, but we must get the cart out of the way. We should try."

The men set to removing as much loose rock as possible. An hour later, as they attempted to position a timber in the enlarged cavity beside the cart, Tom noticed a faint light in the passageway. "Somebody is coming."

Roscoe turned to look. "There isn't much space for more people."

The light became two lights that grew brighter. Finally, Stephanie and Eli's faces became visible. Eli explained why they had dragged in two travoises. "We brought supplies. Do you think we can get any of it to the trapped men?"

Miguel poked a green container that flexed under his finger. "What are these?"

"India rubber," replied Eli, "canteens of water. All of you need some. We brought plenty."

Miguel took off his sweat-saturated shirt. "Tie one and some food inside my shirt. We can fasten it to the end of one of these poles and slide it between the cart wheels to my men." He opened a container as he walked to the cart. "We're sending in food and water. What do you need to help the injured men?" Miguel sucked down cool water.

"We need splints, bandages, a first aid kit, and more oil for our lamps."

Miguel turned toward Alex. "Did they happen to bring any of that?"

Alex informed the new arrivals of the request.

"We have what they need. First, let's get them water and food." Stephanie laid smoked trout wrapped in duck cloth on top of two large india rubber canteens. She buttoned up the shirt Eli had knotted at the bottom and then fastened it to a travois pole by its sleeves. "I hope this will go through."

Supporting the pole, Stephanie followed Eli, who carried the shirt. He pushed the package through the small space between the wheels.

"We've got it!" exclaimed the grateful man trapped in the pitch black. He unbuttoned the shirt and unscrewed the plug of the canteen. "Is this all the water?"

"We have several more," replied Alex.

The man inside gulped water and passed it on

before he removed the duck cloth package. "Send in more water, food, lamp oil, and lucifers."

Eli looked at the obstruction. "Raising this rock with that timber won't work. We should get the mobile forge and one of the ore carts from outside. We can take a cart apart, heat it, and fold the sides to fit underneath. Once we have this one supported, we can take off its wheels. The cart and inserted side plates will prevent the stones from caving in. If the men lie on the travois, we can use the donkeys to pull them out through the space under the cart."

Stephanie didn't wait to hear anybody else's opinion. "Darling, you are the most intelligent man on Earth. I'll keep sending in supplies while you get started."

Alex pulled gravel from around the cart and examined how the wheels attached. Stephanie sat cross-legged beside him in her buckskins. "Ask to describe the injuries."

Alex inquired and then translated the reply. "Paco was hit in the head. They tied a shirt around the injury. He's not bleeding anymore, but he hasn't woken up. They say he IS breathing. Alberto's leg is crushed. Efren has a broken arm. Roberto can't move. Everybody has cuts and bruises."

Stephanie whispered to her husband. "Eli, if Noah seems to be getting better and there is any way to get him and his medical kits in here, these men need help as soon as possible. If he can't, he needs to be ready to help when we get them out. Bring more water and lamp oil, and we'll need another travois because three of the men can't walk."

Eli hugged her. "Thank you for believing in Noah."

"I'd have to be stupid not to know how capable he is after the dust storm disaster. Ask Ann first. You know how Noah is. He'll want to help even if he isn't well enough."

Roscoe walked toward his donkeys. "We can put the forge and tools into the cart and use Little Jack and one of the foals to bring it in."

Tom helped Roscoe untie the selected animals from the lead rope. Roscoe commented, "You have a smart son, Tom. Did he get that from Hattie?"

Tom laughed. "He must have. I'm not that clever, and she was a remarkable woman. I love Emily, but nobody can compare to Hattie. I still wish she hadn't died."

"A part of me still wonders what life would have been like if my first love had loved me back, but your mother is wonderful. I'm very glad that she married me. Eli must have gotten some of his sweetness from her. He obviously got his good looks from you."

Tom patted Roscoe's shoulder. "Well, at least I was good for something. See you when you get back, my friend."

Twenty Nine

Much later, metal wheels squeaked in the mine shaft. Stephanie turned her head. "Finally, I was beginning to wonder if they were coming back." Faint flickers of light grew brighter as the "irir irir" of the ore trolley grew louder. Stephanie plunked her hands onto her hips. "Where is he?"

Eli explained, "Ever since the spider bit him, his mind is getting foggier. He's afraid he'll do something wrong, and besides that, he can't walk this far."

Roscoe and Tom set up the forge in case they had to modify the folded iron plates Roscoe had made outside. They didn't light it. Eli and Miguel unloaded the rest of the items in the cart. Alex and Stephanie kept the trapped men informed of their progress. Alex slid in a new supply of water, food, and lamp oil. "Fernando, we're ready to take off the wheels. The cart is going to drop a little. We don't know what will happen. Get everybody as far away as you can."

Fernando dragged his fellow miners to the far side of the cavern. "We're ready."

Miguel detached then pulled out the first axle

124

with the wheels still attached and shoved it toward Tom. He pushed his body into the open space and then flung bolts and nuts from the cavity as he removed them. The wrench and hammer followed then Miguel. "I'm going to try to kick the axle and wheels out the far side. If you can do it safely, jerk me out when I tell you."

Alex assured him. "I will."

Feet first, Miguel slid back under the cart with his hands extended toward safety. Alex clenched one wrist and Tom the other. The loud clang of boots slamming metal rang out. "Now!"

Holding Miguel tightly, Alex and Tom scrambled away from the cart. Miguel lay in the open cave. The axle and wheels remained firmly in place.

"I'm going to try again." Miguel wiggled back into position. He didn't have much space to raise his knees. Therefore, he couldn't exert much force. He tried several times to kick the wheels out but failed. "This is my responsibility. I have to do this, but if I die, tell my children I love them." He accepted the risk of getting crushed, picked up the blacksmith's hammer, and squirmed into the small space. He beat on one wheel and then on the other. The wheels slowly moved toward the far end of the cart. "This one might do it. Can you reach my feet?"

Alex assured him, "Yes."

Miguel requested, "Pulled me out if you can," then swung the heavy hammer. "Now!"

The obstruction went out. Stones crashed in. Sharp gravel tore into Miguel's face as Alex and Tom pulled him through the billowing dust. Stephanie gagged and coughed. "Did you get him out?! Is everybody all right? Is it completely blocked now?"

"I'm out!" Miguel waved his hand in the direction from whence he had come. "I don't feel anything." He crawled forward and felt around. His hand dumped something. "I feel one of the plates you made." He ran his hand up the edge and along both sides. "It's open under there at least part of the way! Fernando, can you hear me?"

"I do! The dust is thick. I'll try to find out what happened."

Both men reached under the cart. Their fingers touched. Fernando exclaimed, "Thank you, God!"

"I'm going to try to get a travois through. Send Paco out first." Miguel turned to the people on his side of the cave. "Hook one of the donkeys to the travois."

Stephanie saw his face through the clearing dust. "You're injured. Come here!" She opened the first aid kit.

The men set to getting the trapped miners through the small space under the cart. "There is barely any space. Clear it out under there." Miguel let Stephanie tend to him.

Alex crawled in. As he advanced, he swept the gravel toward Eli. Eli pushed the rubble to Tom, who shoveled it into the cart they had used to bring

126

in the forge. Alex's head entered the space on the inner side. "It's tight. Take my hand and pull me in."

Tears made tracks down Fernando's dusty cheeks. "You are the best thing I have ever seen!" He grasped Alex by the wrist.

Alex got up on his knees before he turned back toward the way out. "Send in a travois." He pulled it in before he helped Fernando get the most injured man ready for transport. He turned Paco's face to the side. "So he can fit through. Paco is loaded. Pull him out."

The mountain rumbled as Paco left the trap. Even with a broken arm, Efren scrambled into the tunnel behind him. Stephanie led Little Jenny up the mine shaft far enough to allow space for all three travoises. The broken timbers creaked. Efren grabbed ahold of the rope and started out.

The tunnel shook. "Stephanie, take Paco out, NOW!" Eli pushed the second set of poles with canvas stretched between them to Alex.

"I'm not leaving without you!" Stephanie replied.

"We'll catch up. Get going."

Stephanie refused, "No! We all go together."

Tom and Roscoe loaded the forge into the ore trolley. On the other side of the blockage, Fernando and Alex gently lifted Roberto onto the canvas. The walls of the cave cracked. Fernando ordered his friend, "Alberto, drag your broken leg and get out now."

"It hurts too much. You need to pull me out."

"It doesn't matter how much it hurts. Some of us might not get out if you don't go now. GO!" Fernando called into the tunnel. "Pull out Roberto. As soon as Alberto is out, get him into the cart and get going. Alejandro and I are coming right behind him."

Tom ordered the miniature donkey colt, "Forward Ho." He looked at his son. "Eli, you keep him going. Get Stephanie out of here." A new bellow of dust filled the cavern. "I'll get Alberto and come right behind you."

Alberto stopped moving. "I can't do it."

Alex commanded, "Alberto stretch out your hands. Tom, he can't push with his leg. Pull him out. Save Little Jack for last."

A loud pop emanated from the surrounding mine shaft. "Hurry!" Tom reached in and grabbed one hand.

Roscoe got the other. They pulled Alberto through the tiny opening under the cart.

"Let's go." Fernando slid into the space under the cart.

Alex remained on his hands and knees. "Send in the last travois right after Fernando gets out."

Tom demanded, "Forget everything and come out."

"No, don't waste time."

Fernando returned to the space beside Alex. "Send it now, load Alberto, and go."

Alex loaded all the supplies onto the travois

still at the exit. "Fernando, hold the poles and let it pull you. I'll hold your ankles, and Little Jack can pull us all out." Once they were all positioned, he called out. "We're ready."

The mountain roared and shook as the last man slid through the space under the cart. Alex and Fernando jumped to their feet. The plates under the cart spread. The mountain slammed the trolley to the hard stone floor. Roscoe ordered, "Forward, run!"

Thirty

The group ran stooped over. Their escape wasn't fast. Little Jack, however, was only four feet to the tip of his ears and well below the ceiling. The donkey galloped. In the dust, Roscoe lost sight of him. "Halt!" The people screeched to a standstill. Roscoe clarified as he dashed past his friends, "Not you!" Roscoe called out at the branch of the tunnels, "Come!"

Little Jack had obeyed Roscoe's command just as the people had. He rotated his ears where he stood.

"Come!" Roscoe called out again.

The donkey attempted to turn in the narrow passage. The travois stuck and then turned over. Little Jack brayed his frustration when he couldn't go forward or backward.

Roscoe heard his donkey. "Everybody go on. I'll get him!" He charged back into the mountain.

Miguel ordered, "The rest of you get these injured men out." He went the same way as Roscoe.

Alex followed Miguel. Not far in, they found

130

Little Jack and the spilled-out supplies. The men turned the travois and started reloading. The loudest crashing yet filled their ears.

Miguel turned his head. "I hope that was back at the original cave-in. Leave the rest. We have to get out."

"I'm not leaving anything we can't replace." Alex threw canteens on top of the supplies they had already recovered. He left smoked trout, squares of duck cloth, and matches on the ground. "Go."

Miguel kept his right hand on the wall and his left hand in Alex's. Alex held onto Roscoe. Roscoe kept a tight grip on Little Jack's harness as they hurried to the shaft with the rope.

Miguel stopped at the completely dust-clogged tunnel. Dirt filled their nostrils and stuck to their sweat. They fastened bandanas over their mouth and nose. Roscoe took off his shirt and tied it over Little Jack's head. They were barely able to see as they followed the rope. Rumbling, cracking, and roaring spurred them on.

Thirty One

Efren exited the tunnel. "I made it!"

Chipeta spoke to him in Spanish. "This man will help you."

Noah examined him. *I hope I don't make a mistake.* "Little sister, you know how to do stitches. See to those." He signed to Chipeta and her sons. "Do any of you know how to set broken bones?"

Kanosh answered, "We can."

Sally saw the odd angle of Efren's forearm and signed to Chipeta, "Tell the man to drink." Chipeta did so as she held out a tin cup filled with the sedative that they had made while waiting

Efren drank the liquid, sat down, and held out his arm. "I'm ready."

Sally set a pot of antiseptic beside the man. She slowly cleaned the cuts on his arm, neck, and back to give the medicine time to work. Twenty minutes after Efren ran from what he had thought would be his grave, he started to lean. Sally already knelt in front of him. He slumped onto her shoulder. She waved Kanosh and Noah over. They carried the man to a pallet.

In a daze, Noah set and splinted Efren's arm with Kanosh's help. *That one was easy. I hope I don't make a mistake.* Noah picked up the medical book he had reviewed while they waited outside the mine. He didn't remember any of it.

Sally sat beside Efren with a needle and a package of catgut sutures. She started stitching.

Stephanie and Eli led Little Jenny's oldest colt out the mouth of the mine. Eli reported, "Paco was hit in the head. He's still unconscious. Noah, you woke not long after Roy cracked your head with the rifle. I don't know what's wrong with this man. It's been much longer."

Not far behind them, Fernando exited with Roberto on a travois pulled by the other yearling colt, followed by Alberto in the mine cart pulled by Little Jenny with her youngest colt and Tom beside her.

Sally looked their way. "Where are Alex and Roscoe?"

"Little Jack ran off, but we heard him." Tom led the donkey to Sally. "They went to get him. I'm sure they're coming right behind us." As Tom helped Alberto get out, he noticed something. "It's hot out here." He took off his shirt and threw it over the rubble.

"Roberto can't move his legs." Fernando stood beside his friend.

Noah quickly looked over the four miners. "Sedative, cleaning, and stitches for all of them. We'll have to open Alberto's leg to see what needs to be done. Leave Roberto on the travois. He's been moved too much already. I know you didn't have any other choice. Chipeta, tell Fernando to lie on a pallet. Tell them to drink what you give them and that we are going to sew the cuts on them. Then come here."

When Chipeta arrived, Noah touched the tip of Roberto's pointer finger. "Ask him to try to move this finger and tell us if he can feel me touching it."

Roberto did not move the finger. He informed them, "It doesn't hurt. It's just a pressure."

Noah repeated for each finger before he probed Roberto's neck. "What does he remember about what happened?"

Chipeta listened to Roberto and then signed to Noah. "He and Paco pushing cart. Hit the support. Mine fall in all over him and Paco. One hit back of neck. He fell to ground. He want to crawl, but nothing works now. Fernando pull him and Paco away."

I think it's safe to take off his boots. Noah did so and tested Roberto's toes.

Once again, Roberto felt the touch but was unable to move. "Tell him I'll come back." Noah went to his wagon and flipped through the pages of <u>Contribution to Physiological and Pathological Anatomy</u> by John Godman that he had gotten from Dr. Seibel at Fort Smith.

134

Sally slid up beside Stephanie. "Are you sure Alex and Roscoe are all right? Maybe somebody should go back in."

"They were fine."

"There's been a lot of noise and dust. I'm worried."

"Let's give them five more minutes."

Sally walked to the entrance and called in. "Are you there?" She heard no reply. She went back to closing wounds on the sleeping men. *The skin of humans is much easier to sew than a mule's.* In response to thinking about mule skin, she heard a heehaw. "They're here!" She jumped to her feet and dashed to the mine. Little Jack's shirt-covered head came into view. "You made it!" She hugged Roscoe. "I was worried." She turned to Alex and blushed but hugged him anyway. "Is everything all right?"

Alex held her for a moment. "We lost some supplies but nothing important. I don't think anybody should ever go back in there. It's not safe." He stepped away from Sally because she felt much too good.

Miguel hurried to the pallets where his unconscious men lay. "Except Paco, they were fine. What happened?"

Chipeta put her hand on his arm. "We put them to sleep to fix them."

Ann and Ehawee had all the babies, Oscar, and Nikki, in a wagon. Noah said, "Ann, come here." She walked to the rear. Noah put his finger on some words in the book. "What do you think this means? Am I supposed to do something?"

"Don't say our names." Ann read. "It says swelling around the spine might cause paralysis."

"His neck is swollen. So he should be able to move once it goes down?"

"Maybe."

"Should I ask somebody else to look at this? I might be missing something."

Ann knew they had a problem. "God, thank You for helping us get everybody out. Clear Noah's mind and help him know what to do to help these men. In Jesus' name I pray. Amen."

I do not know what to do! Noah added, "God, please bring somebody to help them. Amen."

"God answered your prayer, Papa. Other people are coming." Nikki had been keeping a lookout with his brass telescoping spyglass.

"Thank You, God!" exclaimed Noah and Ann.

Soon, Kanneatche and a man from Miguel's pueblo galloped into camp. Asking questions in Spanish, the unknown man quickly swung off his horse and dashed to the men on the ground.

Miguel answered the man, "I do not know."

"They gave them something to make them sleep, and they've been sewing cuts," replied Chipeta.

Miguel added, "Paco has been unconscious since the accident."

The Spanish doctor went to Paco. "How long has he been like this?"

Miguel stood beside him. "Four hours."

"His skull is not fractured. His brain has to be swollen. I don't have the tools I need. There is nothing I can do."

Noah looked into space. *Don't we have some tools?* He looked at Stephanie. *She doesn't want me to do anything. What would I do if it wouldn't make her mad?* Noah blankly looked at his sister-in-law.

Stephanie walked toward Noah. "Get your trepanning set."

"My what?"

His mind is fogged up! Doc shaved and stitched Gus after Noah cut off a section of his scalp. In this case, they're going to drill a hole clean through the man's skull. "I'll get it." Stephanie went to Noah's wagon, spoke to her sister, returned, and handed the Spanish doctor a wooden box.

Eli motioned for his father and Roscoe to follow him.

The man opened the box. "You already have a doctor here?"

Chipeta signed the doctor's question to the others then pointed to the man standing beside Paco, looking into the distance. "A spider bit him. Now, he not think well."

"Oh!" The Spanish doctor held out his hand toward Noah. "Dr. Antonio Vega."

Noah shook his hand. "Dr. Luke Smith."

"I'm glad you have this. Have you done this surgery before, Dr. Smith?"

"Ann, have I done this before?"

Ann scowled. *He's saying my name again.* "You

have not. Chipeta, tell Dr. Vega he can't help because a spider bit him, and now his mind is gone. Ask the doctor if he can help my husband?"

The doctor replied to Chipeta's translation. "Sometimes people never recover. There is nothing that can be done. Somebody help me get Paco into a wagon. I need to drill a hole through his skull as soon as possible."

Chipeta told Ann, "Keep drinking the saltbush tea," and then she signed what Dr. Vega planned to do.

Noah and Dr. Vega carried Paco to the wagon with the removable rear boards that Eli, Tom, and Roscoe had just taken off. Emily and Helen hurried to move the bedding.

Already in the wagon, Tom suggested, "Put him in feet first. The doctor can stand outside the wagon and work on Paco's head."

Thirty Two

Dr. Vega looked at Sally, stitching patients. *So beautiful!* "What is in the cup beside you? It looks dirty."

Sally shrugged her shoulders. Chipeta answered for her. "Special water for washing."

"Do you have more?"

"I'll get some." Chipeta carried an empty tin cup to the pot beside the fire.

Dr. Vega examined Fernando's stitches and then looked at Sally. *She would make a wonderful partner for a doctor.* "Woman, continue your good work. Somebody, shave Paco's head and wash it."

"I will do it." Chipeta carefully shaved the injured area and then the rest of the man's head before she poured the liquid over the injury.

The doctor picked up the drill. Stephanie put her hand on his and pointed to the washbasin. She signed and said, "Wash your hands and tools."

Chipeta passed on the message. The doctor exclaimed, "What a good idea!" and then did so.

He wasn't sure why, but Noah felt this was something he should watch. He stood beside Dr. Vega as the man placed the drill at the center of the

139

damage. The grinding sounds of the circular bone-chipping saw set everybody's teeth on edge.

In Ann's wagon, Nikki told her, "I don't like that sound. What are they doing?"

"They are trying to fix Paco's brain. It's inside his head bone. Dr. Vega is sawing through it."

"I don't like it. I wish they didn't have to."

"I don't either, but they think they do. Would you like to go to the dunes?"

"Yes!"

Ann asked, "Ehawee, may we leave all the babies with you?"

Oscar stood up. "I want to go. We should bring our goggles and spyglasses."

"You three go on. If I need help, I'll get Emily or Helen."

Ann and the boys stopped at a creek at the foot of the dunes. A small wave that barely covered his feet crashed in front of Oscar. "It's so hot. I want to play in the water."

"Me, too." Ann sat down, took off her shoes, and then put her hand against the ground to get up. "Oww! The sand is hot! Don't touch it!"

Nikki examined her red palm. "Are you going to be all right, Mama?"

"Yes. I should check the water." Ann stepped into the creek, reached in, and then splashed the boys. "It's fine."

They whipped water back at her and each other, rolled in the cool wetness, and then lay on their backs in the shallow stream. Oscar rolled to his belly. "Ann, we always ask God to help us, and we thank Him for things."

"Yes, we do," replied Ann.

"Why do we only ask Him to do things for us? Why don't we ask Him what we can do for Him?"

"Humm. We should. Would you like to pray about that for us right now, Oscar?"

"God, thank You for all the help. You got us over those high and dangerous mountains, and You saved us from the puma. I want to know what we can do for You. Please show us how we can help You."

Nikki added, "And make me like your Son. Because He would have helped Paco, but I didn't even want to listen to them making a hole in his head. I asked Papa to teach me how to fix people then I didn't stay to learn, and I almost got Oscar and me eaten by that puma because I was bad and left camp. I almost said that word Cleo told me, and I keep almost saying it. Why can't I be good? Oh, no! God, we want to know what we can do for You, but I'm asking for something again. Why can't I be good?!" Nikki started to cry.

"Nikki, honey! Everybody does things wrong sometimes. Satan puts thoughts into our minds, and we can't stop that, but God puts the Holy Spirit into us, so when that happens, the Spirit helps us to do the right thing. You said you almost said that word, but you didn't. You let the Spirit guide you. That's all any of us can do."

"Really? The Holy Spirit is helping me?"

"Yes, but you can ask God to put Jesus's spirit into you more fully. We should all ask for that."

"God and Jesus, it's me again, Nikki. Please fill me up with Your Spirit. Don't leave any space for Satan to put thoughts into me. I don't want him around me. Help me be good and help me to do things for You, just like Oscar said."

Oscar got on his knees and folded his hands under his chin in prayer. "Me, too."

Ann did the same. "And me as well. Use us in Your service, fill us with Your Holy Spirit, and make us like Jesus. I just remembered. The Bible does say something about this. We'll read it when we get back to the group."

"Somebody is here!" Nikki looked around.

"Stay right beside me." Ann reached for the revolver she had stuck into her shoe.

Oscar whispered, "I hear it too. What is it?"

"It doesn't sound like a person." Nikki looked toward the noise. "The sand is sliding!" He jumped to his feet. "Run!"

Ann put her hand on Nikki's arm. "The sand can't come this far. The dune is humming! I think our prayers made the sand sing. I'm sure God heard us and loved what we said!"

"I think so too." Oscar lay back in the water. "I want to climb to the top of the dune before we go."

"The sand is too hot, and it's not stable. It was just sliding. It can't get over here, but it might bury us if we were on it."

They enjoyed the creek until Ann stood up. "The sun is getting low. We better start back."

Thirty Three

After repeated rests for cleaning with the antiseptic to cool the skull and examine the depth of the circular groove, a small disk of bone came out. Fluid joined the blood running over the floorboards onto the ground. Dr. Vega remarked, "I was right. Even though the skull didn't crack, there was swelling and fluid on his brain."

After Chipeta signed the message, Noah asked, "What are you going to do now?"

"Apply dressing and then look at the other men again. I'd like to learn how to make the special wash and whatever you used to sedate everybody."

When Chipeta signed the request, Noah wondered, *how do we make those?*

Roscoe replied, "I can show him."

Chipeta told Dr. Vega what Noah had done to test Roberto and that Noah had said they needed to cut open Alberto's leg to see how to fix it. Dr. Vega knew they had already set Efren's broken arm and that Sally had stitched many injuries. He thought the men were blessed that these particular individuals had been here. "Miguel, you need to pay these people well. How much gold do you have in the sluice?"

"It's empty. All I have from the mine is what we pitched into that." He pointed to the cart they had used to bring out Alberto. "It's just rubble, but they're welcome to have it." He told Chipeta to tell them. She did so.

"We are glad we have been able to help, but we'll take the rubble and look through it." Tom got some bags and a spade from his wagon. He collected every bit of the material in the cart and placed it into his wagon.

Dr. Vega examined Alberto's leg. "There is a lot of tissue damage and crushed bone."

Noah looked at Stephanie. "Didn't somebody we know have this problem?"

"Doc cut open our friend's leg. He removed the little pieces and positioned the rest." Stephanie looked at Alberto's leg. "I don't think you can put this leg back together, but you should open it up and see. If you don't try, you will have to cut off this part of his leg."

"How much longer will he stay asleep?" Dr. Vega inquired.

Helen spoke up. "We can get him to drink more sedative even while he's asleep, but it takes some time to get it into him. If you are going to do that, we should get started."

Once Helen finally got another cup of sleeping potion into Alberto, Dr. Vega picked up the scalpel and sliced through his friend's skin. Bone fragments presented a puzzle. Small chips soaked in the pooled blood. "Maybe the larger ones will knit together. If they don't, I can amputate later. At least we'd have given him a chance." He positioned the big pieces with forceps, dropped the tiny ones into a cup, and then stitched ripped muscles.

Sally handed Dr. Vega a handmade book. "We have this about blood vessels."

Antonio Vega flashed a dazzling smile at Sally as he took the book.

As a frown grew on Alex's face, Oscar ran through their herd of animals to be the first to the family. He signed to Chipeta, "We heard a noise. Does the dune hum?" He tried to mimic the sound.

"Yes, when sand falls," she confirmed.

Nikki joined them. "When we were playing in the water, we heard it after we prayed."

Emily remarked, "You did not get in any water. You are dry as a bone."

"It's so hot that we've already dried." Ann climbed into a wagon. She returned, flipping the pages of the Bible. "Here it is. Philippians 4:6-7. Be anxious for nothing, but in everything by prayer and supplication, with thanksgiving, let your requests be made known to God; and the peace of God, which surpasses all understanding, will guard your hearts and minds through Christ Jesus."

Nikki was still learning to speak English. "What is supplication?" he asked.

Stephanie joined them when she saw Ann get the Bible. "I think it's a type of prayer. Prayer is anything you talk to God about, but when you are desperately asking God for help, that is supplication."

"Supplication is like when we asked God to save us from the puma, but a regular prayer is like what we said to God in the creek?" Nikki asked.

Ann said, "When you asked God to fill you with His Spirit, keep Satan away from you, and let you do something for Him, you were desperately asking God to help you. That was also supplication."

Stephanie put her hand on Nikki's shoulder. "So God will give you His peace and guard your heart and mind."

Oscar said, "I asked for that too. I think I just got God's peace. I've been worried, but now I'm not because I can pray and supplication."

Emily corrected Oscar. "You say supplicate when you are stating that you are doing it."

"Golly, Ma! God knows what I mean."

"Of course. We all do. I just wanted you to know how to say it correctly."

Oscar dropped his shoulders and walked away.

Stephanie remarked, "It might have been better to have told him later."

"Oscar, I'm sorry!" Emily went after her son.

After Alberto's surgery, they moved all the sleeping men into the wagons. Dr. Vega stood beside the injured. "Do you have spare blankets to cover them while we travel? It gets very cold at night."

Thirty Four

Night fell before the group arrived at the miners' pueblo. Efren hurried away with his wife. Fernando and Miguel helped carry the three most injured men into Dr. Vega's house before they left.

Dr. Vega informed Paco's, Alberto's, and Roberto's families, "They need to stay with me. Come back tomorrow." He turned to Sally. "I need a nurse's help tonight."

Alex put his arm around Sally. "None of our women go anywhere alone, and she won't understand anything you say." He moved her toward her family. "I will help you."

Dr. Vega knew how helpful Alex had been. "Thank you." Sitting beside the full hospital beds, he asked, "Do you think Sally would stay here? We have plenty of money in this pueblo. I could buy her. She would be a wonderful second wife."

Alex balled up his fists. "Sally is not for sale, and she isn't going to be anybody's second wife!"

"I was just asking. My first wife passed last month."

"Oh. I'm sorry you lost her. Still, Sally won't want to stay here."

"I'm a charming fellow. I might persuade her. Right now, though, help me make some antiseptic and sedative." Dr. Vega left the room with the ingredients he had purchased from Roscoe.

Thirty Five

Alex spoke with Ann the following day. "Antonio is going to try to get Sally to stay here. We need to do something."

"Don't worry, Alex. Sally has never stayed behind for any man. She won't do it now."

"Other men have tried to win her?"

"Yes."

"Antonio says he'll even buy her if he has to."

Ann's face turned red. "Sally is NOT for sale!"

"That's what I said. Maybe around other people she needs to hide her beauty. Not that you and the other women aren't attractive, but Sally is incredibly gorgeous."

"Thank you for the compliment to all of us. I'll speak with her." Ann got out of the wagon where she had been changing Chris's diaper.

Chipeta joined Alex as he returned to Dr. Vega's house. "I heard talking this morning. Miguel bought a hundred sheep in Santa Fe. He was going to send Alberto to pick them up, hire some men to drive them to California, and sell them. Alberto can't do it now, and nobody else

149

here knows how to be a drover. Your family cares for your animals. Maybe you could buy the sheep from Miguel."

"Thank you for telling me about this." Alex went into Antonio's home.

That afternoon, Eli knocked on the doctor's door. "Hello, Alex. How are the patients?"

"Paco is still unconscious. Alberto is awake, but Antonio is going to sedate him because his leg hurts so much. Roberto wiggled his fingers, so his family carried him home."

"I came to tell you that we're leaving in the morning. Do you still want to go with us to the western sea?"

"Of course, but I need to tell you something." As Alex led Eli away from the house, he repeated what he had explained to Ann and passed on Chipeta's knowledge about the sheep.

"I'll let you know what we decide." Eli left.

Alex walked into the hospital room. He called out, "Antonio!" but heard no reply. He searched the house. Dr. Vega was not home. Then, he saw him through the window, outside with Sally. *What can I do?! I'm not letting him have her!*

Alex pondered. Before long, he heard Sally's voice in the house. "Alex!"

Alex hurried to the foyer. Sally smiled at him. "If Dr. Vega has any books he will sell us, would you be willing to read them to us?"

"Of course."

"Antonio doesn't understand me. Please ask."

150

Alex explained what Sally wanted. Dr. Vega waved for them to follow him. "If Sally would become my wife, I will get her all the books she would like."

Alex took Sally's hand. "He will only give you books if you marry him."

"Marry him! I don't even know him. Are you sure that's what he said?"

"Actually, he said if you marry him, he will get you all the books you want, but last night he said he wanted to buy you."

Sally's cheeks flamed up. "Buy me! I am not for sale!"

Dr. Vega stepped out of his library, "Are you coming?"

Alex pulled Sally away. "You can't buy her with money or books."

Sally acted as if she was putting a ring on her finger, shook her head, then pointed into the room and acted as if she was opening a book. She took a coin from her pocket and nodded yes. "Marriage, no. Buy books, yes."

Antonio's face lit up with a charming smile. "She will marry me for books?"

Ice crystals dropped from Alex's words. "She said she will buy books, but she will NOT marry you."

"She will change her mind in time."

They walked into the library filled with medical books and one novella. Dr. Vega handed the book to Sally. "Para tu mano en matrimonio."

151

Alex translated, "He said it's yours for your hand in marriage."

"I am NOT going to marry you. You can keep your book." Sally threw it to the floor. "Men! They only ever want one thing!" She turned and stormed from the room.

"I told you she is not for sale, and she is not going to marry you. I will not be helping you anymore, but I do hope the men heal well."

Dr. Vega called from the library door. "Sally, if you get to know me, you will love me!"

"We are leaving in the morning. She will not be able to get to know you." Alex followed Sally out of the house.

Sally stomped her foot as she spoke with her sisters. "I can't ever ask a man for anything. They always want my favors. All I wanted was to buy a book. I even had Alex with me. Dr. Vega still insisted that I had to marry him. It's so infuriating!"

Stephanie put her arm around her sister's shoulders. "It seems that men aren't able to resist your beauty."

"Alex isn't like that."

Ann stated her opinion. "Alex is a respectful and good man, but he's in love with you too."

"He is?!"

"I think so," Ann continued, "but don't think all men are the same. None of the others here have acted poorly. It's just Dr. Vega, but in all fairness, his wife did just die, and he's hurting."

"That's no excuse. I wish we could leave now."

Stephanie spoke up. "If Roscoe, Eli, and Tom work out a deal to buy the sheep in Santa Fe, maybe you could dress like a man and pretend to be a sheep drover."

"Good plan, Stephanie. I am so tired of this."

"You could marry Alex." Ehawee saw Eli, Roscoe, and Tom. "Here they come."

"He'd have to ask me first." Sally turned to hear what the men had found out.

Roscoe kicked the dirt. "Miguel didn't want to sell the sheep contract unless I sold him our miniature donkeys, but he doesn't take care of his mines. I'm not going to let him have my animals. That would be a death sentence for them."

Eli smiled largely. "Buuuut…success! Miguel knows he has no way to get the sheep to California. Selling the sheep to us is the only way he can recover even part of what he has invested. We did better than that for him. We bought them for half of what he hoped to get if Alberto sold them in California. A man named Hernandez has them in Santa Fe. He expects a person with the contract to come for the sheep, but he doesn't know or care who it will be."

When the men heard about Dr. Vega's behavior, the family quietly left town. To Sally's dismay, without any new books. However, they did have the contact for one hundred sheep, sacks of rubble from the gold mine, and a wagon load of four-wing salt bush.

Thirty Six

On a mid-September day, three hundred armed men camped a day's march east of Santa Fe. They discussed their orders to capture Santa Fe and thereby annex the territory of New Mexico into the Republic of Texas.

Staying out of the light of the small army's campfires, Roscoe Bacon gathered information. Farther back, Tom Yates maintained his ability to run for help if Roscoe got captured.

"We head out at first light. As soon as we get there and the night conceals us, we'll take Santa Fe," stated one of the Texans.

The commander of the Texan militia slammed his cup on the log upon which he sat. "Stop trying to give orders, Johnson! President Lamar put me in charge of this expedition. We don't know the situation in Santa Fe. Therefore, we will NOT move out before Carlyle gets back, and then we will decide what to do."

Johnson slung coffee from his cup. "I'm telling you, we're worn out and hungry. We can't put up a good fight in this condition. We need to take them by surprise, and we NEED TO DO IT NOW!" He turned heel and strode away from the fire.

Commander Dennison wiped hot coffee from his trousers. "I've had it with that man undermining me. Carmichael, arrest Johnson."

"Yes, sir, but how will we contain him?" Carmichael asked.

"Never mind." Dennison muttered under his breath, "I'd shoot him if I were sure we won't need every one of us to take Santa Fe."

Roscoe slithered away and joined Tom. At their family's fireless camp, Roscoe disclosed what he had discovered. ".... We should forget the sheep and leave. We don't want to get dragged into a war."

Tom countered, "They're waiting for one of their men to return. If we go in the morning, we can get our sheep and be long gone before the Texans get there."

Two days later, Roscoe, Alex, Eli, Noah, Tom, and Adahy rode into Santa Fe, hoping to get out of town quickly. Eli rose in his stirrups and glanced around. "There's a store. Maybe we can find out where Hernandez is and get provisions at the same time."

Inside the store, Roscoe casually strolled up to Eli and whispered, "That's Johnson by the bacon barrels."

Eli turned toward the men. "Get a barrel of bacon." He pointed. "It's over there."

Roscoe and Tom examined multiple slabs of

the fatty meat to listen to Johnson. "Well, Carlyle, did you see anybody who's going to resist or not?"

"Not a soul. Tell Dennison to bring in the men. We can occupy Santa Fe without firing a bullet."

I wish I had money to buy some of that bacon. I'm so hungry; I could eat it raw. Johnson hurried away.

A local man watched which way Johnson went before he slipped into the space between the buildings.

Not long after, Carlyle slipped his hand into the pickle barrel. A wet patch steeped through his trouser pocket as he hurried out the door.

Tom looked at Roscoe. "Did you see that?"

"Yes, and I'm not letting him get away with it. Bring the storekeeper!" Roscoe ran.

Alex turned to the man and woman behind the counter. "¡Te han robado! ¡Sígueme ahora!"

Everybody in the store dashed outside as Roscoe tackled the culprit only a few yards away. He rolled Carlyle over. "I hate a thief! I can't tell you how much I've lost to people like you."

The soldier chewed as fast as he could and swallowed the evidence.

Alex drew the store owner's attention to the wet pocket. "Compruebe el bolsillo de Carlyle."

The pickle juice on his pants and the aroma of his breath incriminated the soldier. "Lo siento. No he comido en días."

"Eso no te da derecho a robar." The five-foot-six-inch storekeeper grabbed Carlyle's arm and pulled the hungry Texan down the road.

156

Alex went back into the store with the shop owner's wife. The rest of the crowd made their way to the sheriff's office.

"Gracias a ti y a tus amigos. Les daré a todos un buen precio." The woman lowered the section of counter top between herself and Alex as she thanked him.

"De nada. Sé lo que queremos." Alex asked, "¿Cómo podemos encontrar a Hernández?"

"Regresará eventualmente. Él es mi esposo, Joaquín. Soy Carla." The shop owner stated that Hernandez was her husband.

Alex purchased and loaded everything the family needed onto their mules then sat with a peppermint stick to wait for his friends to help strap the barrel of bacon packed in bran flakes and the barrel of eggs nestled into corn meal onto their largest mule, King.

"¿Tienen libros a la venta?"

Mrs. Hernandez went to the back and got the only book she had, which happened to be El Periquillo Sarniento, written by José Joaquín Fernández de Lizardi.

Alex flipped the pages. "Interesting. ¿Cuánto cuesta?"

"Puede que los tenga por ayudarnos."

"Gracias." Alex stepped outside, tucked the gift into the packsaddle, and then saw Joaquín and the men of his family headed his way.

Thirty Seven

Three hundred Texans swarmed into the dusty road. Dennison ordered the townsfolk at the top of his lungs, "¡Ríndete y nadie saldrá herido!"

Alex screamed, "RUN!"

Building doors flew open on both sides of the road. Armed men slipped behind the carefully positioned barrels, water troughs, and wagons. Fifteen hundred rifle barrels pointed at the men in the street. Having been warned that Texans were marching on Santa Fe, Filipe Espinoza –the commander of a detachment of the Mexican army– yelled in English. "PUT UP YOUR HANDS! TRY TO RUN, AND WE WILL SHOOT YOU!"

Alex backed into the store.

They're not after us. Eli raised his hands.

Dennison surrendered. "We are laying down our guns." *Johnson set us up!*

"Get their weapons," ordered Espinoza.

"We're not part of them," explained Roscoe.

The commander replied sarcastically, "Of

course you're not." He waved his pistol. "I'm not that stupid," he commanded, "All of you, put down your guns."

Dennison carefully drew his revolver from its holster. "Those men are not with us."

Espinoza knew the store owner. "Joaquín, get away from them." He pointed his rifle directly at Roscoe's forehead. "You're American. DISARM NOW!"

Joaquín hurried to the boardwalk. All the men in the road put their weapons in the dust.

Inside the store, Alex begged. "Hide me, please!" *God protect all of us!*

In the back room, Carla rolled a barrel off a hole where a knot had popped out. She put her finger in the small opening and pulled up a section of boards nailed together from the underside. Alex quickly slid under the floor. Carla repositioned the bacon over him.

Espinoza snarled, "Show the Texans what happens when somebody disrespects a Mexican."

His soldiers knew that meant to subdue with extreme force. They lit into the Americans.

Tom blocked a punch. "GOD, HELP US!" He landed a left on his attacker's jaw.

The sound of breaking bone and then a wail of pain emanated from the solider as he backed away.

Knocked to the ground by a subsequent blow to the back of his head, Tom kicked off the man who jumped on him, only to be grabbed by another.

The Texans swung into groups with their backs toward each other. Half starved, they went down fast, but not until they had laid out many Mexican soldiers.

Eli jump-kicked the man holding his father. The men tumbled away as a Mexican boxed Eli's ear. Eli's powerful return punch sent the man reeling. Eli planted his right foot behind him and swung his fist into the mouth of the man running toward him with a fist ready to make contact. Teeth flew out of the Mexican's head. Two men grabbed Eli from the rear, but Eli pushed with his planted foot, rotated, and flung them off.

A few feet away, Noah swept his leg out and jerked it back in. The man before him fell only to be immediately replaced. Noah's lip split as a Mexican's balled-up hand connected. Noah's foggy mind cleared like a cloudy sky under the bright sun of the adrenalin that coursed through his veins. He was Tahatankohana, the well-trained Quapaw warrior. He stuck the jugular vein of the man who had set his blood flowing. The man collapsed. Noah went for everybody within range of his lethal powers.

The right fist of Adahy connected with a Mexican eye. The socket crushed. He reared back and then threw his body into the Mexican. They crashed and then rolled in the dusty road trying to get the upper side. Adahy came up on his knees above his opponent and then landed a crushing blow to the man's temple. The soldier lay motionless in the dirt. Adahy sprang to his feet and lit into a new foe.

Beside him, Roscoe slammed his fist into a Mexican stomach. He received the same in return and doubled up in pain but quickly recovered and boxed the back of the neck of the man still bent over before him. The man went down. Others swarmed in and overpowered Roscoe.

Tom, Eli, Noah, and Adahy got their backs together. No individual could break their defense. As the surrounded men attempted to protect themselves, the store's door slammed open. Espinoza bellowed in Spanish. "Any more of them in here?"

Carla assured the man glaring at her. "None of them are in the store anymore, but two were here earlier. One is in our jail. He stole pickles from us." She stared back into the eyes of the Mexican commander. "Those men who were with my husband are not with the Texans."

"Maybe not, but if they are, and we let them go, they'll get more men. I'm not taking any chances."

Carla stood up straight. "Don't hurt them, Filipe. They caught Carlyle stealing, and they wouldn't have turned on one of their own."

Espinoza looked into the corner for a second. "Any gringo out here is trying to take our land. They deserve to be beaten. Search the store, Jorge." As his second-in-command moved around the store, the commander watched Carla for heightened agitation.

Carla paid Jorge no attention. She looked out the window at the vastly superior force attacking the invaders. "Stop fighting them. Please."

Jorge entered the storage room. Espinoza followed him. "Get in here, Carla."

Carla's breaths remained smooth, she didn't wring her hands, and her eyes blinked at the same rate since he had walked into her store.

Outside, the inner edge of the Mexican swarm fell to the fists and feet of Noah, Eli, Adahy, and Tom.

¡Déjame pasar! A soldier with blood dripping from his mouth pressed through the crowd with a tree branch. He screamed in Spanish. "Nobody busts out my teeth and lives!" He swung both arms back and then rammed the stick into Eli's side. He pulled it out to repeat the attack.

He's going to kill me! Eli threw his body into the man before he could stab him again. Five men dropped on top of him.

A giant Mexican rushed into the space created by Eli's departure. *How did you get there!?* Tom swung his arm to block the man's rifle butt. The gun flew away. The colossal man grabbed Tom around the waist, lifted him off the ground, threw him to the dirt, and then stomped him.

Completely exposed at their rear, men rushed Noah and Adahy and slammed them to the road. *A boot!* Adahy turned his face and took the blow on the side of his skull. Mexicans piled on top of him.

As he went down, Noah instinctively raised

his arm in front of his face. He landed on and pinned his arm under himself. Several Mexicans pummeled him. *I've got to get my arms over my head.* A man grabbed Noah's head and slammed his face against the packed earth.

Inside, the search moved to the quarters above the store. After a thorough examination, Jorge informed his commander, "She's the only one."

"Notify me if you see any other strangers, Carla." Espinoza proceeded down the stairs and then out the door. Not a single invader was conscious. However, his soldiers continued to beat four of them in retaliation for their injured comrades. He roared, "That's enough! Tie them up."

Thirty Eight

In the blackness of the moonless night, Alex escaped Santa Fe and fled to their camp not far away. "Everybody!" Alex reported the events that brought him there alone. "… I don't know what condition any of them is in, but I'm sure it's not good."

"I doubt we can steal them away from an army that large," remarked Helen.

Sally tapped her jaw as she looked into the night sky. "If they didn't believe Carla, they won't believe us if we tell the commander they are NOT Texans."

"I have an idea." Ann climbed into her wagon. She returned with two envelopes. "These are the letters Colonel Howland gave us back at Fort Gibson. It's not that a Mexican would care about a United States colonel's opinion, but Colonel Howland did describe us. These should prove our men aren't Texans."

"If Alex goes, Filipe will capture him too. It should be a woman to go. Give me all the letters." Sally took the envelopes.

Helen snatched the letters out of Sally's hand. "That man will surely capture a woman too. You have your whole life ahead of you. I've already lived a good life."

"Would soldiers bring their wives and children? Would they have this many animals to slow them down? Would they have a contract for sheep that shows we are working for a Mexican? I think we should all go," suggested Stephanie.

Ann hugged her sister. "You're always so smart. I think we CAN save our men. We'll move out as soon as we're packed."

Thirty Nine

The large caravan of wagons, animals, and people approached the Mexican soldiers. A sentry called out, "¡Detener!"

At the front, as ordered, Alex halted. "Hemos venido a buscar a nuestra familia," explained Alex. The conversation continued in perfect Spanish. "Some of those men are the husbands of these women. We came to Santa Fe to pick up sheep for Miguel Lopez. He hired us to sell them in California. I have the contract."

"The López gold mine López?"

"Yes." Alex handed the sentry the paper.

The soldier read the contract and then looked into every one of the wagons. "Leave the animals and wagons. Bring the women and children."

Alex waved. "Everybody has to come."

The sentry marched the people to his commander. He explained the situation to the guard outside Filipe Espinoza's tent. The guard went inside with the contract and passed the story on to Espinoza.

Commander Espinoza sallied forth from the tent to confront the young man, two boys, six women, and five babies. He addressed them in

166

English. "You expect me to believe you are working for Miguel López to deliver sheep to California. You are either extremely stupid or lying. With a lot of work, you might be able to get small wagons over the mountains. You'll never get those massive wagons to California."

Alex explained, "We're ignorant commoners who don't know what we're doing. Miguel's mine caved in. We were there at the time and helped him get the men out. The man who was supposed to deliver the sheep is injured, so we offered to help Miguel by buying the sheep."

"Who was he going to send?"

"Alberto Perez."

Filipe looked into Alex's eyes but spoke with the sentry. "Mix the men in question in with twenty other men and bring them here." He waved another soldier over. "Take twenty men up to Alamosa. Help my cousin rebuild the mine."

Ann gasped in horror when she saw the twenty-five bloody, shackled men with mangled faces limp into the light. "God, help all these men!" she exclaimed.

"Papa!" Nikki ran to Noah and wrapped his arms around his legs. He glared at Espinoza. "He's already been bitten by a black widow. He won't live through this."

Oscar, however, knew what large groups of murderous men could do. He had watched his father die. He stood paralyzed with fear. Espinoza ordered him, "Go pick out your father." Oscar kept his eye on the commander as he went to Tom.

The commander pointed to Stephanie then a man who claimed to be innocent. "Give your baby to that man."

With Hattie on her hip, she approached the man who was not her baby's father. She held out her child. Hattie turned her face into Stephanie's shoulder and screamed.

"Now, the next man."

Stephanie did so, resulting in the same response from the baby.

"The next."

The words, *two more,* popped into Ann's mind.

Stephanie repeated the commanded procedure until they arrived at Eli.

She won't recognize me with my face like this. Hattie started to turn away. "Come to your pop, Hattie." The baby turned back and looked at the stranger. She held out her arms and leaned toward her father. Eli took his child into his arms. "I love you, Hattie." His tears washed the blood on his face onto his child.

TWO MORE screamed into Ann's mind. She pulled Helen close and put Adele's hand into Helen's. "She loves Roscoe." Ann secretly handed Joy to Sally. "God wants to use her to save one of those other men. She will pick him."

"You," Espinoza pointed at Ehawee, "have your baby pick his father."

Adahy's baby correctly identified his father. Adahy cuddled Etu. "You just saved my life," he whispered.

Espinoza ordered Ann, "Him." He pointed to the person he had indicated first for each of them. Ann approached the man with her son. Christopher reached out to the man. Ann whispered, "Claim to be Chris's father."

"I love you, Chris, my son." The man gently clutched the boy to his chest.

Next up was the woman with a toddler clinging to her legs, "Take your baby to him." Once again, he pointed to an incorrect man. Helen picked up Adele and did as ordered. The child turned away in fear of the unknown person. Once at Roscoe, Adele quickly went to him. Helen explained, "This man is the baby's grandfather."

Sally stood with Joy on her hip. "You, start there." He pointed to the far end of the line of men." Joy refused the soldier. At the ninth stop, Joy leaned toward the man. Sally whispered, "Go with it."

"Release their husbands." Espinoza turned to Alex. "What is your name, young man?"

"Alejandro Divine."

"Alejandro, I appreciate you helping my cousin. My soldiers need food. I will buy the sheep from you."

"I need to speak with the others."

Alex soon returned. "They are pure breed Merino sheep. We will sell half of them for two dollars each in gold or silver coins. Some of your men will need to go with us tomorrow."

The commander ordered Jorge, "Tomorrow, take men and get my fifty sheep."

Alex continued, "And you owe us much more than an apology. You practically beat our men to death. And that is after they saved your cousin's men!"

"What do you want?"

"Medical supplies, books, and somebody who knows the way to the western sea."

"The best guide would be you, Jorge." Espinoza looked at his second-in-command. "I could order you, but it would be better if you volunteered."

That sounds like an order to me, thought Jorge. "They need to be willing to make changes."

"We will do so within reason," agreed Alex. "Tell me your suggestions."

"I don't know everything yet, but you need to get rid of your wagons."

"We need wagons. However, we could get smaller ones if there are enough in Santa Fe. Speak with us tomorrow. Right now, we need medical supplies to help our men."

"Follow me." Jorge headed to the center of the camp.

Alex stepped into the hospital tent. Hundreds of Mexican soldiers sat beneath the ministering hands of their medics. "You've brought your injured men with you instead of sending them home?"

"All these men received their wounds here, most of them by your family. We should have known they weren't part of the Texan Militia shortly after the fight began. None of those Texans could fight as some of your men did!" Jorge turned to the chief doctor. "Espinoza ordered medical supplies to be given to this man to treat the mighty four and the rest of their family."

"I haven't looked at them. I don't know what they need. Bring them here."

Alex refused. "No. Just give me some of everything."

The doctor called for a medic. "Give Jorge enough sutures, forceps, needles, splints, scalpels, bandages, bromine, quinine, mercury, and honey to treat seven badly injured men."

"We'll need soap," said Alex.

"And anything else they might need for treatment," added the doctor as Jorge and Alex followed the medic.

Ann loaded Noah and the man Chris had selected into the wagon. "What are you doing?" Noah asked his wife.

"Trust me," Ann replied.

God must have spoken to her again. "All right," Noah delivered his good news. "By the way. I'm awake."

"I know. You're talking to me."

"I mean, the fight woke up my mind."

"That's wonderful. I see that both of you need stitches. Are you able to tell me what else needs to be done?"

"Tell Alex to take us to the store. I'll look over everybody there. Right now, sew up the cut under my eye, so I can see."

The Texan quietly exclaimed, "I don't know

why you did it, but thank you! My name is Stanley Cornwall. Most people call me Stan."

"Pleased to meet you, Stan," Ann explained, "God told me that my babies were going to pick two men to take with us. Chris went to you."

Sally helped Joy's selection into her wagon. She kissed his lips to satisfy Espinoza's unspoken question. She removed her lips from the man, who wasn't the least bit unhappy about the unsolicited surprise. "Sorry. I know I didn't have your permission, but the commander didn't seem convinced that you belong with us."

"I'll gladly take every kiss you want to give!"

Sally assured him, "That was the only one."

Ann went to each wagon and issued instructions. "Sally, I saw Espinoza looking at you. Would you be willing to cut your hair and wear Harry's old clothes again? I'd like you to be Patrick, our sheep drover, not a beautiful young woman who men can't resist."

"After Dr. Vega's behavior, I surely will."

Ann hugged her sister. "Thank you. When we get to the store, make the antiseptic and sedative. Helen, we'll need hot water and all our washcloths. Stephanie, Emily, and Ehawee set up palettes."

Alex extracted from the Mexican army every person in their family, everything they owned, additional crates of medical supplies, and the Texans God added to their group.

Forty

Alex banged at the store. "It's Alejandro," he called out.

Joaquín came to the barred door. "What do you want?"

"Espinoza gave us our men, but we need a place to take care of them."

"I don't know that you didn't steal them. I don't want him to come after me. Go someplace else."

"Where? Do you think we're so powerful that we could have rescued them from thousands of soldiers?"

"I suppose not. Come in, but stay in plain view. I don't want Espinoza to think I'm trying to hide you."

"Thank you. We'll need access to a stove to care for the injured."

Carla stood at the top of the stairs. "Give me a moment before I get you."

Alex waved to Ann.

She opened the door. "Much obliged."

Stan helped Noah into the store. "He's badly injured. I don't think he'll be able to take care of anybody."

"I only need to look them over. My family will do all the work." Noah sat in a rocking chair with a price tag hanging from its arm. "There's going to be a bloody mess. We'll need a lot of towels and more heat in here."

"I'll get towels." Joaquín headed to his storage room with Alex.

No longer in her night clothes, Carla came down the stairs. "I'm ready. Come to the stove."

Sally entered dressed as a man with her hair cropped to an inch. She answered in a gruff voice. "Thank you, ma'am. My name is Patrick." As her family settled into the store, she carried sacks of plants up the stairs.

The second Texan walked in with his arm around Eli's blood-drenched body. "Hello, everybody. My name is Trivet; Tennessee Trivet from the great Republic of Texas, which is very confusing, so I answer to Trivet. Where do you want this brave man?"

Noah tapped the pallet at his feet. "I'll look him over then you pull him and his pallet over there." Noah asked, "Where do you hurt, brother?"

"Everywhere."

Stephanie knelt over her husband. "He's been stabbed in the gut with a stick. It looks like bark is still in the wound. I tried to clean it on the way over here." Her tears dripped onto Eli's chest. "What should I do to help him?"

"Undress him so I can look him over. Cover his unmentionables."

Stephanie did so.

Noah knelt beside his brother-in-law. He rolled him from side to side to look over all of him. "Put him to sleep. Clean all of him very well with the antiseptic. Stitch all the lesions except the stab. Use tweezers to remove every bit of the bark you can find. Move the flesh around to search. Try to find some moldy bread. Sew the stab wound after you crumble a little of the mold on it, and then make a poultice with the rest of the slice and put it on every cut, especially the stab. Trivet put him where I told you. Stan, bring that one next."

Not knowing how long Roscoe had been engaged in combat, Noah pointed at him. *He's older than the rest of us. His body may not have been able to take as much abuse.* "Tell me what you think is wrong while you undress. Keep covered what you should."

"One of them hit me hard in the stomach, and I have blood on my head. I don't remember fighting for very long."

"How much do you hurt?"

Having been overcome relatively quickly, Roscoe was not very injured. "Not much."

Noah examined Roscoe. "Wash your whole body and hair with soap and then rinse with the cedar wash. Unless you feel you can't, help with stitches."

"I'll do whatever you want after I clean up.

You need to look at this man next. Roscoe pulled Tom to Noah. "He doesn't look like he'll make it. I'm glad you're back. I've been very worried about you."

"You're a very good friend."

Emily knelt beside Tom. "Don't let him die. I can't lose another husband."

"I– I mean, WE will all do our best. We all love him."

"Do you want me to undress him?"

"Yes."

Tom moaned, "Giant crushed my chest at the end. Can't breathe."

"Yes, you can." Noah gently felt Tom's ribs. "It hurts because you have broken ribs." Noah turned Tom's head from side to side. "Your face and head are beat up." He ran his hand down Tom's left arm. "Your arm is broken, and you must have been kicked a lot. You're bruised all over. We'll give you the sedative, clean you up, stitch you up, set your arm, and wrap your chest." Noah instructed Emily. "Take him over there. Get your daughter-in-law to tell you about the bread. You and your young son do the same for your husband. She also knows how to bind his chest."

Trivet helped Emily move Tom while Stan and Ehawee brought Adahy to Noah. Joaquín and Alex returned to the store with stacks of towels. Alex went to Noah. "The Mexicans gave us bottles marked bromine, quinine, and mercury. They gave us a gallon of honey too. Do you know how to use any of that to treat injuries?"

176

"I know many uses for honey. Quinine won't help these injuries. Mercury is in thermometers. I don't know what else to do with it or the other one." Noah opened a bottle of bromine. "That smells awful! Maybe we could open the bottle, and it would keep away mosquitoes. Pack it up for now. Keep out the honey. We might eat some of it."

Stan spoke up, "Will you fix food tonight? We haven't eaten in days."

"Wife, as soon as you can, bring food." Noah turned his attention to Adahy, who had already undressed.

"My wife has already started fixing me," said Adahy, "but it's going to take a long time. There isn't much skin on me that isn't ripped open."

Noah looked at Ehawee. "Are you cleaning the cuts first?"

"I am, my brother. The Mexicans gave us a lot of soap. I heard what you said about using moldy bread. Carla is going with me to the Cantina to ask if they have any."

"Much obliged for doing that. Take Alejandro with you. As late as it is, everybody already had too much liquor."

Joaquín slid on his poncho. "Alejandro and I will go."

As they left the store, Noah finished looking over Stan's wounds. "Trivet, come here. My son, you too."

Nikki got off the floor where he'd been observing how to help people. "Yes, Papa."

"Bring some antiseptic. After I look over Trivet, I'll show you how to help me."

Ann smiled at her husband. "I'll clean and stitch up Stan and Trivet." She called up the stairs. "Patrick! We have enough antiseptic. Is the sedative ready?"

"We're bringing it now." Sally carried a large pot down the stairs. Carla followed with a tray of cups. She dipped one into the pot and handed it to Stephanie.

"Drink up, my darling. Once you're asleep, I'll work more on the stab." Stephanie helped Eli sit up and held the cup to his lips.

Trivet stood before Noah. "How bad off am I? Am I going to die? I don't know what's on the other side of death. I never found God. I'm afraid."

Noah examined the man. "Why haven't you found God? If you try, He'll reveal Himself to you."

"I want Him to sit beside me, so I can see Him. I want Him to say, 'Here I am.' He never has, so I can't be sure He's real."

"I think you'll recover with stitches and time, but death is a storm we WILL all face. Whenever that day arrives, we have to answer for our choices. Everybody has done something wrong somewhere along the way. Our only hope is for Jesus to forgive us, and then our spirits will be reborn. That can only happen before our physical life ends. All we have to do is ask Him to forgive us and rule in our lives, but we have to mean it. Have you read the Bible?"

"No, but my mother told me what's in it."

"Through the centuries, many people have had, and some people alive right now have a hard time believing in what they can't see directly. We have a Bible we will give you. Read it, and you'll find out that God did exactly what you want Him to do. He manifested Himself in physical form as a man named Jesus."

"Jesus was just a man like me."

"Except that Jesus said, 'I and the Father are one. If you have seen me, you have seen the Father,' and He did many miracles to prove that He is God too."

"I didn't know Jesus said he was God. I surely would like to have a Bible. The Mexicans proved that a person doesn't know when his life will end. We thought we'd take Santa Fe without a fight, but look at us." He pointed at Tom. "That man might not live through the night, and he didn't even have anything to do with what we did."

Nikki had been listening. "I'll get one." He left the store, returned, and held a Bible toward Trivet.

Noah prayed, "God, as this man reads the love letter You inspired people to write through the centuries, show Yourself to him."

"Amen," added Nikki.

Joaquín and Alex returned with a basket of what the cantina owner regarded as worthless. They found the store full of sleeping men being sewn by the women and Roscoe. Noah clenched the rocking chair arm. "Nikki, you watched me fix our cat. Do the same for me as I did for Whiskers."

"I might not do it right."

"I'll be watching, and I'll tell you if you aren't."

Nikki got a large package of sutures, opened it carefully, laid it on Noah's lap, and then washed his hands thoroughly with the antiseptic. He picked up a strand of catgut and threaded it through the needle. "You ready, Papa?"

"I am. Thank you for helping me." Noah pressed the flaps of skin on his right arm closed with his left thumb and pointer finger.

Nikki poked the curved needle through the skin, up and out through the laceration, and then pulled the suture until he had only a short portion left. He looked at Noah.

Noah assured him, "Perfect. Go on."

"Back into the cut, up through the under of the skin, and pull. Once the thread is all up, wrap it around the other end, and pull tight to close skin with knot. Not too tight. Come down a little and go down through the skin on other side. Up from inside the cut and pull tight. Not too tight." Nikki continued narrating his work as he sewed his papa's lacerated arm.

"My wife!" Noah called out. "He knows what to do, and he does very good work. Give me the sedative."

Ann quickly made her way across the room and handed her husband a cup of liquid oblivion. "You are a wonderful papa and teacher. I love you more than I can ever tell you."

"I love you too, my wife, and you, my son. Sew up every place I'm cut. Nikki, if you get tired, ask Mama to take over."

"Don't worry. I'm going to fix you, Papa." *And then I'm going to take Chetan and shoot Espinoza.*

An hour later, Nikki still worked on his father. Ann touched her son's head, "It's getting late. Do you want me to do some, Nikki?"

"I'm fixing him. That way, I know he's fixed right."

Ann looked at the precision of the stitches in the light of her lantern. "You're doing the best work of all of us. How many more places?"

"One."

"All right, my son. May I hold this light here for you?"

"Yes, Mama, that helps."

Half an hour later, Nikki tied the last knot. "There is a lot of blood. Should we put him on a clean pallet?"

"Let's wipe it up with towels so we don't wake him."

"Would you do it? I'm ready to go to sleep."

"I will." Ann pointed. "Our mattress is over there. Sleep against the stairs. Be careful of the babies."

Forty One

Long before first light, Jorge and a small group of soldiers knocked on the store door. Alex's bedding blocked the way. He raised his sleepy head. "Who is there? ¿Quién está ahí?"

"Lieutenant Jorge Bueno. We're here to get the sheep."

"I don't know if Joaquín is up. Wait out there. I'll find out." Alex raised the edge of his blankets and swung his legs out. He sat on his mattress and rubbed his eyes.

"You don't need to come looking for me. I've been cleaning for an hour." Joaquín tossed a handful of red towels into a wicker basket. "If you're ready, we can get the sheep now, or he can give you the money, and I'll take him to get however many they bought."

"Give me the money, Jorge. I want to go back to sleep."

Alex opened the door and held out his hand. Jorge opened a small leather pouch. He put twelve gold escudos and four pieces of eight into the hand close to the ground.

"Let's go," said Joaquín from behind Jorge.

Jorge jumped. "How did you get there!?"

"I went out the storage room door."

Alex drew in his hand and counted. "He bought fifty sheep." He shut and barred the door before he snuggled back under the warm covers.

When he woke again, the sun was up. The smell of cooking bacon and frying eggs filled the air. "Jorge, get their sheep?"

Dressed in a clean set of Harry's baggy clothes, Sally answered in a deep voice. "Joaquín says he gave them a different type of sheep that's better for meat. He says they roasted and ate every one of them then moved out at first light with the Texan prisoners and Jorge too. We can still get a hundred Merino sheep if we pay for the sheep the army got."

"Dirty cheats! Now how are we going to know the way?"

"We didn't before, so nothing has changed." Sally held out a large tin cup.

"At least we know we need smaller wagons." Alex took the coffee.

"Do you think you can trade ours or buy small ones?"

"I will try. Where is everybody?"

"We moved into the storage room so Joaquín and Carla can run their store. Go ahead and move your bed in there."

"All right, and then I'll see about the wagons." Alex set down his cup and dragged his mattress across the floor. "How much does Joaquín want for the sheep the army got?"

"He said he usually sells them for one dollar and seventy-five cents each."

"Would you rather drive fifty or a hundred sheep?" Alex handed Sally eleven gold escudos. "That's worth eighty-eight dollars."

Sally gave Alex a plate of bacon and eggs. "We'll need to get a sheepdog either way, but there hasn't always been enough grass, so I say fifty or none, if possible."

Alex looked for the man he thought was competition for Sally's heart. "Where's Trivet?"

"I suspect he's on the trail to Texas. He left after everybody was asleep," Sally replied, "but Stan is still here. Right after eating, he drank the sedative. I think he doesn't like pain."

"Who does?" Alex carried his empty plate to the tub of hot water. "After I wash this, I'll be off to see about wagons and dogs."

Just before nightfall, Alex walked into the storage room, followed by a dog with yellow, white, and brown hair. "Her name is Samantha, but her previous owner called her Sam. I spent most of the afternoon learning her commands."

Sally knelt beside the young animal and rubbed behind its ears. "She's so beautiful. Teach me everything you learned."

"We'll have to do it tomorrow. I have a buyer for our Conestoga wagons, but he needs them tonight for his trip back east. I've rented a house where we can unload everything and stay there as well."

Noah got up from the crate upon which he sat. "Now is the time to move since we're all awake."

Stephanie put tamales from the cantina in front of Alex. "Eat while we load our bedding."

"Finish this up for me." Helen poured coffee into the injured men's cups.

Forty Two

A mile from town, Alex stopped Goliath. "This is it." He jumped off the wagon in front of a ranch house.

"How wonderful, we've got fenced fields. Are those the sheep we bought?" Still pretending to be Patrick, Sally leaned into Alex's hands to get off the wagon. "Let's get the sedated men inside before we start unloading."

"Sedated men? And yes, most of them are our sheep."

"We women thought it would be best if our injured men didn't try to help, and you know they would if they were awake. We put the sleeping potion in the last of the coffee."

With the help of Roscoe, Alex, and Stan, the women got the men into beds and then went to work. Before the buyers arrived with a team of horses, all the animals grazed in the fields, no india rubber cover remained on a Conestoga wagon, and one wagon was almost empty.

Alex shook the tallest man's hand. "We're almost ready for you to take the first. Look them

186

over and decide if you'll buy them. Don't forget about all the modifications."

By morning the barn held the provisions from the four Conestoga wagons the family no longer owned. Roscoe owned three hundred more dollars, and Eli and Noah one hundred and fifty dollars each from the sale. Alex's and the hidey-hole wagon were packed to the limits and secured in the barn. After the second mostly sleepless night, the family locked all the shutters, barred the doors, and lay in warm beds.

When they woke, Stan no longer accompanied them. Sally plunked her hands down on her hips. "I don't know why God wanted us to save those Texans. All they've done is run off."

Ann replied, "They both helped us the first night. Stan also lent a hand last night, and we needed them both nights. Besides, God's plan doesn't have to meet our expectations, and He doesn't have to let us know what it is either."

Ten small farm wagons sat beside the house in the morning light, and thirty-seven additional horses grazed in the field. Noah plucked a piece of paper nailed to the wagon closest to the door. "Much obliged for the rescue, the stitches, and the very tasty food. I was powerfully hungry! I need to go after my friends. Can't take these wagons or horses, and you need them, so I took vitals for a few months in exchange. Sorry we got you into this. Stan."

Noah folded the note. "This is a pleasant

surprise. Alex, come with me to Santa Fe. We'll use a couple of these wagons to haul parts."

Adahy walked toward the house. "I'll put on my chaps and look over the horses."

"I'll check the wagons." Roscoe lay on the ground under the one beside them.

Hours later, Noah and Alex returned from town with pitch, axle grease, linseed oil, and wagon parts. Noah found Adahy. "Why did you put up the animal tents?"

"It wasn't just the men who were starving. The horses were too. To make sure each of them got a good amount of oats, I set up the tents, put one horse in each section, and filled the grain bags. I put money on the kitchen table to pay for the animal food. The horses should be done eating. They need watering now."

Roscoe stood up. "I'll take them."

Ten days later, every wagon had axles that could turn or be fixed into position, a falling tree able to be attached at either end, good brakes, and dry pitch. The india rubber wagon covers had been halved and installed over four of the small wagons. The horses had regained much of their strength, and the injured men were recovering well from the Mexican thrashing.

The family sat around the dining room table. Alex scooped black-eyed peas onto his plate. "I told you Santa Fe was a bad place."

Noah took the bowl of peas. "I'm sorry we got a beating, but I'm happy to have my mind back."

Helen slathered butter on a slice of the bread she had baked that morning. "And now we have the wagons we need. How horrible would it have been to have had to abandon the wagons and their contents along the way? I want to keep the piano."

"And the cast iron stove, and I'd like to take this one too," added Ann

"Can we get a map?" wondered Ehawee.

Emily poured milk into a china cup. "Surely somebody in Santa Fe has been to the western sea. Alex should go to the store tomorrow and ask about a map."

"I thought we were loading the wagons tomorrow." Alex cut into the prairie chicken on his plate.

Roscoe swallowed. "A map would be EXTREMELY helpful."

"We'll do the best we can to load without you," said Noah.

When Alex returned to the ranch the following day, he possessed a large piece of butcher paper. "Joaquín knew that José Luis had been to San Diego. I paid the man to make this." After the children had gone to bed, Alex unfolded and spread a map on the dining room table.

Eli tapped the words written on the left side of the map. "What does this say?"

Alex looked him in the eye. "José Luis said there is no water in that desert. We have to take all we'll need for the animals and us, or we WILL die. He said we should not try to go there with so many animals and these wagons. I told him God would get us there. He said there is no God, and we won't make it."

"We know God is real. Still, is there another way?" asked Eli. "I don't think we should go that way with Pop the way he is."

"Maybe, but this is the only way he knows. He said we'll need to bring tools to cut away plants along the way and even the mountain in some places to get wagons through, but he doubts we can do it."

Roscoe reminded them, "We still have the dynamite."

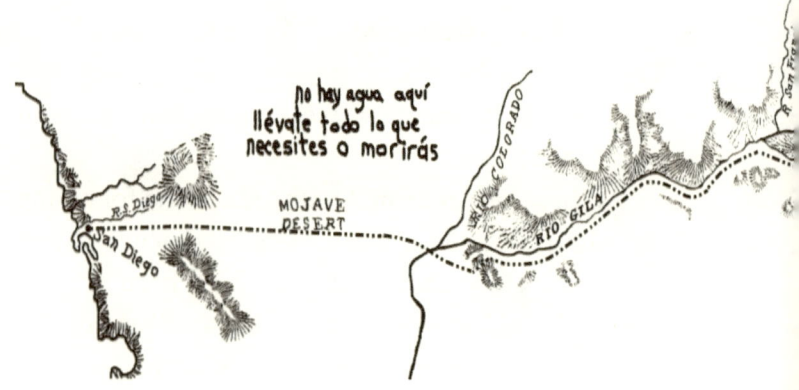

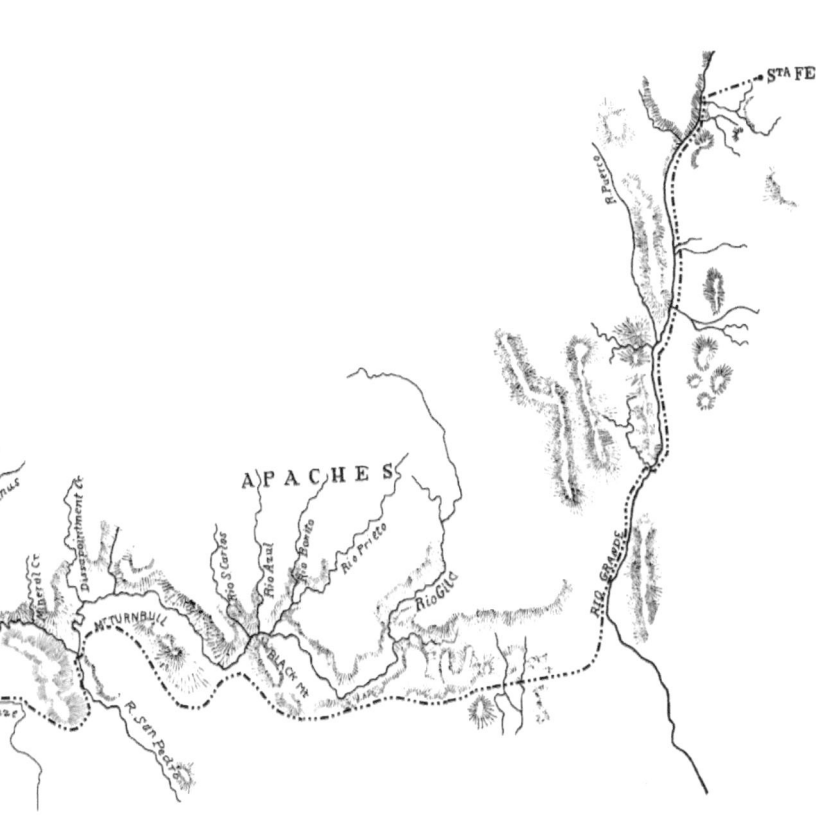

"I bought the tools José Luis recommended. I'm supposed to get them from Joaquín when we leave." Alex put his finger on the mountain just west of the San Pedro River. "He said we can't pass between this mountain and the river. He went up and along the top, but he said we can't get wagons up that way, so he suggested that we go south of the mountain and then follow the Santa Cruze River north back to the Gila. From there, we should go along the Gila. He also said to make sure we stay south of the river to avoid the Apaches."

Sally put her hand on Alex's on the table. "We are so blessed to have you with us. You are the only one of us who could have gotten this." She kissed his cheek.

Alex beamed with pride. Even though her hair was cropped close to her head and she was dressed in pants, a loose shirt, and work boots, heat filled his body from Sally's kiss. "You are very welcome. I'm glad to be of some use." He focused his mind on something other than his thoughts about the beautiful woman he saw beside him. "How did the packing go?"

Noah replied, "Only two are loaded. Ann insisted that Eli, Adahy, and I stop helping soon after we started."

Ann informed everybody, "I'm not allowing our injured men to reload. It's going to take however long it takes, so if you have to get the tools quickly, take an empty wagon and get them. I wish we had a place to stay. It would be best if we could wait until spring to travel."

Noah asked, "How long will we be able to stay here?"

"Carla told me her brother owns this ranch. I'll ask her tomorrow." Alex folded the map.

Alex reported his finding at the supper table

the following day. "Carla said her sister-in-law demanded that they go back to Mexico City, so her brother wants Carla to sell this ranch and send him the money. She said we can rent this place until she finds a buyer. Since I found some money in the wagon where I found the knife, I solved both problems. I bought the ranch. That includes all the animals and everything else that's here."

Sally's heart raced. She couldn't breathe. "Are you staying here!?"

"Absolutely not! I hate Santa Fe. I'll sell the ranch in the spring."

Sally gulped air. "What if nobody buys it?" she stared at her plate.

"Then I'll give it to Joaquín and Carla. Now that we have even more sheep, maybe we should teach Nikki and Oscar how to ride the Texan Steeldusts. They can help drive them when we're traveling again."

Nikki sat up straight. "Can I, Papa? Please."

When everybody's attention was elsewhere, Alex put his hand on Sally's. He softly assured her, "You are more important to me than anything else. I have no plan to leave this family."

Sally knew what he meant. Her radiant smile led Alex to believe she felt the same.

Forty Three

With broken ribs, it was too hard for Tom to speak. He wrote: Get the bags from the mine. I saw glittering when I got Alberto out of the cart. I think it's full of gold. Pulverize the rubble and smelt it. He handed the note to Emily.

Emily brought the paper to the breakfast table and placed it beside Eli.

Eli looked at the message. "Family, I have news." He read the words aloud. "...Although, we aren't well enough yet."

"It doesn't have to be men who pound the rocks to smithereens," said Ehawee.

Roscoe took the note. "With the big forge in the barn, I can smelt. We can use the bullet mold to shape the gold."

Alex swirled his coffee in his cup. "There's an assay office in Santa Fe. After breakfast, I can ask which way is best."

"I doubt it matters what shape we make."

Noah stopped his fork halfway to his plate and waved it side to side. "I think it's best if nobody knows what we have. Somebody may try to steal it."

"Maybe we only need to get it out of the rubble while we're here," said Roscoe, "We can take it to California as pure gold."

"How will we, or anybody else, know how much it's worth? We should have coins of known value," Ann wiped crumbs to the floor for Samantha, who begged beside her.

"Good point. We have many months before we'll leave. We can take our time. Still, we should get all of it ready before we let anybody know what we have." Noah helped himself to a third piece of breakfast mutton.

Alex took the platter. "And we should get everything we can from this farm. I can ask Joaquín if there is something we can plant this fall."

"Only something without plowing, please. We can only do so much," stated Stephanie.

"We broadcast winter wheat in Raton. If you think that's a good plan, I could buy the seeds right away," suggested Alex.

In Santa Fe, Alex considered Joaquín's suggestions. *Adahy and Noah could sling tiny mustard seeds using our donkeys to lug the heavy seed bags. The women would have no problem spreading the heavier lentils.* He purchased seeds.

The family sowed winter crops. The work completed, those able to ride practiced herding sheep in the surrounding lands. Nikki called out, "Hee-haw!" as he made a sharp, quick turn on his favorite Steeldust, the one he named Cornwall after Stanley Cornwall. He drove a wandering sheep back to the flock.

Forty Four

In December, the mustard pods turned brown. Noah, Alex, Roscoe, and the women cut the plants at the roots and then crammed them onto hanging poles in the drying barns to finish maturing. Many more plants remained in the fields, but they had no more space to process them. Alex rode to Santa Fe and walked into Joaquín's store. "Hola."

"What brings you here this time, Alejandro?"

"We planted too much mustard. We can't fit it into the barns. Do you think anybody would like to buy some? They would have to harvest and dry it in their barns. How much should we ask for it?"

"Some people noticed how much you planted and already told me you would have this problem. I'll negotiate a fair price for you and collect the money, but I want ten percent. How much do you have left?"

"Probably two acres."

"I'll have your buyers and their workers here at six tomorrow morning. I'll let you know how much each bought and give you your share of the money."

"I'll rent a room in town tonight and be here at six."

Carla came in from the storage room. "You may sleep in here if you want. We won't charge you anything, and I'd love it if you would join us for dinner."

"Only if you let me help you while your husband makes the arrangements."

Joaquín walked toward the door. "That would be a perfect trade."

Six AM arrived, along with a crowd of men. Five of them talked with Joaquín at the counter. Alex stood beside Joaquín. Outside the store, the workers dangled their feet over the edges of the wagons and joked with their friends.

José Luis turned to the man beside him. "Señor Salazar, it doesn't matter that I have more men or how fast they pick. We can rope off the divisions and then go however fast or slow our men go. Each group can only harvest the mustard inside their section."

"That's fair. Joaquín, may we use rope and bring it back?" asked Alvaro Salazar.

"You may. Twenty-five reales a day per rope."

Wondering what Alejandro and his family — who believed that there was a God who helped them — were doing, José Luis had ridden past the farm multiple times. He knew the fields were adjoining squares. He handed over fifty reales. "I'll need two one-hundred-foot ropes. The few extra feet to the edge will be obvious. I'll put my ropes across the middle, and Hector can run his ropes across halfway to the end of our side. You three mark your side into parts as you want."

Carla entered the room with a wheelbarrow full of the desired item. She allowed José Luis to take two. As each man paid Joaquín, Carla doled out the ropes.

All the men knew the way to Alex's ranch. Alex still led the way with his share of the sale in the form of goods purchased from Joaquín and then loaded into Alvaro's wagon. "Señor Salazar, do you have any brothers or sisters?" Alex asked.

"I have a sister, but I don't know where she is or if she is alive."

"Why not?"

"She left Santa Fe many years ago."

"What was her name?" Alex thought he already knew the answer.

"Rosa."

"Was it eighteen years ago?" asked Alex.

"Yes! How did you know?"

"I knew somebody named Rosa Salazar."

"Where is she?! Is she well? Is she happy?

"What does your sister look like?"

"Long black hair. Beautiful brown eyes."

"That describes every woman in Santa Fe. The last time I saw my Rosa, she was very happy. She was putting bread into the oven." *Mama told me not to be late getting home, but Grandpa and I wanted to finish that clock. I never saw her again. I miss her.* Alex choked back the sorrow that the memory brought.

"My Rosa loved to make bread. Where is she? I will go and see if she is my sister."

"I am sorry. A landslide killed her."

A tear formed in Alvaro's eye. "Maybe she wasn't my sister."

Your youngest son looks very much like my mother. "I would love to hear about your sister."

At the ranch, José Luis saw the Texan horses and Merino sheep. *Those horses are Steeldusts. They're the best for cattle tending. I sure could use some. Those are the sheep with the soft wool. If God is real, did He give them to Alejandro because he believes in Him? God, if You are there, give me some of those horses and sheep, and then I'll believe in You.* He and his men started harvesting a quarter of the offered mustard plants.

Alex helped Alvaro and his sons, listened to stories about Rosa when she was a child, and learned to wrap the plants in their barn in cloth to catch the seeds. Long after the other men had carted off their shares, the sun set on empty mustard fields. Alex waved goodbye as Alvaro and his youngest son drove their wagon home. His other son rode to Santa Fe to turn in the ropes. They hoped Joaquín would consider it the same day if it was before the following morning.

Helen looked out the window as they rode away. "I so wanted to help that family. I don't know why, but I'm sure they are important to Alex."

Roscoe stood beside her. "They spent less

money for their plants because they were willing to do the work themselves. We should allow them their self-pride because they accomplished it themselves."

"With Alex's help."

"Yes. Let's eat some of that imperial cake Ann made."

Helen turned from the glass pane. "All right, I'm sure it will be good." She whispered to her husband, "Although I like your cakes better."

Alex washed up before sitting in the only empty chair. "I'm sure Alvaro Salazar is my uncle. I didn't tell him because I didn't know what would happen if I did. Alvaro invited me to his hacienda for Christmas Eve. I think I'll go. I might as well spend time with my mother's family since I'm here."

Forty Five

Alvaro's hacienda adjoined Alex's ranch. It was still an hour's ride to his house. Alvaro opened the door with his wife by his side. "Karmen, I want you to meet Rosa's son."

"I never said Rosa was my mother!"

"But she is. I see her eyes when you look at me."

Karmen scooped Alex into her arms. "Rosa was my good friend. She introduced me to Alvaro. I told Papi not to disown your mother, but he wouldn't listen. He regretted it in the end. He died crying for Rosa to know he was sorry and that he loved her." She released Alex. "Come in, nephew."

Alex stepped into the warm house that smelled of cinnamon. "Your home smells like my mother's churros."

"Rosa and I use the same recipe. I hope you will enjoy them."

"I am sure I will, Tía Karmen. I haven't eaten any for years."

That Christmas Eve, Alex told stories about his parents, his grandfather, and himself as a child. "Since the landslide, I haven't been able to talk about my parents without tears, but telling you about them makes me happy."

Late that night, Alvaro laid his arm across his nephew's shoulder. "We love you, Alejandro, and not just because you are Rosa's son. We have heard about everything you have done since you came here. We love you because you are a good man."

Karmen hugged Alex. "I am so glad you live in Santa Fe now!"

"I love all of you as well." As Alex rode Blackie through the adobe archway in the wall around their large yard, he wondered how he would tell them that he wouldn't be staying.

Forty Six

The mustard seeds fell from the thoroughly dried pods into the cloth pouches. The bottom lentils rattled in their yellowed pods only a couple of weeks after they stored the last mustard seeds. A few days after that, the same group of men from the mustard harvest arrived at the ranch. As arranged, they roped off their sections of the two acres offered to them and paid Alex directly. As instructed by Alvaro, Noah and his family pulled up and laid their three acres of lentils in windrows. Those who had purchased plants carted their portions away.

Three days later, Noah hurried into the house. "The sky looks threatening. We need to get the lentils in!" The entire family sprang into action. They tossed the plants into their barns and every unused inch in the house.

Stephanie followed Ann as they carried snow-covered plants into the kitchen. "I'll dry these before I lay them on the dresser in my room."

Ann's basket still hung from her arm. "Too bad we couldn't get them all, but it's coming down too heavily now."

Sally looked at Ann's brimming basket. "How many rows are still out there?"

Stephanie dabbed her plants with a dish towel. "One whole row and about half of another. Considering how much was out there, we did well."

"I think these will be all right once they dry." Sally put dripping plants by the fire.

Noah joined the girls. "Anyway, we got what we got. If it hadn't been the weather, deer might have eaten it all, or something else might have happened. Nobody ever gets everything, and now we have so much more than we bought."

Sally hugged her brother-in-law. "At least Gus didn't burn everything to the ground this time."

Noah held her tight. "Don't think about that, Sally. Besides, in a way, he did us a favor. Look what we have now because Gus took the farm away."

"I know, but I still wish I could make him pay for what he did." As Sally said, "I'd like to kill him myself," Alex walked in with an armload of snow-covered lentils.

He stopped in his tracks. "You want to kill somebody!? Who?!"

"I'm referring to Gus." Sally pondered for a moment. "I wanted to do something horrible to him at the time. Thinking about it now, if he were here, I don't know. I would never have met you if Gus hadn't destroyed our farm. That's worth everything he did."

Ann looked at Noah and mouthed, I told you, over Sally's head.

Noah let his sister-in-law go. "I'm also glad we know Alex."

Alex remembered what Sally and Noah had told him about Gus. "From what you've told me, he was very despicable." Alex looked into Sally's eyes. "Are you saying I'm the same amount likable as he was unlikable?"

"Yes," Sally stated emphatically.

"Wonderful! Since you want to kill him, I think that means you love me."

"That is sensible logic." Sally sashayed to the kitchen door, turned, and batted her eyes at Alex just before she disappeared down the hall.

Mesmerized, Alex stared at the empty doorway. *I think she said she loves me!* Three other people had witnessed the profession. "What did she mean?"

Ann assured him, "I think she meant exactly what you think she meant."

"I love her too."

Noah escorted Alex from the room. "We know you do. Remember what I told you. Keep yourself under control. Marriage first. You won't like what I do to you if you don't. Do you understand?"

"I do. Should I ask her soon?"

"She's only sixteen, and you're just seventeen. Perhaps you should wait."

"She's sixteen and a half, and I can provide everything. I even had enough money to buy this ranch, and I'll get that money back when I sell it in a few months. We'll all have even more money when we sell the wool and turn in the gold bullets."

"Talk to Ann and Stephanie. It wouldn't be good to upset them. Besides, we may be completely wrong about Sally's feelings."

"I don't think I'm wrong. I'll talk with her sisters. I can't believe how blessed I am!" Alex went to the barn with Noah to help drape lentils over the hang rods.

Inside the kitchen, Stephanie asked, "Should we go talk to her? That was very forward."

Ann heard Christopher crying. "Later, my son is unhappy." She walked down the hall to the room where Ehawee and Emily were watching the babies.

Sally had already entered the room. She bounced her nephew as she held him to her chest. "He's hungry, Ann."

Ann held out her hands. "Alex thinks you just told him that you love him."

"Good because I do." Sally gave Chris to his mother. "I love all my nieces and nephews, but I want a child of my own. I don't love Alex because I want a child. I love him just for himself. Remember how I felt about Melvin?"

"Yes," answered Stephanie and Ann.

"I love Alex more. I can't imagine a better person. I've kissed several men, but not Alex. I want him to kiss me."

Stephanie nursed Hattie. "I thought I would die from wanting Eli to kiss me, but Alex might be like Eli. Eli told me he wouldn't be able to stop himself if he kissed me, so he wouldn't until we were married. Waiting made that first kiss so delicious. I still remember it. So be careful about what you're doing, Sally."

"I'll marry him today if he wants to."

As Ann fed Chris, she remarked, "A child is highly consuming of your time and energy. Once you have a child, everything you do is influenced by how it will affect your child, so enjoy your freedom."

"It's not that bad in this family. We help each other. Besides, you have four children because you kept every child we found for yourself. Did it ever occur to you that I might have wanted any of them? No, you just let me suffer."

"I had no idea! I thought you were unhappy about leaving Melvin and Chaska. I didn't know it was about the children."

Ehawee spoke up. "God led Ann and Noah to Joy, Nikki, and Adele. He did not send you to find them. And also, I have only one child, and I think a child takes all your time and energy."

Sally continued arguing. "Noah had to cut Etu out of you. That's why it was hard on you."

"I'm sorry that you're hurting. I don't want that, but nobody is preventing you from loving any of our children. We all want you to love them and for them to love you." Ann rocked in a chair as she fed her son.

Sally hung her head. "I should have kept my mouth shut. I'm going to help hang lentils." She made a hasty retreat from the uncomfortable tension she had created.

Forty Seven

Sally strung plants on a hang rod and passed it to Alex. Eli noticed that the way the two of them interacted had changed. He got between them and worked Alex to the other side of the barn. "I warned you, and I meant it. I'll shoot you through your heart if you have or even try to sleep with her!"

"I haven't, but I am going to ask her to marry me."

"She's too young. Back off."

"It's her choice, not yours, or is it just me you have a problem with?!"

"It's not you. You don't need to go full chisel. I don't want her to get married, and then you don't turn out to be the right person."

"So, how long would it take for YOU to be sure?"

"Certainly not the mere six months we've known you. If you truly love her, travel all the way to the western sea with us. See if you still think you love each other after all the hardships we'll go through."

"Arrrghh!" Alex kept himself across the barn from Sally, who continually wove under the foliage in his direction. Alex didn't know how to prevent her family from turning against him and also not upset Sally after she had made it obvious that she had feelings for him. He maneuvered away and racked his brain to come up with a good way to proceed.

Alex's standoffish behavior continued for weeks. Sally hid in the barn and cried. *I'm such a fool to have thought he loved me. I'll never find somebody.*

Alex made his way to the corn crib to get feed for their chickens. He heard soft sobs emanating from one of the stalls and peeked inside. "Sally!" *I'm breaking her heart! I don't care what Eli thinks. I'm not doing this to her!* He jerked open the door and hurried inside. "Don't cry. I've only been trying to give you time to be sure I'm the right man. I don't want to hurry you." Alex helped Sally to her feet. "I love you with all my heart! I'm so sorry that I've been hurting you. Forgive me!"

Sally threw her arms around Alex's neck and looked into his face.

"You are all I want." Alex kissed her passionately.

"I love you too." Sally moaned with pleasure.

Alex stepped back and knelt. "Sally Williams, you remember how we were both so mad at God for taking everything away from us? You said God gave things back to you, and I told you He had never given me anything. I love you. I want to spend my life being the man God is giving you for taking away your parents and farm. I hope you are the woman God will give me. With you by my side, I'd be the most blessed man on earth. Please marry me."

"Oh, Alex, yes, I will." She dropped to her knees beside him and pulled him into the clean straw. "Kiss me again."

Alex struggled with the intensity of their kiss. "I want to, but your brothers will kill me! Can you wait so your family won't turn against me? They want us to find our home at the western sea before we get married."

I should ring their necks. "I don't want to. What if something happens?"

"Let's not borrow possible troubles from tomorrow. We need to work with our current circumstances and believe we will get married when it won't cause your brothers to shoot me or do something worse. If they killme, then you really won't have me."

"I don't think they would if I told them it's my choice. However, I want you to be happy, so we will wait. I'll be spinning pirouettes of joy in my heart now that I know how you feel."

"I will too, my love!"

Alex stood up and reached down to help Sally to her feet. *God, oh, God, she is so beautiful in every way. Help us wait!*

Forty Eight

On the mild winter day of February 18th, Karmen went to the Devine ranch to teach the women how to make mustard paste. Halfway through the day, Emily put her hand on her large belly. "One of you better go tell Tom. Oscar was born quickly, and I've heard the next ones are even faster."

Sally dropped her spoon. "Is this the day?!" She left the wooden utensil on the floor, ran from the kitchen, and flew into the barn. "Tom! Emily is having the baby!"

"I'm on my way!" Tom handed Eli the spade he had been using to fill a duck cloth sack with lentils.

It's my brother or sister! "I'm coming too!" Eli put them on the floor.

Noah remarked, "It's going to be hours before the baby arrives, and we're almost done."

Eli picked up the spade, thought for a second, and then shoved it into the sack. "This can wait." He hurried to the house.

Tom skidded to a stop on the slick wooden

213

boards of the kitchen floor. "Are you doing all right? Are you having any problems?!"

Emily kissed Tom soundly. "Be calm. Everything is fine. I just want you to be here."

"Is everything going correctly?!" queried Eli as he dashed into the room.

Karmen laughed. "Like father like son!"

"I'm going to keep making mustard until the contractions are five minutes apart. We probably have a few hours," Emily informed the others of her best guess.

"I'll stay here. What can I do to help?"

Ann pointed at a crate of mason jars. "Put those into the boiling water."

"What about me?" Eli looked around the room for something obvious to do.

"You do the jars. Tom, come help me," replied Emily. She spooned a tiny amount of yellowish-brown paste out of a pot. "Is this too strong, my love?" She raised the spoon to Tom's mouth.

Tom touched his lips to the thick mixture. "Whew! Much too strong! I'll get more water."

Karmen held out a jar. "I told you we added too much vinegar and not enough turmeric."

"Yikes!" Emily pressed her baby again.

Sally stopped pouring water into the prepared mustard they were making. "That wasn't much more than five minutes!"

Oscar came into the room. "Noah told me you're about to have my brother. I told him you're making me a sister."

Nikki followed his friend. "I'm practically a brother, so make us a sister."

Emily patted her son's head. "I don't get to choose. Whichever it is, is what we get."

"All right, Ma. I'll still keep it."

"I'm glad to know that!" Emily rubbed her abdomen. "Maybe we should start getting everything ready. Eli, would you mind entertaining the boys in the sitting room while Tom and the women help me in the bedroom?"

"I will certainly do that. First, we'll help carry whatever you need into your bedroom. Come on, boys?"

No sooner were the towels, clean sheets, and bowls of warm water strategically positioned than Emily informed everybody, "I'm having this baby right now!"

"No, you aren't," said Helen, "having a baby takes time."

"Yes, I am. Eli, get the boys out. Ann, help me into the bed." Before the door completely shut behind Oscar, Emily started unbuttoning her dress.

"Lay down. I'll undo your dress." Ann helped Emily across the room to the bed. From the other side of the bed, Helen helped her daughter-in-law lie on her back.

Emily panted. "It's here! Pull my pantaloons off!"

Tom approached his wife to do so.

Emily snapped, "Not you!"

"Do you want me to leave?" Tom asked.

"Of course not!" Emily breathed rapid shallow breaths.

Tom plastered himself against the wall.

"Here it comes! Tom, hold my hand!"

Tom darted to his wife's side. He placed his hand in hers. She just about squeezed his fingers off.

Sally, Ehawee, Stephanie, and Helen grabbed the four corners of a sheet and tried to lay it over Emily's lower half. "No time!" Emily screamed wordlessly as the new arrival exited, also wailing.

In the sitting room, Oscar jumped from his chair. "Mama is dying! I have to go to her!"

Eli grabbed his hand. "Your Ma is fine. It just hurts when the baby comes out."

"Did I do that to Ma?"

"Yes, we all did, but it's all right. Women forget the pain the second they hold us."

Ann wiped the blood from the crying baby. "Oscar will be happy. He has a sister!"

Helen dabbed the sweat from Emily's brow. "You did great! I didn't know a baby could arrive so quickly!"

Tears of joy and relief trickled from Tom's eyes. "Emily, my love, you can stop squeezing my hand now."

Emily did so. "Sorry. Do you have any skin left?"

"I'm fine. Do you still want to name her Carol Ann?"

"I do."

"Carol Ann, meet your mother and father." Ann laid the clean baby on Emily's chest.

Tom stroked his new child's bare back. "I'll never say a woman can't handle anything ever again. Every one of you is a remarkable person. I was scared to death!"

Emily's tears followed. "Welcome, Carol Ann." After several minutes of nursing and cuddling, she said, "Help me sit and make me presentable. I want everybody to meet our daughter."

Helen walked into the sitting room, where the entire family waited. "Emily and Tom want all of you to come and meet Carol Ann."

"I told you Mama was making me a sister!" Oscar ran down the hall. He slammed open the door.

Tom saw Oscar about to take a flying leap onto the bed beside his mother. He sprang up and caught Oscar in the air. "Careful, son. Carol Ann is right where you were about to land!"

"Oh! I don't want to hurt my sister."

Emily moved Carol Ann. "We know. From now on, make sure you know where she is first." She patted the bed beside her. "Bringing in your sister was hard work. I need an Oscar hug."

Oscar sat snuggled to his mother with his sister on his lap when the rest of the family arrived. He informed them, "This is my sister. Isn't she the prettiest?" He looked into Carol Ann's face, who studied her brother's smile at the same time.

Eli looked at his father, Emily, Oscar, and Carol Ann together, with Helen hovering behind the bed. *He doesn't need me. He has a whole new family.*

Tom had already imagined that this scene would occur, and nobody could ever take the place of his oldest son. Without looking up, he said, "I need my entire family to be a happy man. I NEED my oldest son, daughter-in-law, and grandchild's love! Give me hugs. " He looked up and opened his arms.

Remembering how his broken ribs had felt even months after his accident, Eli gave his father a gentle hug and spoke softly into his ear. "I need your love too. Thank you for making sure I know I still have it."

Tom pulled Eli tightly to his chest. "You have it forever."

Forty Nine

March arrived. Only a few provisions remained after five months at the Devine Ranch. The family hoped to get enough money from their wool to purchase all the supplies they needed for their upcoming journey to the western sea. Roscoe explained the proper sequence of purchasing and selling. "First, buy without giving a hint that you have a product to sell. That way, you can haggle down to the lowest price the seller will give you."

Tom continued Alex's lesson. "Then, you approach Joaquín to sell our wool while we load. Mention that it's exceptionally soft and that we are the owners of every Merino sheep in Santa Fe. Be clear that you are also asking José Luis, Alvaro Salazar, the other farmers, and the man at the livestock yard if they want to purchase our wool."

When Alvaro arrived to teach the family how to shear sheep, Alex asked, "What do you think about this wool?"

"This wool is much softer than anybody else's. You're going to cause us to get a lower price. Maybe you would wait to sell yours."

"Would you be interested in purchasing all our wool? You could decide when to take it to market. Of course, we still expect a good price. If not, we'll offer it to other buyers."

Alvaro stopped cutting wool. "What if I buy your unshorn sheep and include the value of the wool?"

"Wool only. We're taking the sheep with us."

"What do you mean?"

"The ranch is for sale. We're moving on."

"You are!? I thought you were here forever."

"I'm sorry, Uncle. We can't stay."

"How much do you want? What are you selling with the ranch? Any of the animals?"

Alex translated the questions to the family members learning how to cut wool without injuring the animal or themselves. They had a family discussion.

Noah spoke for them. "Alex, while the others keep sheering, why don't you, I, and Alvaro take a walk? He can tell us what he wants, and the family can decide what we are willing to leave. Tomorrow, you go into town and see if anybody else is interested in buying. If we decide to sell to your uncle, we'll let him know."

After everybody else sold their wool at the stockyard, Alex sold theirs to Joaquín. He brought the money home and informed the family, "I'm going to sell the land, house, barn, forge –with a full array of blacksmith tools– the furniture and kitchen items we decide to leave, two dozen chickens, and fifty Merino sheep to Alvaro."

They also decided to leave mostly rams, all the lambs, their shorn mothers, and ten Texan horses. Alex lost money selling the ranch for the amount Alvaro could borrow. However, he had earned ten dollars during the lentil harvest and purchased a wagon load of supplies with the mustard plant sales. He exchanged or took everything the family wanted from the farmhouse.

They left Santa Fe with mustard and lentils, the animals they had when they'd arrived and their new offspring, twenty-seven Texan horses, one hundred Merino sheep from the Lopez contract, ten additional goats, and the sheepdog named Samantha. Since they had only ten cages, they filled them with younger chickens. Karmen and Alvaro had taught them how to harvest lentils and mustard, make mustard paste, and shear sheep.

Most importantly, Tom, Eli, Noah, and Adahy had an excellent place to heal. With all things considered, Alex figured they had come out ahead. He said a teary goodbye to the people in Santa Fe who loved him: his uncle, aunt, and cousins.

With the wool sale money, the family stocked their wagons with provisions then bid Joaquín and Carla adios with much sadness that they would never see each other again.

They left the assay office with ninety-two

dollars in Mexican coins in exchange for the gold balls they had smelted from the mine rubble.

On March 20, 1842, Alex left Santa Fe with a fondness for the town.

Fifty

The path from Santa Fe to the eastern side of the Rio Grande allowed trouble-free travel. Samantha kept the large herd of animals in a tight pack. Sally commented to Alex, "Who needs a drover?! You picked a superb herder." She encouraged the dog. "Good work, Sam!"

Sam trotted to Sally for scratching behind her ears. Having also been well trained, Sally happily rewarded the dog with the requested behavior.

"You two work together better than any of the rest of us. I do understand Sam, though. I'll do anything you ask for your affection!"

Sally looked around to determine if anyone could see them. "You both have ME under YOUR control. Here's a kiss for you." So they didn't get caught by others or carried away by themselves, Sally made it brief. "I'm very proud of us."

"About what?"

"I know you love me, so I'm patiently waiting for God to tell us when we can get married."

"Right, but I hope it doesn't take too long to get to California!"

"Me too!"

Three days after leaving Santa Fe, the wagons and animals bunched up at Galisteo Creek. "This isn't good. The only way forward is in the creek." Noah took his spyglass from his eye. "With no way out as far as can be seen."

"Fill our containers and let the animals drink while I scout ahead. If it's shallow enough, we might be able to travel in the stream." Eli urged Ace into the water.

"Is this part of our journey going to be harder than crossing the mountains?" asked Oscar.

"We don't know what's ahead," replied Tom. "We'll deal with whatever as it comes. We are all very capable people, including you."

Nikki led the mules, Rose and Molly, into the creek. "But Mama is making me a new sister, and I don't want her to get hurt. I'm worried."

Holding the lead lines of Beauty, Dolly, Edwin, and Martin as they drank – the mules she had acquired in Little Rock— Sally remembered what Alex had told her in the barn in Santa Fe. "Don't drag possible problems from the future into the present, Nikki. We have this minor issue to deal with right now, and that is traveling in this stream. None of us knew this would happen, just like we don't know what will happen next, so why make up imaginary problems?"

Alex smiled at the passing of his message. *Sally thinks I have meaningful things to say. I love her!*

The last animal drank its fill an hour before Eli returned. "Galisteo Creek is shallow all the way to the Rio Grande, but the bed is uneven. It's going to be slow navigating. We'll have to travel between the mountains and the river when we come out on the south side. Water can rise quickly, and we don't want to get trapped between the river and the mountain. I suggest we be on our way."

Stephanie held out a bowl. "Dinner is made. Eat while we clean up."

Even with a six-mule team pulling the very heavy wagon, it immediately bogged down. Roscoe unhitched the team. "We have to rethink this. Maybe we need Mexican cattle to pull the wagons and probably six per wagon."

Alex brought their Jersey cattle into the water. "José Luis might not let us have any. He was furious when I wouldn't sell him the ranch."

Tom helped hitch the team to the back of the stuck wagon. "I thought he was going to shoot somebody when we told him we gave Steeldust horses and Merino sheep to your uncle. Maybe he will trade cattle for some of them."

"We'll need six oxen teams, I think." Noah stood on the land and held the reins of their only bovine team. "That would be seventy-two cattle. We'll probably need to give him money as well."

Sally watched. "Since we're going to drive more animals, maybe you should find another dog or two. Are we all going back to Santa Fe?"

The men looked at each other. None of them wanted to leave the women and children they loved. "Yes."

Fifty One

José Luis sat on the veranda of his hacienda. A large cloud of dust rose on the horizon. When the dust settled, it was around seventeen horses, fifty sheep, and the six men in front of him. "I thought you were on your way to San Diego."

Alex answered, "We appreciate all that you did for us, and we thought you might like to have some of the Merino sheep and Texan Steeldusts. Maybe you would trade for some of your cattle?"

"Maybe. How many cattle? I have piebalds and Andalusians."

"Before we decide, we need your advice again. What would we need to be able to drive a hundred of them to San Diego?"

"Along with all the rest of your animals?"

Alex got off his horse. "Yes, minus what we trade with you."

"Even though Steeldusts are superb cow horses, each of you men would need two. It would be best if you traded them out every other day. Still, it's probably impossible."

"That would leave us five horses to trade."

"Maybe with six well-trained dogs. My Arrogante, Camilla, had a litter of eight last fall. We started training them as soon as their eyes opened."

Alex leaned against the veranda rail. "Six of them available?"

"Yes."

"So, for six Arrogante sheepdogs and one hundred piebald cattle, mostly oxen, we have five Steeldust horses and fifty Merino sheep. The horses can do more than just herd cattle, and the sheep will give you wool every year."

"That what you have with you now?"

"We will keep the horses you said we need."

José Luis looked over the offered animals. "I want these four females and this male Steeldust. Most of these sheep are males. I don't like that."

"If you let the females breed only with these males, their offspring will remain pure. However, if you let these males breed with your other sheep, even your regular wool will get better."

"I want more female sheep."

"We will trade the five horses you want for the six sheepdogs if we can pick the dogs, and then we'll ask Joaquín to find somebody to trade oxen for these sheep."

"I'll trade the dogs and cattle if you give me one more female Steeldust."

"How about the five horses and fifty sheep for the six dogs and only seventy-five piebalds? You have thousands of cattle, and you won't even miss seventy-five. We pick the cattle."

One horse for twenty-five cows! I am good! "You can pick your dogs while I get these horses into my barn. They are under the veranda. Drive the sheep into that paddock, and then we'll go out on the range and get your cattle."

Alex pointed and spoke in English. "One of you, use the standard signal to tell the dogs under there to drive these sheep into that. He says they're trained. Watch how they work, and pick six young ones." He handed over the lead ropes of the five horses José Luis wanted. "We will keep the halters and lead ropes. Do you have any six-ox yokes?"

"The only one I will part with is broken. You can buy it for two reales. Do you want to see it?"

Alex caught Eli's gaze. "Look at José Luis's yoke and decide if it's worth two reales."

Adahy called out the needed command. Arrogantes popped out from under the veranda and herded the animals. The men observed the dogs while Eli, Alex, and José Luis went to the tack room.

Roscoe, Tom, Adahy, and Noah each had a dog beside them when Eli carried the yoke and harness from the barn. Noah said, "We recommend those two." He pointed.

Alex looked at the darkest of the five remaining dogs. "Jump," he commanded. The dog sprang up, landed, and then returned to sitting. "Come." Alex gently slapped the side of his leg. The dog hurried over, sat in front of Alex, and looked into his eyes. "Good girl!" Alex scratched the dog behind the ears.

Eli did the same with the other recommended

canine. However, the almost entirely blonde runt of the litter responded. "All right, Blondie. I guess you picked me."

"What are their names?" asked Alex.

"Not named. I knew I would be selling them eventually."

Out on the range, José Luis rode beside Alex. "I have to tell you. I thought God was not real, but I've seen how your family lives and helps others. I said, 'God, if you're real, give me some of those Steeldusts and Merino sheep, and then I'll believe in You.' Well, I just got some of them. How do I find out about this God of yours?"

"First, I have to let you know that we were on our way, but God uses this family to reach out to those He calls, and He wouldn't let us go forward. He sent us to you because He showed us that we need oxen to pull our wagons. And who happens to own most of the cattle? You. God is definitely real and is calling you to believe. So, buy a Bible from Joaquín and read it every day. Go to the church in town. Talk to the preacher and the other people who attend."

"I will. Since God sent you to me, and you are going to use my oxen to pull your wagons, we need to be sure none of them have hoof problems. Do you have time to put shoes on them? You won't get far with lame animals."

Alex passed the message to the other men. Noah suggested. "Some are bound to go lame even if we shoe them. Perhaps we should negotiate for more and trade two more horses. We'd still have twenty."

José Luis was thrilled. "Two more! As you said, I have thousands of cattle. I'll give you twenty-five more for female Steeldusts. One more thing; when any of them go lame, if you can't trade them with a local along the way, eat them."

The dogs and men cut out seventy-five four-year-old steers and twenty-five cows José Luis identified as heifers, but Noah picked some he thought looked pregnant. The men made sure they did NOT round up any bulls because they would be too hard to manage while traveling. They herded the cattle into the small field beside José Luis's barn. Roscoe walked inside. "That's a large forge," he looked around, "but you have only two anvils. This is going to take days."

"I'll get more anvils." Alex rode to Alvaro's ranch. "We're going to shoe the cattle we bought. Alvaro, may I use your anvil out at our old ranch and then put it back? I'm going to take ours and our mobile forge too. We'll have seven men, five anvils, and two forges."

Alvaro stood up. "My boys and I will help. Let's go."

The ten men brought in the cattle, trimmed the hooves, shaped the shoes, nailed them on, and then took the shoed animals to the other small field. They stopped not long before darkness set in.

Alex paid for the shoes, use of facilities, and help. José Luis bid goodbye to and commanded the six dogs he had traded to go with and obey the men taking them.

Once back at Alvaro's ranch, the family loosed their cattle into the field with the rest of their animals. As they shared supper with Alvaro's family, they paid him for using his anvils, helping, and grazing their animals. They spent the night in their wagons.

Carla heard the bell on the door jingle and glanced over. "What are you doing here!?"

Alex informed Carla, "We need to buy twelve six-oxen-yokes, harnesses, and two hundred cattle shoes."

"I didn't know you had cattle."

"We just got them."

"Joaquín! Bring in twelve six-ox yokes and harnesses." Carla walked to a stack of small barrels. "Each barrel contains one hundred cattle shoes." She pointed. "Those hold horseshoes."

Joaquín brought the requested items in a wheelbarrow. "What are you doing here!?"

"That's what I asked," said Carla.

"Final purchase before we go. Two barrels of each kind of shoe," Alex drew a bag from his breeches. "How much?" Joaquín named the price. Alex counted out the money. "We wish you many blessings."

The six men strapped the purchase on the pack mules with them and waved goodbye. "Adios, amigos."

Fifty Two

The caravan arrived at Galisteo Creek for their second try. "Travel at the speed of oxen learning to pull wagons is slow." Stephanie looked at the blessedly still shallow waters. "Shall we just wade on in?"

Eli sat on Ace. "We should get the heaviest wagon through first. I'll come back before we get the other wagons going. We can decide if it's better to have the babies in a wagon or cradle boards."

Roscoe followed the wagon on King.

Emily spoke up, "Carol Ann is riding in a wagon. It may get stuck, but it won't trip and fall."

"Exactly right, all the babies need to ride, but we'll wait until we know if the cows can pull the wagons in the creek. They still aren't very cooperative, and this will be even harder for them," said Ehawee.

Ninety minutes later, Roscoe returned. "Did you fix dinner?"

Helen filled up a plate. "Here is yours. What happened?"

"We got through fine. Eli is waiting with the

wagon. Douse the fire and pack up. Secure your babies in the wagons."

Their seven dogs worked together as one fully functioning pack to drive the unharnessed horses, mules, goats, donkeys, sheep, and cattle down the creek. Once all the animals were safely grazing, the dogs ran to Sally for praises and rewards.

Navigating toward the campfire's light, Noah drove the last wagon out of the water south of Galisteo Creek. "Problem solved. It was a blessing that this happened so close to Santa Fe. I'm sure other obstacles are ahead that will require a lot of pulling power, and now we have it."

Nikki stood beside the wagon. "Go eat, Papa. I'll unharness the oxen and take them to the grass."

"Is Oscar going to help you?"

"No, he's playing with Carol Ann. I didn't know she would take him away from me."

"He loves his sister, and she is new."

"I love Adele, Chris, and Joy, but I didn't do that to him. I'm just not lovable."

Noah knelt on one knee, put his hands on his son's shoulder, and looked into his eyes. "You are very lovable. No matter what, Ann and I will always love you, and so will God. It won't take very long for Oscar to be back to playing with you. Let's take care of these cows together."

Fifty Three

The following four days rendered twenty oxen lame. Alex laid out their map. "José Luis said to try to exchange them with the locals. When he made the map, he told me Albuquerque would be a good place to trade if we needed supplies. We should get there tomorrow. Do you think they can walk that much farther without re-shoeing them?"

Roscoe sat beside the fire. "Probably not, but we should remove and keep their shoes if we trade them."

Helen handed him a tin cup. "Give them willow tea in the morning."

"This one's hoof is cracked. Let's try the painkiller and see if we can get them into town." Noah lowered an ox leg. "Alex, will you go into town and find out if we can trade before we do anything."

Alex folded the map and slid it into his pocket. The following morning, he rode Blackie to the center of the community. He asked the women at the fountain, "Do you know anybody with cattle they might trade? We have oxen that would be wonderful animals for somebody, but they have sore feet right now. They will be perfect after healing. We need oxen that can pull a wagon now."

"No, señor, we have only mules," said one.

Another replied, "We use our ox every day. We can't."

None of the women knew a farmer— certainly not their husbands or fathers— who could help.

I guess we'll have to kill them and smoke the meat. Alex hung his head. *That's too much for us to carry. This isn't good at all.* He turned toward their camp. On the north side of Albuquerque town square stood San Felipe de Neri church and convent. *Might as well stop and ask.* He knocked.

Eventually, the parish priest opened the large door. "How may I help you, my child?"

"Twenty of the oxen that pull our wagons have gone lame. Would you know of anybody who might exchange some in walking condition for ours?"

"Where are they?"

"We're north of town. We decided it would be best to find out if somebody will trade before we have them walk any farther."

"Our Heavenly Father wants none of his creatures to suffer. How far away are the lame oxen?"

Alex perked up. "By galloping horse or lame oxen walking?"

"Well, both, I guess."

"Twenty minutes by horse, probably all day for the oxen to walk here."

"We might trade. Wait here." The priest

started to close the door but paused. "I am Father Manuel Ortega."

"My name is Alejandro Devine, but my family calls me Alex."

A short time later, Father Ortega and a second man came around the side of the convent mounted on mules. Father Ortega stopped beside Alex. "Friar Emil takes care of our animals. He will look at your oxen."

Alex alerted the father and friar on the way, "Don't be alarmed when we get there. My family is large, with many wagons and animals. None of them speak Spanish."

"Why is that? Your Spanish is excellent."

"I've always known this language and English. I joined this family after I was grown."

The three men approached the camp just over an hour after Alex had left that morning. Eli spotted Alex before any of the approaching men saw him. He loudly called out, "Come into the camp, Alex!" and thereby notified the men almost upon them and his family that they would soon meet.

Father Ortega's forehead lifted. His eyes opened wide. "This isn't what I assumed you meant by big. I thought twenty was your entire herd. You have so many animals and such a variety of our Heavenly Father's creatures. We'll never find the lame ones."

"Our dogs are keeping them separated from the rest."

Alex and the men with him rode into camp.

His family was doing whatever they needed to be doing at the moment: nursing children, changing diapers, meeting the two unknown men, or secretly pointing rifles at them from under the edge of wagon canvases.

Noah had learned some Spanish. "Hola, amigos. No hablo español."

"Hola, that is all right. My name is Father Ortega. I speak English, and so does Friar Emil. Alex has explained your situation—."

Surely not everything thought Noah.

Father Ortega continued, "with the oxen. He tells me your dogs are keeping them separated. May we see them now? Your voice sounds different than the one we heard telling us to come into your camp."

"The other man remains on guard duty," replied Noah, who did not comment on the lame oxen.

Friar Emil inspected the animals. "I would not call these oxen. Yes, they are steers, but I doubt they had ever worked before you hooked them to your wagons. If the rest are the same, you'll soon have more problems. Perhaps I should look at the rest."

Noah and Alex looked at each other and silently agreed. "That would be fine," replied Noah.

The four men weaved through the herd. Friar Emil stopped beside a cow. "This one isn't even a steer! And it's pregnant!"

"We meant to get some heifers."

"She's not a heifer. Her udder is too large. Who did you buy these from?"

Noah said, "It doesn't matter. We picked the ones we wanted."

The friar suggested, "You need animals accustomed to working. You should trade all your steer for our oxen. How many do you have?"

"Are yours tough and used to working? How old are they?" asked Noah.

"There are some that are six. Most are seven or eight."

Alex ran his hand along the back of the pregnant cow. "We will get fewer years of use out of them because yours are older than ours."

"Teaming our oxen with your untrained animals will improve the work. Would you want to trade any more than the already lame? We could take your worse animals."

Noah remembered what Roscoe had said the night before. "We want to keep their shoes."

"Ours have shoes. Some of these are missing. You'd have more than you do now."

"Let me talk to somebody before we decide. I'll be back." Noah went to the wagon where Ann and her sisters were out of sight. "Girls, you had a cow for years…." Noah explained the offer. "What is your opinion?"

Ann bounced Christopher on her knee. "I think two seasoned oxen per wagon with four of our best rotated with our horse, mule, and donkey teams would work, so twenty-four."

Stephanie stated her opinion. "What if we had to use oxen teams several days in a row? We need to be able to swap at least every other day. We'd need forty-eight of the friar's oxen and ninety-six of our cattle."

Noah pondered for a minute. "Friar Emil said theirs work hard every day. We wouldn't have to swap theirs. Maybe we should swap the forty-eight. We'd only have to use two of ours on those days and could rotate them every other day."

Sally said, "As we go, ours will become actual oxen as well."

Noah walked back to the field. "Yours are years older than ours. Sixty of yours for fifty of ours."

The father and friar talked out of hearing and then rejoined Noah and Alex. "If you give us the missing shoes. One more thing you should know; there are Banditos stealing cattle, and the Federales are stopping anybody traveling with cattle. You need proof of ownership. Do you have a bill of sale from the previous owner?"

"No," replied Alex.

"We suggest you pay us to mark all these animals with our brand. We will give you a bill of sale for all of them."

Noah said, "Except for the cattle, we already owned the rest of these animals."

"It's your choice, but you can take the branding iron and make it your mark if you're far away from here."

"We'll be back." Noah signaled Alex to follow.

In camp, Noah sounded the meeting whistle. Everybody joined at the wagon where the women and children sat. Noah explained the second proposal. The family came up with a counteroffer.

Alex and Noah found the father and friar looking over the cattle. Alex informed them, "Sixty of your oxen for fifty of ours. We will pay you for the missing shoes. It will take time to brand all these animals. We want grazing in your fields, oats for all our animals, and safe harbor and meals for our family in the convent. The women and children will stay in our rooms. We will pay you for boarding our animals and us. There are fourteen people to feed. You see the animals."

Father Ortega held out his hand. "Agreed." He turned to Friar Emil. "As soon as I get home, I will send the men and supplies you want." He looked again at Alejandro. "Alejandro and unnamed family member, who does not need to tell me his name, we had your dogs separate other cattle we think will soon be lame. There are more to look at before you pick the fifty worst."

The potential trading group had two cows that looked pregnant. Noah sent them back to the animals they would keep. "We will work on their feet and brand them first then let them heal while we work on the rest."

Under the supervision of Friar Emil, the fifty steer to be left in Albuquerque remained where they were. The rest of the people and animals went to town.

The week they branded the animals, the uncle of one of the women Alex had spoken to at the town fountain returned to Albuquerque. His niece asked, "Do you know anybody willing to exchange working oxen for lame animals?"

Javier stroked his goatee. "Maybe. Where are they?"

"I don't know, but they should be near."

"I'll see if I can find and help them."

Javier discovered the additional animals at the convent. *This will be easy. The Navajos with us will be able to pick up their trail. I'll get my men.*

Fifty Four

Sally locked the door to her room with the dogs inside. "We want them to obey us, not fear us. I will not let you inflict that kind of pain on them."

Noah stood outside her door. "All right. I hope Federales don't think they're stolen."

"Just have Father Ortega write: and the seven sheepdogs that answer to the names of Sam, Blondie, Blackie, Honey, Frisky, Bliss, and Tiger."

"I'll also have him say: and will do anything Sally Williams asks them to do."

"Are you going to use my name?!"

"Of course not. I was joking with you."

"It wasn't funny."

"I'm sorry. I'll have him write what you asked." Noah went to find Father Ortega.

The dim light of sunrise found the family leaving without any person in Albuquerque having seen any of the women or children. Roscoe had the slightly modified branding iron. Father Ortega drew the new brand on the bill of sale, stating that all of the animals were marked with the shown brand and that seven unbranded sheepdogs were also part of the group.

Noah looked into the wagon from the driver's seat. "This time, we should truly be ready."

Nikki replied, "I hope those pieces of leather Eli tied on those two cows keep their feet from going bad. I've walked more than those cows, and shoes have kept my feet good."

"I hope so too." Noah flicked the reins.

Javier watched the caravan move out.

The family kept the cattle at it to accustom them to the task because the horses, mules, and donkeys couldn't pull the wagons in the excessively deep sand beside the river. The Albuquerque oxen took the brunt of the work while the Santa Fe steers yoked with them learned. Each ox walked one day out of three without pulling. The steers pulled every other day. Since they cooperated instead of fighting against the work, they fared much better than before Albuquerque.

Fifty Five

Beside the campfire at the Rio Grande ford, Sally asked, "Ann, may I sleep beside you? It gets so cold at night, and I'm all alone. I can't get warm even under three blankets. I don't know how Alex is staying warm, but Noah and Eli won't let us get married, so we can't keep each other warm."

"Did Alex ask you?"

"He did, and I said yes. Alex told me Noah and Eli said they would kill him if we married before we get to the western sea."

"They did?! Do the two of you want to wait?"

"I don't. I don't think Alex does either."

"Sleep beside me tonight. Tomorrow, I'll talk to Noah and find out why he said that."

In the faint light of a tiny sliver of moon, Sally pulled her feather mattress next to her sister's.

Noah asked, "My wife, why is Sally coming over here?"

"She's cold, and I told her to. I'll talk with you about it in the morning."

244

Sally snuggled to Ann's back. "Good night," she pulled the blankets over them.

"Good night, Sally," replied Ann, Noah, and Nikki.

Midway through the night, Samantha slid under the blanket beside Alex. When the morning light touched her eyes, the dog returned to duty. Blondie should have been coming into camp. Sam called out with a single bark but got no reply. She barked frantically.

Everybody woke. Alex and Noah raced after the dog. Every dog, except Samantha, and a large portion of their cattle, was gone. They dashed back to inform the others. "We didn't find any bodies, so we think the cattle and other dogs were stolen last night." Noah climbed into his wagon.

Alex added, "Noah wants to go after them, but we shouldn't all go. It's probably the banditos Father Ortega warned us about."

Noah returned to the fire pit where everybody had gathered. "Indians must have come in first and captured the dogs. We need them and the oxen, and it's easy to see which way they went. Adahy, come with us. The rest of you men and Sam drive a large group of animals two miles south and then into and out of the river before you bring them back. As soon as you get packed, you women take the wagons and all the other animals across the river right here. When the men get back here with their animals, cross over.

"Everybody go straight west, so we can find each other. Get out of view as quickly as possible and then wait. Wipe out the tracks of your crossing at this place. Leave those going south. When we return with our stolen animals, we'll cross here too. I'll try to take their horses and any other animals they have to make it harder for them to come after us. When the rustlers finally get here, they should think we went south. Hopefully, we'll be able to get away. Get started now."

Noah, Alex, and Adahy rode north without the dog that had escaped capture due to Alex's encouragement to sleep with him.

Everybody went to their assigned task without breakfast. The unharnessed animals were accustomed to following the wagons and gave Roscoe, Tom, and Eli some trouble. However, they moved right along once they were out of sight of those crossing the river.

Fifty Six

The thieves drove the stolen cattle toward Javier's hideout in a cluster of mesas northeast of the ford. Even strapped on the Navajo's horses, the sheepdogs bounced hard in the sacks used to capture them. Blondie's captor pummeled her every time she trashed.

Eyanosa, Blackie, and Adahy's horse, Paint, had traveled almost every day for years. The pursuit was nothing for them. Following the wide trail of cattle tracks, they caught up when the bandits stopped for the night.

The three men tied their horses out of view. Adahy slipped away to reconnoiter the area around the animals.

"You need to learn this, and I need you to listen to what they say, so do exactly what I do." Noah slowly slithered into hearing range of the bandits. Alex mimicked every move and freeze.

Javier bragged, "This was my best find. We got so many. With all the other animals they have, they'll never come after us, and men can't leave women alone either."

Alex almost laughed. *You don't know our women.*

An hour later, the three sneaking around the camp returned to their horses. Adahy reported, "They had our cattle hobbled and a rope around them. I removed the hobbles. There are twelve horses tied to a single holding line. I retied the rope with a quick-release knot."

Alex repeated what Javier had said about the women. Adahy snickered. "A person should never underestimate our women."

"I think the Navajos only want the dogs and rum," remarked Noah. "They're already halfway to passing out, and so are the bandits. Getting the dogs is going to be the hard part. We can't just grab them and run because they have them in bags. We'll have to go into their camp and free them. Be sure the dogs know it's us so they don't attack us when we let them out."

"If we wait until all of the men are asleep, we might be able to get far away before they discover that they've lost," said Alex.

"Maybe we can help them get some good sleep." Noah pulled a flask from his shirt. "Sedative."

"How are we going to get them to drink it?" asked Alex.

In Javier's camp, a Navajo heard a sound. Noah pressed himself to the ground only twenty feet away from the man and two open rum jugs. The Navajo peered into the darkness. Noah studied his surroundings while he waited. Each time the
248

Navajo looked away, Noah advanced. An hour passed before he had worked his way under the stack of packsaddles. He poured the flask of sedative into one of the jugs before he quietly knocked the other over.

Javier leaned down to get a jug. He cussed, grabbed the other vessel, and jumped up. "Who knocked over the rum?!" He fired wild shots into the air. "I'll put a bullet in ya!" Everybody stared at Javier as he staggered toward the fire and then slurped liquid from the jug that still contained something.

A Navajo grabbed the rum before it met with the same fate as the one that had caused Javier to pitch a conniption fit.

Noah remained hidden under the rustler's noses. Thirty minutes after Noah spiked the grog, all seven men had passed out in strange configurations. Alex went into camp and prodded one of the men with his boot. The man didn't respond, so Alex leaned down and spoke to a sack. "Good dog. We're here to save you." He commanded, "Stay." The animal recognized the voice. Its tail flipped up and down inside the bag. Noah and Adahy did the same at other sacks.

As Blondie crawled out of her sack, the five other dogs licked the faces of Alex, Noah, and Adahy. Blondie saw the men on the ground and then ripped into a leg.

"No!" ordered Noah.

"Come." Alex picked up a packsaddle.

Noah stitched up the Navajo's leg. He bandaged it with strips of material he ripped off Javier's shirt while Alex and Adahy prepared for their departure.

Once all the horses had been saddled, bridled, and fastened to the lead rope, Adahy released the cattle. "Forward, ho!" He pointed south to let the dogs know which way to drive the animals.

Alex led the string of horses loaded with all the supplies of the bandits except one bag of beans and the empty jugs. In order to not give the thieves a death sentence, Noah left seven guns, but with ammunition only in the chambers.

Fifty Seven

Having already been very intoxicated and passing out before consuming much sedative, the injured Navajo woke with horrible pain. He looked at his leg wrapped in strips of cloth, removed the bandage, and saw the stitches. He glanced around. Neatly stacked by the fire were one sack, a few jugs, and some guns. He said to himself. "Why weren't we killed? What happened to my leg?" He got up and examined the tracks. *The dogs helped them. The one I carried probably wanted to rip me to shreds. Even though we stole their cattle and dogs, they stopped it and fixed my leg. What kind of people are they?* He saw Javier's ripped shirt. *I am sure Javier did not give me any of his shirt, but a man who should not help me did.*

The man pondered before he shook Javier. "Wake up." Javier remained asleep. Javier's heart beat, and he still breathed. He tried the other men. None of them were able to wake. "Owner of cows has strong magic!"

Fifty Eight

The morning sunlight woke the sedated men. Javier put his hand to his head. "Worst hangover ever!"

"Was spell," said the injured Navajo.

Javier noticed the absence of animals. "Your people put a spell on me and stole my cattle!"

"Then why I still here?"

"And they took everything else too!"

Soon the whole group knew their state of affairs. The Navajo suggested, "Start home."

"Home! I'm going after my cattle and horses!" Javier spat into the dirt. "Dirty cattle thief!"

One of the other men put his hand over his eyes and looked south. "I don't see them. We have only one bag of beans. We don't have enough to go after them and get home."

"We'll get our supplies back. This time we'll kill them and take everything," snarled Javier.

"We not catch them. They gone long time," said the man who had been awake for hours.

"How do you know how long they've been gone?" asked a man named Xavier.

"Woke up long time ago. Dog chewed leg. Cows already gone." He raised his pant leg to show the bloody bandages.

Javier looked at the river. "The water is rising. It will be too high when they get to the ford. They'll be trapped on this side. I'm going after them!" He picked up the beans.

One of the men grabbed the bag. "You're not taking the only food we have!"

Javier shot the man.

As the man and beans fell, Xavier put a bullet through Javier's forehead. "Did you think you could shoot my brother and live?" He kicked Javier. "You always were stupid! And you ain't taking our food."

The Navajo asked, "Home?"

Xavier scooped up the bag. "Home it is. Bring the jugs. We'll need them."

As the men gathered the empty rum jugs and corks, Xavier looked down at his brother. "Sorry, but I don't have a way to bury you."

The five remaining bandits started north.

Fifty Nine

Far to the south, Adahy contemplated the crossing. "Must have been a lot of rain north of here. I don't know if we can cross before the water sweeps us away."

Alex considered the water then looked north. "I don't see a dust cloud. I don't think they're coming. We should NOT try."

"We need to get across. Let's see how fast it's rising." Noah gouged a deep line in the sandy bank.

Fifteen minutes later, Noah still squatted beside the mark. He touched a different finger with each statement he spoke. "The water is up less than one finger. We don't have wagons. The animals can swim. It would be very bad to be here when the banditos return. If we are already on the other side, we'll be safe. They won't be able to cross for days. Even if we are swept far south of here, we can come back up. We should go."

"All right." Adahy urged their recovered cattle and new horses into the Rio Grande. As soon as Paint started to swim, Adahy wrapped its tail hair around his hands and slid off. He and the horse floated downstream as it swam toward the far shore. With Paint acting as the bell mare, the animals followed.

Alex entered downstream of the herd, hoping to keep them together.

Noah again looked at the mark he had made. *Three fingers up.* "God, get us safely across!" He drove the last of the cattle into the water.

Much farther downstream than Adahy had imagined, Paint reached a place where she could climb out. All the dogs and most of the cattle and horses arrived at the same location or shallow water close enough to walk over. Adahy called them to the land above.

Alex prodded the animals until all of them had gone up the bank. He and his tired horse climbed the bank behind them.

The river current became treacherous. Much farther south than where he had seen Adahy and Alex exit, Noah and several animals still struggled toward the shore. Noah saw no place to escape or even a shallow place to rest. He knew Eyanosa was exhausted, and the other animals had to be as well. He needed to find a way out of the river fast. "God, show me the place to get out!"

The current swirled Eyanosa into a fallen tree. Noah noticed his horse's motionless feet. *We're held by the current and this branch. We can rest!* He yelled, "Forward, gee!" and waved his arms. The animals struggled toward him. A cow slammed into the tree then another and then a horse.

Some are too far out. I'm too tired to go after them. Maybe I can lasso the horse still out there and pull it over. Three steers floated past as Noah's loop went around the horse's neck. The current jerked the rope from Noah's hands. The horse drifted away. *Crimony! It had a full packsaddle.* He yelled to the horse he had known for less than a day. "I'm sorry! I hope you and the cows find a way out!" Noah screamed, "Come!" to those that still had a chance.

The tree caught six cows, two horses, and Noah in its embrace. "God, three steers and a horse are gone. Even though we'll never have them, save them, please." Noah told himself *we have all the rest. It was the right thing to cross. That is if I can get those of us in this tree out.* He looked at the animals with him. *I don't want to lose whatever is in that packsaddle.*

Noah took the bridle off Eyanosa, pulled himself onto the tree trunk, and then wove around the branches to the bandit's horse. He tied the bridle to a thick limb, the saddle pommel, and a handle of the packsaddle before he unbuckled and opened the flap. Noah found a rope, tied it to the pack handles and the saddle pommel, and buckled the flap before he made his way to the shore.

Noah returned to the horse with the rope around a tree on the land. He secured the rope above the horse, slipped under the water, and released the girth strap of the riding saddle to which the packsaddle was attached. It started to slide off, so Noah shot to the surface and jerked the rope hard. The gear remained on top of the horse.

Soon, the waterlogged saddles dangled from

the branch. Noah took a few items at a time to the shore and emptied the saddle, so he could carry it.

"I'm coming for you now, Eyanosa." Noah moved the rope, hauled in his saddle, and set it on top of the others. "I'll use the rope to pull you out. I wish I had our pulley. How am I going to get you around the branches?" Noah sat and leaned against the saddles to contemplate.

"Noah. Noah."

"What?" Noah opened his eyes and saw Adahy standing over him. "Thank God you're here. I must have fallen asleep. How are the animals?" Noah looked toward the river. All eight animals remained pressed to the tree, but one cow's head drooped into the water. "Oh no! If I hadn't fallen asleep, it might not have died!"

"It would have anyway. The tree stabbed it."

"Where is Alex? Is he all right?"

"He's fine. He, all the dogs, and the rest of the animals are resting. They will start north without us if we're not back by the day after tomorrow."

"We need to get these animals out of the river as soon as possible."

"It's a good thing I brought my axe. I'll chop first. The branches are too big beside the trunk, and we wouldn't be able to move them out of the way. It will be fastest to go straight out. Pull the brush away as I chop it off."

After three hours of chopping and dragging branches, they had what they hoped was a path to the bank. Even though Eyanosa wasn't the one closest to the shore, Noah strapped the packsaddle around him and tied him to the rope.

Adahy stood upstream in front of a standing tree. Noah pointed, "Go to Adahy," then climbed along the fallen tree and joined Adahy. "Come!" Eyanosa tried to swim as the men pulled. The strong current pushed against the horse, but they struggled on. Eyanosa's hooves eventually touched the riverbed.

Not many minutes later, Eyanosa put his front hooves on the steep bank, pushed with his back legs, and jumped partway up the bank. The pull of the rope kept the horse from sliding back. Eyanosa tried to scrabble up. When he finally got the front of his body supported on the top of the bank, he laid his head down. It seemed to be forever before he made another push and got his whole body to the land above the river.

Noah's horse needed stitches, but the most important thing for his most loved animal was to rest. Noah stroked Eyanosa's neck and head as the horse lay motionless on the dry ground. "Good boy. I'm glad you're out."

"I don't know if we can get the cows," remarked Adahy.

"Go downstream and see if there's a better place. I'm going to wrap Eyanosa's legs." Noah went to the pile of drying packsaddle items.

Adahy returned and sat beside Noah. "Not far ahead are rocky rapids that surely would have killed you. We have to save however many animals we can right here. We should at least be able to get the other horse. Maybe we should name it Lucky."

"I didn't see any bad injuries when I got the saddles, but I want to look again. If it's too damaged to live, we shouldn't waste our energy, but if we do get it out, we'll name it Lucky."

The second horse lay on the dirt above the river an hour later. Adahy rubbed its neck. "I'd like Lucky to be mine."

"That's fine with me." Noah looked at the sun. He looked at the cows in water up to their backs. "Before we try to get any of them up here, we should get all of them to the shore."

"Good idea. If we get them to a place where they can rise with the water, we might be able to save all of them."

"We only need to cut one more branch to get that one." With the axe on his shoulder, Noah walked the tree route to the cow closest to a path they had already cut. He set to the difficult work of chopping a limb in deep water.

While he did so, Adahy rigged the packsaddle to fit on the larger animal. Once ready, the men pulled. Adahy called, "Gee," to get the animal to come toward them. The cow tried to swim away from the tree. The men barely pulled it against the raging current.

"I don't think we'll be able to get them," said Noah.

Eyanosa rose and walked to the men.

"We've pulled animals from a river before. I

think he remembers and wants to help. I don't want to let him. He needs to rest, but I have an idea. We clear another path then hook up two cows. We get Eyanosa to pull the farthest cow the distance it will take to pull the closer cow to the bank. If we let the current pull the first cow backward, it will pull the other cow to us."

The water was halfway up the necks of the cows when they were ready. "Eyanosa, pull," commanded Noah. The farthest cow approached the fulcrum tree. "Backward, ho."

Due to the force of the current, Eyanosa backed quickly. The other cow zipped to the shore and then stood on its feet well above its drowning point. They got three cows to the shallows before Eyanosa gave out.

Noah unhitched his horse. "Lay down, boy. Good horse."

The sun was setting as Adahy hitched Lucky into the system. The gelding dragged the pull cow away from the capture tree while the last stuck cow pushed its nostrils up to reach the air. "This one is almost completely under." Noah saw the whites in the cow's terrified, underwater eye. "Let the pull cow go."

The underwater cow popped to the surface as it zipped through the water, thrashing frantically. The cow realized it had touched the ground and then kicked.

"Calm down!" ordered Noah.

The cow slammed its hoof into the steer beside

it. The victim dropped into the water and floated toward the tree.

Noah again ordered, "Calm down!"

The frantic cow reared and bucked dangerously close to another of the cows already at the shore. Noah sat on the bank and watched. At precisely the right moment, he kicked the cow into the current. The pull cow drew closer until the terrified cow hit the tree. Lucky pulled the calm cow the rest of the way. They again had three cows at the shore.

Adahy went to the tree. "A branch skewered it."

"Crimony! Well, it was a choice that had to be made. She might have made us lose all the cows."

"Not that one. The one she kicked."

"At least the living one is still in the harness. Lucky can pull it over and hopefully get all of them up the bank before sundown. Would you start a fire? We might as well eat some of the one that just died."

By the time a cow leg cooked on a spit, four cows and two horses grazed in the lush grass beside the river. Noah sat at the fire. "We lost five cows and one horse, but the rest of us made it over, and it will be days before those rustlers can cross. I think we made the right choices." Noah looked at his brother-in-law for his opinion.

"I agree. If we hadn't gone after them, we would have lost all the cattle they took AND six dogs. And the bandits might have killed some or all of us if we had stayed on the other side of the Rio Grande."

That night, they skinned both cows and hacked up the recently killed one. They dragged over branches they had chopped from the fallen tree and hung the cow meat, packsaddle, and riding saddles in the smoke.

Sixty

Adahy opened his eyes. *The animals look strange.* He focused. "Noah! There's a horse with a packsaddle!"

Noah bolted to his feet. "The saddle must have protected it in the rapids."

The two men approached the horse that had found its way to them during the night. Adahy put his hand beside the flesh dangling from the horse's face. "It needs stitches badly. It's a wonder that it wasn't strangled." He removed the rope and bridle.

"Its legs are cut as well." Noah removed the packsaddle and examined the rest of the animal.

"I hate to make it suffer, but we don't have any sedative. We'll have to tie it down."

Noah patted the horse. "The additional pain would probably be more than it can handle. I'm going to look for plants to help us."

"I'll see if there's anything usable in this packsaddle."

"Most of what was in the other one is still good." Noah put his hand above his eyes and peered along the riverbank. "I'll be back."

Adahy opened the saddlebag flap. *This is a*

blessing. He pulled a coffee pot from the pack, filled it with river water, put it in the fire, and then dumped in wet coffee grounds. He put waterlogged pinto beans in a pot, rice in a second one, and hung them on the spit he got from the saddlebag. While the beans, rice, and coffee cooked, he dried potatoes. Next, he lugged large flat rocks close to the fire and washed them off. He spread the remaining coffee and all the black peppercorns over them. He hung empty sacks that were marked salt and sugar over branches. *The rice and beans won't be good for long.* He emptied them into plates, tin cups, and other cooking containers and hung the sacks to dry.

The final bag held soggy meat. Adahy tried a bite. *Buffalo jerky.* He hung all of it, the empty sack, and the packsaddle in the smoke.

Noah returned empty-handed. They let the beef smoke cure and cared for the living animals as well as possible without sedatives or sutures.

To use as much salvaged goods as possible, the men ate beef, beans, and rice every meal. The second morning, they drank extra strong coffee and gave plenty to the animals as well. All revved up, they put the packsaddles on cows and started north.

Near the end of the day, Alex saw them through his spyglass. Filled with relief, he rode toward his friends.

Noah walked beside Eyanosa as he spoke to Alex. "I wasn't sure if I would get out of the Rio

Grande alive and thought, what is the matter with me? I know life is short. Eli and I shouldn't have told you to wait to marry Sally. I'm sorry I threatened you. I want you to be my brother-in-law. When the two of you decide the time is right, I'm happy to perform the ceremony."

Alex jumped off his horse and hugged Noah. "I love you too." He turned to Adahy and opened his arms. "All of you."

Adahy stepped into Alex's embrace. "I do too." He backed away. "Tomorrow morning, we go to the rest of the family. I'm sure they're worried."

During the night, the highly vigilant sheepdogs thought they heard rustlers. They snarled and barked.

"Come!" ordered Eli in a loud voice. The instantly happy dogs ran to him. "Good dogs!" Eli knelt and rubbed their heads.

The men in the camp heard Eli's command. Noah called out, "Come into camp, brother!"

Eli embraced and patted the backs of all of them. "The others sent me to look for you."

Alex replied, "Good. It would be better if you brought them here than for us to drive these animals there and back."

Noah inquired, "Did you bring medical supplies?"

"What do you need?" Eli took off his pack.

"Those stupid banditos had absolutely no medical supplies." Not expecting an answer, he asked, "What would they have done if any of them was injured?"

"Probably just shot him," said Alex.

Noah continued, "Anyway, we want to sedate and stitch injuries. One of the horses has a horrible wound on its face."

Adahy asked, "Did you travel close to the river? Did you see any sign of the banditos?"

"I did follow the river. I didn't see any sign of them. You probably shouldn't have a fire in case they are over here." Eli handed Noah a flask.

Noah took it. "There is NO way they got across. We barely made it over. We lost some of the cows in the high water. Don't tell the women that we crossed in rising water."

Adahy removed the strip of his shirt that they had wrapped around the face of the horse they had decided to name Miracle. The flesh flapped down.

"That is bad," said Eli. "Are you going to do the work tonight or in the morning?"

"This one, right now. The others can wait until morning." Noah poured the liquid into a pot of water and carried it to Miracle. "Eli, I'd like to speak with you." While he sutured the horse's lacerations, Noah soaked all the bandages in antiseptic water, but more importantly, he explained his change of heart about Alex and Sally. "…but don't say anything to Sally. Let Alex decide when to speak with her." After Noah and Eli reapplied the sanitized bandages to the animals, they slept.

Eli spoke with Alex at first light. He mounted Ace after eating. "Wait here. We'll join you in four or five days." He took five of the dogs with him.

Sixty One

The first thing Alex did when he saw Sally was kiss her. The second was to tell her what Noah and Eli had said to him. He then asked Sally if she wanted to marry immediately or wait until the journey ended.

Sally talked it through with Alex. Since it was no longer a mandate to oppose and the nights were getting warmer, they decided to take the family's advice and wait.

Noah kissed Ann and then told her what he and Eli had first said to Alex, but that they had changed their minds and had told him so.

Ann decided not to tell Noah what Sally had disclosed the night she had slept beside them.

Eli held his wife in his arms, explained everything, and assured Stephanie that he would apologize to Sally when Alex told him to go ahead.

Adahy kissed Ehawee and Etu.

After supper, Noah told the story of the cattle

rescue. He said the river had risen after they were in the water, which was true. He also reported that they had gone into the Rio Grande before the water was high, which was a lie.

That night, Noah had a dream. He set up one totem after another. Upon the circle's completion, the center glowed. Like those he had seen during the sweat lodge ceremony in his home village, a demon stretched its clawed hand from the light and then its arm. The top of its skull emerged. A bulging eyeball peered into the world. Noah screamed, *NO!* kicked over the totems, and then woke in a sweat. *It was only a dream. Why did I dream that?* He tried to go back to sleep, but adrenaline coursed through his veins.

Sixty Two

Morning arrived with a stillborn calf. "I'm not surprised," remarked Noah. "That cow was slammed into the tree twice. That's probably what killed it."

"Can we eat it?" asked Emily.

"We can. And we'll use it to make cheese next year." Ann looked at her husband. "Please let me have its stomach." She went to milk the mother.

Noah handed Ann the requested part. "How can you use this to make cheese a year from now?"

"I'll cut out the lower section of its stomach, put this mother's first milk into it, tie it off, and let it sit overnight. Tomorrow, I'll empty it, clean it, salt it, and then hang it on the clothes drying rack on the side of our wagon. Once it's dry, I'll cut it into chunks and jar it in salt. Next summer, we add a few pieces of it to milk. We'll be able to make a lot of cheese."

Eli held the small hide of the calf. "I'll scrape off the hair, tan this, and string it up on my wagon."

Roscoe, Helen, and Sally prepared rib

barbeque. Tom, Alex, Emily, Ehawee, Stephanie, and Adahy cut the rest of the meat into thin slices. Oscar and Nikki packed them in salt.

Sixty Three

Across the prairie, the hinges of an iron door creaked. The warden of the Arkansas Penitentiary barked, "I've told you to knock!" He looked up to see who had so grievously disobeyed his standing orders. "Your Honorable Justice Clemont!" He shot to his feet. "Sir, I didn't know you were coming. I wouldn't have spoken so sharply."

"Why would you think anybody would inform you? This is the only way to determine a penitentiary's true state of affairs. My men will need the keys and unrestricted access."

"Of course!" Rufus Knapp hurried to the large metal box welded to iron bars buried deep inside the structure of the wall.

Micah Clemont, Chief Justice of the United States Supreme Court and the country's highest-ranking judicial official, commanded, "Keys to the records room."

One of the men with Justice Clemont already stood beside Warden Knapp with his hand out. Having studied the prison plans on the way there, he pocketed the key and went off to take command of the records before anything could be altered.

"Infirmary." As soon as the doctor with the

Chief Justice of the United States Supreme Court held the key in his hand, Clemont demanded the next. "Kitchen." He continued as his men scurried away. "Library, outside exercise yard, cell block, guards' quarters, your quarters."

Two days of inspecting all the visible functions proved everything to be as it should be. The third day into the records review Justice Clemont sat at the table that held the scrumptious meal in Warden Knapp's dining room. Corporal Fisher knocked on the door. "Begging your pardon for interrupting your meal, Your Honorable Justice, however, we found a very unusual prisoner release,"

"What is it?" asked Warden Knapp.

The Chief Justice glared at the warden.

"Judge Daniel Hall of Little Rock requested a transfer to The Quarry of a convicted murderer named Joe Smith."

"Daniel Hall. Little Rock. There is something." Justice Clemont thought for a moment. "Oh yes, The Quarry. I asked him to look into a potential uprising at the Hard Labor Camp in Missouri. What do you know about this, Warden Knapp?"

"I didn't like giving him private access to the prisoners or releasing Joe Smith to him, but he had a document stating that you authorized him to take whatever steps he deemed necessary, and he found this to be a step that he had to take. I have the transfer papers."

"I did tell him that. You complied as you should have, but I can't think of a reason to reduce the sentence of a murderer to hard labor." Justice Clemont folded and slid the document into his vest pocket. "That was a good find, Corporal. Keep up the good work. You're dismissed." He transferred a steak from the serving dish to his plate.

Corporal Fisher returned to the records room. "I told you he would want to know. He told me it was a good find."

Dickerson, a penitentiary guard ordered to assist, said, "It was just a transfer."

"I think Judge Hall is as crooked as the letter Z."

I better warn Uncle Daniel.

Sixty Four

Noah, his family, and their animals traveled south along the western side of the Rio Grande. His dreams became terrifying. A translucent horror projected from between his shoulder blades—the sharp teeth of the vile apparition bit into his face. Noah rarely evaded the sharp claws that sunk into his flesh. An eternity of pain passed as he fought and struggled to pull the revulsion from his body. Almost ripping his heart through his back, Noah finally tore his tormenter from his body and flung it as far as he could. Instantly, a more vicious demon formed to torture him.

Afraid to sleep, Noah took the night watches. Dark circles formed under his eyes. Exhausted, he barked about everything. Even the animals avoided him. When he could no longer stay awake, he dreamed of falling backward into Hell, screaming: *Jesus will save me.* Noah fell and fell and fell. He dropped the entire depth of the earth, but help never came. He woke and wept. *Why didn't you help me, Jesus!?*

Just north of the copper mine at Santa Rita del Cobre, Noah sat at the fire and stared into the distance. He barely heard Stephanie reading. Oblivious of his surroundings, he didn't notice Christopher toddling toward him. The child fell and then wailed.

Ann picked up her son. "I've never seen you act this way, Noah. What's wrong? You've been mean for weeks, and now you let our son get injured!"

"He fell so fast. What do you expect of me?" Noah stomped to the other side of the camp. *It's your fault. You expect too much of me. I can't even tell you the truth.*

Ann watched Noah sulk. *God, something is wrong. I don't know what it is, and maybe he doesn't either, but You do. He's suffering. Please help him.* Another dose of nightmares tormented Noah. In the morning, the family left the Rio Grande and went west.

Sixty Five

Two weeks after Justice Clemont's surprise visit to the Eight District Penitentiary, Dickerson knocked at the Hall Mansion in Little Rock. The judge opened the door. "Alger! Come in. What are you doing here?"

"Are we alone?"

Daniel Hall called out, "Honey, I'm going to the courthouse. We'll have one more person for supper tonight."

Judge Hall locked his chamber door. "Speak softly if that would be prudent."

Alger fidgeted.

"Out with it, son."

Judge Hall's nephew wrung his hands, "I'm sure it's nothing, but I thought you should know. Micah Clemont ran a surprise inspection at the prison."

Judge Hall's eyes narrowed. "Aaaaaand?"

"He knows about the transfer of Joe Smith, and he's on his way to The Quarry to find out why you downgraded the sentence of a convicted murderer."

Judge Hall started to sweat. "Are you certain it was Joe Smith?"

"Yes, and he's fixed his flint to find out why. Perhaps you shouldn't be here after he finds out Joe isn't at The Quarry."

"I planned to take Joe to The Quarry when he returned for his pay. This is his fault. He should have come back a long time ago."

"Tell Aunt Pearl that you're going with me on a court-assigned mission. We'll find Joe Smith and bring him in."

"I'm not suffering the elements. I'll tell Clemont that Joe escaped during transport and write up a backdated capture order to prove it. What else can a man do after being overpowered by a murderer?"

Judge Hall informed only one bounty hunter. The capture order authorized three months to find Joe Smith and one month to bring him in. Colt Barrett set off before the sun was up.

Judge Hall carefully wetted the contract and dabbed the ink. *Ann Williams! I hope Joe found you and cut off your head. Then what good will that pretty body of yours be to that heathen?* Once the date 15 May 1842 no longer had the last digit, he slid the paper into his desk and locked the drawer. *Once the paper dries, I'll write a zero in place of the two.*

Sixty Six

The Quarry had not been on Micah Clemont's original list of facilities to inspect. The detour to Missouri added two weeks to his time away from home. *I promised my daughter I would be there this year. I'm going to miss her birthday again.*

Justice Clemont set the inspection of The Quarry into motion. Warden Forest Ronan looked squarely into Micah Clemont's eyes. "I surely do remember Judge Hall. Thank you for sending him. He carried those troublemakers out of here. I haven't had any problems since. Nobody wants to go to the penitentiary, and now they know that will happen if they get out of line."

"And nothing changed when he transferred Joe Smith to The Quarry?"

"Judge Hall never brought anybody here."

"You don't have Joe Smith in custody?!"

"No, sir."

Now, I have to go to Little Rock too! Hall, you better have a VERY good explanation.

Sixty Seven

Below Guadalupe Pass, Noah looked at the lofty peak beyond the gap.

Camped at a large spring, Stephanie read, "He that hath my commandments, and keepeth them, he it is that loveth me: and he that loveth me shall be loved of my Father, and I will love him, and will manifest myself to him. John 14:21"

The words smacked Noah in his face. *Jesus didn't come because I failed to keep His commands. I opened a door with that lie about the Rio Grande. Satan is using it to attack me. I need Jesus more than anything. I have to tell the truth.*

Noah stood up. "I have something to say." He looked at Adahy and then Alex. They nodded. "I lied about the Rio Grande crossing. Alex and Adahy didn't want to go into the river because it was already high when we got to the crossing. I was afraid to stay on the east side of the river because the bandits might have killed us. It was more likely that some of us would die in the water because it was rising, and nobody can fight a river. Anyway, because of me, we lost three cows to the river, and a tree killed two. I should have asked God to lead me, but I didn't. I lied to all of you because I was afraid that my wife would stop loving me if she found out I was stupid and reckless again. I'm sorry. I'm asking all of you and God to forgive me."

Ann hurried to her husband and wrapped her arms around him. "Noah, my husband, my love, I will never stop loving you, never. And just to let you know, I probably would have made the same choice. I also forgive you for lying, and please don't ever again feel that you have to because you are worried about my love. I also forgive you for the horrible way you have been behaving since that lie."

Everybody joined in a ginormous hug and assured Noah that he was forgiven and loved.

Later that night, Nikki lay in his usual place between Ann and Noah. When he thought Ann was asleep, he touched Noah's arm. "Papa, I'm so glad to know that I'm not the only one who makes mistakes. I'm glad to know that a person can be forgiven when they do. Like Mama, I will never stop loving you."

"Thank you, my son. Your love means everything to me."

Ann gently squeezed Noah's hand, which was on her hip. He lightly pressed his hand against her.

They said no words yet spoke volumes of love to each other.

Before long, they all slept. Noah cried out to God in his dream. *God, I need you desperately. I'm helpless and fallen without you. I'm sorry that I sinned against you and my family. Please forgive me. I can't survive without your love.* A cross approached him. Red dots of love pulsed around it before they faded away. *Thank you for forgiving and loving me!* He slept peacefully and soundly.

Sixty Eight

The family woke amidst a herd of wild cattle that had surrounded them during the night. Covered by buffalo hides, Noah and Adahy lay across the backs of their horses. With their bows close to their sides, they casually rode to fat heifers with spinal humps almost a foot high. From under their hides, they shot arrows into the hearts of two beasts. The animals silently dropped where they stood. Not a single cow spooked. While the herd continued to graze, the invisible hunters dropped two more.

They threw off their hides. "WHOO! GET OUTTA HERE!" screamed the men.

The cattle stampeded toward the pass.

The family set up to skin, butcher, and preserve the fallen animals. Roscoe roped a rack together. "Tom, you want to ride to the pass and see if we can get wagons through?"

"Yes, let's," Tom went to saddle Spirit.

They found a hundred-foot-high yellow and brown façade of rock covered with green moss on one side and high mounds of bare rock on the other. Wild cattle drank at a large stone basin surrounded by a thicket of mesquite and Spanish bayonet.

This looks like a yucca, but it's a tree. Roscoe swung his machete into a fifteen-foot-high plant with leaves like swords and central stalks like spears topped with clusters of white bell-shaped flowers. White, great southern butterflies scattered from the flowers. Roscoe felt a sharp pain in his forearm. "Crimony!" Blood dripped from a gash. "Those leaves are sharp! I'm cut right through my shirt. I need to get back to camp."

"Let's go." Tom directed Spirit away from the water. "This is the only way through. We should send a team to start clearing a path while we dry the beeves. Even though it's going to be hot, we'll have to dress in thick leather."

In the valley, Sally cut intestines into sections. "I'm used to this now." She and Helen knelt beside ten-gallon tubs they had set up several yards away from the others. Roscoe and Tom approached the camp as the women brought cleaned guts back into camp. "Eli, will you help me pull the outer layer off this piece?" asked Sally.

"I surely will." Eli got a good grip on the fleshy tissue.

Sally held the inner lining tightly and pulled. "There's a lot of fat on these cows. We'll make yummy sausages."

Helen saw Roscoe's bloody shirt. "Let me see the injury." She looked at the wound on the back side of her husband's wrist. "What happened?"

"A plant with very sharp leaves did it. I need stitches."

Helen kissed Roscoe's hand. "I'll get the sedative and sew it up once you're asleep."

Ehawee fried back-strap medallions in their large cast iron pans. Emily nursed Carol Ann. Ann and Stephanie watched the four toddlers careen around a large netted area inside the wagon circle. Oscar and Nikki played together in the dirt beside the women.

After eating the mid-day meal, Noah, Adahy, Tom, and Alex dressed in buckskins and went to clear a path through the plants.

Sixty Nine

Four mornings in a row, they ate beef sausage crumbles with eggs lain by their chickens and milk from the piebald cow that had given birth to the stillborn calf.

After a long, hot day clearing dangerous plants, Noah rode into the cool below Guadalupe Pass. *It's so much better in the shadow of— Oh! That's what Psalm 91 means!* He informed the family that he wanted to read that night. After eating, Noah picked up his Bible. "I'm going to read Psalm 91, and then I want to tell you what I thought about today."

"All right, Papa," replied Nikki.

"Psalm 91. He that dwelleth in the secret place of the Most High shall abide under the shadow of the Almighty. I will say of Jehovah; He is my refuge and my fortress; My God, in whom I trust. For He will deliver thee from the snare of the fowler, and from the deadly pestilence. He will cover thee with his pinions, and under His wings shalt thou take refuge. His truth is a shield and a buckler.

"Thou shall not be afraid for the terror by night, nor the arrow that flieth by day; nor the pestilence that walketh in darkness, nor for the destruction that wasteh at noonday. A thousand shall fall at thy side, and ten thousand at thy right hand; but it shall not come nigh thee. Only with thine eyes shalt thou behold, and see the reward of the wicked.

"For thou, O Jehovah, art my refuge! Thou hast made the Most High thy habitation; there shall no evil befall thee, neither shall any plague come nigh they tent. For He will give His angels charge over thee, to keep thee in all thy ways. They shall bear thee up in their hands, lest thou dash thy foot against a stone. Thou shalt tread upon the lion and adder: the young lion and the serpent shalt thou trample underfoot.

"Because he hath set His love upon me, therefore will I deliver him: I will set him on high, because He hath known my name. He shall call upon me, and I will answer him; I will be with him in trouble: I will deliver him and honor him. With long life will I satisfy him, and show him my salvation. Psalm 91.

"I want to tell you what I think this means. When I came off the hot mountain, I thought it's better in the shadow. We have to stay close to be in the cooler air. Then it occurred to me that it is also better in the shadow of the Most High. I did something wrong when I lied. Then I moved away from God to hide what I did. When I did that, I had nightmares because I was far away from what keeps me safe. It's just like this Psalm listing all these things that could hurt a person, and it says the person close to God is safe. To be close to God, I have to be obedient. I am protected if I behave as God tells me in this book. That's what being in the shadow of the Most High means: reading about Him, knowing Him, and doing what this book tells me to do."

"I'm glad to know that," declared Oscar.

Nikki echoed the sentiment, "Me too."

Even though brush still blocked the way to the other side, they filled the nets under the wagons with ash tree branches and climbed to the gigantic pool of water in Guadalupe pass. They paused to fill their water containers before they moved deeper into the passageway.

A wagon tongue broke less than a mile across the rough terrain of the pass. Roscoe examined the damaged part. "This is the third tongue that's broken since Raton. We don't have another."

Tom suggested, "We've used a lot of what we brought. Why don't we move the supplies, take whatever parts we can from this wagon, and then leave it?"

Alex laid out their map. "It looks like we're only halfway. Still, the animals would get more days off with one less wagon to pull."

Everybody agreed, so the men chopped mesquite and Spanish bayonet while the women moved the supplies and prepared supper. When the men returned, all the provisions, as well as the hounds, wheels, axles, and other wagon parts, were stored for transport. They nailed the emptied jockey box to the side of a different wagon to serve as another animal feedbox.

Ann wiped axle grease from her hands. "All the hubs are packed again."

"And you've put its linseed trough under a wheel." Noah put his machete in the tool wagon. A breeze ruffled his hair.

So handsome! "I wish I could drag you into this wagon right now," Ann pressed her body to Noah's and sought his lips.

After a long kiss, Noah whispered, "I do too." They walked to the fire holding hands.

As the family ate supper, a frightful wind came up. They positioned the wagons to provide as much protection as possible, drove their herd and flock into the cove, then huddled together in the wagons.

Thirty hours later, the wind lay. Like every morning, Noah dressed and belted his long knife to his side. The family ventured out without their bows or guns to see what had survived the gale.

The Apaches that had secured their cowhide shelters in a well-known outcropping of rock also left their enclosures weaponless.

Both groups suddenly found themselves face-to-face with unknown people. Everybody froze. All their minds took in the positions and possessions of everybody else.

Noah and his family immediately signed. "We mean no harm."

The Apache patriarch realized he didn't have

his usual advantage in an encounter with white people. *Cannot sign instructions. All speaking this way. What kind pale faces these?* He returned the greeting. "We mean no harm. Come to get yucca. You cutting down?"

They're mad that we're destroying their plants. Noah put his hand on the pummel of his knife. "Yes. Want get through pass."

He have weapon. Need be careful, but they have no respect for spirit of the yucca. The Apache asked, "Why you not use?"

"Came from rising sun. Don't know how. You show us for antelope horns?"

"Bring horns," the Apache pointed to a Spanish bayonet lying on the ground, "and yucca."

Noah added, "Everybody in the open. No weapons. Send one woman get tools. I send one woman get horns. What we need?"

"Axe, digging stick, scraping stick, flat stone, pounding stone, baskets, fire, clay pot."

"Show them. My woman bring same thing if we have."

An Apache woman wearing a four-inch wide, intricately beaded necklace retrieved the needed items and placed them at her husband's feet.

Ann looked over the tools. *That digging stick looks like a spear to me.* She went to the out-of-view wagons in the cove.

Potential weapons are gathering. Noah said, "Son, bring Chetan wrapped in a blanket."

Nikki climbed into the wagon with Ann. "Papa wants me to bring his gun in a blanket."

"No, he doesn't. He said no weapons, but it might be a good thing to do."

"When Papa had that spider bite, and you went to hide the bear root, Papa and I named his revolver Chetan and my pistol Otto."

"Oh! We'll have to make it seem like a baby." Ann pinched Chris. Her littlest son did his part of the deception and screamed as Ann rolled a goose-down pillow into the shape of a small child and then wrapped it and the loaded revolver in Adele's blanket.

Nikki went back to Noah, bouncing the bundle. "Chetan was crying."

Ann saw the way the woman held the axe. *She could easily throw that at one of us.* Ann spread a blanket at the feet of Adahy, looked up into Adahy's eyes, and winked. She laid out an iron axe, one of their trading knives, a butcher board, a wooden mallet, a woven basket, a clay dutch oven made by Noah's grandmother, a bottle of matches, tinder, and kindling. She signed, "Be back with wood and a shovel." *I can use a shovel if they make me.* "Nikki, give Chetan to Papa and help me with the wood."

Nikki held out the blanketed bundle. "He doesn't feel good. Rub his belly, Papa."

Noah slid his hand into the blanket and got ahold of his revolver.

Ann and Nikki returned. They sat on the blanket with their yucca and tools before them. "My son like learn," signed Ann.

The Apache woman signed, "Watch and do same." She set to making a fire with a spindle and fire board.

Nikki lit his tinder with a match and had a good fire going before the Apache had a hot spark. He carried a burning branch to their instructor. "For you." He held out the fire.

The woman took the branch and lit her fire. "Come." She walked to a nearby Spanish bayonet stump.

Ann and Nikki followed.

With her digging stick, the Apache scratched at the dirt about a foot from the plant's roots.

Ann placed the shovel on the earth at a nearby plant. She put her boot on it and pushed it into the ground.

The Apache struggled to dig while Ann quickly created a trench around the plant.

"This deep?" asked Ann.

The Apache held up three fingers. "Times deeper."

Ann removed the specified amount of earth, slid the shovel under, and pried the root ball from the ground. "You want Nikki get one for you?" She rested her foot on the shovel.

The woman vigorously nodded her head. When Nikki brought it, she took the shovel with a smile. *This will make digging easy.* She unearthed the yucca root in a tiny fraction of the usual time. "I keep?"

"Maybe."

The woman carried the shovel to her fire

before she went back for the roots. She stood beside her yucca tree with her axe, placed her fur boot on the lower leaves to hold them down, and then hacked at the bottom edge of a leaf.

Ann cut several from her plant with her hunting knife before the woman had three.

Hers much better. The Apache placed three leaves beside her clay pot. "Your pot very beautiful."

"Husband's grandmother made."

"She one of us?"

"Yes, but Quapaw."

That explains how they know sign. "You trade for pot and tools?" The woman pointed to the shovel and then the knife that Ann held.

"Grandmother at rising sun. Never see again. Cannot give this pot. Have different pot. What you have?"

"I show later." *What do I have for these good things?* "Now, wash roots."

Ann looked at the dirty mess. "Sons get two other pots." She pointed at herself and then at the Apache. "Me and you use to wash?"

"Yes." The woman's whole body fell into a relaxed and hopeful position.

"Nikki, you and Oscar, go to our trading supplies. Please get two large iron cooking pots with legs and bring their lids too."

All the Apache jaws dropped when they saw the cast iron dutch ovens. The woman asked, "What you want for these?"

"Buckskin clothes and moccasins little larger than sons." Ann pointed at Nikki and Oscar.

One of their instructor's sons had outgrown his clothes. She had recently made him a new set. "I have only one."

Ann pointed at the group of Apaches who had not moved since they and the pale faces had spotted each other. "If other have, I trade shovel, knife, and pot to you and other."

The Apache called out, "Lozen, come!"

A tall woman walked over. "Yes, Awinita."

The Apache teaching Ann told her cousin what Ann offered.

Lozen nodded her head.

Awinita spoke in Apache. "Ask Baishan for his old clothes and bring them with yours."

Lozen returned with two sets of beaded clothes and moccasins. Ann placed them on her blanket. "Everybody could start working on yucca."

Relaxed and smiling, Awinita looked up at her husband, Tarak. "We trade and work fine."

Tarak looked at Noah.

Noah said, "We smoke peace pipe for good trading and harvesting of yucca. I bring Kinnikinnick and pipe, or you want to?"

"We have no medicine man."

"I am mystery man. I bring. Everybody smokes."

Thirty-four people with their eleven babies sat cross-legged around the two fires. Noah returned wearing his buckskin pants with his mink cape over his shoulders, his mystery man bones in his hair, his medicine bag lying over his bone breastplate, and his moccasins with the ermine tails on his feet. He placed his tongs on a stone beside Nikki's fire, drew a pipe stem from the bag around his neck, and raised it to the east.

Ann signed what her husband said. "Pipe is man, his clear thought, and cunning. Feathers are the winged ones." Noah touched the turkey and eagle feathers, flapped his arms, and circled the group. He stroked the bundle of hair fastened to the pipe stem, "Horsehair, all four-legged ones that walk Mother Earth." He bent down and brought the pipe toward Mother Earth.

After touching the alligator hide wrapped around the wooden tube, he continued his dance. He brought his hands together and then spread them apart as if swimming and parting the water. "Alligator skin is swimming ones. Wood is everything that grows." He raised the pipe stem to the south. "Together with two-legged ones, all are one."

Noah retrieved a pipe bowl shaped like an eagle's claw holding the earth. He raised it in the west. "Bowl is woman and the sun. Both bring life. Claw is eagles the Great Spirit told to watch over this family."

In his right hand, Noah pointed the pipe stem to the east. In his left hand, he held the pipe bowl. He joined the two, and the Calumet was born. He raised it to God—the Great Spirit who lives in Father Sky—then lowered the Calumet toward

Mother Earth. "Our feet rest on Mother Earth. Pipestem reaches into Father Sky. We are bridge between sacred above and sacred below. Earth, sky, the two and the four-legged, the winged ones, swimmers, trees, and all plants are one. Pipe binds us together."

Noah brought forth his pouch filled with the herbs of power: sage, cedar, tobacco, and sweetgrass. He twirled and circled, sprinkled a pinch of the herbs on the ground, put a bit in the pipe bowl, and then raised the pipe to the East. "East is thunderbirds and rising sun. We thank you for each day you allow us walk on Mother Earth."

He repositioned and raised the pipe again. "South, thank you for strength, healing, and new spring life. Spirit of wolf, bring happy and peaceful trading." Noah repeated the plant offerings and circled the fire.

"West, we thank you for spiritual wisdom and spirit helpers. Connect us to spirit world."

At the top of the circle, Noah said, "North, we thank you for endurance and health. Fat Buffalo, sense the troubles, hardships, sadness, joy, and good times to come. Provide layers of fat for us, so we survive coming cold."

In the place where he had begun, he finished, "Circle to spirit world complete. God, in Father Sky, we ask You; hear us."

With his tongs, Noah took a small glowing coal from the fire. He lit the pipe, dropped the ceremonial ember back into the fire, drew in the sacred smoke, and then blew it out to God above. "On this fragrant smoke, we send prayers to Great Spirit in Father Sky. Hear our prayers. I smoke for peaceful trading. Aho."

He offered the Calumet to Tarak.

He is a medicine man. I wonder if he could help Itza-chu. "Great Spirit, I offer thanks for sending this family. I ask for peaceful trading and healing for family." He dropped his offering of tobacco into the bowl before he inhaled.

As the pipe passed, each person drew in the smoke and then sent their prayer to God as they breathed out.

Seventy

Awinita placed a long slender leaf on the flat rock she used when in the pass. With a stone, sharp on one side and rounded to fit in her hand on the other, she cut off its pointed tip with a long narrow strip of the leaf still attached. She carefully scraped long strokes down the length of the narrow strip and then wiped off the green flesh with her fingers. "Keep this." She placed it in a bowl.

The woman flipped the leaf. "And this side." She scraped until all that remained were several long, yellowish fibers attached to the sharp thorn. She picked up the rest of the leaf, removed the flesh from both sides until all the fibers were free, and then held up the torn with the fibers in one hand and the bundle of loose fibers in her other. "Make," Awinita placed her right hand in the basket she had brought from her tent, "into this."

"It's beautiful." Ann ran the sharp side of her knife down her leaf. It cuts the fibers. *That won't work. Duller is better.* She flipped the knife and used the backside. *Much better. Maybe I should use a stone. I don't want to cut myself, either.*

Nikki watched both women. He went in search of a couple of good stones.

Awinita had her three leaves finished before Ann had one. She put a piece of root on the stone. "Peel. Chop. I use you knife?"

Before Ann handed the woman a hunting knife, she held a root. "Little or big pieces?"

Awinita demonstrated. Soon she had a small pile of half-inch pieces of the peeled root. She placed several in the palm of her hand, added a little water, and then squeezed. Suds formed in her hand. "Wash." She set down the root chunks, rubbed her hands together, and then rinsed them in water. "Feel." She held out her hand.

Ann rubbed the back of the woman's hand and then turned it over to see if her palm was completely clean. "Nice. Can keep for later? Or only good right now?"

"Can use now and keep for later. And it clean hair." She picked up the bowl of leaf slime. "This clean too." Many of the plants lying on the ground had long purple fruit. Awinita cut off several with the knife. "We eat now, and we bake some."

Awinita ringed her fire with stones and then packed them with dirt. After she placed a large flat rock in the center and positioned several fruits on it, Tarak placed a huge flat stone with a hole bored in the center over the pit.

While the fruit cooked, Awinita picked young flower stalks, peeled them, cut them into sections a few inches long, and dropped them into the water boiling on Lozen's fire. Awinita led the women as they collected the white yucca flowers amongst the hummingbirds that came to drink their nectar.

In the dark of the night, White yucca moths pollinated the flowers on the living and the cut-down plants.

Lisa Gay

Seventy One

In Maumelle, Colt Barrett went straight to the sheriff's office and showed his contract to Norman Sweeting. "Did Joe Smith come through Maumelle two years ago?"

"That might have been the man who helped rid us of Roy's ghost. Murry and Candy Strong will know. We'll go ask."

Nobody answered the door at Murry Strong's home. *I think this is the week Edwin goes to get the plants. Murry and Candy are probably visiting with Horatio and Esther.* Lawman Sweeting turned from the door. "We'll try one more place."

Smiling sweetly, Esther greeted the men at her door. "Norman, what brings you to my home?"

"First of all, I haven't had a chance to tell you, but I'm happy that you came back to Maumelle, and I'm so glad that Dr. Canfield was able to help you with the pain. The other reason we're here is that this man is looking for Joe Smith. Was that the man at Lucy's with you that night?"

Everybody in Maumelle knew when "that night" was. Esther opened the door wide enough

300

for the two men to enter. "Come in and tell us why you're looking for Joe."

Colt held out his contract with Judge Hall. "He's a wanted murderer."

Candy walked up the hall toward their guests. "Joe seemed like such a nice man."

Once they joined Horatio and Murry in the library, Colt explained. "When Joe Smith was a child, he murdered his father. Two years ago, he escaped when being transported to The Quarry. He killed a stable hand in Little Rock, and there's no knowing what he's done since then."

Murry, his wife, sister, and brother-in-law already knew about Joe. They knew why he had killed his father. They had learned that Joe had not killed the man in Little Rock. However, Judge Hall should never find out that Robert was not dead or that the Joe Smith, who had left Little Rock, was now a man with a new heart. They also knew that Raymond Pence had assumed the identity of Joe Smith. However, if they passed on any of their knowledge, two men with a chance for a good life would be ruined. "He went to Perryville with S.R. and Edwin Snow. They came home and told us that Joe Smith went north from there."

"Much obliged for your help. I'll go to Perryville tomorrow. Is there a place in town where I might get a room?"

"Lucy's Boarding House. It's blue," said Candy.

Seventy Two

It was his daughter's birthday, and he wasn't with her. Micah Clemont angrily paced in Judge Hall's chambers. "Hall, why on God's green earth did you take Joe Smith out of the penitentiary, and where is he?"

"He seemed to be repentant, and he was so young. I thought he should have a chance. I was wrong. He attacked me, overpowered me, and escaped. I've had a bounty hunter searching for him ever since."

"You had to be out of your mind to overturn the sentence of a murderer. It makes no sense. What are you up to, Hall?"

"Nothing, it's just as I said. I hired Colt Barrett to find him. I'll get the contract." Daniel Hall pulled open a drawer. *I hope he doesn't look closely. The change is almost visible.*

Micah Clemont snatched the paper and a cloth from the drawer. "What is this?"

"I lost my blotter. I have to use that."

Micah's eyes narrowed as he looked over the document. "Don't leave Little Rock." He sneered,

302

"JUDGE Hall." He dropped the cloth on the desk then turned on his heel and strode from the room.

Daniel Hall used the cloth to wipe Justice Clemont's fingerprints from his door knob. *I'm too clever for him to figure out what I've been doing.*

Justice Clemont returned to his room and redressed as a commoner. *People talk when they're drunk, but I don't know who won't tell Hall what I'm doing. I'll have to do this myself.* Having learned that Judge Hall always went to the Hillcrest Inn to drink, Micah looked over the patrons as he descended to John Peabody's bar.

Micah spent several evenings playing a mudsill with Little Rock's uneducated working men. He spent just as many days reviewing court records before he staggered into the doggery beside a man who had occupied the same barstool every evening that Clemont had been in Little Rock. "I'm buying anti-fogmatics tonight."

"A man couldn't have a better friend." Bruce McHay hugged Micah before he attempted to sit on a barstool.

Micah held out his hand, pulled Bruce up from the floor, and intentionally slurred his words. "We'll ride that sinner out of town on a rail tonight!"

"No need. Ol' widow Simmons went out of print this morning. Tomorrow, we're gonna put some blue plums into his idea pot and dump Tom Henry into her eternity box without anybody getting peery."

So, that's how he's been doing it! "I don't want to get found out by the wrong person. Anybody new getting involved?"

"Same bunch since the beginning. You're the new one!" Bruce's eyes narrowed.

I can't lose him now. Micah looked at the man beyond his drinking buddy's shoulder and then wailed into the man who happened to be in the wrong place when Micah needed to prove himself as a rowdy. The inn erupted into a rambunctious exchange of fisticuffs.

"You're out of wit, out of money, out of credit, and completely out of manners." Mr. Peabody's son threw one gentleman of four outs after another from the inn.

Bruce landed on his drinking buddy. He and Micah staggered down the road with their arms around each other's waists. "So, who's gonna be with us tomorrow?" asked Micah.

"The whole group Hall got together. We'll be meeting at the Crisp Railyard."

I thought so. Micah helped Bruce into his wife's arms.

"Spent everythin' again, didn't ya? What the children gonna eat now?" Bruce's wife spat into Micah's face. "I hate the whole lot of ya!"

"I didn't, Mavis. Look in my pocket." Bruce fell onto his face as his wife attempted to retrieve their means of survival.

Poor sot. Micah made a hasty retreat.

The next time darkness fell, Micah again made

his way in raggedy clothes. He melted into the back of the small crowd at Crisp Railyard.

A bloody, dark-skinned man knelt in front of Judge Hall.

"Tom Henry, I told you to stay away from our women!" Hall drew a Sharpe 1760.

"I was just lookin'!"

Micah nodded his head. Men behind a locomotive rushed onto the scene. Micah Clemont and the murderous men scattered. At Justice Clemont's orders, all the men were chased but allowed to get away. Captain Cornish told the man they had saved from imminent death, "Keep your eyes down and stop thinking about what you were thinking about."

"Yes, sir. I surely will!"

"And get out of Little Rock!"

The man disappeared into the darkness.

Captain Cornish joined Justice Clemont behind the Insane Asylum. "I told you he was killing everybody he could catch. I doubt Joe Smith overpowered him and escaped. I think Judge Hall sent him after someone who got away."

"Tomorrow, I'll start searching the records for people who passed around the time Hall had an anti-miscegenation case. We'll exhume the graves until we find extra bodies."

Seventy Three

In Guadalupe Pass, both groups remained camped where they were. Inside a cowhide tent, Noah looked at Itza-chu's foot with Tarak. "How long like this? How happen?"

The man with two black toes and a purple foot held up three fingers. "Moons. Tiníléí bite."

"What Tiníléí?"

"Big Lizard." Itza-chu's held his hands about two feet apart. "Black and yellow. Hard circles all over. Breath smell awful. It bite me. Not let go. Tarak kill and pry open mouth with stone. Stay away from them."

"It here." Tarak picked up the tanned hide of a Gila monster.

"If we see any, we stay away. These two toes need cut off." Noah pointed. "I make you sleep. You not feel it. I teach how make sleep potion and other potion to heal rest of foot."

Itza-chu looked at his brother, Tarak, then Noah. "I ever walk again?"

306

"Not soon. Not easy without these. You can learn how. If not take toes away, you die not long time from now."

"What you want to do this?"

Noah looked around the tent. "That quiver and the arrows."

Itza-chu nodded his head. Tarak went to the quiver with a design beaten into the hard cow leather. He picked it up and held it out toward Noah.

"Make fire here, bring both pots my wife gave your family, boil water in one, get a rope, and your shovel. I come back with sleep magic." Noah counted twenty arrows as he carried the payment for his services to his wagon. To acquire maggots, Noah put a hunk of raw cow meat on a large cliff protrusion before returning to his patient. He brought two flasks with ribbons tied on them, a clean towel, a tin cup, forceps, a tourniquet, sutures, a box of bandages, a chair, a large flat stone, and Nikki. "My son help."

Nikki poured fluid from the flask with a yellow ribbon. He covered the bandages he had placed in the empty iron pot and then filled a tin cup with the sedative in the flask with the red ribbon. Nikki passed it to the patient.

Itza-chu drank it straight down. "Tarak, watch them. Do not let them kill me."

"They will not try, but I will watch."

Nikki dropped the surgical implements into the pot of boiling water. Noah propped his knife with the blade end in the water and then positioned a few branches to have only one end in the fire. "Everybody stay away from his blood and whatever comes out of his foot. It lizard poison."

When Itza-chu snored, Nikki washed his hands in antiseptic water, removed the surgical implements from the water, and laid them on a clean towel. Tarak helped Noah rope the patient into the chair with his leg secured. Noah positioned Itza-chu's gangrenous foot on the stone they had put in a depression dug in the dirt. He tied the tourniquet around Itza-chu's ankle, put on gloves, and gave Tarak a pair. "Tarak, hold foot still."

Noah positioned the tip of his knife blade between the big toe and the one beside it, lowered the blade to the black flesh, positioned one hand on the top to hold it between the toe bone and the foot then slammed the handle down. The toe dropped into the depression. "Perfect. Exactly where I wanted." He released the tourniquet, watched the blood flow until it appeared free of pus, and then retied it. "Give me one of the burning branches."

Nikki handed his father the requested item.

Noah cauterized the blood vessels and then looked up at Tarak. "Now the next." Noah removed the other dead toe. He seared the blood vessels closed with the burning wood after all the visible poison had flowed out. "Forceps and sutures." Noah pulled the flesh and held it together with forceps. "Nikki, I would let you suture this, but I don't want you to get this poison on you. Would you hold the forceps?"

"All right, Papa."

Noah sewed the skin and dropped all the surgical tools and his knife into the boiling water before he wrapped antiseptic-soaked bandages around the foot. He removed his gloves and put them in the hole. "Tarak, put gloves in. Help pick up chair and move away from poison." They moved Itza-chu. Noah looked into Tarak's eyes. "We not want poison on anybody or anything. Bury hole, put boulder over, move tent after we get tools."

For days, the yuccas felled to make a path for the wagons were dissected, scraped, eaten, or dried for later use. The wild cattle killed by Apache men were processed. In the evenings, Stephanie read the Bible. The rest of the family signed what she read. Everybody heard God's words.

When the last Spanish bayonet that blocked the wagons fell, each Apache family owned an iron dutch oven and two knives. Every one of them owned an antelope horn. Awinita and Lozen also owned a shovel.

Even though Itza-chu had not needed the maggots, they explained how to use the tiny creatures, taught how to find the necessary plants, and how to make the two potions. Itza-chu's foot was almost the same color as the rest of him, but they instructed them to find and put leeches on his foot if it started to become purple again.

Noah rode away with the bow and arrow-filled leather quiver. The family had ten variously-shaped, large black and tan woven yucca containers stuffed full of yucca twine, and each of them wore newly made yucca-fiber shoes. Oscar and Nikki waved goodbye to the children who had played and worked with them.

Seventy Four

Years of hostility between the Tipai-Ipai people and the Mexicans erupted at the western sea. Settlers from the surrounding land fled to the fort. The small contingent of ragtag soldiers stationed at the San Diego Presidio possessed only two cannons, one spiked with an iron stake and the other without a carriage. Doubting that they would hold off the swarm of angry natives, soldiers and settlers loaded their muskets as the women and children dashed into the inner rooms.

The barred gate held fast as the Tipai-Ipai laid siege. Unable to breach the walls, the Tipai-Ipai and their allies occupied and patrolled the surrounding land. Any invader caught west of the Colorado River was to be put to death. The Mexican men, women, and children trapped inside the presidio prayed that help would reach them via their seaport.

Seventy Five

Night had long since fallen when Colt arrived at Adeline's Inn in Perryville. He saw the sign on the back wall that said to knock on the door under the stairs. He made his way past the dining tables and did so. A small square in the door opened. "I need a room," said Colt.

The man on the other side said, "Two bits for a room and breakfast." He slipped his hand between the bars of the opening and then counted the coins before he handed Colt a key. "Room three at the top of the stairs. Breakfast will be at six in the morning. My wife is a wonderful cook. You'll enjoy the meal."

Adeline hummed as she made coffee. Her happiness made her a better cook than she had been even before Raymond Pence had been in her life. She chopped sausage and scraped it from the cutting board into a large skillet. Zane came into the kitchen and kissed her cheek. "Good morning, wife. What are you making? The kitchen smells even better than usual."

"Since we have a full house, I made sausage gravy and biscuits. This batch of sausage you made at the farm is the best I've ever eaten."

The coffee and sage sausage aroma quickly brought the patrons to the dining tables. Colt swung his leg over the back of his chair and plopped into the seat. "I'm looking forward to whatever is cooking in the kitchen."

"Adeline makes the best breakfast money can buy. It's even better than food our mama might cook."

"While we're waiting, maybe you can help me."

"I'll try. What do you need?"

"I was told that a man named Joe Smith came through here. I'm trying to find him."

Zane almost gagged on the spit in his mouth. "I don't remember the names of all our guests. I can look in the registration book. Do you know when that might have been?" Zane walked toward the bar. "Why are you looking for this man?"

Colt pulled out his contract and laid it on the counter. "He's an escaped killer, and I'm gonna bring him in."

Zane read the paper. *Dirty, rotten, double-crossing liar.* He scowled. *He's as bad as any of the men in that prison and worse than many.* "So this Judge in Little Rock says this man, Joe Smith, escaped, and now he wants him dead or alive." He flipped through the Inn's registration book. "Here he is. I remember him now. He stayed a few days. He said he was looking for an Indian and a white woman and that Judge Hall wanted him to bring back their heads."

"Did Joe say where he was going from here?"

"He was also looking for a Spaniard and a white woman. He said he was right behind them and figured they would cross the Arkansas at Point Remove Creek. He must have gone up to the ferry."

Adeline came into the room with two large coffee pots. "Zane, please pass out the cups, plates, and silverware then carry the gravy pots to the tables."

"I'll get right at it." Zane reached under the counter for a tray of cups. "Good luck to you, mister. I hope you find him."

"I think I will. He's been leaving a trail a mile wide. It's unusual for an escaped convict to do that."

"Something doesn't seem right about it, does it?" Zane went off to do as asked by the woman he loved.

At Point Remove Creek, the Ferryman remembered Joe Smith very well. "I'm not surprised that he's a convict. Joe Smith was the rudest man I have ever taken across the river. A bad storm was coming in, and he did NOT even offer to help me get my ferry out of the river. He raced off down Military Road going west."

Seventy Six

The Oakland Cemetery groundskeeper disturbed the dead for the sixth night. "This is too much work. It ain't easy digging this much dirt. I don't even know why. I'm not doing it again."

Captain Cornish enlightened the man, "Then you'll have to hire somebody if we have to exhume another grave."

The shovel broke a pine board in the hole beneath the gravestone marked:

Gideon Hess

September 15 1799- August 29 1835

You passed too soon, beloved son.

"We're at it. It won't take long now." The gravedigger put his shovel under the broken wood and pried it up. "Good Lord! How did that get in there?!"

"You won't need to dig up another. Go to Peabody Inn and knock at room 1. Tell the man inside that we found one then come back here," ordered Captain Cornish.

When Justice Clemont and Sheriff Taylor

arrived at the graveyard with a wagon, the grave digger asked, "Am I in trouble? I don't know how that other body got in there."

The sheriff assured the frightened man, "You are not. Finish digging it up."

The coffin with all its contents was transported to the town jail and locked into a cell.

The morning after the coffin with two bodies had been exhumed, Sheriff Taylor, Justice Micah Clemont, and Captain Cornish knocked on Judge Daniel Hall's door. His servant opened it. "Shall I get the Judge?"

"Yes," replied Sheriff Taylor.

Judge Hall came to the front door, saw which three men were there, slammed the door, threw the bolt, and sprinted across his house. He threw open the back door and ran straight into the arms of two Little Rock deputies.

The three from the front rounded the house corner. "Daniel Hall," informed Sheriff Taylor, "you are under arrest for the murder of Samuel Adams and for aiding in the escape of the murderer Joe Smith."

Seventy Seven

Well over a thousand miles to the west, the wagons descended a long, rough defile to a wide valley of gamagrass filled with thousands of wild cattle at a spring. They pushed through the herd toward the water. A raging, pure back Andalusian bull charged full speed toward the lead wagon. "Shoot it!" screamed Sally as she braced for impact.

While Nikki and Oscar shot their pistols, bullets flew from Roscoe, Alex, and Tom's rifles. The Lefaucheux revolver bullets fired by Emily, Ann, Stephanie, and Helen sunk in, but Adahy, Eli, Ehawee, and Noah's arrows protruded from the bull. The animal, determined to end the intruders, did not die until its collision with the wagon broke its neck. The corner of the wagon dropped.

Roscoe surveyed the rest of the massive herd before he called out, "Reload and stand guard while we replace this wheel."

Tom cautiously made his way through the pressing cattle to the closest spare. "The rest of them seem calm enough. I wonder why that one charged us."

"We'll never figure that out." Roscoe jacked up the wagon while Tom brought the replacement.

Eli quickly spilled the guts from the downed bull. "I wish it was safe to stay here and skin it. We'd get a huge piece of leather."

"We're here until we can move, so skin it." Tom set the wheel.

Noah, Alex, and Adahy axed off the legs and head. Eli quickly and expertly sliced the hide from the rest of the carcass and laid it on a wagon seat. He scraped away traces of flesh and fat while the other men hacked the skinned carcasses into manageable pieces and loaded them onto the seat floors.

The women created what they hoped would be a safe path to the water with a row of wagons joined by hundred-foot nets and a second row ten feet over. The dogs drove their animals through the corridor into the spring. While they drank, the family took the wagons around the spring and made a passageway out the other side. They swapped animals so those harnessed could get a drink while the people filled water containers and prayed to escape without losing any of their cattle to the wild herd.

As they traveled away, Nikki and Oscar counted. Once beyond the cattle bunched around the spring, Nikki reported to Noah. "Papa, we added five black ones with big humps on their necks and two calves."

Oscar stated his conclusion. "So we didn't lose any. I wonder why they came with us."

Noah thought for a moment. "Maybe they smell the bull in the wagon."

Ann bounced Chris and Joy on her hips. "Maybe you should hang its rear end from the wagon. We might gather more."

"We certainly can try it." Noah cut the suggested parts from the hind quarters and carried them away.

Sally set up their drying racks. "We didn't need this one, but we shouldn't waste what we kill."

"It killed itself." Ann set to helping Sally with the mountain of meat.

Emily made a fire pit, roasted yucca fruit, and a back muscle of the bull.

Because they needed a few days close to the water to preserve the meat, they set up the stove. Helen baked bread.

Stephanie and Ehawee picked cloudberries on the masses of low scrubs growing nearby. Stephanie popped a raspberry-looking berry into her mouth. "The red ones are sour."

Ehawee tried a few of the bright gold berries. "The yellow ones are sweet and juicy. I think they're the ripe ones."

Stephanie sampled a few. "You're right. That's good. Most of them are golden. They'll be delicious in milk."

Ehawee stood up. "Oscar, Nikki, bring baskets and help!"

More wild cows joined their herd as they gathered berries and dried the beef. The family ground the dried meat and made pemmican with numerous cloudberries and the bull's copious fat hump. They wrapped the mixture in the hairless rawhide that they convinced Eli was its best use.

Adahy threw beef scraps to the dogs and surveyed the land ahead. "I don't see animals ahead. I think it will be a long way to the next water hole. We should fill up." He sat to eat the morning's berries, bread, milk, and steak.

They took the wagons back to the spring, gathered all the water they could carry, and then departed with more than a hundred pounds of newly made pemmican and their yucca baskets full of cloudberries. The dogs brought a dozen Andalusian cows, their four calves, and the rest of the animals.

Twenty-seven dry miles and three days later, they reached the San Pedro River. After making an easy crossing, they caught a big mess of black-speckled, yellow Apache Trout.

Seventy Eight

Every person Colt spoke with at Spadra Bluffs had terrible things to say about Joe Smith. "Two people died trying to save the mill he set on fire," said the innkeeper. "If you catch him, bring him here for trial."

At the store, the owner reported, "I think he went up to Harmony. If you catch him, you'd be better off shooting him. He is a mean and surly fellow."

Later that day, Colt went back to the store. "I don't see a road going north from here."

"Did you notice Spadra Creek?"

"How could I miss it?"

"Stay on the west side and follow it north. You'll end up in Harmony. I'm sure he didn't find any loose women up there. I told him to go to Little Rock."

A day later, Colt rode into Harmony. Sheriff Smitty Wyman didn't care for the prying of Colt Barrett. *Judge Hall sent a bounty hunter! What is wrong with that man? Why can't he leave them alone?*

Everybody in Harmony knew that the man

who had come to their town posing as Joe Smith was Raymond Pence, the man who had shot Sebastian. Sebastian would have died if Noah hadn't happened along and saved his life. Ray had also kidnapped and then beaten Lola almost to death. Sebastian and Lola had received a letter stating that the man had died. They were overjoyed but telling Colt what they knew about Joe Smith could lead the bounty hunter to the Williams sisters. They feared the bounty hunter was after them as well, and the townsfolk didn't know how far their friends had gone.

Colt stood in Carpenter's Mercantile. Earl and Clara reported that they knew nothing about Joe Smith, just as everybody else in town had told him. Colt returned to Spadra Bluff.

He was unsure if he was going in the correct direction, but it was only May 31st. Not accustomed to failure, he headed west on Military Road, hoping to pick up new clues.

Seventy Nine

For two weeks, the Williams sisters wound through the lush valleys between the stony hills west of Rio San Pedro. As they started north along the eastern side of Rio Santa Cruz, Colt Barrett arrived at Fort Gibson in Indian Territory. He stood in the office of Colonel Howland with his contract in his hand. "I've been looking for a particular escaped murderer. If I don't find him, I will have failed."

"We don't ask questions. We sell supplies and keep the peace with the Indians. Rarely do any of us know the names of the people who come here, but let me take a look at your paper."

"To tell you the truth, after everything I've been told about this man, I can't understand why Judge Hall was transferring him to The Quarry." Colt held out the contract.

"Judge Hall!" Colonel Howland read the name. "Joe Smith!" He smiled. "Mr. Barrett, I have good news. You have not failed. Joe Smith was here. I threw him into the stockade for fighting with one of my soldiers. After a few days, I let him go but banned him from my fort. He crossed the Neosho."

"That doesn't mean I have found him."

"Some of my men came across his frozen body and buried him. You can tell Judge Hall that Joe Smith no longer needs to be captured, and you don't have to put up with that terrible man taking him back to Little Rock."

Eighty

A week of easy travel brought Colt to Van Buren, Arkansas, with a sealed letter from Colonel Howland. Far to the west, the route of Noah and his family proceeded in and out of dry ravines that prevented access to Rio Santa Cruz. The occasional seeps they found did not provide enough water. Their thirsty sheep and cattle bleated and lowed incessantly every uphill mile through the mesquite and agaves taller than those they had encountered while traveling through the Sonoran desert below them.

When the last wagon arrived at the top of the bluffs above the river, Tom's voice rang out, "Halt! Clouds are gathering. Put out everything you can to gather the rain, and load the empty wagons with all the dry wood you can find."

Stephanie prayed, "God, give us the storm we need to recover."

They dug trenches they hoped would puddle gallons of the life-sustaining liquid and set the wagon covers to funnel rain into their barrels and ten-gallon tubs.

Helen danced in the gentle rain that drenched her. "Thank You."

Roscoe joined his wife for a few minutes of joy before the heavy clouds rolled in and shrouded the mountain in darkness. The downpour continued through the night and the following day. The animals drank from the trenches. The people dipped water from the rain barrels attached to the sides of their wagons and drank their fill. When the barrels filled, they transferred the rain to their water mattresses. The dogs kept the animals together in the thunder, lightning, and rain and took turns sleeping in the empty wagons.

The second morning, the men left their wagons fully armed. Only their well-hydrated animals surrounded them in a wet world of ponderosa pines and Douglas firs. Roscoe and Helen prepared a breakfast of coffee and flapjacks made with the last of their flour. It had been days since they'd had water for anything except cooking and drinking. Lack of clean diapers had become a significant problem. Ann, Stephanie, Ehawee, and Sally washed and hung dozens of them on the lines attached to the sides of their wagons.

Hours after the sun rose, the wagons covered in rectangles of white cloth proceeded along what appeared to be a road. They made good progress with the revived piebalds and Andalusians they had trained to pull the wagons.

Alex scouted ahead. In the late afternoon, he came across an adobe house surrounded by reed huts and dozens of chopped-down agaves lying about. He called out, "Hola amigos en la casa!"

Two drunken men stumbled out the front door. A boy snuck out the back, jumped on a horse, and rode away in the woods along the side of the road. Alex noticed rifle barrels just inside the windows. He assured the men who could barely stand, "I am a friend passing by. What is this place? I will trade with you if you have flour."

"You don't need to know what we are doing. We only have enough of anything for ourselves. Go into Tuscan and buy what you need."

"How far is that?"

"Keep on this road for two days."

"Is this the only way?"

"Yes, and you must go through the town if you are going to the Gila River." *But the soldiers at the presidio will capture you.*

"Thank you for the information." Alex rode back the way he had come.

A drunkard yelled, "The town is the other way!"

Back at the wagons, Alex reported what he had come across. "… It's probably not safe to go past them."

"Let's stop here. Noah can sneak over and find out if we can," suggested Ann.

Noah mounted Eyanosa. "I need Alex to listen to what they say. Remember, it will take a long time to do this. We probably won't be back before tomorrow. Wait here."

Ann handed her husband a flask with a red ribbon. "This is probably the solution. I wish I could go home and thank Mina for causing us to learn how to make this."

"Mina did a horrible thing no matter what good came from it. She tried to kill you, you have the scar on your collarbone to prove it, and she almost killed Christopher before he was even born."

"She ended up being a decent person, and I understand why she loved you so much because I do."

Noah kissed Ann's lips. "I love you to the moon and back, mother of my first and soon-to-be fifth child. I don't know why Eli and I thought it wouldn't be safe for you or Stephanie to travel while pregnant. Nothing can stop either of you."

Nikki stood beside Ann and looked up. "Papa, teach me how you find out about things."

"The first lessons need to be safer."

Noah and Alex did not approach the house from the road. Alex mimicked Noah's slow, careful, winding path through the mesquite and towering saguaro cacti until they lay in a clump of plants at the side of the house.

Men in the front yard chopped the leaves from the dug-up agave plants. One of the men picked up an agave heart. "This batch will fill up the last hut. You start the fire. I'll carry these in."

The second man had already walked toward the hut with a heavy agave core. "After I get it going, I'll carry the roasted ones into the house to be crushed."

The boy who had left the adobe house on Alex's first visit cantered from the direction of Tuscan with a man by his side.

The man stopped in the yard. "Esperanza's son told us a man was here asking questions."

"Yes, but we didn't tell him anything."

"I didn't pass anybody."

"He went back the way he came."

"Did you hide the mescal you've already distilled?"

"We buried twenty jugs beside the saguaro with all the arms, but Esperanza has two barrels fermenting that are too heavy to move."

The man with rations from Tuscan got off his horse. "Let's eat first. Then I'll help you dump it."

"It's almost ready to distill, and there's so much. Paco will line us up in front of his firing squad if we waste it."

"You're right. I'll see if I can find the man and get rid of him."

Alex signaled to Noah to move away from the house. At a safe distance, he reported what he had learned. "...We can't let him find our family. I don't see a way to get the sedative into all of them. Let's set an ambush and catch him."

Noah watched the man tie the horses to pegs sticking out of the adobe wall and then go into one of the reed huts. Ten minutes later, all three men went into a second hut. "Maybe I can get the sedative into something. See if you can dig up one of those jugs."

Alex slithered to the loose dirt beside the saguaro. Noah squirmed to the horses. When the men entered the third hut, Alex dug with the spade he had learned always to carry.

Noah peaked into the window. A woman and the boy stirred the goop in two large barrels. A still spanned the entire wall across the room, a large table with several chairs sat in the center, and two men lay asleep on the floor of the one-room house. Noah noted which hole the saddle bag buckle was using before he opened it. Inside, several large cornhusk-wrapped parcels were wedged beside two jars of red sauce. Noah carried the jars to the back of the house, poured some of the liquid over his finger, and touched his tongue to it. Tamale sauce. He emptied more into the dirt and replaced it with the sedative. The rest of his flask went into the other jar.

As Noah slid the jars into the bag, the men came out of the hut. He dropped to the ground and crawled to the backside of the building.

"Bring the food in ten minutes," said the newly arrived man.

The boy came out of the house, removed the packages and jars from the saddlebag, and handed them to the other men. "Put these in the roasting hut to warm up."

I don't think he thought about the fact that the bag was open. Noah still worried that his plan was ruined.

When the men heard the activity in the house cease, they took the food inside. Esperanza had set seven places. She put tamales on each plate and covered them with hot sauce. "Who wants mescal?"

"I do!" replied all of them.

She filled six cups with liquor and one with water. "You know I won't let you have any," said Esperanza to her son. "This sauce is extra tasty today!"

Her son agreed. "May I have another tamale?"

"Maria made a lot. You can have more."

Before they finished the food, all of them had crashed to the floor or dropped to the table. Noah and Alex laid out the bedrolls and dragged everybody onto one. Alex commented, "We probably didn't put them on the right pallets."

"We'll fill our bottles with the two we're taking and leave their empties when we come past. They'll think they drank too much to care." Noah dropped the feet of the last man.

The wagon train approached the mescal distillation house. At the same speed as his initial visit, Noah, Nikki, and Oscar followed the path Noah had previously taken. He told the boys, "We go this slowly, so our motion doesn't draw attention. Most things, including humans, notice movement. If birds, horses, or something senses us, it will change its behavior and possibly alert the people. These men were too drunk to have noticed, but you don't know what the conditions will be beforehand, so always assume the worst. Did you wipe out our tracks like I showed you?"

"Yes, but make sure we did it well, Papa."

Noah examined the soil and mesquite. "I can tell, but most people wouldn't."

"How can you tell?" asked Oscar.

"This leaf is pointing in the opposite direction, and I see the back-and-forth motion of the dirt. You should pick up some soil and sprinkle it." Noah demonstrated and then dropped a few dead leaves as the finishing touch.

"Oh! That is better!" Oscar dropped another few mesquite leaves. "I like this!"

"Me too," Nikki covered the subsequent steps of their path with sprinkled dirt and leaves.

At the house, Noah and the boys peeked into the window and verified that everybody was unconscious. "Look for the place I poured the sauce on the ground. It's along the back of the house."

Nikki finally declared, "I can't see anything, but this ground feels a little gushier. This is the place."

"I agree," said Oscar.

Noah knelt beside the boys. "Very good, you are right."

"Will I be like you someday?" asked Nikki.

"I think so."

"I'm glad." Nikki hugged Noah's neck.

"I'm happy that you want to." Noah stood. He looked into the window again before he led the boys past.

As the wagons and animals passed, the people examined the entire area, went into the house, and gathered the tamales still wrapped in cornhusk packages untouched by the sauce. Noah placed the two empty mescal jugs on the table. "We don't need to worry about tracks around here. There are so many going every direction nobody will notice a few extra, and it doesn't matter that our wagon train passed because nothing will seem to be missing." He left the ground by the cactus disturbed. "They'll think they dug one up and drank it."

"We need meat. The soldiers at the presidio left to put down the Papago and took all our animals. We only have flour, cornmeal, eggs, cigars, wheat, cheese, habanero peppers, and salt."

"We will trade three wagons and ten steers for a fifty-pound barrel of cornmeal packed with 100 eggs, another with wheat flour and another 100 eggs, three wheels of cheese, twenty strings of peppers, two bushels of salt, two dozen bushels of wheat, four bushels of whatever fresh vegetables you have, and 200 cigars."

"Three wagons and fifteen beeves."

With three fewer wagons, we'll need eighteen fewer steers. "Then double everything."

I could get much corn from the Apaches for mescal. "Do you have mescal from the house on the road?"

"No, we passed a house, but everybody was asleep."

"We will do this if you have mescal to trade."

I don't want Paco to find out that we took any of his mescal. "We have whiskey."

"Let me see."

Eli heard the word and got a gallon of it. He handed it to the Mexican, who took a swig.

"Three wagons, twenty beeves, and four of these."

Four is all we have. "Three wagons, eighteen beeves, two jugs whiskey, and oxen harnesses for the three wagons."

"Agreed."

Some of the townsfolk took the worn-out steers that Roscoe brought over. As others loaded the last of the traded supplies into the travelers' remaining empty wagon, three soldiers from the presidio approached the newcomers with a message from the commandant.

The negotiator read the paper in his hand. "Surrender twenty-five cattle and an equal number of sheep in exchange for unmolested passage on the main road." Alex translated the message for the others and added that most of the soldiers were not in Tuscan.

"No," declared Noah.

The soldier who held the paper opened his eyes wide in shocked disbelief. Thrusting a pointing finger, the man informed those resisting him, "We will not allow you to disrespect the people of Sonora. We will take everything."

The hand gestures and tone of the soldier's voice made it obvious what he had said. Eli shot the paper from the man's hand. Noah sent an arrow between the red swag hanging from the pompom at the top to the brim of the tall hat perched on the soldier's head. Both men barked, "NO!"

The other twelve family members drew revolvers, pistols, and rifles from under the wagon canvases. Fourteen armed people stood ready to defend their possessions.

Not these people. "Would you trade goods for animals?"

Alex passed on the soldiers' new strategy. "Now, they request a trade. We have more steers we can give up from those broken wagons we abandoned. It would be better if we didn't have to worry about them coming after us."

"And we could use more ammunition. Tell them that we will discuss a trade as we travel north."

At the fort, Roscoe gave the soldiers the twenty worse steers still in their possession. Alex received 100 rifle balls, 24 flints, 4 horns of powder, 1 jammed cannon, and 5 cannon balls.

The commandant watched his much-needed supplies ride away. *The Sonoran desert will kill them. When the rest of my men get back, we'll find them and take everything they have.*

Eighty One

The path from Tuscan was difficult, but the commandant had seemed less than sincere in his assurance of friendship. Noah wasted no time as he hurried his family down a dry creek bed of deep sand then through thickets of mesquite growing in the clay, baked hard by the scorching summer heat.

They came across no water the first day or the second. Sweat poured from Adahy. "We can't sweat like this. The moon is full, and it's cool at night. We should keep going like we did last year when the water hole was dry. If we come to water, we'll stop. If not, we should continue until we find a place out of the sun."

Ehawee dripped beside her husband. "And I'm still worried about the soldiers in Tuscan. I want to get far away as quickly as we can."

Everybody agreed, so they marched across the parched clay plain until the early morning when they found themselves between a set of singular peaks. Roscoe stopped the column. "The eastern mountain will shade us in the morning and the western in the afternoon. After we rest, we can look for water in the mountains."

Sally commanded the dogs. "Hold."

They unharnessed the animals, climbed into their wagons, tied scarves over their eyes, and lay down to sleep. When Noah woke, there were no animals near the wagons. He looked across the flat land and saw them in a group about a mile away. *Why did the dogs keep them over there?* He trotted through Artemisia. *This looks like a kind of mugwort. We need to harvest some.* The herd stood in a shallow depression. *They probably got a little water before they trampled it into mud.*

Noah returned to the wagons. The rest of the family was awake, so he told them about the plants and the mud pit. Adahy and Tom left in search of a better water source. Everybody else emptied the fifty-eight bushel baskets they had gotten in Tuscan, sewed calico cloth inside them, or dug holes and forced them into the mud. The water slowly seeped through the fabric.

When the first basket contained enough water, Eli yelled, "Come!" The dogs ran to him. "Drink." The dogs lapped up the water they needed to continue to work.

It was difficult to prevent the animals from ruining the baskets while the water slowly gathered, but the dogs kept the thirsty beasts back until their turn. Roscoe led a cow to a full basket. "I wish we had traded more cattle. It's going to be hard to find enough water in this desert."

With babies in cradleboards on their backs, the women gathered sage. Adele, however, refused to be trapped. She pulled at plants beside Ann.

"Come." Ann took Adele's hand and walked

away from the rest of the people. Ann pulled up her dress and squatted. Adele closely watched as Ann did her business then she pulled down her diaper and did the same. "Good girl!" Ann cleaned up, waited for her daughter to finish, and then wiped the child's bottom. "You are so smart. I hope you keep doing that." Ann hugged and kissed Adele repeatedly. "Good, good girl! If you are out of diapers before the next one is born, that would be so wonderful. Maybe all three of you will be."

They found no other water, but they had a wagon full of drying sage. Except for the dogs, chickens, and the cat, which had much less, every animal drank a basket's worth of water and ate a quart or two of wheat. Cleaned diapers again hung on the wagons.

When the moon rose, they rolled out and marched through the night. Artemisia and mesquite were the only other life within many miles of their path. When the sun rose, they were far from the second set of mountain peaks they saw ahead. There was no place to get out of the coming blistering sun, so they trudged on through the day.

They believed they would reach the mountains halfway into the night, so they doled out a ration of water at nightfall—with a double portion going to Emily because she was nursing Carol Ann— then resumed travel.

The mountains were farther away than they had appeared, but they reached them before morning. Hoping to find water, the men immediately set off. A thick stand of saguaro spanned the plane between the peaks. Lesser long-nosed bats sat on and ate the pulp of popped-open fruits that grew high on the cacti. Sally ducked as a bat swooped over her head. "I wonder. If they can eat the fruit, can we? It would be some moisture."

Stephanie picked up one of the green-skinned —tapered down at both ends but fat in the middle— fruit with bright red insides that lay on the ground. "I'll give this to a chicken and see what happens." The hen pecked apart and gobbled up the fruit.

"Look at this." Helen stood over a fallen, many-armed, seventy-foot-long cactus. She swiped some red pulp from a fruit and touched it to her tongue. "Oh! This is sweet and tasty!"

The animals munched the fruits lying on the dirt and ate the surrounding cacti that had not reached a foot in height. The cat, Whiskers, bounded after a pack rat it discovered nibbling fruit, and the dogs chased a jack rabbit.

Since none of the animals or Helen exhibited any ill effects, Helen chewed up and swallowed a whole bite of the sweet pulp with thousands of tiny embedded black seeds. After another wait, she felt slightly revived from her thirst. She extracted a long rib from a dead saguaro and used it to chase away the white-winged doves that had arrived with the dawn and harvested fruits she could reach.

Everybody in the camp got a rib from the dead

saguaro and gathered the pods. They filled themselves and then wrote a note for the men to eat the big pile of the harvest they left for them.

Oscar placed the paper on the saguaro fruits. "I want to learn how to write messages."

"I do too," Nikki climbed into the wagon where Ann's other children slept.

"I'll teach you." Sally then ordered the dogs. "Hold."

They slept with their mouths and sticky fingers stained saguaro pink.

Having finally located water, the men returned only to discover that the cacti had hydrated the camp's inhabitants. They tucked their full canteens into a wagon and ate saguaro fruit. People and animals alike were worn out from the four-day sixty-mile trek from Tuscan and slept soundly in the shade of the mountains.

Late in the day, they gathered thousands of saguaro fruits and chopped the ribs of the dead cactus into firewood. "This has a bird's nest in it." Emily salvaged a cup-like object from the remains. "They must have dug into the cactus, and the plant scabbed over the exposed area."

Stephanie looked at the hard bowl. "I saw a woodpecker making a hole in a cactus."

"Do you see any more?" asked Tom. "We can use them to scoop water." He looked for more fallen cacti.

The basin the men found at the base of the mountain contained the water from the recent untimely rain. They and the animals drank every drop. Then, by the light of the moon, they left the twin peaks and headed toward what looked like cottonwood trees.

Cottonwoods did line the Gila River ten miles from the saguaro stand. Pima Indians saw the wagon train. Accustomed to trading with Spaniards, they swarmed from their villages, speaking Spanish and what sounded like English but wasn't. Noah and Adahy signed that they were friends and would like to trade as Alex informed the friendly people the same in Spanish.

The mob of people excitedly agreed. Tom and Roscoe set out a sample of what they had on a blanket. The premade clothes, cloth, thread, sewing kits, and beads thrilled the Pima. They offered sweet corn, water and musk melons, crookneck squash, pumpkins, mesquite beans, chickpeas, fresh clams, clams in brine, and Saguaro wine and syrup stored in fired clay jars sealed with clay plugs.

Tom and Roscoe did not have enough to satisfy the desires of two thousand Pima. To have trade goods for the remainder of their journey, they offered only three-quarters of their inventory. The people who offered the most goods won the bidding war.

Speaking Spanish, the chief offered Alex advice. "Go west beside the Gila. Drink river water. Cross Santa Cruz. Walk four days straight west back to Gila. From there, do NOT drink from river or eat anything around it all the way to Rio Colorado because salt everywhere."

The cattle drank the most water and didn't do well eating desert plants, so they traded twelve steers and one wagon to the Pima for them to carry produce from the saguaro stand between the mountains to their villages. Alex acquired more vegetables, forty-eight bushels of shelled corn, and the privilege to cut and fill two wagons with grass.

For days, the animals grazed on lush grass and drank river water while Ann, Stephanie, Emily, Ehawee, and Helen dried vegetables under the intense sun and heat of the desert. They gathered thousands more saguaro fruits, learned how to grind their seeds into flour, make the fruit into syrup and jam, and the pulp into lightweight toasted cakes.

With Chris on her back and Adele by her side, Ann helped make pumpkin molasses. As she chopped pumpkins, Adele removed her diaper and proceeded to relieve herself. *I don't want to discourage her.* "Good girl." Ann held out her dress to make a curtain around the child. Ann cleaned Adele's bottom when she finished and then took away what her child had deposited on the ground.

As if nothing out of the ordinary had happened, the Pima women continued to cook pumpkin and toast the seeds. Once the flesh tenderized, they poured the liquid into a separate pan to boil and placed the cooked pumpkin meat aside. Ann stirred and stirred as the juice reduced.

Once thick strings started to form in the dark syrup, she poured it into her mason jars and sealed them with melted beeswax. As they had done with the saguaro fruits, Ann pressed the pumpkin pulp into bars with added ginger and cinnamon.

Roscoe built a bonfire on the clay ground. He heated the cannon and hammered it until the jammed ball came out. After everything cooled, he measured the bore and the other five cannon balls. "These will fit. What should we do with the big one?"

Tom test-fitted the cannon in the carriage he built. "Maybe we can trade it."

Nikki and Oscar opened new binders full of unused paper, pencils, and erasers. Sally toted her most recent binder of notes about the flora and fauna they had come across since she started the procedure at Fletcher Creek in 1840. "On the first sheet, draw a grid. You make one like this." Sally drew a horizontal line across her paper two inches from the top. "Leave a space up here to write the grid designations. Then draw more lines going the same way all the way down about this far apart." She made lines spaced half an inch apart.

The boys filled their pages with horizontal lines and then made vertical lines like Sally drew.

"Now comes the learning how to write. Words are made with letters. We are going to write some of them above each column we made. We start with the first letter, which is A." She wrote a capital A above the left-most column. "Next comes B...."

Once she had the first eight letters of the alphabet on the paper, she said, "There are also things called numbers. One of the things numbers do is designate how many of something there is. We are going to write them down on the side of our grid. This is 1." She picked up a saguaro fruit. "It means this many." As she wrote the numbers down the left side of her paper, she moved fruits into her counted pile. The boys did the same with their sheets and fruit.

"Now," continued Sally, "before we start recording what we find around here." She pointed to the top left box of her grid. "Above this column is A, and to the left is 1. This box is the A1 box." She pointed to the box below it. "This is still the A column, but now the 2 is on the left. It's the A2 box." She pointed to the third box down. "What do you think this box is named?"

Both boys said, "It's A, but I forgot what that number is called."

"Very, very good. You figured out that everything in this column will be A and then the number on the left. This one is three."

Nikki blurted, "It's A3."

The lesson continued. The boys knew the capital letters A through H and the numbers 1 through 20 when they carried their binders to their parents.

Oscar showed Emily and Tom what he had made and named every letter and number on the page to the praises of his parents.

Across the village, Nikki showed Noah what he could do. "You learned all that in one day!" Noah picked up Nikki and swung him in a circle. "You are a brilliant person."

Nikki squealed with delight. "Each box stands for a little piece of this village. Tomorrow, I'm going to learn how to mark what we find in each box. I love Aunt Sally. She's so much fun!"

Sally heard Nikki and remembered what Ann had said at Alex's Santa Fe ranch. *Nikki and I share a love for each other even if I am Aunt Sally and not Mama.* Her heart warmed. She looked at Alex cutting grass by the river. *But I still want to have children of my own.*

Eighty Two

Justice Micah Clemont returned to Little Rock on a lovely mid-July morning. He rented a house and settled in with his wife and daughter.

Not long afterward, Sheriff Taylor went to the home of Bruce McKay. Mrs. McKay opened the door with a baby on her hip.

"Is your husband here?" asked the sheriff.

"I haven't seen 'em since he started sharing the grog with Alger. 'Em comin' home every morn' with a fimble-famble about people diggin' up graves. Most likely that thatch-gallows dirked him an' sent my poor husband to an earth bath."

"I hope he comes home soon, Mrs. McHay. Good morning to you, ma'am." The sheriff went off to the next house on his list.

To make the arrests as quickly as possible, his deputies simultaneously knocked on doors all over Little Rock. They rounded up seven of the sixteen men on their list. Some of those who they could not find were reported to have gone missing. After hearing from several family members that the men had become friends with Alger shortly before their disappearance, Sheriff Taylor went to the Hillcrest Inn. "Cornell, is a man named Alger staying here?"

"He's in room 14."

"Bring your key." Sheriff Taylor drew his Waters flintlock pistol.

"What's happening, sheriff? The scuttlebutt is that you're arresting people."

Taylor stopped at room 14. "Just open the door."

Inside the room, Alger had already pulled on his boots.

The sound of slamming wood came from the inside of the room. "Open it!" ordered Sheriff Taylor.

Cornell turned the key. The sheriff barreled into the empty room, darted to the window, and looked out. "ALGER, STOP!"

With a Pepperbox pistol in his hand, Alger turned toward the window.

Taylor saw the gun. "Duck!" He flung himself to the floor.

Alger fired. As he rolled, a loose spark ignited the other barrels. The whole volley of projectiles flew into the wall and through the window.

Blood flowed from Cornell's belly. "I'm hit!"

"Get down, you fool!" Taylor scuttled across the floor and out the door. He bounded down the stairs. "Nobody leave! There's a murderer outside! Bessie, Cornell is shot. Be careful going into the room." The sheriff peeked out from under the swinging doors.

Alger sprinted toward the stable.

Taylor dashed through the kitchen and out the back door. He raced along the alley and then skidded around the corner into the stable. He planted one foot forward and his other behind him and then pointed his pistol toward the big opening at the front of the livery.

Sunlight streamed in. The smell of manure permeated everything. Flies buzzed around him, but he still heard the sound of running, drawing closer. He wiped the sweat from his eyes.

Alger didn't even try to slip in at the edge of the door. He dashed straight through the middle of the entryway.

I need him as a witness! Taylor shot wide. "Halt! The next one will be through your heart!"

Alger's pepperbox was useless. All the barrels had fired when he had shot at the sheriff back at the inn. He screeched to a standstill and held up his hands.

"You are under arrest for the murder of Bruce McHay and probably several others."

Eighty Three

The bailiff called the Little Rock court into session. The defendant, lawyers, and just about every other person in Little Rock rose. A new judge came in, sat, and then tapped his gavel. "People of Little Rock, we are here today to determine what happened in Little Rock on June 16th of 1842. The charges are the murder of Bruce McHay by Alger Dickerson. Richard Atwood, Arkansas State Judge, presiding. This court is now in session. Micah Clemont, please call your first witness."

Micah rose. "I call Mrs. McHay."

Judge Atwood addressed the woman. "Raise your right hand and place your left hand on the Bible." A deputy stood beside the chair and held out a Bible. "Do you swear to tell the truth, the whole truth, and nothing but the truth? So help you God."

"I do. So help me God," said Mrs. McHay."

"Did your husband ever drink at John Peabody's Inn?"

"Yes, sir. 'Em there almost every night. I told 'em to bring our money home, but would he? Not on his life. He couldn't keep from wastin' it on ale."

"Did he have any friends at the inn?" asked Micah.

"Yes, sir. You was one of 'em 'til you brought 'em home with money in his pocket. I bought my poor babies some food."

"Anybody else?"

"After you, it was that one." Mrs. McHay pointed at Alger. "Then Bruce stopped comin' home at all."

"What day did he stop coming home?"

"June 16th."

"Thank you, Mrs. McHay. That is all my questions."

Judge Atwood said, "Christmas Bell, do you wish to cross-examine this witness?"

Esquire Bell stood. "Please call me Esquire Bell or Chris Bell. Thank you." The defense lawyer approached the witness. "Mrs. McHay, did you ever go into Peabody Inn when your husband was there?"

"No."

"So you are guessing that your husband was with Mr. Dickerson in Peabody Inn."

"No, sir. I saw 'em—"

Esquire Bell cut off the witness. "That will be all."

"But I saw—"

"That is all!"

Mrs. McHay went to her seat.

Micah Clemont rose. "I call John Peabody."

Judge Atwood addressed the innkeeper.

"Raise your right hand and place your left hand on the Bible. Do you swear to tell the truth, the whole truth, and nothing but the truth? So help you God."

Mr. Peabody replied, "I do. So help me God."

Micah asked, "Did Bruce McHay drink alone, or did he usually drink with another person when he was in your inn?"

Peabody reported, "He always drank with somebody. He liked to put his arm across a person's shoulder and sing when he was three sheets to the wind."

"Are any of the people he drank with in this room?"

"Yes." Mr. Peabody pointed at various people in the room. "Him, him, him, him, him, and you as well."

Micah said, "Please note that one of the people identified as drinking with Mr. McHay was Alger Dickerson. Do you remember who was drinking with Bruce McHay on June 16th of 1842?"

"I do. It was Alger."

"Are you sure?"

"Yes, because Mrs. McHay came to my inn looking for Bruce the next day. That made me think about who he was with. I told her that he was probably with Alger because they had left together."

"Did you ever see Bruce McHay after he left with Alger Dickerson?"

"No."

"Did Alger Dickerson or Bruce McHay ever take a room at your inn?"

"No."

"That will be all. Thank you, Mr. Peabody."

Richard Atwood looked at Esquire Chris Bell.

Esquire Bell strolled across the muggy courtroom. "Did you ever hear Bruce McHay talk about his home life?"

"All the time." Mr. Peabody looked at Mrs. McHay. *Poor woman. I hope he doesn't ask me to repeat any of it.*

"What did you hear Bruce McHay say about his home life?"

Mr. Peabody sighed. He locked eyes with Mrs. McHay. "I'm sorry." He turned his gaze to the lawyer. "He said his wife was making him as poor as Job's turkey, but he pocketed her aggravation because he liked her cat-heads and drumsticks. He said he thought about leaving her, but he got his tail down every time he was going to tell her."

"So you heard Bruce McHay say he wanted to leave his wife?"

"Yes."

"That is all my questions. Thank you, Mr. Peabody."

Micah called his next witness. "Sheriff Taylor."

Judge Atwood swore him in.

"Have any abnormally buried bodies been found in Little Rock?" asked Micah.

"Two so far."

"In what way were they different?"

"One was in a coffin with another body. The other was in a shallow grave."

"Do you know who these people are?

"We believe the body in the coffin was a man named Samuel Adams. The other has been identified as Abel Polkinghorne."

Judge Atwood noticed that Alger started to sweat.

"How many people have been reported as missing during the last two weeks?"

"Ten."

"How many have been reported as missing in the previous ten years?"

"Three."

"Are you saying only three people were reported as missing in a ten-year period of time until two weeks ago, and then there have been ten?"

"Yes."

"That is all my questions." Micah returned to his seat.

Christmas Bell rose. "Has the body of Bruce McHay been recovered?"

"No," answered the sheriff.

"That is all," Christmas Bell sniffed his nose as he turned from the witness. "You can't have a murder without a body, can you, Sheriff?"

"I call Cornell Hillcrest." After Mr. Hillcrest swore to tell the truth, Micah asked, "Did Alger Dickerson ever take a room at your inn?"

"Yes. He checked in on May 15th of this year. He stayed at my inn until he was arrested."

"Who paid for his room?"

"Mrs. Hall."

"What happened July 17th of this year when you and Sheriff Taylor went to room 14 and knocked on the door?"

"We heard the window shutter slam open, so I unlocked the door. The sheriff ran across the room and looked out the window. Alger fired many shots all at once that flew in through the window. One of them went into my stomach. Then Sheriff Taylor ran down the stairs and told my wife to help me before he ran out the kitchen door."

"Thank you, Mr. Hillcrest. Those were all of my questions."

Esquire Bell rose. "Mr. Hillcrest, did you yourself see who was in the room before you opened the door?"

"No."

"Did you personally see the man who shot toward the window?"

"No."

"Why do you think Alger Dickerson jumped out the window and fired a volley of bullets?"

"Sheriff Taylor said he saw him."

"So you didn't see the person. You only heard that it was Alger Dickerson."

"I guess so."

"No more questions, your Honor."

Micah rose. "I have no further witnesses."

Judge Atwood said, "Esquire Bell, call your first witness."

The defense lawyer called several witnesses

who all testified that, on numerous occasions, they had heard Bruce McHay say that he wanted to be free from his wife's constant nagging about money.

The only point Micah drew out was that Bruce McHay had said he wanted to leave his wife for seven years but had gone home to the women every night.

Judge Richard Atwood stared at Alger Dickerson then Micah Clemont. *I don't want to let a guilty man go free again. I'm sure he killed Mr. McHay and all the other men on my docket of cases. He'll keep killing people like Roy did if I let him go, but there is no body, and so many people heard him say he wanted to leave his wife. Maybe they'll find the body someday. Mr. Dickerson won't be free until all the cases are heard. I'll hear the Abel Polkinghorne's case last and hang him on that one.* "Micah Clemont, approach the bench." Micah stood before Judge Atwood. "I want nolle prosequi. We can revisit this case if you find Mr. McHay's body."

Micah nodded, walked back to his table, and turned toward the bench. "The State of Arkansas enters the plea of nolle prosequi regarding the Bruce McHay murder case."

"Very well, if that is what the state chooses, so be it. The case may be picked up again if further evidence is found. Court is dismissed. Take the defendant back to his holding cell."

Eighty Four

Noah led the wagon train from the Pima villages to the Maricopa, who lived beside them along the Gila. For two days, the family drank water and harvested clams from the river and the inner bark from the cottonwoods. They traded six steers for crookneck squash and melons that they stored under the grass in the wagon.

The following four days, they fed the animals and themselves with Pima and Maricopa provisions as they cut through the dense mesquite back to the river. A light coating of salt covered the mesquite and young cottonwood trees. Just as Alex had been told, the Gila had become brackish.

They traveled up and down soft, clay gullies. On numerous occasions, they were forced into the sand of the shallow river. Rarely did they find drinkable water or grass that could be eaten. Most days, the animals drank the water and ate the grass, shelled corn, or wheat they had brought.

Two weeks after leaving the Maricopa, Eli returned from scouting in time to help set up camp. "The river butts a rock cliff not far ahead. We have to pull the wagons up a steep bluff to a plain of clay or float the wagons in the river. The Gila is fast, but it's only been a few inches deep a few times. It might be a good idea to stop here and find out how far we have to go before we can get back to the river from above or back to the land from the river."

Tom scratched his head. "We've found a little fresh water close to the river. We've only got enough with us for a few more days. We can't go the upper way if it's a long way to water. I'm willing to take several canteens and find out. Who will scout out the river route?"

Emily rocked Carol Ann. "You need to go in pairs."

"I'll go with Pop," volunteered Eli.

Adahy looked at Noah. "You want to go together and see if we can make it down the river?"

Noah answered, "Yes, but first, we should take our heaviest wagon in and see if it floats. Right here, we can easily get into and out of the river."

"The wagons are going to leak." Roscoe placed a spit over the fire. "The desert was so dry that the boards separated. We'd need to cut down that dead cottonwood, make two poles, and lash them to it for the wagon to float, but I think everything will be ruined by the salty water that will get in."

"Maybe we can use this," Sally picked some of the fluffy white fibers off a cottonwood, "and clay to plug the gaps. There's a lot of both everywhere."

Tom unharnessed the last team. "It will take

days to prepare the wagons. We'll use all our water before we even get started. Let me take a look above tomorrow. God, please show us the right way to go."

"We have to cross the Colorado River. We should work on the wagons anyway." Sally went to get a sack.

Stephanie called out, "Bring several. I'll help you gather."

Tom, Eli, Noah, and Adahy reconnoitered while the rest of the family rearranged the items in the wagons. They loaded the two that hauled cast iron stoves with the blacksmith tools and anything that would not be damaged by salty water and stuffed cottonwood fluff followed by clay between the boards of one of them. They drove both wagons into the river to see if the wood would swell up and seal the gaps in either of them. The water was barely deep enough for them to float, and the sandy bottom made them hard to pull.

When he returned, Noah reported, "Up the river are sand bars only a few inches under water. Remember how hard it was to get the wagons over the sand bars when we floated down the Arkansas?"

Sally remembered very well. "At least the water is warmer if any of us fall in."

"And all you'd have to do is stand up and walk out," added Adahy.

Tom and Eli rode into camp. "We should take the high road. There are pools with fresh water to drink and probably enough to refill everything."

Helen asked, "Do we have time to pitch the wagons?"

"Let's see how well either of them is doing after the night in the water." Eli swung off Ace.

It required a six-mule team attached to a six-ox team to pull the caulked, leak-free wagon up the bluff. Eli and Noah unhooked the wagon above the camp, took the animals to the water hole to drink, left two dogs to keep them from wandering, and then used the extra donkeys they had brought to carry barrels of water back to the river. "Prepare the other wagons for the Colorado River crossing."

Eighty Five

Finally home in Little Rock, weary of the whole matter and glad it would be wrapped up in a few minutes, Colt Barrett went to what he thought would be Judge Hall's chambers at the courthouse. A different name was stenciled on the door. He walked to the clerk's office. "I want to speak with Judge Hall?"

"It's not visiting hours. Come back tomorrow between 10 and 3."

"What!?"

The clerk remembered what he had been told to do if Colt Barrett came looking for the Judge. "What is your name?"

"Colt Barrett."

"Please come into my office and have a seat. May I get you some coffee?"

"Yes." Colt walked into the room.

The clerk poured Colt a cup of steaming liquid.

"Please wait here." The man left the room, bolted it from the outside, and then went to the jail.

"Sheriff Taylor, I've got Colt Barrett locked in my office."

"You shouldn't have locked him up. He's not a criminal." Sheriff Taylor went to the coat tree and retrieved his gun belt.

"He's not? Then why do you want to know he's here?"

"That's not your concern." The sheriff buckled on his gun belt and went to the building beside the jail. He unbolted the clerk's door and walked into the room.

Colt cupped his coffee with both hands. He looked up. "Sheriff Taylor, after I speak with Judge Hall, I want to collect my bounty for Joe Smith."

"I don't see Joe Smith."

Colt withdrew the sealed letter from his pocket and passed it to the sheriff, who read it.

"Dead. I guess his sentence didn't get reduced. What makes you think there's a bounty for Joe Smith?"

Colt pulled his contract with Judge Daniel Hall from his other pocket. The sheriff looked over the paper. Everything was the same as the contract Justice Clemont had given him except for the date. "How long ago did he hire you?"

"I know I'm late, but that shouldn't keep me from collecting."

"This contract says you have four months from the date on this document. Are you saying this was when Judge Hall sent you after Joe Smith?" Sheriff Taylor pointed to the date.

Colt's face turned red. "You can't expect me to time this to the minute!"

"Calm down, son. I'm going to pay you. I'm asking these questions for a different reason."

"What reason is that?"

"You have not done anything wrong, but I am going to confine you to my house. I need to assure non-contamination of your testimony."

"My testimony! About what? I told you Joe Smith is dead. Colonel Howland said so."

"Be calm and come with me."

Eighty Six

Alger sat in the witness box and realized the verdict wouldn't be the same as the previous nine trials. This time they had the body with pepperbox pistol slugs in it. He looked at Judge Atwood and then Micah, who stood beside him. *Clemont is too smart. I better lay the blame elsewhere.* "Uncle Daniel told me to do it. He said he didn't want any Angels of Righteousness alive because they knew too much."

Micah's eyes narrowed. *Once the pressure is on, people always crack and tell everything they know. That's why I put all of Alger's other cases first.* "Who are the Angels of Righteousness?"

Alger looked at Judge Atwood. "I want you to promise to go easy on me if I talk."

"I will take it into consideration," replied the Judge.

"The Angels of Righteousness are a group of men committed to keeping the white race pure by eliminating men or women who continue to be an abomination by mating interracially."

Micah handed Alger a sheet of paper. "Are all these men members of that group?"

Alger read the list. "Yes."

"Did you witness any of the Angels of Righteousness' executions?"

"Only the first one."

"Who was executed, and who did it?"

Alger looked at Judge Atwood again. "You'll protect me from my uncle?"

Judge Atwood assured him, "You will not have to worry about Daniel Hall."

"Uncle Daniel shot Samuel Adams in 1835."

Micah Clemont turned toward Judge Atwood. "May I approach the bench, your Honor?"

"Come."

"After you hear Daniel Hall's case, I plan to bring charges against Alger Dickerson for the murder of Samuel Adams."

"Thank you for informing me."

Micah returned to his chair.

Judge Atwood asked, "Is there any further evidence or testimony to be presented by either of you?"

Both lawyers answered, "No."

Judge Atwood didn't have to consider. "Alger Dickerson, I find you guilty of the murder of Abel Polkinghorne. As promised, I am giving you a reduced sentence in exchange for testifying against Daniel Hall. You are sentenced to life in prison."

"Life in prison! That's not going easy on me! I was a guard at the Eighth District Penitentiary. The inmates will kill me."

"I'll let you stay in Little Rock," said Judge

Atwood. "Sheriff Taylor, take Mr. Dickerson back to his cell."

On the other side of town, Rufus Knapp, Corporal Fisher, and Forest Ronan checked into rooms at the Peabody Inn.

Eighty Seven

The day Alger Dickerson received his life sentence to the Little Rock jail, six donkeys, five oxen, and one mule managed to get the last wagon to the clay plain above the Gila River. They spent the day beside the water pools, drank all they wanted, filled all six water mattresses, and left with all but four of their twelve barrels full.

For two weeks, the goats, sheep, mules, horses, and donkeys ate the mesquite beans the Pima Indians had introduced to them. The cattle, however, would only eat the grain rationed to them, hay from the wagons, and what little edible grass they found as they traveled up and down in the hills that followed the river. They twice crossed the Gila and hacked down mesquite, willows, and young cottonwoods until they arrived at the lush bunchgrass above the Gila's convergence with Rio Colorado. No water or stored animal food remained.

After a peaceful night, Stephanie sat up and rubbed her eyes. "Darling, look at the glittering grass. The dew is beautiful."

Surrounded by high mountainous layers of black stone, they butchered two lame steers, ate back straps, and smoked the rest of the meat. Their living animals grazed on wet grass.

The following day, they waded through the salty black waters of the Gila River for the last time and then traversed the sparsely vegetated wedge of land between the two rivers.

Before the sun went down, they stood at the bank of Rio Colorado. Alex looked at their map. "On the other side of this river is the Mojave desert. We need to fill up with water. The Colorado looks different on the far side. It might be drinkable."

"I'll test it when I get over there." Adahy took his turn at a potentially dangerous task. He rode Paint into the river with one end of a rope fastened to the pommel of his saddle. The horse walked most of the way in water no deeper than his belly, swam three fast channels, and then waded out onto a flat, sandy beach.

Adahy secured the rope they would use to bring the wagons to a large cottonwood. He waved to signal readiness and fresh water.

Tom stood beside the cottonwood poles they had made. "No way of knowing how deep the water was in the places where Paint swam."

"I hope the wagons are still watertight." Eli picked up one of the logs. "Let's lash these to the most questionable one."

Once ready, Roscoe flicked the reins. "Forward, ho." King guided his team into the Colorado. They approached the first channel. Roscoe instructed the animals, "Forward, swim."

Goliath and King were much taller than Paint and never reached a depth that required them to swim. At the second deep channel, Roscoe issued the same command. Even Goliath swam, but his hooves were not far from the riverbed. Only Goliath walked when they crossed the third channel. The wagon rolled on its wheels the whole way across.

The family members on the eastern bank loaded the little animals that might be swept downstream into one of the wagons that no longer held hay, attached it to the harness, and used oxen to haul them. Ehawee and Etu rode across with them.

Eli used Ace to pull the wagon back. On each trip, they harnessed a new set of draught animals. They repeatedly crammed the animals they thought might have trouble swimming into the wagon. Helen took the last of the small animals across as the sun went below the horizon.

In the twilight, Sally piloted a wagon full of provisions. Stephanie took Hattie across in the next wagon, which was also full of supplies.

Because they refused to be still, Ann strapped down Chris, Joy, and Adele while Emily tied Carol Ann into a ten-gallon tub. They crossed by moonlight.

Noah, Eli, Tom, Alex, Nikki, and Oscar rode horses as they drove the remaining loose animals into the river. With the help of the dogs, they got the entire herd to the west side of Rio Colorado.

Noah lay down his head. *I'll worry about the desert tomorrow.*

During the night, the animals drank fresh water from the river and ate the grass they found under the bushes and mesquite bean pods that looked like tight screws.

Eighty Eight

Across thousands of miles, mountains, rivers, and the prairie, the man responsible for the family's flight to the west, sat on the opposite side of the bench than when he'd sentenced Ann Williams and Noah Swift Hawk three years earlier.

Ecstatic that the trial of Daniel Hall was finally underway, Colt perched on a bench in the rear of the jammed-to-the-gills courtroom. Sheriff Taylor had assured him that he'd get paid for bringing back the proof of Joe Smith's death and for the time he spent confined in the sheriff's home. However, if anything drove Colt out of his mind, it was boredom. He was more than ready to return to his life.

"Daniel Hall, you are accused of aiding the murderer Joe Smith in his escape from the Arkansas Eighth District Penitentiary. Arkansas State Judge Richard Atwood, presiding." He rapped his gavel on the desk. "This court is now in session. Daniel Hall, where is your solicitor?"

"I will represent myself," answered the accused.

"Very well." Judge Atwood shifted his eyes to the other side of the room. "Esquire Bell, please state your case."

Christmas Bell sat on the prosecutor's side of the courtroom for this case. "The state of Arkansas alleges that on June 10th of 1840, Daniel Hall did request that the convicted murderer named Joe Smith be transferred from The Arkansas Eighth District Penitentiary to the hard labor camp in Missouri known as The Quarry with the intent to release Joe Smith to hunt down and kill Noah Swift Hawk and Ann Williams."

Judge Atwood looked at Daniel Hall. "You may state your opening remarks."

They can't prove I had any particular plan, thought Daniel Hall. "I am not guilty. I intended to take Joe Smith to The Quarry but was overpowered by him, which allowed him to escape against my will, and I have tried to recapture the man."

Judge Atwood had spent years looking into the eyes of his outlaw brothers-in-law, Hank and Roy Butterfield. He believed he could see a lie on the face of a liar. He kept himself from rolling his eyes in disbelief. "Esquire Bell, call your witness."

"I call Rufus Knapp." After Warden Knapp was sworn in, Esquire Bell continued, "Please tell us what you do to earn a living."

"For the last ten years, I have been the warden of The Arkansas Eighth District Penitentiary."

"Did the defendant, Daniel Hall, come to The Arkansas Eighth District Penitentiary in 1840?"

"Yes, he did."

"Exactly when and what did he do?"

"Judge Hall arrived June 3rd of 1840. He brought men from The Quarry to finish their sentences in the Arkansas penitentiary. He looked over the facilities and spoke with many of the inmates. On June 10th, he requested that Joe Smith be transferred to the hard labor camp."

"Did you release Joe Smith into the custody of Daniel Hall?"

"Yes, he had a paper from Micah Clemont authorizing him to take any steps necessary to solve the problem at The Quarry, and Judge Hall said the transfer was necessary."

"Did Joe Smith and Daniel Hall leave The Eighth District Penitentiary together, and were there other people with them?"

"I saw them leave together by themselves."

"Thank you. That is all my questions."

Judge Atwood did not bother to look at the defendant. "Mr. Hall, you may cross-examine the witness."

Daniel Hall sauntered to the witness and handed him a paper. "Is this the document from Micah Clemont that you referenced?"

"Yes."

"I enter this as evidence that I intended to fix the unrest at The Quarry as ordered by His Honorable Justice Clemont. I have no further questions for Warden Knapp." Hall handed the letter to Judge Atwood.

1, May 1840

Honorable Judge Hall,

It has come to our attention that discipline at
the hard labor camp in Missouri has grown lax. As
a result, unrest and chaos have led to a request for
more guards. I find myself indisposed and unable
to travel. As you are the closest court official, you
are ordered to inspect the facilities at The Quarry.
Make corrections where needed, arrange for the
transport of troublemakers to The Eighth District
Penitentiary in Arkansas, and take whatever other
steps you deem necessary. Report your findings
and corrective actions to this office as soon as
feasible.

Sincerely,

Micah Clemont

His Honorable Justice
United States Supreme Court
Alexandria, Virginia

Judge Atwood scanned the face of the witness.
"Step down, Warden Knapp. Esquire Bell, call your
next witness."

Esquire Bell rose. "Forest Ronan."

Mr. Ronan promised to tell the whole truth and then sat.

"State your position at The Quarry," ordered Bell.

"I am the warden."

"Has Joe Smith ever been incarcerated at or brought to The Quarry?"

"No."

"That is all."

Atwood looked into the eyes of Daniel Hall. "Any questions for Warden Ronan?"

"No. Warden Ronan is correct. I never brought Joe Smith there because he got away from me." Daniel Hall smirked. *And nobody has any way to prove that I purposely did not take him to The Quarry or that I took him to my home in Little Rock.*

Atwood didn't look up from Micah's letter. "Step down. Call your next witness Esquire Bell."

"I call Colt Barrett."

Daniel Hall dropped the glass of water he had raised to his lips. *Oh no! I didn't know he was back!*

Colt took the stand.

Esquire Bell asked, "Were you engaged to look for Joe Smith?"

"Yes, Judge Hall told me that Joe Smith had overpowered him and escaped. He hired me to find Mr. Smith and bring him to Little Rock. He gave me expense money and said I would be paid the bounty when I brought in Joe Smith."

"Do you have a contract stating the terms of the agreement?" asked Chris Bell.

Colt drew the document from the inside pocket of his vest.

Daniel Hall jumped to his feet. "I OBJECT!"

"To what!?" asked Judge Atwood.

"We don't know if that is the actual contract or if he altered it. I request that it be ruled as inadmissible."

Colt looked at Judge Hall with shocked disbelief on his face. "It's the one we signed. You're trying to get out of paying me! I was only three days beyond the contracted date to bring him in, but I did the work and found out that Joe Smith is dead!"

Daniel Hall hoped deeply. *Maybe Joe found them and killed that miserable woman.* "Did you kill Mr. Smith when you found him, or did you speak with him first?"

Judge Atwood banged his gavel on the desk. "Mr. Barrett, do not answer." Atwood breathed deeply and glared at Daniel Hall. "It's not your turn to question the witness. You should know that. Mr. Barrett, hand me the contract."

Colt passed the paper to the judge. Judge Atwood examined the document. "I don't see any evidence of tampering. Esquire Bell, do you have further questions?"

"Mr. Barrett, you said that you were only three days beyond the date you were contracted to return. What is the date that you returned?"

"September 18th."

"Of what year?"

"This year, of course."

"What is the date you were hired?"

"May 15th. I was supposed to return with Joe Smith or evidence that he was dead by September 15th, but I think I should get paid."

"What year were you hired?"

"This year. The date is right there on the contract."

"I have no more questions for Mr. Barrett."

Judge Atwood frowned. "Judge Hall, you may proceed."

"Mr. Barrett, did you speak with Joe Smith?"

"I did not speak to Joe Smith. Colonel Howland of Fort Gibson told me that some of his men found Joe Smith's frozen body. I gave his sealed statement to Sheriff Taylor."

#Q%^^W^ *She got away!* "Mr. Barrett, admit that you changed the date on your copy of the contract. Admit that you are two years late, and I will still authorize payment of the bounty."

"I am NOT two years late! And another thing, Joe Smith was a terrible man. Everybody told me how horrible he was. He burned down a mill, killed two people, and left a trail as wide as the Arkansas. Escaped convicts don't do that. And why would you want to take a man like that out of prison and allow him to get away with serving only hard labor?"

"Stop talking. You don't get to ask questions! You are lying about the date I sent you because you want to get paid even though you are woefully late.

You should be ashamed of yourself! You won't get a single penny!"

Judge Atwood's jaw dropped. *This man was a Judge! He's behaving like a child! He's sure enough guilty of something.* "Mr. Barrett, you may step down and take a seat. Esquire Bell, do you have any more witnesses?"

"I call Sheriff Taylor." Sheriff Taylor took the stand. "Do you have the document Mr. Barrett says he gave you?"

"I do." Sheriff Taylor gave Colonel Howland's letter to Judge Atwood.

Bell asked, "What is the date of the letter?"

"June 23rd, 1842."

Daniel Hall jetted up again. "Joe Smith did not leave a clear trail. It took Colt two years to figure out that Joe had gone to Fort Gibson."

"You rotten liar! I left May 15th of this year!" shouted Colt.

Judge Atwood loudly banged his gavel. "You are both out of turn! I will charge you with contempt of court if you do so again. That goes for both of you."

Colt's face flamed red. "I can get people from every town I went through to come here and testify." Colt remembered something. "Or you can ask Mr. Hillcrest if I've been in his inn this year."

"Mr. Barrett, you are hereby charged with contempt." Judge Atwood issued orders. "Sheriff Taylor, you are dismissed from the stand to get this Hillcrest fellow."

Cornell Hillcrest sat in the witness chair. Chris Bell asked, "Do you know Colt Barrett?"

"Sure I do. Every Monday, he brings Amanda to my Inn for supper. Well, at least he used to. He hasn't done so lately."

"When did he last bring Amanda to your inn?"

"Let me think." Mr. Hillcrest tapped his jaw. "I guess about six months ago."

"Do you see Colt Barrett in this room?"

"He's right there." Mr. Hillcrest pointed at Colt Barrett.

"No further question for Mr. Hillcrest, your Honor."

"Mr. Hall, do you have questions for this witness?"

Daniel Hall asked, "How much is Colt paying you to lie for him?"

"What?" Cornell Hillcrest thought *one more proof that Daniel Hall has serious problems.* "Shall I tell of all your drinking bouts in my inn and the horrible way you treat people? People like that slave Abraham. It must have cost him months of wages to buy those jars of honey. You knocked him down, broke them, and then insulted his owners. And now you're accusing me of lying about something I can get multiple people to confirm. You've completely lost your mind."

Judge Atwood stopped him. "That's enough, Mr. Hillcrest. You may step down." He looked at the documents before him. "Judge Hall, do you have any witnesses to call?"

Daniel Hall looked at the multitude of people in the room. *None of them can help me.* "No."

"I think I've heard enough. Daniel Hall, please rise. I find you guilty of lying about the date of your contract with Mr. Barrett. It only makes sense that you are guilty of allowing Joe Smith to escape and then trying to cover it up. I sentence you to ten years in The Arkansas First District Penitentiary. Nobody you sent to prison should be in that one. Sheriff Taylor, take the prisoner to his cell. Tomorrow, I'll hear The State of Arkansas's case against Daniel Hall for the murder of Samuel Adams."

"What?!" His eyes as big as saucers, Judge Hall pulled out of Sheriff Taylor's grip and attempted to make a run for the door.

Colt Barrett tackled him. "Lady Justice isn't blind, Hall."

Eighty Nine

A warrior of a Tipai-Ipai scouting party voiced his opinion. "We can't allow anybody to get to San Diego. We need to scout the whole length of the Colorado, and that is too much land to watch. We should ask the Mojave to help us. They want shells. We want to stop anybody from bringing supplies to the soldiers. Some Mojaves are here today. I can ask them."

"Nobody will try to cross Hayikwiir Mat'aar. We don't need help."

"We should ask anyway. We can get shells from the ocean, but what will we do if the pale faces drive us from our homes?"

The leading chief agreed. "Make the trade and get them to kill anybody who tries to get to San Diego by land."

Good. I arranged for the Mojave to help us months ago. My chief would have had me executed if he had found shells gone. "I go right away."

Ninety

Richard Atwood perched on a tall chair behind the judge's bench. "We are here to determine if Daniel Hall murdered Samuel Adams on or around August 29th of 1835. Esquire Bell, call your first witness."

Chris Bell rose. "I call Alger Dickerson."

Why is he calling Alger? He's on my side. Daniel Hall saw his nephew advert his face when he passed. *That's not good. He was there.*

Judge Atwood swore Alger in and then instructed him to sit.

"Mr. Dickerson," asked Chris Bell, "Did you live in Little Rock in 1835?"

"Yes," answered Alger.

"Did Daniel Hall live in Little Rock in 1835?"

Alger again affirmed, "Yes."

"What is your relationship to Daniel Hall?"

"Daniel Hall is my mother's brother."

"In 1835, did you and Daniel Hall belong to any social group?"

"No."

Chris Bell furrowed his brow. *I thought they*

killed Samuel Adams together as Angles of Righteousness. "Did you regularly get together with Daniel Hall for nighttime activities?"

I might luck out. I'd never have to talk about Samuel Adams if he doesn't ask the right questions. "No, Uncle Daniel usually went to Hillcrest Inn at night, and I was too young to go there."

"Was there any particular night that you and Daniel Hall met and broke the law?" asked Esquire Bell.

"One night, Uncle Daniel let me drink moonshine out in the backyard."

Micah Clemont huffed in frustration. *Just ask him straight out!*

"Did you see Daniel Hall shoot a Samuel Adams on August 29th of 1835?"

HA! Still the wrong question! "No."

Micah looked at Sheriff Taylor beside him. He mouthed WHAT?

Taylor drew his lips down and shrugged his shoulders.

He said he would, but he is not cooperating. Chris Bell looked at Judge Atwood then looked over his shoulder toward Micah. "No further questions."

Hall isn't going to risk Alger saying something, but I have to allow him his turn. Judge Atwood refused to call Hall an esquire. "Daniel Hall, you may cross-examine."

"I have no questions." Hall breathed a sigh of relief.

I hope Bell grows a brain. Atwood instructed, "Call your next witness, Esquire Bell."

"I call Parley Taylor." Once Parley sat in the witness chair, Bell bade him, "State your occupation."

"I am the sheriff of Little Rock."

"Have you ever been in this courtroom when Alger Dickerson was on trial?"

"I object!" said Daniel Hall, "Alger Dickerson's trial is not relevant to this case."

Esquire Bell countered, "Mr. Dickerson made statements during his trial that are relevant to this case."

Judge Atwood instructed the witness, "Answer the question, Sheriff Taylor."

"Yes, I was in the courtroom during every one of Alger Dickerson's cases."

Esquire Bell asked, "Did you hear Alger Dickerson state that he had witnessed Daniel Hall murder Samuel Adams?"

"Yes, I did."

"Exactly what did he say?"

"Alger had been asked if he had witnessed any Angel of Righteousness executions. Mr. Dickerson replied, 'Only the first one. Uncle Daniel shot Samuel Adams in 1835.'"

"I have no further questions for this witness."

Judge Atwood continued, "Mr. Hall, you may cross-examine."

Daniel Hall crossed the room, pushing the chair upon which sat the ball attached to the chain around his leg. "Sheriff Taylor, has Mr. Dickerson been found guilty of murder?"

"Yes."

"Do known murderers habitually lie?"

"Some do."

"Is it possible that Mr. Dickerson lied when he said he saw me shoot Samuel Adams?"

"Yes."

"I have no more questions." Daniel Hall pushed the chair back to his seat.

"I would like to recall Alger Dickerson at this time," requested Esquire Bell.

Judge Atwood explained, "Mr. Dickerson, do you understand that you are still under oath and must tell the truth?"

"Yes."

"Be seated," ordered the judge.

Chris Bell stood beside the witness. "Did you witness the Daniel Hall shooting of Samuel Adams in 1835?"

"Yes."

"Describe what you saw."

"Uncle Daniel caught Samuel Adams and made him kneel in front of him while he pressed a pistol to his forehead. He said, 'I told you to stay away from Labella, but you didn't, and now she's ruined. Tell me where she is, and I'll only send you to The Quarry.' Samuel said, 'You'll hurt her. I'll never tell you where she is.' That's when Uncle Daniel shot him."

"I have no more questions."

Atwood waved his gavel at Daniel. "You may cross-examine."

As he approached, Hall's eyes shot daggers into his nephew. "Was it night when this supposed shooting occurred?"

"Yes."

"What was the color of the supposed victim's clothes that night?"

"I couldn't tell. It was dark."

"So, it was too dark to see clearly?"

"Yes."

"Did you feel for a pulse on the supposed corpse?"

"No."

"So, you didn't verify that the man was dead, and you couldn't know who shot Samuel Adams because it was too dark to see clearly." Daniel Hall believed he had proven Alger as an unreliable witness. "That is all my questions. Step down from the stand."

Alger stood. "We went to the barn—

Daniel broke in, "STOP TALKING."

Alger continued anyway. "We were together when we caught him. I'm sure he was dead because he had a hole the size of my hand in the back of his head."

Christmas Bell said, "I have no further witnesses for now, but I reserve the right to call witnesses after hearing Mr. Hall's witnesses."

"Very Well. Mr. Hall, you may call your first witness."

Nobody can give me an alibi for that night. My only hope is to show that Alger is a liar. "I call Patience Dickerson."

Judge Atwood swore in Patience.

Daniel Hall asked his sister, "What is your relationship to Alger Dickerson?"

"He is my son."

"Did Alger lie to you when he was growing up?"

"He did. All children do."

"I don't mean occasionally. I mean, even when Alger had no reason to lie, did he tell you things that were not true?"

"Yes."

"How often?"

"A lot."

"Did you ever tell me that you couldn't believe a word Alger said because he lied so much?"

"Yes."

"How old was Alger when you told me this?"

"Twenty-five."

"Are you saying that Alger Dickerson is not a trustworthy source of the truth?"

"Yes."

"No further questions."

"Esquire Bell, cross-examine."

Chris walked over and put his hand on the rail of the witness box. "So your son, Alger Dickerson, has never once in his life told the truth?"

"Yes, he has. He tells me things all the time that are true."

"Give me an example?"

"He told me he got the job at The Eighth District Penitentiary, and I know he worked there."

386

"What do you think is the ratio of truth to lies from Alger Dickerson?"

"I think he tells the truth eighty percent of the time."

"So anything that Alger Dickerson says has an eighty percent chance of being a true statement?"

"I would say so."

"That is all."

Judge Atwood looked at Daniel Hall.

"I have no further witnesses." Hall hung his head. *That double-crosser is going down.* "But I would like to make a statement on my behalf."

"Go ahead."

"I did not shoot Samuel Adams. I spent that night drinking at the Hillcrest Inn. Alger is guilty of murdering or helping to murder Samuel Adams. He told us so himself."

Richard Atwood had known the verdict before the trial started, and nothing he had heard during the trial had changed his mind. "After hearing what these people have said, I find Daniel Hall guilty of the murder of Samuel Adams and sentence him to be hanged by the neck until dead.

"Also, Alger did tell us that he participated in the shooting death of Samuel Adams. I find Alger Dickerson to be a co-murder of Samuel Adams and sentence Alger Dickerson to be hanged by the neck until dead."

Patience screamed, "NO! YOU CAN'T TAKE MY BROTHER AND MY SON!"

Ninety One

Stephanie poured the morning coffee. "I don't think we can get across without making a water cache along the way."

"How would we accomplish that?" asked Sally.

Eli looked up from his binder. "I'm making a chart. We need about fourteen hundred gallons of water a day, but we know we can get by with less for a few days." A few hours later, Eli passed around his chart. "Here is what I suggest."

day	at dusk	at dawn
1	**team 1** Leave river w/ all supplies, water mattresses in 3 wagons, water barrels in last.	**team 1** Arrive mile 25. Leave everything & start home. **team 2** Leave river with fresh animals.
2	**team 1** Arrive river. **team 2** Leave 4 full barrels at mile 25. Take wagons w/ everything else.	**team 2** Arrive mile 50. Drink 4 barrels water. Unload supplies.

3	**team 2** Leave 3 wagons, all mattresses, 4 full barrels. Take 4 empty barrels, 1 wagon.	**team 2** Arrive mile 25. Drink 4 barrels water. Take 8 empty barrels and 1 wagon.
4	**team 2** Arrive river. **team 4** Refill barrels. **team 3** Leave river with fresh animals, 8 refilled barrels, 1 wagon.	**team 3** Arrive mile 25. Leave 4 full barrels. Take: 4 full barrels and 1 wagon.
5	**team 3** Arrive at mile 50. Drink 4 barrels water, dig depression, and line with india rubber wagon covers.	**team 3** Drink 4 barrels water. Empty water mattresses into india rubber lined ponds. Take 4 wagons, 7 empty water mattresses, 8 empty barrels.
6	**team 3** Arrive mile 25. Drink 4 barrels water. Take 4 wagons, 7 empty water mattresses, 12 empty barrels.	**team 3** Arrive river. **team 4** Refill barrels and mattresses.
7	All people and animals leave river well hydrated with every water container full.	Arrive mile 25.
8	Arrive mile 50. Drink the ponds dry, reinstall the india rubber wagon covers, & load all the supplies.	Leave
9	Arrive mile 75. Drink half the carried water.	Arrive mile 100. Drink half the carried water.
10	Arrive at San Diego.	

"We can't leave it out there alone. People or animals will ruin everything," declared Oscar.

Tom assured him, "Nothing is out there for the same reason we have to go through all this. There is NO water. Also, I recommend waiting a few days after team three returns. They'll need to recover, and also, we should gather all the mesquite bean pods we can find while we're here."

Helen swallowed the last of her breakfast. "Can we leave the wagons with the stoves here? I want to make bread."

"The four small wagons should hold the supplies we need to take out there, and I'd enjoy fresh bread with saguaro jam." Noah noticed the glare bouncing off the sand ahead of them. "We need to find our goggles. Let's do some testing before we start."

Ann returned from a short trip onto the nearby desert sand. "It's like the dunes at the Lopez gold mine. It's going to burn the animal's feet."

"What about making foot covers like Eli made at Albuquerque?" suggested Oscar.

"We have 232 animals that will be walking. That's 928 booties!" exclaimed Eli.

"I don't see that we have any other choice," Tom started toward a wagon. "I'll count how many antelope hides we have left."

"Thirty-Seven," said Eli, who always knew how much they had of everything. "We can probably get eight small circles out of each. That's only-" Eli thought for a few seconds. "Two hundred and ninety-six, but that's only enough for the dogs, goats, and sheep. We also have six cowhides. We can probably get three hundred out of them and protect seventy-five more animals."

Eli pondered on. "Donkeys have small hooves. We should be able to get the sixty-eight circles we need for them from the Andalusian bull hide. We can eat the last of that pemmican today. That still leaves sixty-three horses, twenty mules, forty-one cows, and twenty-four oxen with large hooves. We'll need three hundred more sixteen-inch circles."

"Crimony!" said Nikki, which was the word he had picked up from Ann to use instead of the cuss word he had learned from Cleo.

"We'd solve three problems by butchering oxen. We'd have more meat, we'd have more hides to make booties, and we'd need less water and booties." Noah added, "This is why I told everybody not to get attached to the oxen."

Nikki patted his father's hand. "We've already eaten some. Go ahead and do it. I won't be upset."

Eli cocked his head. "Let's start making booties with the hides we already have and see how many feet we get covered before we butcher an animal. Working together, we should be able to make the ninety-six we'll need tonight."

"We should walk the animals in the sand close to camp today," suggested Roscoe. "If they do all right, we could start shuttling supplies and water into the desert this evening."

As soon as foot coverings were installed on an ox, Adahy saddled it. He put on his blue goggles and broad-rimmed felt hat, covered the back of his neck, and then rode the animal into the hot sand. Next was Noah on a Steeldust. Sally rode Big Jenny into the desert. Beside her, Alex sat on the mule named Diamond. The animals circled in the sand until dusk.

In the blazing sun the longest, Adahy slid off the steer into the river. "The heat is terrible. I barely made it the whole day, and all I did was ride. I don't think anybody would be able to unload supplies in the heat of the day.

"Team 1 and team 2 should leave at the same time. We swap to team 2 animals in the morning and go on to mile 50 during the day. Team 1 can still bring the animals that pulled the wagons home the next morning. That way, we can unload in the evening. This ox seemed to suffer more than the others. Maybe we should use them as team 1 and bring them straight back to the river."

Eli pulled the last rawhide string through the last circle of leather he believed they needed before sundown. "We don't have boots for a second set. Team 2 will have to wait until tomorrow evening."

Helen put the one she had just finished into the pile. "God, please get us twenty-five miles out with the wagons and back with the oxen. Keep us safe. Please show us what we need to learn. May the crossing of this desert bring You glory. Amen."

Everybody echoed, "Amen."

Ninety Two

Sally, Alex, Roscoe, and Helen struggled five miles across deep sand to the crest of the last dune. "Thank you, God!" Roscoe slid down the slope and waited for the wagons to descend safely before continuing across the flat desert. A few hours before dawn, Helen saddled the ox Roscoe removed from the yoke. "That went well!"

Sally did the same with a second ox. "Now comes the hard part."

"We should be able to travel much faster with no wagons." Alex tied the lead rope of a string of oxen to the saddle pommel of the ox on which he sat. "With any luck we'll get most of the way back before it gets blistering hot."

Only minutes after they arrived at the twenty-five-mile point, the group set off along the tracks they had made on the way out. In the remaining cool of the night, the riders double-timed the oxen and covered half the return distance. As the air and sand warmed, the animals slowed. Two hours before the sun shone directly overhead, they reached the dunes. The ox that had spent the previous day in the hot sand bellowed its discontentment.

Helen commanded the animal, "Quiet. You're losing water making all that noise. I'm miserably hot, tired, and thirsty, but you don't hear me complaining!"

The ox keeled over.

Helen wailed, "We're going to die!"

"No, we aren't. This is the second day that one was in the heat. We're only five miles from the river. We can do it." Roscoe wiped a river of sweat from his face and neck. "But we do need to get off and walk." He took the halter and footwear off the dead ox.

Sally plodded through the scorching sand beside Alex. As she sucked the last water from her canteen, a second ox dropped to its knees. Sally stood beside the dying ox. "I've changed my mind. We've overcome many difficulties, but this desert might be too much. I want to get married before we start across. We'd have at least a few days together before we die."

Alex removed the dying animal from the string. He put the booties from its feet into his pocket. "All right, my love. We do have a good plan, but this sun could cook us if we have water or not."

Hours later, Nikki shouted, "I think they're back." He dashed away to get his spyglass.

Ann had hers in her pocket. She jerked it open and scanned the western dunes. When Nikki arrived at her side with his looking tube, Ann hugged him. "My eagle-eyed son, you're right."

The tiny figures grew closer for an agonizingly

long time. Once finally back, man, woman, and ox collapsed in the cool river. The ministering hands of the family tended to the four people who had barely survived the deadly heat.

Ann knelt beside her sister. "Are you all right!"

Sally whispered, "I don't know."

"What can I do to help?" Stephanie held Sally as the water flowed around them.

"Don't let me float away!" barely made it out of Sally's mouth.

Nikki dripped water over Sally's forehead.

Stephanie slid her legs under her sister and wrapped her arms around her armpits. She looked at her husband. "Eli, you need to rework the plan."

"I'm already thinking about it." Eli wiped Alex's cheeks with a cloth as he held him in the current.

Beside him, Tom cared for his mother with the help of Oscar and Emily. "I knew I shouldn't have let you go."

Noah held Roscoe in the cool, fast water. Roscoe reached up and wrapped his fingers around Noah's arm. "The dunes are only five miles wide, but they're much hotter than the rest of the desert. The heat killed two animals on the way back. We can't be out there during the day."

"Ehawee, the animals need to be looked over." Adahy waded toward the oxen. His wife followed him.

When everyone had revived, Eli passed around an updated schedule. "Here's my new plan.

Pop and I will take mules and donkeys. I hope it's not more than a hundred and fifty miles to the sea."

day	at dusk	by dawn
1	**team 1** Leave river w/ all supplies, water mattresses in 3 wagons, water barrels in 4th.	**team 1** Arrive mile 25. Leave everything & start home. **team 1** Arrived river 2 pm.
2	**team 2** Leave river with all 12 canteens full. Get over the dunes then canter to mile 25. Take everything except 4 full barrels and 4 ten gallon tubs to mile 50. Unload the supplies if we have time.	**team 2** At mile 50 spend day in shade of wagons. Animals drink 4 barrels water. People 3 canteens water each.
3	**team 2** Unload if needed. Leave 3 wagons with all the full mattresses and 4 full barrels. Take 4 empty barrels and 1 empty wagon. Canter to dune and then walk. Stop at mile 25 if we have to.	**team 2** **Hopefully** arrive at river but spend the day at mile 25 in the shade of wagons if we have to. People 3 canteens water each. **team 4** Refill barrels
4	**team 3** Leave river with 4 refilled barrels, 12 full canteens, 1 wagon. Cross dunes then canter to mile 50. Start digging 4 wells. (4 feet deep and 3 feet around)	**team 3** At mile 50. Animals drink 4 barrels water and each person 2 canteens. Spend day in shade of wagons.

5	**team 3** Finish wells and line with india rubber wagon covers. Empty water mattresses into wells and cover. Drink 4 barrels water and 2 canteens. Take 1 wagon, 7 empty water mattresses, and 8 empty barrels. Canter to mile 25.	**team 3** At mile 25 spend day in shade of wagons. Drink 4 barrels and 2 canteens water.
6	**team 3** Take wagon, ten-gallon tubs, empty barrels, water mattresses, and canteens to river.	**team 3** Arrive river. **team 4** Refill barrels
7	Leave with all wagons, full water containers, and people and animals well hydrated. Travel to mile 25.	At mile 25 spend day in shade of wagons.
8	Travel to mile 50. Drink the wells dry, reinstall the india rubber wagon covers, and load all the supplies.	At mile 50 spend day in shade of wagons.
9	Travel to mile 75. Drink half of carried water.	At mile 75 spend day in shade of wagons.
10	Travel to mile 100. Drink half of the water.	At mile 100 spend day in shade of wagons.
11	Travel to San Diego. Drink town water.	

Ninety Three

Hand in hand, Sally and Alex stood before the rest of the family. Sally took a deep breath. "I'm afraid we won't make it across the desert. I want to get married now, and Alex agreed. Noah, would you perform the ceremony?"

Noah asked, "This very second? I'd like to have time to plan something nice."

"If Eli and Tom leave tomorrow evening, we can get married tomorrow. If they have to leave tonight, then yes, this very second."

Stephanie hurried to the couple and wrapped her arms around them. "I'm so happy for the two of you. I've been thinking about your wedding for months. I have all kinds of ideas. Let me tell you."

After Stephanie's presentation, Alex hugged her. "I think this would be perfect!"

Sally vigorously nodded her head. "I love this! Thank you."

Stephanie pulled her sister into the hug. "Wonderful. We'll get started."

Ann wrung her hands. "Sisters, I'm sorry, but everything we have is twenty-five miles away, and we didn't keep enough food to stay an extra day. Noah can marry you now, but we'll have to celebrate on the other side of the desert."

Sally looked at her sister. "Oh! Where is my brain?"

"Maybe you cooked it today," answered Ann.

Stephanie still held her sister and soon-to-be brother-in-law. "That doesn't explain why I didn't think about that."

Noah put a hand on Sally's shoulder when she turned from Stephanie. "I always have my ceremonial clothes. Therefore, right now, it is. Give us a little time to prepare as best as we can. You and Alex get yourselves ready."

When Noah and the others separated, they had a plan. They placed river stones in a large ring before each person went to his or her assigned task, including the band of Mojave Indians up the river. Using a hollow reed to breathe, a scout approached under the water. Full of curiosity, but prepared to signal for his compatriots to eliminate the group that might be bringing supplies to San Diego, the native's eyes rose above the water. The Mojave in the water saw something no pale face would do.

A man, who wore buck skin pants, a mink cape, ermine tail moccasins, mystery man hair bones, and a medicine bag around his neck, fanned the air inside the circle with eagle feathers that he withdrew from his medicine bag.

The Mojave saw a cluster of brush at the river's edge. He hid there before he allowed his ears to rise above the water.

The mystery man spoke. "Father God, command disharmony, negativity, and all other forms of evil to leave the wedding circle." He sprinkled a trail of tobacco as he treaded the ring of stones. "Take this tobacco offering in exchange for your blessings on this ceremony. Stones give your permanence to this marriage."

The family gathered outside the circle. Noah stood next to a short tobacco-free opening. "All those who support and bless the union of Alejandro Devine and Sally Williams enter the wedding circle and stand at your position."

Noah smudged each of them with a cluster of smoldering sage as they entered the circle.

The Indian in the water had traded with many Mexicans before he realized they planned to force him from his homeland. He had learned the language and knew the man performing the ceremony wasn't a Mexican. *He not speak the language and eyes the color of the sky. He not one of us either.*

"Alejandro and Sally, if you want to join your lives, come into the circle." Noah waved his hand from them toward the place where they should stand. Alex and Sally passed him, each draped in a small blanket.

Noah closed the tobacco ring. "Holy Father, seal evil outside." He took his place in front of the bride and groom. "Alejandro Divine and Sally Williams, marriage is a sacred union created by our heavenly father as a symbol of the union of Christ and the Church. This is a forever commitment. Just as Jesus will never forsake us, you should never abandon this marriage. Weave your lives together around our Blessed Savior in the power of the Holy Spirit. As the Bible tells us, 'Husband, leave your mother and father, cleave unto your wife, and the two shall become one. Wife, respect and honor your husband as the head of you. In the same way, your husband should respect and honor Christ as the head of him.

"Although storms will come, and disagreements will arise, support, love, and forgive each other all the days of your lives. If you are willing to exchange your individual lives for a joint life, take the first step toward Nikki and Oscar."

Sally and Alex turned and stepped over to the boys.

Nikki looked into Sally's eyes and then Alex's. "I love you exactly the way you are, but Papa told me you have to be willing to change from being only you."

Oscar spoke his part of the prophecy. "You will become something better than either of you could be alone. Together you will be a family. By removing your blankets, we symbolize the old you going away." He and Nikki stepped behind the couple and took the blankets when Alex and Sally dropped them from their shoulders.

This is a wedding! The man becoming waterlogged watched intently. *This is a family, but why do they have so many animals?*

"If you are willing to proceed, take step two," instructed Noah.

The couple moved to Eli and Stephanie. Stephanie spoke first. "Baby sister, I have watched you grow from a person afraid of everything into a strong young woman who has faced and overcome many obstacles, a woman who believes in herself and her family, a woman well able to be a great wife and mother. Alex, I have known you for only a year. During that year, you have shown yourself to be a brave, intelligent, resourceful, caring, sharing provider who will be an excellent husband and father."

Eli said, "I speak to Alex first to tell you that I don't apologize for attempting to protect Sally. I do apologize for not seeing that your intentions have been to love, honor, and protect Sally from the first day you met her. I see the depth of those feelings, and I am delighted that you will become her husband.

"Sally, you are my sister as well. Although I don't personally remember, I heard the story so many times that I feel like I remember you reaching for the silver mirror and pulling it to you when you were just a baby in a basket on your mother's arm. Without damaging the mirror or yourself, you acquired what you wanted. I have watched you make what you want happen many times. Remember when you told us that you wanted Noah and me to be your brothers? While Stephanie and Ann had a lot to do with that, you did everything in your power to keep us together as a family, and here we are, all together, despite Daniel

Hall and everything else. You love and want Alex, and look where you are right now. With that much ability to make happiness happen, I'm sure you and Alex will be very happy."

Together Stephanie and Eli went behind Alex and Sally, draped a large blanket over their shoulders, and spoke in unison. "This blanket symbolizes our hearty approval and blessing over this joining of your lives."

"Alex and Sally, if you still desire to join your lives, take step three to Roscoe," instructed Noah.

Those two pale faces, but the husband might be one of us. Mystery man so strange. I find way talk to him. A bubble of gas escaped from the Mojave's rear. He quickly dropped.

Noah noticed the ripples. *That's not a turtle!*

Roscoe spoke. "Many, many years ago, I met a woman and wanted a large family. That was when I started researching and learning about the uses of plants, minerals, and animals. I learned about mandrake, and I bought some from a Chinese man. I ground it, planning to put it in the tea of the woman I wanted to be the mother of my children. That wasn't meant to be. This mandrake never brought me children of my body, but I have a family of my heart. I give this mandrake to the two of you as a blessing. May you have many children." Roscoe held out a bowl in which sat a small pouch containing mandrake.

Sally and Alex took the bowl.

Noah proceeded despite the eyes he thought

he saw just above the water. "Take the fourth step if you still want to bind together."

The couple proceeded around the circle to Adahy and Ehawee. Adahy held a bow and quiver of arrows. "Alex, when we first came across you, we thought you were defenseless. You had no gun, bow, or knife, so we believed you could not protect yourself. However, we were not correct. You immediately charmed us with your humor and good nature. You removed any threat to yourself by making us friends. However, many things in this world will not be overcome that way, so I give you this bow and quiver of arrows along with a promise to teach you how to use them so that you'll be able to defend and provide in this marriage."

Ehawee rubbed something between her clasped hands. "Sally, when I met you, I was starving. You sat in the middle of the blanket upon which I sat and served us smoked elk, salted goose legs, bear meat sausages, cheese, dried apples, apricots, sassafras tea, goat milk, and honey. You exposed your most secret fear to an entire village of people you didn't know when you allowed my brother to tell about what happened in the Indian with the rope to the moon and back cave. You opened your heart to Kimimela and helped her overcome her fear of caves even before you could do so. You opened your heart to all of us girls as you took us mapping the land and plants around the village. You have a heart as big and open as the universe. Alex, you have used your knowledge of español—

404

She said español! I can speak with him.

"and people to help this family again and again. You have always done so happily and many times at your own expense. That is why I know that the two of you will have a wonderful marriage and life together and why I give you my heart stone." Ehawee placed a small heart-shaped stone into the bowl that Sally and Alex held.

"Your heart stone! You've had that since you were a child. Are you sure?!" exclaimed Sally.

"Yes. I love you. Both of you."

"Thank you."

Noah was sure they were being watched. *I don't think we're in danger. He's been there a long time.* "Sally and Alex, if you wish to take the fifth step, go to Tom and Emily."

Emily placed a folded paper in the wedding bowl. "Like Alex, I'm rather new to this family, but I see the love the two of you have for each other. I heartily support this union. Marriage will not always be happy with never a problem. There might come a time when you think you don't love the other anymore. But I believe both of you don't just love the other, but that you like each other as well. Remember, it's a commitment you have made to each other and God. Hold on to the promise you are making today, stay together in the bad times, and God will bring you out the other side. That is a copy of the letter my mother gave me the day I married Warren. It has helped me many times. Both of you read it and hold the words in your hearts."

Tom spoke with a dreamy voice. "Sally, you had an excellent example of how to be a mother. Emma loved you and your sisters so much. You'd sit in the chair in my store while she brushed your hair. I wished Hattie had lived long enough for us to have a daughter. I watched you, Stephanie, and your mother and imagined Hattie loving our daughter the way Emma loved you. I don't have them here, but I want to give you many ribbons to put in your daughters' hair."

Those have to be their animals. Their condition is too good for them to be bringing them as meat. And they have only two wagons for fourteen people. They cannot be taking supplies to San Diego. It would be better if I go to them openly. The Mojave put his breathing reed into his mouth and swam underwater like a frog.

Noah looked straight at the river when he saw the dark shape moving under the river's surface. *He might be going to get others.* "Take step six to Ann if you are still committed to marrying." Noah went a few steps over to stand beside his wife.

Ann exchanged the bowl for a board with three long clusters of different colored horsetail hairs attached: a yellow section from Helen's horse, Lemonade, black hair from the tail of Biscuit, and red from Lucky. The hair was secured together at the top and then divided by color. "The two of you are well suited for each other. You are both individually full of strength and power. Both of you have lost much but have found even more in each other. Together you will be a power with which the universe will have to reckon. Noah and I give you this unity cord as a symbol of our blessing."

Noah hurried the ceremony. "You will take the final step and forever join as you speak your vows to each other. When you braid this cord, you also weave the strands of yourselves together. With your love and commitment to God, your marriage will be a cord not easily broken."

The couple took the seventh step into life together and went to the tree stump set up to hold the plaque. Alex secured the board on a nail hammered into the wood. He laid the black hairs across the yellow into the middle. "Sally, in good or bad times, I promise to live my life in devotion to you and God."

Sally pulled the red hair over the black ones. "I promise to live my life in devotion to you and God, whether the times be good or not."

"I pledge myself to you alone and will forsake all others." Alex weaved the yellow hairs over the red into the middle.

"I will give myself unto you only." Sally brought the black hairs over the yellow.

Alex weaved the red back. "I promise to let God show his love to you through my body, actions, and love."

"I pledge to wrap God's love around you with my body and love and everything I think and do." Sally continued the braid.

Noah saw a lone man approaching from the

direction that the swimmer had gone. The man stopped far away.

Alex braided in black. "I promise to share my dreams, joys, troubles, worries, and sorrows and never to close myself away from you, to be open for you to share with me, and to love you at all times. Thank you for agreeing to spend your life as my wife and allowing me to spend mine as your husband."

Sally smiled as she laid the yellow hairs across. "This is the cord of God that I am using to promise to you that I will share all the good and bad inside me and to hear, care, and help you in everything you share with me and to always in all things love you. Thank you for marrying me."

Noah raised the board from the stump and handed it to Sally. "I pronounce you husband and wife. Alex, you may kiss your bride."

As Alex kissed Sally, the man at the edge of their awareness resumed his approach. Noah wiped a break in the stones and tobacco. "Go forth weaving your lives and this cord together. Right now, though, everybody get into the wagons. Get your rifles ready, and then do nothing else unless I tell you."

Sally dropped the unity cord. "What?! What's happening?"

"Pick that up and get into a wagon. Somebody watched this ceremony, then swam up the river, and is now walking toward us."

"Why did you keep going? You should have

warned us!" Ann grabbed Chris and Joy from the baby corral. "Sally, please get Adele!"

Noah explained, "He wasn't going to attack us, and I wanted Sally and Alex to have a perfect and complete ceremony."

Sally hugged her brother-in-law. "Thank you." She picked up Adele and ran to the wagons with everybody except Noah.

Ninety Four

The approaching man called out in Spanish, "Soy amigo!"

Alex stopped halfway into the wagon. "Sally, I have to go. That man spoke Spanish. You stay below the sideboards."

The people in the wagons peered out from under the wagon covers with their guns at the ready. Alex called out in a loud voice. "Hola, soy amigo tambien!"

As the man drew near, the concentric blue tattoos that covered his body became visible. "Soy Tálpo. Mi gente es Pipa Aha Macav. Esta tierra caliente es de nosotros."

Alex explained, "He says his name is Tálpo. His people are called Pipa Aha Macav, and that this hot land is theirs."

"Tell him we mean no harm. We don't want his land. We're crossing to the western sea."

Alex passed on the message.

"Why you going to sea?" asked the Mojave.

Alex thought he knew the answer but asked Noah. "What do you want me to tell him about why we're going to the sea?"

"Tell him that an evil man tried to kill my wife

and me because we married. We want to go far away to love each other safely."

Alex stated Noah's reason and added, "I am here because my parents and grandfather are dead. I do not want to live with the people of that village. Then I fell in love with the sister of this man's wife, so I came with them."

"You go to San Diego to take these animals to the soldiers for food?"

"No. These are our animals, but would you want some of these oxen?"

"Maybe."

Alex said, "I think he might like to have the oxen. Would you want to trade? Would we still need the skins of any of them to make booties?"

"Eli said we would need some of them when he thought we would take the oxen. Let me think." He scratched numbers in the sand, added, multiplied, and divided. "We need two hides."

"I've seen vultures circling but only in one place. We might be able to get some of the hides of the two that died today."

"We can't be sure. We should keep two. Tell him we will trade twenty-two oxen if he has something to trade. Don't tell him about what we have in the desert."

"We will trade…" Alex flashed all ten fingers twice and then two individual fingers, "twenty-two ox." He pointed at one of the animals.

"Why?"

"They cannot walk across —" he pointed at the dunes; "desert, and they need too much water."

"You cannot take enough water for this many animals even without ox, and days are too hot."

"Do you know another way?"

"Go around. The nights are very cold. You have blankets?"

"We do."

"Food? Jars? Baskets?

Alex asked Noah, "Do we want food, jars, or baskets?

"Our wagons are almost bare. If he looks, he'll see very little food. What kind of food? How large are the jars?"

Alex asked. The man ran through a list of items which Alex repeated to Noah. "Pumpkins, mesquite beans, salmon, trout, eels, clams, crabs, rabbits, squash, corn, roots, herbs, berries, and muskmelons."

Plants here are different. I need to learn about the place where we'll live. "Ask if he knows a medicine man by the sea willing to share his secrets with me. I will share what I know in return. Tell him I am a mystery man sent to the world."

Alex translated Noah's words.

The tattooed man signed, "If you speak this language, I tell you."

Noah signed back, "I speak this way."

"I thought you mystery man, but eyes wrong color," signed the Mojave.

"I special messenger of Great Spirit. He poured the sky into my eyes."

"OH!!! You prove this?!"

"You have snake with tail that rattles?"

"Yes."

"You show me where. I drink rattlesnake poison. It not kill me. You will be sure."

"All my people and your people watch. If you die, all your people die."

Alex spoke in English. "Nobody can do that. Why would you say that you can? You'll get us killed!"

"Trust me."

God in heaven knew that this encounter would happen. He had provided Noah with the same small animal capture device he had used to catch a rattlesnake out on the prairie. That stringed board was used to open the stove door every time they made bread. Since they had decided to keep the stoves with them, it was in the wagon. "How far?"

"Two fingers move of sun."

"When I catch it, how long to get your people?"

"We will go past them. Warriors will return with us."

"You and me smoke to agree to this before we go."

"I have no pipe."

"I have." Noah pulled his pipe bag and pouch of herbs of power from the medicine bag hanging from his neck.

"Your family must smoke too."

"I agree." *I better explain this to Ann.* Noah went to their wagons and related the situation. He looked into Ann's eyes. "I know you will be afraid. I know I can do it. I have done this before."

"You did it when you saved Emily and Oscar."

"How long have you known?!"

"I found out after the sandstorm. I understand you are saving us again. Do what you have to. I trust you. But if you die, I'm going to kill you!"

Nikki looked at Ann. "He would already be dead."

Noah explained. "It's just an expression. It means I better not die."

"It's getting late. Are you going to have time to do this before it gets dark?" asked Roscoe.

"We will go on horses. Alex, tell him to ride one of the Steeldusts."

Alex passed on the message.

"Don't know how," replied Tálpo.

"I guess you have to walk." Alex turned to Noah. "He doesn't know how to ride a horse."

Noah waved for Tálpo to come over. "We will smoke. You ride with me. When we get to your people, tell them start walking here. They here when we back. If they try hurt my people, I kill them with magic." Noah filled the calumet, lit it, drew in the smoke, and blew it above him. "Father Sky and Mother Earth, hear the agreement we make. God, bless me with Your power to drink the poison of the rattlesnake and live. Cause all of the people in my family to honor this agreement to go peacefully to the western sea. Cause the people of Tálpo to allow us to pass. Help us to cross the

414

desert. Show Tálpo what to offer for the oxen." *And have them take away the oxen tonight so we can start the next part of our plan.* Noah passed the pipe to Tálpo.

Tálpo smoked and then said, "Great Spirit, when my people see this man drink the snake poison, show them that my decision is right. I keep the right to kill them and take all their animals if he dies, they attack, or help Californians." *Show me what to offer for ox.*

The rest of Noah's family, including the two boys, but not the babies, Eli, or Tom, smoked in acceptance of the agreement. Tálpo did not seem to realize that two men had not joined them. Noah and Tálpo rode away on Eyanosa. Noah discretely signaled to move forward with the plan if they could get away before Tálpo's people arrived.

When Tálpo was out of hearing, the family discussed the request to stick to the plan. Stephanie tapped her jaw. "If we get food for the oxen, we can spend the extra day here, but then Eli and Tom will have to remain hidden, or Tálpo will want to know why they didn't smoke."

Tom said, "It might be better if we go. If we leave before sundown, we should be able to get all the supplies unloaded tonight and spend only one day out there drinking water. We'd have more when we get there with all the animals."

"It will be good if the oxen are gone, but having more water is good either way. I hope we get large water jars, but I agree with Pop. We should go as soon as it's cool enough. Since we'll be

415

riding directly into the sun, we should zig-zag behind the ridges as much as possible."

"Good thinking, son. Let's get ready."

They strung together the needed animals, covered them with blankets to keep the sun from scorching them, laid canteens of cold water over twelve mules, mounted King and Ace, and then rode into the burning sand.

Ann pulled Sally aside. "You and Alex sleep in the wagon tonight. It will probably hurt the first time. Hopefully, Alex will be gentle." She hugged her sister. "Tonight, when the time is right, enjoy sharing love."

Ann strode across the camp. "Kill an ox and start roasting it. We need to make a lot of bread before the Mojave warriors arrive."

Ninety Five

Noah pushed the board with the rope loop into the snake nest.

Tálpo watched in awe. "These kill my brother with one bite."

It wasn't a pit, so the capture was painstakingly difficult. Noah finally managed to snag the line on a root in the roof of the hole. He let the device lie still until a rattler slithered onto the board, and then he jerked the rope tight and held the snake fast.

"You got it!" exclaimed Tálpo.

Once Noah had the small snake out of the hole, he used a long, forked branch to pin its head to the ground. He moved his capture device forward along the rattler until the rope safely and securely held its head and body to the board. "That took long time. We hurry back. Your people probably already at my camp. Hold this." Noah placed the head end of the board on the ground and leaned the other toward Tálpo.

"I not want carry that."

Noah wanted Tálpo to feel fear, increasing the man's reverence for Noah's courage. "Hold like this until I get on. Then I take it, and you can get on."

They cantered back to camp. Noah saw that the mules were gone. His family sat beside a dozen Mojave warriors eating freshly baked bread and hunks of the ox roasting over a large fire.

Noah smiled to himself. *Everything is going well.* "Let me quench my thirst before I perform the ceremony."

Tálpo slid off Eyanosa and sliced himself a portion of meat. Noah drank milk as he put on his mystery man clothes. While the others ate ox meat, he carried a bowl past his audience to prove that it was empty before he tied a bootie around it.

Before he released the rope, Noah pinched his fingers tightly behind the rattlesnake's head. The snake thrashed. As if fighting to control the wild creature, Noah brought the deadly animal close to many Mojave warriors, who flinched to escape the snake. Then, to capture its venom, he forced the mouth over the edge of the bowl. The fangs pierced the hide. Every time Noah jetted his face toward the snake, it ejected its venom into the bowl. He pulled the snake away and tipped the bowl toward the man Tálpo had identified as the leader of their party. "Adahy, remove the hide."

Adahy had watched the ritual the first time Noah had performed it. He released the thong that held the hide over the bowl.

418

The lead warrior leaned forward and looked inside. He signed, "Rattler poison in the bowl."

Noah walked the bowl around the circle to let everybody see that the bowl they knew had been empty now held rattlesnake venom. Still holding the thrashing snake securely behind its head, Noah opened his mouth, held the bowl high above, and poured in the contents that glittered red in the light of the setting sun.

Ann stifled a scream of despair as her husband swallowed.

Noah opened his mouth, stuck out his tongue, and moved it from side to side while he circled to display that he had consumed the rattlesnake poison. Noah slid his blade under the rattler's skin and drew it down the pale belly. He flung the incapacitated snake to the ground. "I am Mystery Man sent to the western sea by the Great Spirit. As agreed, we will go into the desert within five days and be gone. You signal to all your people between here and western sea to allow us to cross."

"My people live here beside river. Tipai-Ipai people by sea. If you living when moon rises, I will send message, but we are we, and they are they," replied the war party leader. "Tálpo told me you will trade many of animal we now eat."

"Son, bring me an empty bushel basket." Noah flashed all his fingers twice and then held up two. "Ox. What you offer?"

"For each what you call ox," he held up one finger as he named each item, "muskmelon, pumpkin, basket corn, basket beans, basket red barberries, basket squash, large jar salted eels, large jar salted clams, smoked rabbit, smoked trout, smoked salmon..." he held up two fingers, "smoked crabs."

Noah countered with a closed hand. "No eels. No beans." He raised three fingers, "Crabs," then two fingers, "salmon, trout, rabbits with furs, pumpkins, muskmelons."

He kept up his two fingers and raised the bushel basket that Nikki had brought over. "Baskets red barberries, baskets squash," He displayed four fingers, "baskets corn." Noah again signaled two then spread his hands one above the other as far apart as he could, "Jars clams."

The Mojave negotiator held up three fingers. "Crabs. Only," he held up one finger, "rabbit, trout, salmon. All the others." He poked out two fingers. "We take ox and one wagon to village tonight. You get what we agreed. Come back here before hot again tomorrow."

"The moon is up. I am alive. I agree."

Adahy and Roscoe already had a wagon hooked to six Steeldust horses. Adahy sat in the driver's seat. "I will go. You stay here."

Noah felt fine but accepted in English. "Much obliged. I will stay and drink milk."

Adahy asked, "Which way we go?"

The man pointed north.

Adahy instructed the dogs. "Blackie, Honey, drive oxen."

The Mojave marveled as the dogs nipped only at the legs of oxen and drove them in the designated direction.

Roscoe slipped a halter over the head of the final ox they needed and held the lead rope.

Finally able to be alone, Alex and Sally slipped into the wagon and pulled the puckering strings closed. They shared physical love for the first time in either of their lives.

Six hours after leaving, Tom and Eli stopped at a cluster of rocks they believed was fifty miles into the desert. Accustomed to unloading goods at their store, they quickly moved the contents out of each wagon, stacked everything together in the sand, and then drove the wagons containing nothing but full water mattresses into two parallel rows forty feet apart.

They suspended the four india rubber covers between the rows at the top of the wagon bows, tied them to each other, and then added the canvas covers on top. After they got the mules and donkeys under the sunshield, they doled out half the allotted water. Eli and Tom placed all but the last bolt of cloth they planned to lay over the empty wagon, consumed their third canteens of water, climbed over the seat, and slid under the thick cloth roof. They pulled the last bolt into position and lay down to sleep.

Adahy returned to camp with the dogs and a wagonload of food. "Tálpo added a jar. He said it's not for the oxen. It's a wedding gift for the two he watched take the seven steps. It's the black one." He crawled under a bush close to the river, lay in the cool dirt, and slept while the people who had rested during the night processed the wagon's contents.

Sally shook the black jar. Its contents sloshed. "I think it's more clams." She dug the clay plug out with a knife and looked inside. "I guess we get to try eel after all. Everybody has to eat some."

Oscar pinched his nose with his fingers. "It's your present. I don't want anything in that jar."

"I'll take a no-thank-you serving," Stephanie got a whiff and wrinkled one side of her nose. "You never know until you try. Too bad we didn't get a recipe."

"Chowder may be good," suggested Helen.

"I'm going to slice one down the middle and fry it." Sally reached into the jar and pulled out an eel. "Slimy. This thing has to be four feet long, and it's heavy. It probably weighs fifteen pounds. This is a lot of meat. I'll cut off a foot of it."

In only a few minutes, the soft but firm meat was ready. "Looks like fish." Sally stabbed a chunk with a fork, blew on it to cool it enough that it wouldn't burn her, and popped it into her mouth. She gently chewed for a second. "Yum!" She chewed it up and swallowed. "We should NOT have refused them. I'll cook more."

Everybody ate a portion. Sally set some aside. "Adahy can eat this when he wakes up. We'll cook more when Tom and Eli get back."

They set to work and spread the forty-eight jars of clams over the wagon canvases they moved to the ground.

Sally smiled at the husband she had lain with and then slept beside. She put her hands on her hips and stretched her back. She glanced at the canvas covered with wet clams before looking at Alex. "I'll bet you that they'll be baked by sundown."

"I'm not taking that bet. I know you're right." He kissed Sally's lips. "Who will help me rinse out these jars?"

"Aren't they pretty?" Nikki ran over and carried one to the river.

Oscar held one in the slow current close to the shore. "They might think these are large jars, but I don't. They aren't going to hold much water."

"Probably around three gallons. I think a hundred and forty-four more gallons of water will be helpful. I'm glad we got them."

"I am too." Oscar looked inside the jar. "It's just that I thought they would be as big as me."

Nikki informed his friend. "Forty-eight jars that big would hold all the clams in this whole river."

"Probably not," said Alex, "but it sure would have been a lot of clams."

Nikki sniffed the jar. "It still smells. I don't think these will ever be clean. We should use the water in them to clean diapers."

Stephanie, Helen, Emily, Noah, Ann, Ehawee,

and Roscoe had cut up all the squash and pumpkins and placed the slices on other canvases. After they strew the barberries in the sun, they sat in the edge of the river and made animal booties. At day's end, they stored the food that had indeed baked dry during the day and hunkered down for the night.

Tom and Eli drank four more canteens of water while they prepared to depart. To protect their supplies, they untied the covers from the west set of wagons and drove the first eastside wagon just west of the pile of goods on the ground. To make the fourth corner, they forced two wagon bows into the sand, leaning against each other at the top. They tied the covers right above the sideboards. Before they started back, they allowed the animals to drink the last two barrels of water.

With six mules pulling a wagon with only four empty barrels inside and the other eighteen animals tied lead rope to lead rope and then fastened to the rear, they made it back to their camp in the cold of the night.

When everybody was awake, Sally plopped the rest of the eel she had started the previous day into the frying pan.

Clunk.

"The eel clunked!" Sally picked it up. Something fell from its mouth. "It's beautiful. Blue, white, and orange."

"It looks plain and gray to me," remarked Ehawee.

424

"Not the eel." Sally passed around a stone the size of the first joint of her finger.

Ann placed the blue stone with orange and white webbing back into Sally's hand. "Exquisite. It must have taken a long time to get it this smooth. The eels were nice, but giving you this is surprising."

"Maybe Tálpo put it there, but why put it in the eel's mouth? Jesus had a fish bring a jewel to pay his taxes." Sally placed the Mojave turquoise in her pocket. "I think God had the eel get it. Thank you for getting the beautiful stone, eel, but we're eating you anyway." She coiled the eel in the pan and placed it in the coals of the fire.

Ninety Six

Noah, Adahy, and Alex planned to get every scrap of ox hide, and the dunes were too hot to stop during daylight hours, so they waited until dusk.

"There wasn't much the vultures hadn't eaten." Tom handed Noah the reins.

Adahy drove the wagon down the last slope of sand. "Not even bones. Maybe that's better. We'll get to the supplies sooner. I hope we make the wells tonight and be here only one day." They quickly traversed the remaining forty-five miles.

"Let's get started." Alex held out one of the shovels Tom had left at the edge of the supply pile.

It soon became apparent that they had a problem. Noah leaned against a shovel. "This is the same thing that happened when we tried to dig a hole in Cadron Creek. The sides wouldn't hold together then either."

"What did you do?" asked Alex.

"Made a dam and moved the water. We'll have to make this one wide and then bring the tarp up and fill in around the outside as we add the water."

It took the rest of the night to dig one wide

depression three feet deep in the middle. They secured the wagon covers between the wagons while the sun rose. After watering and corralling the horses under the sunshield, they lay in the wagons beneath the bolts of calico already sun-bleached from Eli and Tom's trip.

Midway through the second night, they had made one india rubber-lined well three feet deep and four feet wide filled with the water of four mattresses. Alex wiped his brow. "Let's cover this with india rubber. If we leave now with the empty mattresses and barrels, we should be able to get back to the river not long after dawn."

"With four extra mattresses of water, the next team should be able to work two nights and dig two wells because they won't waste time trying to figure out how to do it. They can pick up the extra barrels at mile twenty-five and have enough water to fill the third well." Adahy finished the last of his third canteen.

"We wouldn't use more than the fourteen hundred gallons Eli said we need, and we have a lot of water in this well. We don't want to trap an india rubber canvas under hundreds of gallons of water. Actually, let me think." Noah found his binder and a pencil.

Noah figured out how much less water they needed without the oxen and how many more gallons they would need in the second well. "We'll take the wagon to the twenty-five-mile water barrels. Adahy and I will return here with the wagon, two horses, and four full water barrels. Alex, you take the six empty barrels tied on three horses and ride the fourth horse back to camp.

"Tomorrow night, we'll make a smaller well with the last three mattresses. We'll drink the water in the barrels we brought back from twenty-five. That will be enough until somebody brings six fresh horses and a wagon with six barrels and all the canteens full.

"We'll need to drink some of that water as soon as it gets here and during the next day. Then we take one wagon, the empty mattresses, and barrels back to camp the next night. We'll lose only one extra day. That is if both of you agree."

Alex rode into camp alone. "Don't panic. Everybody is fine. It was harder to dig a well than we thought. This is the plan…."

Roscoe spoke up. "I've been back from the desert the longest. I'll go." That night Roscoe rode out with the requested water in one of the two wagons that had remained in camp.

The morning of the second day after he left, Roscoe returned with Noah and Adahy. Ann hugged her husband.

"I'm so glad you're back!" Nikki wrapped his arms around the legs of Noah and Ann.

"Me too!" replied Noah. "It's much too hot."

Nikki held on tight. "Are we leaving tonight?"

Noah shook his head. "I think we should give the horses that just got back a rest until tomorrow night." *Me and Adahy too.*

Ninety Seven

Under the waxing moon, Noah, Ann, and their family prayed for God's protection. They crossed the Algodones Sand Dunes for the last time and then started into the desert that might kill them.

Everybody and the animals were in top shape as they drank water from the pond that Noah, Alex, and Adahy had made fifty miles into the waterless wasteland. The family extended the sunshield by the two wagons they had just brought. Even so, they couldn't fit all the animals under the sunshade.

Roscoe suggested. "We'll start some of them west of the wagons. Around noon, we can take some that had been in the shade to the east side and bring in those that were out."

"The little animals will stay shaded the longest. Let's get it done and get some sleep." Noah tied short animals to the west side of their wagons. He slept as well as he could before he moved the animals.

As the sun went down, Helen, Ehawee, and Emily scooped water from the second well. Even doing almost nothing, the dry air and blistering heat sucked vitality from the living. They drank cached water and ate bread they had made beside the river, clams cooked into chowder with milk from the cow they assumed would dry up crossing the desert, and fresh muskmelons. The animals ate mesquite beans the family had gathered at the river and drank the second pond dry.

With the wagon covers reinstalled, the supplies loaded, and everything possible full of water, the family started their second serving of what had not yet seemed like a deadly desert.

They traveled across the flat land hindered by the desiccated air that sucked moisture from everything. The animals slugged along for thirty miles that night. Tom looked over a lamb. "We have to stop and give them water. Let's set up the canvas. We can use the bows and make a bigger covering. It won't be as thick, but it's better than any of them having nothing."

Sally looked at the mountains ahead and patted the head of the lamb. "Some animals won't make it without a good amount of water, and the mountains don't look that far away. It looks like we can get there this coming night, so maybe we should let them have more than half the water."

Eli figured in his head. "Five mattresses and one barrel will give them a thousand and fifty gallons, and if we use only one barrel of water, we'll still have a thousand and forty-four gallons left, plus what's in the canteens. I'll start with the animals that seem the most exhausted."

"Lamby and I are most obliged. I'll help," Sally followed Eli.

Roscoe pulled some creosote bush branches from the net under a wagon. "We have another cold hour to cook. Beef rib barbeque sounds good?"

Stephanie answered, "All your barbeque is great. I remember the elk ribs you made at Pine Bluff. Sure we were starving, but it would have been the best even if we had gorged the day before."

Noah put his arm across Roscoe's shoulder. "I'd love some. I'm going to start making the shelter. I can use some help." He walked away.

Nikki and Oscar climbed into the wagons and untied the covers.

Ninety Eight

The scorching day in the arid desert under a beautiful blue but utterly cloudless sky left them all desperate for water. Chris and Joy cried, which made them lose more water. "I'm afraid they'll kill themselves crying!"

"Give them my share," Noah pulled the canteen over.

Ann gave all four of her children water.

Noah's tongue stuck to the roof of his mouth. He spoke with cracked lips. "I'll get a ten-gallon tub and pour in a jug of clam water. Maybe that will give us some moisture in here. I'll tell the others to try it too."

It was the hottest day yet. The tub of water barely helped, but Noah's babies did stop crying. Etu, however, continued to scream.

The sun finally went below the flat horizon that had kept them in the hot sunlight until the last torturous second. Everybody came out of the wagons. Adahy held Etu's limp body. "We put him in the tub and forced him to drink, but he doesn't move anymore."

"Save him, Noah." Ehawee's tears flowed.

"Stop crying this instant. You can NOT lose that much water! Adahy lick it off her face."

Noah put his ear to the boy's chest. "His heart is beating. Put a tub under him. We need to pour water over him."

Ehawee turned her face to Adahy. "Drink my tears."

Adahy did so while Stephanie poured water over Etu. The water evaporated and pulled heat as it ran down the child's torso.

Ehawee wrung her hands. "Is it helping?"

"It's hard to know," replied Noah, "As long as he keeps looking at us, I believe we'll save him."

The clam water in the tub disappeared as they poured it again and again. A few minutes after they started the second tub, Adahy looked up. "He smiled."

The second tub was almost dry when Etu wiped his face. Everybody clapped. Ehawee hugged her son. "He moved!"

Sally put her arm across Ehawee's shoulder. "The sun's been down for hours. Now that we know he's going to revive, we should move out. We need to get him out of this desert tonight." *Along with the rest of us!*

Noah rose from his place beside Etu. "I don't have a drop of water in me. This desert is sucking it out of us faster than we can drink it, but we probably won't find water the second we get to the mountains, so we shouldn't use all of it. Eli, please calculate how much more water we can use. Ehawee, keep pouring water over your son. Everybody else, start your assigned tasks."

Eli looked at the mountains and estimated. "Five hundred more gallons. Everybody, fill a canteen from a barrel, drink all of it, and then fill it again to drink while we travel. Give plenty to the children too. I'll start watering the animals."

After the scorching day, it took them twice as long to get ready. Sally accidentally knocked an egg from a chicken crate. It cracked open on the wagon bed. "Crimony! They've barely laid an egg since we crossed the river, and I broke the only one!" She scooped it up and flung it onto the cracked clay ground.

Oscar walked past the egg a few minutes later. "The egg cooked! I'm going to eat it." Before Emily could stop him, it was down the hatch. "Yum! Fried egg!"

Nikki play-punched Oscar's arm. "And you didn't even share it."

"There must be a lot of heat stored in the clay to have cooked it that fast. I'm ready," said Ann. Thirteen other readies followed hers.

Eli commanded Ace, "Forward, ho."

Ninety Nine

Two hours later, the lamb that had suffered the most the previous night died. Nikki stroked its fur. "Goodbye, little friend. We're sorry."

"It's much hotter and drier than we thought," explained Oscar.

No sense in wasting meat. Once everybody had passed, Eli gutted the animal, skinned it, and hung its carcass on a wagon. Eli also harvested the two grown sheep that died not long after but took only the hide when the ox they had kept expired. *Even with the planning that got us eighty miles before using any of the water we're carrying, this land is proving to be true to its name: The Desert of Death.*

A Steeldust pulling a wagon stopped, drew its last breath, and then fell over. "Get it out. I'll bring over another." Roscoe headed for one of the animals to which he felt least attached.

Eli slurped water from his canteen and looked at the carcass. *It's too much work.* He removed it from the harness and left it behind.

Still a long way from the western hills before them, they entered a gap between two wide-spread barren hills littered with stones and low plants displaying masses of thorns. A harnessed Andalusian keeled over. "Halt!" called out Adahy. "We have to give the animals the rest of the water while any of them are still alive."

"I'll look for water. Please, God, help me find a lot of it." Noah led Eyanosa between the mountains to a clay plain with scattered creosote and salt bushes. He spotted a black-footed ferret, tied Eyanosa to a bush, and followed the animal to Carrizo creek. "Praise be to God!" The ferret lapped water before it moseyed away.

Noah dropped to his knees, dipped the bowl from his pack into the water, and raised it to his sun-blistered lips. He surveyed the area while he drank. *Even beside this creek, there are barely any more or any greener plants. The kind of plant is different, though. I'll have to remember to look for this.* Noah studied one of the small palms for a few minutes. *I need to get Eyanosa.* He filled his canteen from the shallow stream, backtracked, filled the bowl, and held the water under his horses' mouth. Eyanosa slurped up two bowls before Noah took another swig for himself. They moved to the delicious, life-giving water.

At the creek, they drank their fill. Even though he had taken his horse in case he needed to ride back, Noah walked beside Eyanosa to the wagons. "I found a creek. Now that you watered them are the animals well enough to walk another mile?"

"We should go if they are or not. We need to get to water before sunrise." Adahy handed Ehawee their child. "Keep him cool."

One Hundred

Beside the creek, under the canvas between the wagons, the temperature dropped to miserably hot from deadly. "How much longer until we get to the western sea?" asked Nikki.

Alex pulled out the map. "The map shows us going through this gap and then over. It looks less far than the desert but doesn't show how many miles up and down the mountains. It's probably quite a few more days."

Tom looked over Alex's shoulder. "I've been thinking about what Tálpo said. I don't want to get caught in another war. We barely survived the last one. If Mexicans and Tipai-Ipai are fighting in San Diego, we should go north or south of them."

"Good Point. I agree." Eli rubbed the scar on his stomach. "Should we vote?"

Sally said, "I think we all agree. We don't go to San Diego. We see which way looks easier once we get to the other side of the mountains. After we set up for the winter, we can scout up and down the coast and find the place we want to settle. I can hardly believe it. It's been three years since Gus burned down our farm, and we've traveled so far, but we're finally almost there."

Stephanie smiled, "AND we have wonderful new family members. I couldn't be happier, except maybe to tell you that Eli and I will add another in about seven months."

"That's wonderful!" Emily rushed over and hugged her daughter-in-law.

Everybody congratulated the couple. Ann, due in two months, had to stretch over her big belly to hug Stephanie.

The people and animals that had made it across the desolate and merciless desert slowly revived over the two days they remained beside the creek. Fully stocked with water, they resumed the trek at sundown. On the southern rim of the flat plain ahead, it looked like a gap through the Laguna Mountains, so they set off in that direction. Once again, the animals wore down quickly and barely trudged along. Nikki walked beside Noah. "Are more of the animals going to die?"

"Maybe not if we go at a slow pace. But we need to get to the hills tonight." As quickly as he dared to push the animals, Noah led them under the light of the full moon.

Several hours before dawn, Ann saw Eyanosa stumble. "Noah, we have to water them, or Eyanosa will be the next to die."

"Halt!" yelled Noah. "Full water for all the animals and people now!" He hurried water to his favorite animal. "Don't die." He rubbed Eyanosa's neck before he trotted off to get water for Zi and Rose. "As soon as they're full of water, we need to

438

move on. We need to get completely across tonight. None of us will make it through another day in the desert sun."

Just like the start of the evening, it didn't take long for the animals to fatigue. This time, Noah led them as slowly as he dared. Just after dawn, they nestled into a shallow gully, raised the canvases to add to the shade, and set up for what they hoped would be a much easier day at the foot of the barren, rock-strewn Laguna Mountains.

One Hundred One

After another almost unbearable day, with only the light of the waning moon, the animals stumbled up the rocky mountain. The leg of one of their Jersey cows slid into a space between large rocks. In the harness and pulled forward by the other five cows, Arbuckle's leg broke. It became apparent that night travel was no longer possible.

Sally knelt beside the cow they had found at Fort Arbuckle. "It wouldn't do any good to make another cage like we did for Gimpy. The ground is too rough for that to work. I'm very sad to lose her."

Eli put his hand on Sally's shoulder. "Me too, but we have her calf. I can be the one to do it if you want me to."

"Much obliged, Eli." Sally patted the cow's neck, rose, and walked away.

"After you go over the rise, set up camp," instructed Noah. "We'll have to travel during the day from here on, but I think we'll be all right. The air has cooled as we've come up this wash."

"Do you think we can dig to water?" asked Alex.

"There are palms here, but this looks like a rain runoff creek. You shouldn't waste much energy, and certainly not after the sun comes up."

"We're almost out of water. I'm going to try." Alex grabbed a shovel and put his back into it. The ground had no problem staying together. Soon he had a hole a few feet deep.

The other men joined him. By sunrise, they had a ten-foot-deep but still dry hole.

"Sorry to make you put all that work into this worthless attempt to find water."

"It was worth a try, Alex," Noah climbed out of the hole. "We'll give out the water we have left and then get going. Maybe we'll find some today."

"If we do," said Adahy, "Eli's plan got us far enough to get across."

"It wasn't good enough. We lost six animals," replied Eli.

"Yes, but there's no telling how many animals you saved," declared Roscoe.

One Hundred Two

Micah Clemont stood in the Little Rock sawmill office. "Yes, I want to build it with sturdy lumber, but I plan to disassemble the gallows after the hanging. You can have the lumber back, so I'll only pay half price."

Augustus Pexels held firm. "You pay full price, or you don't get the lumber. I might buy it back after you take it down but probably not. Who will buy the lumber you're going to hang our men on? If I do, there will be a transportation fee to haul the lumber both ways."

"Well then, here's your twenty dollars. Have it delivered tomorrow. The men will start right away."

"I'm surprised you've been able to get anybody to build it. Those men have a lot of relatives who aren't taking kindly to you hanging their kinfolks. Most of them don't think you gave them a fair trial the way you ran them through like that."

"They were identified as Angels of Righteousness, and the kinfolks of the men they murdered didn't take kindly to what they did either. Just deliver the lumber." *The sooner this is over, the better. The men I brought in are costing me money, and it will take days to build a nine-man gallows.*

Later that day, Augustus sneaked through the rear door and up the stairs of Peabody Inn. He knocked at room 1. "It's me, Augustus," he whispered.

Micah opened the door.

Augustus looked both ways down the hall before he slipped into the room. "I can't get anybody to deliver the lumber, and people are talking about burning down my mill. I can't help you."

"I understand." Micah held out his hand.

Augustus said, "I hate to lose the money. What if I arrange for lumber to be delivered from Maumelle? It would take a couple of weeks to get here and cost more."

"How much?"

"They probably would buy the lumber back, but it will be ten more dollars up front."

Micah pulled a sack from his pocket and removed a ten-dollar gold piece. "See to it then. Upon delivery, I'll pay you an extra 25¢ for every day sooner than fourteen."

Not an hour passed before Augustus rode the fastest horse he owned toward Maumelle. He left a large sign on the mill stating, "Absolutely no lumber will be/or has been sold to any person for the purpose of building any type of scaffolding." His grown sons sat watch over the mill in case anyone tried to set it afire.

Before the day ended, tall timbers were being milled, and stock lumber sat in Maumelle wagons set to be delivered to Little Rock. The mill owner had no idea why Augustus needed him to help, but it was a large order, and he didn't care.

One Hundred Three

Noah wound up the dry wash. The higher they climbed, the larger the agaves grew in the ash-gray soil of pebbles and conglomerated rocks. Air from the coast blew wood smoke over the slope. Noah sniffed the air. "It's probably a Tipai-Ipai camp. Wait here. Sally, give me that stone."

"No. It's mine."

"I hope you'll get it back. I won't bring it out if I don't need to, but I might need it to protect me. Then, if I get them to smoke the Calumet with me, they won't attack us." Noah held out his hand.

Sally looked into Noah's eyes for a moment. "Trading has made the people we've met friends. Try that with our other goods, but if it needs to leave me, it does. Be careful." She gently pressed the eel gift into Noah's hand.

Noah carefully made his way to the crest. Many more ridges lay ahead. In the small valley before the next, six men camped. *Long hair, sticks through their noses, nothing on but breechcloths, except that looks like an agave fiber belt and fiber sandals. Well, I'm not going to have the nose ornament, but I have the hair and sandals. I wonder if it would be better to dress*

445

in my native clothes. No, it's too hot. At least I should change my clothing the best as I can.

Noah went back to the wagons. "I want to dress to look more like them, but not exactly."

"Can we sneak around them?" asked Ann.

"No, they'll see us as soon as we crest the ridge. When I come back, stay in the wagons unless I tell you to come out."

A few minutes later, Noah wore a breechcloth. His medicine bag hung between the puma scars on his bare chest with the stone added to his usual items. He slid on the yucca fiber sandals the Apaches had made for him, tied his hair at both sides of his neck, and then donned his belt and knife, along with Itza-chu's quiver of arrows. He picked up his bow and walked away.

Noah whistled a melody as he crested the ridge. All six heads below turned. As soon as the Tipai-Ipais looked his way, Noah signed, "friend."

The men jabbered and gestured excitedly.

Noah continued to sign, "friend," as he stood where he was.

The clearly non-Californian was not aggressive. The Tipai-Ipais calmed and tried to make out what the man signed. They picked up their bows and slowly approached.

Noah signed the same word repeatedly.

The leader of the Tipai-Ipai men studied the intruder. *He wears our clothes. No Californian would have young man initiation scars on his chest.* Still far away, the man signed, "friend, come down."

Noah made his way down the stony slope in

the sandals that did not hold his feet securely. *I hope they're at least helping my image.* He stopped several feet from the other men. "I come in peace."

The man who stood closest asked, "Why you come here? What tribe?"

"Come because people attack me. Tribe is Quapaw."

"Never heard Quapaw."

"From rising sun. Walk many winters to here."

"You lie. You need much to walk many winters. You have nothing."

"I have more things. I smelled smoke and came to see."

"Where you go?"

"Do not know. Want find place live in peace. Right now, want much water."

"How we trust you?"

"I medicine man. I will smoke with you."

"Your eyes wrong color. You lie like Californians."

"I, Tahatankohana," Noah signed swift hawk, "special mystery man of Great Spirit. He pour the sky into my eyes."

He is a hawk?! "Prove it!"

"Great Spirit gave me this in eel mouth." Noah brought the turquoise from his medicine bag.

The Tipai-Ipais recoiled. "The stone of life!"

"Yes," said Noah very calmly. *I didn't know they saw this stone that way.*

"You are shaman!"

"Yes."

"You help us; we tell you where good place to live and where get water now."

"What you need?"

"You tell us what we need. Then we know you shaman."

Noah looked at the men while he put the stone into his medicine bag. *All they have is a travois, their bows, and arrows. They need meat. We own sheep.* "Great Spirit sent me bring you meat. We smoke and agree we not attack other then He Who Talks comes. Others stay. I give one sheep each of you. He Who Talks brings sheep to," he pointed at the other Tipai-Ipai, "you."

"We smoke," said He Who Talks.

The seven men sat. Noah spoke the words in Quapaw as he performed the ceremony to create the Calumet. He raised his pouch of sage, cedar, tobacco, and sweetgrass to the north and then filled the bowl. "Smoke carries our prayers to Father God, the Great Spirit." Noah signed, "I smoke for peace between these men and their people and me and my family, for water now, to give sheep to these men, and for guidance to a new home." Noah shook a match from his jar, struck it on a stone, lit the pipe, drew in the smoke, and then exhaled. "Aho." He held out the pipe.

He Who Talks took the Calumet. "I smoke for peace between this man and his family and us and our families. I take him to water and guide him to a good place to live. He give six sheep."

Each of the other men smoked and signed the

same. Noah smoked the last of the herbs and then took the pipe apart. As he put the stem in its pouch and slid it into his medicine bag, he swung the bowl back and forth to cool it. He packed it and the matches and then signed, "He Who Talks, come."

One Hundred Four

The two men climbed the hill. The eyes of He Who Talks grew wide as they rose above the ridge. *Six wagons and more animals than I can count.* "You do have things!"

"Yes. Now, I give." Noah selected five large rams. "I give your sheep end of travel. Which way we go to water? Follow you over hill or go other way? How long to water?"

"Follow. Three fingers of sun to water."

Noah tied the lead mule of each team to the rear of the wagon in front. He yelled, "Forward, ho," and then walked in front of the lead wagon with the reins in his hand. The dogs drove the animals.

He Who Talks repeatedly turned his head to watch. "Dogs very good. Where family?"

"In wagons until I say come out."

"They safe with me."

"Terrible cross of desert. They stay out of sun."

"You cross Hayikwiir Mat'aar?"

"Yes. Too hot and no water."

"You do have magic. Hayikwiir Mat'aar land of death. Stone of Life brought you across."

"Yes."

"Stay." He Who Talks led the five sheep to his companions. He spoke to them in their native language before returning to Noah. Until the last wagon crested the next ridge and went out of view, the hunters stood where they were, holding the yucca twine around the necks of the sheep.

For two hours, they ascended as they went up and down the ridges. The wind from the ocean brought moisture into the cooler air of the mountains. Finally, after a long descent, they rode to a giant, water-filled fissure in the flat ground. He Who Talks smiled. "Can drink and swim. Water hot." He jumped in.

Noah squatted and felt the water. "Like a bath." He decided He Who Talks was safe. "Everybody can come out. We can draw water and swim."

Thirteen heads poked from one end of a wagon or the other. Nikki jumped out and ran to Noah. "Papa, may I go in?"

"First, we give the animals the last of the beans and let them drink." Noah secretly returned the turquoise to Sally as she watered the chickens.

Soon everybody splashed in the large spring of mineral water. After enjoying the deep and abundant water for a long time, Ann announced, "Diaper cleaning time."

"I didn't mess up those diapers," Nikki swam to the center of the pool.

"Get over here. We all do chores even if it's not directly for ourselves, but you may wash clothes or fill water containers." Ann got out. She carried a Mojave jug to the pool.

He Who Talks flew out of the water. He grabbed Ann's wrist and screamed curses in Spanish. "Where you get this?" he signed.

The jug dropped and shattered. Ann drove her other hand into her attacker's gut. Surprised by a white woman's sudden and powerful return, He Who Talks lost his grip.

Simultaneously, Noah jumped from the water. "Never touch my wife." He tackled the man and rolled on the ground as they wrestled. Clumps of Noah's hair left his head, and blood flowed from He Who Talks' nose. He Who Talks got Noah in a chokehold, but Ann kicked her attacker off her husband. Noah flipped the Tipai-Ipai and then pressed his knee into the small of the man's back, pulled up his arm, and squashed the man's cheek into the dirt. "Sign to him to explain, or we will kill him right now. The rest of you get a weapon. Make him afraid."

Noah drew the man up under the barrels of several guns. He released He Who Talks' arm but kept a chokehold around the man's neck.

Alex stepped in because he had heard those cuss words directed at him back in Raton. He spoke the demand in Spanish.

He Who Talks brow furrowed. *They are Californians!* He replied as well as he could with his neck drawn back. "That Mojave jar. They supposed to kill anybody crosses river."

Alex glared. "Were you supposed to kill everybody?"

"Yes."

"Why you did not?"

"I thought you were not helping Californians at San Diego, and you help us. But you are Californians. You speak in their words."

"I am from the rising sun and not with these Californians. The Mojave saw we are not here for your war. We gave them animals. They gave us clams in jars."

"How do I know you speak true words?"

"We could have killed all six of you earlier? We could have killed you now? We did not. We come in peace to find a home."

True. They could have killed us. "I believe you. How I prove not enemy?"

Alex explained to the family.

Noah let the man go. "Give your weapons," he signed. "Never touch or threaten any us again, or we WILL kill you. You take us good place. Show us where find good plants and things. Family will decide if more as we go."

He Who Talks untied the belt that held his throwing stick and knapped quartz blade. His breechcloth went with the belt he held out to Noah. Noah removed the weapons and gave the strap and cloth back. "You wear this always."

For the remainder of the day, they drew water and cleaned. The wagon's clotheslines filled. Sally pinned a petticoat to dry. "Nothing has been this clean in months."

The family allowed He Who Talks to walk among them. The boys kept their distance, and the women maintained a space between the man and the young children. Ann gave He Who Talks a bowl of sheep and squash soup when they ate supper.

He Who Talks thought, *why do they give me food and not make me a prisoner?*

The men and dogs followed their unspoken watch schedule during the night. The following day, they traveled southwest across the flat valley. He Who Talks led them through a low gap into a valley of scattered oaks below a stony, scrub-spotted mountain.

Noah stopped and stared at the tall peak on their right.

"Kuuchamaa," said He Who Talks.

Noah's shoulders and the back of his head tingled. "That mountain has power."

He is shaman. "That our most sacred place. When Kuuchamaa created world, he made this mountain special place for him to live when he came as a man. He lived on this mountain. He called shamen from all peoples and told them to live in peace and help each other. He taught dances to teach our people how to live. Some other tribe tried to throw power on the mountain to kill him.

454

They didn't hurt him, but they broke mountain right there." He pointed to a split in the side of the mountain. "Kuuchamaa called shamen again and again, but they kept fighting. When he died, they burned him away on mountain top. Spirit of Kuuchamaa still in the mountain. Only Tipai-Ipai shaman He calls can walk there. If any other goes, he dies. But if Shaman is told to take sick people there, Kuuchamaa heals us at Tears of Great Spirit."

"We will respect the mountain," replied Noah. "May we hunt here or collect these acorns?"

"You may."

They knocked down the nuts with the tipi poles they got in a Cherokee village, gathered them up well into the night, threw out acorns that had visible weevil holes or looked rotten, and stored the rest in duck cloth sacks. In the morning, they loaded the full bags and followed the water that started near the holy mountain.

Where the stream folded back, they stopped for the mid-day meal. A red-tailed hawk flew overhead while the animals grazed. He Who Talks pointed. "He is one of four helpers of Great Spirit's son. Hawk, raven, and eagle during the day, and owl at night. They watch everything and tell Spirit of Kuuchamaa what we do." *You are Swift Hawk. Are you watching us?*

The hawk dove into the grass and rose with a meadow-jumping mouse. He and the people watched each other while they ate.

They went south past the creek bend, turned southwest, and then encamped just west of Ejido Mountain. "Tomorrow, we get to ocean. It good place to live."

They ate more of the sheep that had died in the desert, cornbread made from the Mojave corn they ground, and pumpkin soup.

After breakfast, they traveled northwest for fifteen miles and then crossed the Tijuana River at its confluence with the Alamar. Adahy suggested, "We should stay here tonight. I want to get to the western sea during the day."

Sally remarked, "But I'm so excited! I don't know if I can wait another night."

"My village is Milh Ixox. I go tonight and tell them you coming," said He Who Talks.

"NO!" commanded Noah. "You will tell your people to attack us."

"I not do that! I smoke pipe with you," protested He Who Talks.

"You attacked my wife."

"Because I think you hurt Mojave friends. We live here very long time. Californians come. They smoke pipe with us, then catch us, hurt us, make us work, take our children."

"For this Tipai-Ipai fight with Californians?"

"Yes."

"When Tipai-Ipai smoked with Californians, Tipai-Ipai made ceremony. When you smoked with me, I made ceremony. I have Calumet and herbs of power. I know the sacred above and the sacred below. Do Californians know this?"

"They do not," replied He Who Talks. "You live with Tipai-Ipai. We teach you how live here. You teach us what you know from land of rising sun."

"You and your family teach us," Noah circled his hand to show that he meant his whole family, "Your shaman teach me?" He pointed to himself.

"I agree," said He Who Talks.

One Hundred Five

In Little Rock, Micah paid Augustus two dollars. "I don't know how you did it."

"They only needed to mill the four main posts. They had the rest in stock because they were putting together an order for Mr. Strong, but he didn't need to deliver it for two weeks. I told him it was now or never, so he let me take it. Don't tell anybody I had anything to do with getting it."

"My lips are sealed, and Maumelle Lumbermill is painted on the wagons." Micah left Augustus behind the livery and went off to round up the men he had waiting to build the gallows.

Relatives and others, who believed that the convicted had only done what should be done to people engaging in interracial relations, watched the construction of the gallows in front of the courthouse. "What are we going to do?" asked Owen, the grown son of one of the convicted men.

An uncaptured Angel of Righteousness held a bottle of matches. "Burn what they build!"

"We can't set it on fire with a single match. We need something else, so we can get away once the

458

fire is going," said another of the men secretly watching.

The sun was high overhead when the carpenters leaned the floor platform against the jail wall. Two of the twenty-foot support posts sat in their holes. The men put down their tools and went to Peabody's for their mid-day meal.

Owen held a stick with an oil-soaked rag around it. "It's a lucky day. None of them stayed behind. Let's go!"

"So go on and do it," encouraged the man who had suggested that they needed more than a match.

Owen held the door open. "Any of you coming with me?"

"It's a one man job. Any more, and we'll be seen. Go on. We'll keep a look out from here," said the Angel of Righteousness.

Owen looked to see if anybody was in the bar. "There's a man in the bar."

"Use this coat and wrap it around the torch." A fourth man took one from the coat tree in the corner of the room.

Wearing the coat tightly wrapped around his body, Owen casually strolled past the man in the lobby. He doused the newly built floor, lit the torch, tucked it under the oil-drenched wood, and then dashed off at lightning speed.

The oily smoke wafted in the window. Sheriff Taylor sniffed. *What's that?* He looked out the window but didn't see anything. He returned to pinning wanted posters on the wall then sniffed again. *I definitely smell something burning!* Taylor turned and saw flames licking up the wall. He grabbed the bucket he used to bring water to make his coffee, flew out the door, and tossed the water on the wood burning against the building. The fire continued to burn. "HELP! BRING WATER!" Taylor kicked the burning structure into the road.

Nobody came with water. *Stupid people. I'm sure whoever set this fire is watching.* "YOU AREN'T GOING TO STOP THIS HANGING, AND YOU COULD HAVE SET ME ON FIRE. I'LL FIND YOU, AND YOU'LL ROT IN JAIL."

The man in the bar saw Owen run in and up the stairs. *He smells of oil and smoke, and why is he wearing a coat on a hot day like this?* He heard Sheriff Taylor. *Well, that explains Owen, but nobody's going to hear a word about this from me.*

When the carpenters returned from dinner, he sent one of them to get Captain Cornish.

Miles Cornish strode into the jail. "I see the remains. Why do you want me? You're the sheriff."

Sheriff Taylor informed him, "I can't go looking for the culprit and keep a watch on the construction of the gallows. Post a guard here until this hanging is over."

"I guess my men might as well be doing something instead of sitting in the arsenal. How many do you need?"

"Six. I want to make a statement. If you break the law, you pay the price."

One Hundred Six

Two days later, Noah, Ann, and their family skirted the salt marsh of the Tijuana River. They became visible to the people in the large coastal community. He Who Talks' father was a Kuseyaay, a helper to the village leader, the Kwaapaay.

A delegation of men, including He Who Talks' father, rode east before the approaching caravan could come within striking range.

He Who Talks, Noah, and Alex hurried ahead to meet them. He Who Talks called out, "Father! I bring friends," then signed and spoke in Spanish so that Noah and Alex would hear him tell how he had met the group with him.

The Tipai-Ipai men asked to meet the other people and to look into the wagons to verify that everything was as they had been told.

Noah agreed, "Come out, family."

In Spanish, Alex stated how each person was related as he walked past them.

Each of the new arrivals responded, "Hola."

After making sure no soldiers lurked in the wagons, they crossed the flat and rode into a village of domed willow branch homes. The fifteen families in the sib of which He Who Talks was a

461

member swarmed around the arriving caravan. The delegation that brought them in explained to their families that the new people were a family who had come to escape attack and wanted to live in peace with friends.

Adahy signed, "May we go to the western sea? I never seen a sea."

"Come," said He Who Talks' father, Duro.

They proceeded across the wide beach. Out on the water, people fished from shallow, bull rush bundle boats. Ocean waves lapped at the sandy shore. They knelt in a circle and held hands.

Noah prayed. "Heavenly Father, You have brought us thousands of miles to this beautiful beach. Time after time, we faced circumstances that could have been our end, but You always helped us and showed us the way. We have learned to trust You and not fear. Because You have been with us, and You do not change, we know You will continue to be with us.

"We praise You for making this land and allowing us to see so much of it. There are so many different things, and all of it is beautiful in its own way. We also thank You for putting so many people around us to help us and for letting us minister to them too.

"We are forever especially grateful for those who have joined our family. We love them. Five people left Harmony with almost nothing. Three years later, we are a family of nineteen overflowing with animals and provisions. We say thank You, and we love You. Amen"

Everybody echoed, "Amen," and then stood.

He Who Talks pulled a boat into the surf. "The water goes forever. You come with me?"

"Yes," Adahy helped push the boat into the deep water.

Roscoe, Helen, Sally, and Alex stood shoulder-deep in the western sea. The boys ran in the sand and collected shells. Eli, Stephanie, and Hattie built sand structures and then watched the waves dissolve them. Nearby, Tom and Emily dripped ocean water on Carol Ann.

Ann sat in the waves with Chris and Joy as they splashed in the salty water. Ehawee and Etu played beside her.

Noah leaned down and kissed the top of Ann's head, "I love you!" he ran into the receding ocean with Nikki, Oscar, and Adele. They followed the waves out and then ran inland to avoid the returning water.

Out in the deep, Adahy dove into the water with He Who Talks. Ehawee saw them repeatedly surface and drop something into the large basket in the boat. When they came ashore, they brought dozens of lobsters.

Later that day, half the family went to the salt marsh and harvested oysters, whelks, and rushes. The others stayed in the village with Bly, He Who Talk's wife. They cracked open acorns, peeled off the shells, and spread the kernels inside the long trough in a large flat granite boulder. Bly informed them, "We grind them into powder when dried. Tonight, we catch many fish in beach."

Nikki watched the movement of the two tattooed lines that went down from the corners of Bly's mouth and the third down the middle of her chin. He corrected the woman. "Fish are in water, not the beach."

Bly insisted, "They on beach."

"May we catch too?" asked Ann

"Yes."

In the middle of the night, He Who Talks went to get anybody who wanted to catch grunions. Everybody went to the shore and found the beach covered with slender eight-inch-long fish.

Oscar knelt beside a fish buried in the sand. Others flipped and slithered around it. Suddenly the fish, with only its head and upper fins showing, popped into his face. "Ahhh!" Oscar fell over backward. The fish washed into the ocean on a wave. "What are they doing?!"

He Who Talks explained, "Laying eggs in the sand. Grab as many fish as you can. We eat and smoke for this winter."

The fifty people on the beach shoved grunions by the handfuls into baskets. Except for Carol Ann, even the young children managed to keep ahold of some wiggling fish long enough to get them into a basket. Adele squealed with delight.

He Who Talks asked Noah, "You stay here with us?"

Noah looked at Ann. She nodded.

Bly saw. "You need to make lodge. Tomorrow I show you how."

A few hours later, all the fish had returned to the ocean. The tiny fraction the people had gathered amounted to thousands of fish.

One Hundred Seven

That same evening in the civilized city of Little Rock, the nooses were installed on the newly built gallows. Daniel Hall sat in his cell. *I wish I knew if Joe dispatched that horrible creature who calls herself a woman. I hope Ann Williams is feeding the worms and that despicable heathen Noah Swift Hawk is too. At least I'd go to my grave in peace, knowing they went first.*

One Hundred Eight

From the salt march by Milh Ixox, Noah, the other men of his family, and He Who Talks cut sheath after sheath of long tule cattail leaves. In a grove inland from the marsh, they gathered willow branches and saplings. The boys harvested the inner bark of the trees to replenish their dwindling supply.

The women sat together on a large boulder on the nearby Tijuana River bank. Bly dropped acorn kernels into a shallow basket. "Rub together, tap basket, and blow to get skin off."

Once all the kernels were skin-free, Ann, Stephanie, Sally, Ehawee, Emily, and Helen did as Bly did and pounded their acorns into powder in one of the many depressions in the rock. After all the acorns had been ground, they moved to a gravel sand bar. Each of them scooped out a depression. They lined the bottom with a half-inch thick layer of wet, coarse sand and formed it into a large shallow bowl with a raised lip. Over that structure, they firmly patted in another inch of dry, fine black sand. With the leeching bowl constructed, they poured water through the cluster of pine tops to wet the sand. It was then reinforced by a ring of stones around the outer side. Before they added their acorn meal, elder branches were propped around the bowl to prevent dirt from blowing in.

Bly showed the other women one of her smooth, fine-grained cooking stones. "Each of you, find ten. Clean very well." She pointed to the river and then started a big fire while Ann and the women of her family searched for cooking stones in the cold river.

The fire burned down to coals as the women repeatedly ran water through the meal using the pine to break the flow into sprinkles. For hours, they leeched the bitter tannic acid from the acorn flour.

Once the leeched acorn paste passed the taste test, they put their stones in the coals to heat while the water drained. When the acorn meal surface became cracked, they used their fingers and scooped out the acorn paste, which they put into clean, water-tight baskets. Bly stuck her fingertips into and slightly pinched off a clump of the white meal next to the black sand. She held it over her water bowl, scooped up a handful of water, splashed it over the meal, washed away the sand, and then plopped the clean wad with the rest of the acorn meal.

"Oh, that's why you use black sand," said Helen. "You can see when it's gone."

Bly kneaded the acorn meal to release its oil and then added fresh water. She then removed two stones from the fire, washed off the ashes, and put them in the basket with the acorn mix. With looped sticks, she kept the rocks moving. "Add more hot stones when they cool." The acorn meal soon boiled and thickened into shawii. They scraped the shawii from the stones and set them aside to cool enough to handle while they cleaned everything.

Trip after trip, the men had dumped wagonloads of building materials at the section of coastal land assigned to them by Duro. Finally finished working for the day, everybody ate the shawii.

Bly looked at the tall piles of branches and cattail leaves in the morning light. "Today, while the men fish in the ocean, we women will build your e'waa. Draw a circle on ground same size as mine."

Each of the six women drew the twenty-foot diameter outline of their e'waa.

"Every three feet around the circle, pound stake into ground then remove," instructed Bly.

Once all six houses had their holes, they used yucca twine to lash together two twenty-foot-long leaf-covered willow saplings at their top ends, bent the bottom ends down, and inserted them into holes in the ground on the opposite sides of the circle. Bly explained, "We use willow keep out many bugs."

They created high arches in each set of holes

and made a dome. Starting at the ground, they tied two-foot-apart willow branch rings to the uprights. They left out the lower horizontals between two uprights to make a door.

"Now," said Bly, "fold tule over this. Very thick. Goes over outside bottom rings." She pointed to the third ring. "Cut at ground. Next ring up, do same. Comes down over top of this tule. Keep going up. Leave small open at top. When all covered, we tie branches around outside to hold tule on. Keep out animals and wind we put big stones around bottom and cover with Mother Earth."

One Hundred Nine

In Little Rock, Daniel Hall stood over a trapdoor with a noose around his neck.

Pearl looked up at her husband. "How could you have hated so much that you're willing to leave me alone?"

"Everyone I executed deserved to die. I'm not sorry about that, and you'll be all right if you sell the house. You and Ansel can live with your sister."

"You're worse than a louse." Pearl was angry, but she loved him and didn't want to watch. She marched away.

As Ann built a lodge by the western sea for herself, Noah, and their children, the hangman pulled the lever.

Acknowledgments

* Farewell! But Whenever You Welcome the Hour, Words by Thomas Moore, Music by A.F. Keene, published by Oliver Ditson & Co., 115 Washington Street Boston, not dated.

Cover

San Diego Image by:
<aref="http://www.freeimageslive.co.uk/free_stock_image/cabrillo-coastline-jpg" target="_blank"> freeimageslive.co.uk - photoeverywhere</a>

Chapter Headings

W. R. Michael Mattingly

Follow Me Online

https://www.ChanceandChoicesAdventures.com

Did you like this story? Please write a review!

https://www.amazon.com/Western-Sea-Chance-Choices-Adventure/dp/1945858249

Chance and Choices Adventures by Lisa Gay

Pray for Justice
Choose Your Consequences
No Remorse
Means of Escape
Torn Hearts
Xida People
Stone Cold
Goodbye Hideout
Along the Way
The Western Sea
Sally's Sketchbook